MW00850250

THE PRISON

JOE EDD MORRIS

Black Rose Writing | Texas

© 2019, 2020 by Joe Edd Morris
All rights reserved. No part of this book may be reproduced, stored in a retrieval
system or transmitted in any form or by any means without the prior written
permission of the publishers, except by a reviewer who may quote brief passages in a
review to be printed in a newspaper, magazine or journal.

The author grants the final approval for this literary material.

Fourth printing

This is a work of fiction. Names, characters, businesses, places, events, and incidents
are either the products of the author's imagination or used in a fictitious manner.
Any resemblance to actual persons, living or dead, or actual events is purely
coincidental.

ISBN: 978-1-68433-210-6
PUBLISHED BY BLACK ROSE WRITING
www.blackrosewriting.com

Printed in the United States of America
Suggested Retail Price (SRP) $19.95

The Prison is printed in Gentium Basic

PRAISE FOR THE AUTHOR

"*Land Where My Fathers Died* is an amazing debut. It made me think of *All The King's Men, Blood Meridian,* even *As I Lay Dying.* Joe Edd Morris's characters spring from the earth itself. This is a book you won't put down, a story you'll remember for many years to come. What novel. What a writer."
  ~Steve Yarbrough, author of *The Unmade World* and *Safe From the Neighbors*

"First novelist Morris, a Mississippi pastor-turned-psychologist who also writes poetry and short stories, tells a poignant tale of a young man's search for identity...This beautifully upbeat and enduring novel is recommended for all ages, especially in areas with large Hispanic populations."
  ~*Library Journal*

"A truly memorable literary journey...combining a strong plot with first-rate characters and some elegiac writing about the link between families, the land and its history...Morris's obvious talent shines through from start to finish.'
  ~*Publishers* Weekly

"Not long ago I heard a literary critic claim that there are only two stories— a stranger comes to town or a young person leaves home...Joe Edd Morris' terrific first novel, 'Land Where My Fathers Died,' fits neatly into the second category...Morris knows Mexico well, and his descriptions of the landscape and the small towns that dot Jo Shelby's way have the ring of hard-earned observation. Morris, a former Methodist minister, writes with a clear lyricism. Aware of language and what it can bring to a story, he seems equally cognizant of what it can subtract from a story. Here is a simple but completely eloquent description of Jo Shelby's thoughts at the end of the book: 'He thought of where he was and how far he'd come and of his chances and what he had to lose and what he had to gain and weighed both sides of the equation and decided there were times in a man's life where simple arithmetic broke down and nothing was more than something but there was no book that ever taught that.' I doubt that many writers could say it better."
  ~ *Raleigh News Observer*

PRAISE FOR *THE PRISON*

"Prose in the skilled hands of Joe Edd Morris is powerful, lyrical...almost like reading poetry." –Peggy Webb, *USA Today* bestselling author of *The Language of Silence*

"*The Prison* is exciting, smart, and eloquent." –Michael Hartnett, author of *Generation Dementia*

"*The Prison* is high on my list of important Southern literature." –Gerald Walton, author of *The University of Mississippi: A Pictorial History*

"A stunning achievement by an accomplished writer of remarkable talent." –Jim Hutchingson, co-author of *Boundaries*

To Roy H. Ryan

In memory of B. F. Lee

ACKNOWLEDGMENTS

The Prison involved three years of writing and research and during that time several friends contributed ideas and suggestions. I am indebted to the late B. F. Lee for his idea that Cal Ferguson's salvation would come from inside his prison. Millsaps Dye (and his dog Luke), who grew up in the Delta in Clarksdale, drove me over the countryside to ensure I had "the grid" right. His suggestions regarding the story narrative were also invaluable. Buck Falls, a Clarksdale planter, offered helpful information about the land and farming. His brother, George Falls of Memphis, provided space for me to write when my wife and I stayed at the River Inn. A big thanks to David Holcomb of Clarksdale who told me about the school bus beyond the levee and that story.

Much of the legal knowledge came from attorney friends and readers, George Dent and Tom Wicker. Tom helped particularly with information about the state Capitol and Legislative processes. George took me to the Chancery Clerk's office in Tupelo, Lee County, and literally walked me through the the steps and processes involving deeds and wills.

Others who read the early drafts with helpful feedback are: Millsaps Dye, Jim Hutchingson, Drs. Gerald and Julie Walton, W. O. (Bill) Rutledge III. Dr. David White, Dr. John Bryson, Dr. Marion Winkler, Peggy Webb, Sonja Jenkins and Joe T. Wilkins III.

I am greatly indebted to the staff and inmates of the Marshall County Correctional Facility, a private prison located in Marshall County, Mississippi where I served as a staff psychologist. Their descriptions and depictions of prison life and solitary confinement, plus my own observations, resonate throughout the story.

Immeasurable thanks and gratitude go to author Michael Hartnett of Long Island, New York who read and edited the initial, the second and final drafts of the manuscript and recommended it to Black Rose Writing for publication. Reagan Rothe, publisher of Black Rose Writing, and David King, design director, have been excellent shepherds through the publishing process.

In his book *On Writing,* Stephen King advised that to be a successful writer one must stay healthy and stay married. I would add a third: marry an English teacher. Sandi, my wife, reads everything I write and offers helpful critical comments along the way. However, with *The Prison* manuscript, there was no "along the way." She said she could not put it down, something I'd never heard from her. She is also that "stay healthy" part who keeps me on track. Many thanks, Sandi. I'm honored and privileged to have you as editor number one.

THE PRISON

"I have called you in righteousness...to open the blind eyes, to bring out prisoners from the dungeon and those who dwell in darkness from the prison."

~Isaiah 42:7 (KJV)

"It is said that no one truly knows a nation until one has been inside its jails. A nation should not be judged by how it treats its highest citizens, but its lowest ones."

~Nelson Mandela

"...under a government which imprisons anyone unjustly, the true place for a just man is also in prison."

~Henry D. Thoreau...From Leo Tolstoy's *Resurrection*

CHAPTER 1

November 27, 2014

Shell Ferguson drove slowly along the stretch of blacktop, his eyes focused on the curious shapes ahead. He had lived his entire life in the Mississippi Delta but never fully adjusted to its flatness. The endless monotony had a haunting way of playing tricks on his eyes.

The mid-day sun shone brightly in the clear blue dome, but not warmly. It was late November, Thanksgiving Day, and cold. Two months before, he would have seen rows of cotton and soybeans flicking by in geometrical precision, acres of milo and wheat and rice. Now, drab fields of stubbled stalks lay busted and disked, bleak and barren. Along the hedgerows and creek banks, shattered trees scratched the sky. He crossed old bridges over old rivers, serpentine across the limitless alluvial plain. He passed gum-choked bayous and stands of cypress along channels of sloughs, motionless black water going nowhere. No music from this flat-lined land. As if time was in limbo, as if it had stopped and was waiting to be time again.

His appointment was at one o'clock. He glanced at his watch and noted the date. His birthday. Every few years it fell on Thanksgiving Day, but with all that had happened, he'd lost track. It was anything but a day of thanksgiving. It was a death day, a no thanks day. That's how he felt inside. In the past week, he had lost more than he had ever gained in his life. Going from age seventy-eight to seventy-nine was an addition, but it seemed a subtraction. Life's arithmetic might add, multiply, and divide. But in the final analysis, it was all subtraction.

He continued on across the colorless flatscape. The odd rectangles stamped on the taut horizon grew larger.

He drew closer.

And closer.

He pulled into a parking lot the size of a football field and turned off the motor.

Mystified, he sat.

Surely, he had made a mistake, taken a wrong turn. He'd had his share of wrong turns in life, some not by choice. Surely, these two-storied structures, like mammoth Legos set end on end, were warehouses or a commissary complex, a factory or group of factories. But not a prison. He saw no manned watch towers, no uniformed guards clutching .30-30's pacing back and forth along catwalks. There were enclosures all right, but they weren't confined. These walls sprawled, spread like building blocks a giant might have laid down and linked together. They went on and on.

Reinforced wire fences *did* surround the colossal complex. Coils of shiny barbed-wire, sun rays splintering from them, *did* border the fences. The large sign across the front *did* say SUNFLOWER COUNTY REHABILITATION CENTER.

He had heard a privately-owned prison was being built in the county twenty miles west of his home, a square mile of private land sold to a private corrections corporation. He had heard it would house four thousand prisoners, three times the number at Parchman, the state penitentiary that abutted his property. He had heard all of that in 2005. Though he had hunted in the area, he had never ventured to see the new prison. It was off the beaten path on a county gravel road, and the wide expanse of land it occupied had been posted. And before. Long before. He had been in two prisons in his life and had no reason to see another.

Until now.

Prisons have come a long way since my time, he mused observing the mammoth structures. At Parchman, a huge plantation without a perimeter fence, convicts worked under the rifles and shotguns of guards and trustees. He recalled the times he had halted his mule and considered making a run for it and glad he didn't. After six years of a twenty-year sentence for manslaughter, the real killer confessed.

Then there was the prison in Mexico where he was incarcerated a few months for carrying a disabled pistol while in that land searching for descendants of his great-great grandparents, Confederados who had traveled with Gen. J. O. Shelby at the collapse of the Confederacy.

He thought of other penitentiaries, gray stockade prisons he had seen in the movies; ones he had read about in books, heard Johnny Cash and Hank Williams sing doleful songs about on the radio. The monstrosity before him resembled no prisons of yesteryear; of film or fiction or song. If he dreamed wild dreams of what this prison might look like, none would be as wild or as farfetched. *No telling what it's like on the inside*, he thought.

Stiffly, and slowly, he opened the cab door and slid out. His right hip had been ailing, but he'd refused the replacement surgery. He had gotten this far in life, he could keep going. He stepped into the bright cold, pulled his coat around him and tucked his chin between the lapels. He ambled, timidly at first, cautiously, toward a large chain-link gate framed in coils of barbed-wire. His lean shadow wobbled ahead of him. A sign on the gate said DO NOT ENTER GATE WHILE IT IS MOVING, but he saw no sign that told him how to make it move.

From a small square metal speaker to the left of the gate, a woman's voice squawked, "Identify!"

"Shell Ferguson, here to visit my grandson."

"His name?" the voice barked back.

"Calvin Ferguson."

"Press the button below the speaker," she commanded.

He lifted a hesitant finger and pressed the button, worn a dull gloss from countless fingers before.

He waited.

Seconds passed. He heard a loud click, then rumbling. A heavy steel gate began moving in a steel groove. He obeyed the sign and waited until the gate stopped moving then passed through the portal. Like finality, a door of doom, the gate rumbled shut behind him, and he found himself trapped in a fenced graveled corridor. Above and below him, rows of coiled barbed wire added a chill to the brisk cold.

He faced a similar gate, another speaker.

The woman's voice again: "Press the button."

Through a plate glass window, he could see her looking at him. He followed the instructions, waited for the sliding gate to stop, and passed through its steel frame. He had seen a James Bond movie. Steel doors opening and closing, some unseen force or wizard running the show.

Across a wide concrete walk, its white-grainy texture glaring from the overhead sun, he approached double glass doors. They might have been doors at Walmart or a church. Expecting another button, another voice, he stopped in front of the doors and noted the panels of heavy glass. But there was no button, no speaker, no voice. A black male guard on the other side, twirling a ring of keys on his finger, waved him in.

Shell opened one of the doors and stepped into an area the size of a small room. The guard twirling the keys wore a gray uniform with black piping on the sleeves and a black stripe down the outside of each leg.

Another guard, a young black woman with a jutting face and a toothpick in her mouth, wore a starched long-sleeve white shirt with a single bar on the shoulders. She stood in front of Shell, hands on her hips, her feet spread military style. "Remove your hat and belt and shoes, billfold, all other items you have and put 'em in there," she ordered, pointing to a large square bin. "Then put the container on the conveyor belt." She had one gold front tooth that flashed when she spoke.

He did as she commanded and watched the conveyor belt pull the bin containing his possessions through wide flaps and into a black box. He knew enough from television shows and the news he had seen that the box was X-raying everything in the bin. He knew, too, the booth she commanded him to step into and raise his hands was doing the same to him.

A long, shrill tone sounded.

"Your watch," a male guard on the other side of the booth said pointing to his wrist. He was also black and dressed similarly to his female counterpart; dark pants, starched creaseless white shirt, shoulder bars indicating rank, as though this was a military base and the military was in charge. Accessories of battle hung from the guard's belt—holstered canister, black baton, radio. No gun. He asked the guard checking him about the canister.

"Spray gun!" The guard responded.

"What does it spray?" Shell asked.

"Pepper," the guard snapped, slapping his hand on the grip. "You don't never want it on you."

Shell removed his watch and gave it to the guard, backed up and, as directed, passed through the booth again. This time, no alarm. He wondered why it didn't detect his wedding ring.

"Sit on that," the female guard commanded and pointed behind him.

He turned and saw what appeared to be portable steps, the kind one sees in libraries or hardware stores. "Where do I sit?"

"Top step," another male guard standing nearby directed. "On the black circle."

"What for?"

"Don't ask questions," the male guard grumbled.

"What for?" Shell asked again, perturbed. "I'd like to know why." *Are they going to wheel me away somewhere?*

"To see if you got contraband up your butt," the guard said irritated.

Shell sat. He heard a long beep he assumed cleared him. He wondered how it would have sounded if he were near a bowel movement. If it would sound at all.

"Now git up and come around here," the male guard said sternly.

He got up and moved behind the steps.

"Put your chin above the cross mark and move your head side to side, like this." The guard demonstrated.

Shell opened his mouth—

"To check for contraband in your mouth, down your throat," the guard responded, preempting his question.

"Contraband?"

"Drugs, cell phones," the guard replied.

"Cell phones? In my mouth?"

"It's happened," the female guard with the gold tooth snapped.

He looked around at the guards. They were all black. In his time, they had all been white, and all males.

The female guard ordered him to turn around and spread his legs. From top to bottom she frisked him, fluttered her hands over his body, across his chest, around his crotch, down his legs, even his socks, touching him in places no woman had ever touched him. Except for his wife. Athen would never touch him again, that painful thought piercing his heart.

His personal items—belt, shoes, watch, ballpoint pen, Chapstick—were returned. Everything except the money was still in his billfold. The female guard removed forty of the sixty dollars he was carrying.

"I'll keep the two twenties and return 'em to you when you leave," she said. "No one can enter the prison with more than twenty dollars, that includes the warden."

He gave her a two-finger salute. Forty dollars was the amount he had left Parchman with sixty years ago when he had headed for Mexico. Arithmetic has a strange way of bringing life full circle, and he thought again of his reason for being there and wished the sad mission belonged to another.

A different black guard motioned Shell to follow him. He was short and stocky and wore a wide-brimmed floppy hat, a thin strap securing it beneath his chin. The hat seemed mismatched to his military dress, a bit flamboyant. The guard pushed buttons, gates rumbled open and closed. Always, Shell was between gates, no exit until another opened. *A parable of life*, he mused.

"Gates are opened from Central Control," the guard said sensing his visitor's concern. He pointed to mounted cameras spaced at intervals along the ceiling. His Adam's apple bobbed up and down like a cork when he spoke. "The guards in Central Control see who pushes the buttons. No two gates open at the same time. That's why we have to wait," he continued, tapping an anxious toe, the tapping, too, out of sync with his swaggering air. That much hadn't changed in sixty years, the tough macho attitude of the guards, white or black, male or female.

He had a question the guard detected in his canvassing eyes.

"Nobody's ever escaped from this facility," the guard said.

The changes were stacking up. It was no longer called a prison, but a facility. He knew what that word led to: facilitate. Next, prisoners would be called facilitites.

"Inmates have tried," the guard added.

Okay, then. Inmates. He scratched his head.

The gate finally opened.

Shell looked left, he looked right. Long hallways either side. Shiny plastered mustard-colored walls. Shiny polished concrete floor. Smooth, he thought, reflecting on the rough prisons he had been in, the raw deals he'd been dealt, big bumps in that long road. He felt like a man with a festering sore that got all the bumps yet his body, not the sore, felt all the pain.

The guard nodded right, and they began walking in that direction, their heels clicking on the smooth floor, echoing off the smooth walls, smooth clicking in Shell's head like a stuck record.

The guard led him to the end of a hall where they turned left, and he saw another hall ahead of him two football fields long, gates every fifty yards or so.

"We got to go through all those?" Shell asked.

"We do."

"That might take a while."

"Might," the guard clipped. "We got time."

That's what it's all about, Shell thought.

He followed the guard down the long corridor hearing the rhythms of their strides bouncing off the high shiny walls. A strong scent of baked bread suggested they were passing the kitchen; then further down a sign on a green door to his right said WAREHOUSE. At that door, he detected the vague smell of wet cardboard. The prisons he'd been in had only one smell, a mixture of human sweat and waste and what an occasional breeze brought from the land. Here there were no breezes. This place was hermetically sealed.

The guard stopped at another gate and hit a button.

They waited.

The gate finally opened.

Repeating the procedure, Shell followed the guard through the long tunnel of gates. He was continually amused at the differences between this prison and the ones he had been in. Bright lights hung from overhead steel beams. Along the spotless walls stood black, uniformed guards. He asked the guard about the shoulder bars.

"They're ranks—sergeant, lieutenant, captain."

"Got any generals?" Shell inquired.

"That's the warden," the guard said and smiled.

"Who's he?"

"Name's Culpepper. Gov'ner appointed him."

"The current governor?" Shell asked.

"No sir. His predecessor, back in 2005, when the facility opened. I been here that long, too."

"Where's the warden from?" Shell probed.

"Tunica," the guard responded without eye contact or comment as they continued down the long corridor.

Shell had heard of problems in the police and sheriff's departments in Tunica. He persisted. "What did he do before he was the warden?"

"That, sir, I do not know. But I worked for the police department in Drew."

That struck a nerve and Shell went no further. It was the Drew City Police that falsely arrested him on a Saturday night sixty years ago he wanted to forget.

The prisoners Shell passed wore loose-fitting khaki pajama-like tops and bottoms. No zebra stripes. Some of them looked his age. Some looked in their teens. Some had their heads shaved, some had braided locks, and some ponytails. They walked to and fro, casually, arms swinging, as though they had no care in the world. Occasionally, he caught whiffs of body odor. Most, he observed, had tattoos, some covering their bodies, at least what he could see.

"Do they all have tattoos?" Shell asked.

"Most do."

"I've never seen so many."

"In the free world maybe not," the guard said. "But in prison, they're codes."

"Secret messages?"

"Maybe to some. They tell stories they want other inmates to know."

"If I had my story tattooed," Shell said, "I'd run out of skin."

The guard chuckled. "Some in here got long stories. Most are short."

They continued walking, Shell's mind a sponge. "Give me some examples, of the short ones."

"Well sir, a dagger in a neck means they killed and are for hire. A tear in an eye corner, they murdered. Towers," he turned and looked at Shell, "that's how many times they been incarcerated; crosses, sentences paid in full. Cobwebs, and a lot of 'em got these, mean a lengthy term."

"Like spiders trapping their prey," Shell added.

"Exactly. And if you see the numbers 1488 on one, he's a Nazi."

"Nazi!"

"We got 'em. They mean in the free world, meaner in prison."

"Incredible! They must get the tattoos before coming here."

The guard shook his head as they continued down another long corridor. "Some do." He pointed at the floor. "Most get 'em here."

How in the world? Shell thought.

Large, restless dogs held on short leashes by guards roamed the hall sniffing the air.

"Guess the dogs are looking for drugs," Shell said.

"And cell phones," the guard added.

"Cell phones? Dogs can smell cell phones?"

"Yep. Don't ask me how, but they teach 'em. Cell phones and drugs flow like rivers in here."

Reflecting on the security check he'd just gone through, Shell scratched his head again. "A gnat on your ass can't get in here."

"Guards. Employees," the guard said. "Crime pays in prison." He pulled a tennis ball from a side snap pocket on his pant's leg, pointed to the slit where it had been cut open. "Friends outside throw 'em over the fences. Found this this morning, and the gadget inside," he said pulling a small cell phone from the other pants leg pocket. "Hadn't had time to give it to the security chief. Inmates get 'em from inside, too," and he palmed a hand at the other employees in the hall. "Nine hundred folks work here. Most make less than ten dollars an hour. This here phone would sell for eight hundred or more, if you get my drift. Inmates use 'em to pay off their drug debts."

"How?" Shell asked amazed.

"Something called PayPal. Like I said, crime pays in here. But not for me. Like I said, I been here since the year the place opened and never been on the take."

Shell didn't know what to say, so he just nodded. He recalled growing up and reading Dick Tracy comic strips, the caption in them that always said, "Crime doesn't pay." Dick Tracy must not have known about prisons and what goes on behind their walls.

"Ratting on an employee is near sudden death for the ratter," the guard continued. "Workers know it. Like I said, cell phones and drugs flow like rivers in here. Regardless what we do, they don't never dry up. Inmates smart as whips."

Whips. The word sparked a flashback. He had been whipped twice in prison, once in Parchman and again in Matamoros, Mexico. The lashing in

17

Mexico couldn't hold a candle to the one at Parchman. It was with a wide black leather strap dubbed Black Annie. That one damn near killed him. Both were the result of his ignorance, not his smarts. "My, my," was all he could manage.

They continued walking, Shell wondering, How much further?

At the end of the long hall, one more gate. It slid open, and they stepped outside and continued walking, past chain-link enclosed areas where men played basketball, lifted weights, kicked a soccer ball around. Instead of the brown pajama-like outfits he had seen inside, these men wore baggy gray drawstring pants, gray loose-fitting t-shirts, white socks, and white sneakers.

Beyond the recreational area, Shell saw what appeared to be a baseball diamond and pointed. "Is that what I think it is?" he asked the guard.

"Yessiree, a baseball field."

He looked around him, strained his neck. "And all this tall netting around it and the buildings?"

"Fi'ty feet to be exact," the guard said. "Warden just had it put up to stop throw-overs," and he presented the tennis ball again, bounced it once in his hand and returned it to his pocket. "Next thing you know, they'll be dropping from one of them newfangled robot planes."

They left the sidewalk along the rec area and entered another building. Shell saw another long hallway, another series of gates.

"We gotta go through all of those, too?"

"Nope," the guard replied.

They passed a door on his left with a narrow window. Shell stopped and peeked in and saw a huge room the size of several basketball courts. It was filled with rows of bunks, showers along one side and up front, tables and benches anchored to the floor where prisoners sat playing cards or checkers, or talking. Widescreen televisions hung from the ceiling.

"Follow me!" the guard directed, interrupting Shell's reconnaissance. "You not supposed to look in there. Your boy's not in there."

Shell followed him further down the clean glistening hall, past closed, windowless doors that said, Utility Room, Barber Shop, Chapel. The last one had a window. Shell paused and looked in—plywood pulpit, drum set, chairs arranged in a circle. Taped to the wall was an over-sized hand-drawn cross, some biblical pictures, the kind he'd seen in Sunday school rooms growing up. He turned to the guard. "You have worship services?"

"Got two chaplains, two services—Sunday and Wednesday mornings."

The room next to the chapel said LAW LIBRARY.

"A law library?" Shell said in disbelief.

The guard, paces ahead of him, stopped and turned. "Yeah."

"Who uses it?"

"Inmates. They know the law better than the lawyers."

"Why?" Shell asked.

" 'Cause they go in there and read a lot."

"No! Why a law library in a prison?"

"Regulations or the law. Or both. I don't ask questions. I just guard," and he motioned Shell on.

"I guess you have one that says 'Tattoos,'" Shell said.

"Why you say that?"

"You said they got their tattoos in here."

"Not from the prison staff," the guard said. "Tattoos are prohibited."

"How do they get 'em?" Shell pressed.

The guard gave him an irritated asking-too-many-questions look. "They do it themselves." As if anticipating the next question, he continued. "They do it with makeshift stuff. Use melted rubber from shoe soles, ashes, or soot. Inject it under their skin with needles they make or steal in the medical unit. Jury-rig electric razors or CD drives into an injection machine. Like I said, they smart."

Shell had more questions but deemed it best to hold them, at least for now.

They passed a door that said VISITATION and Shell stopped. "Where's my grandson if he wasn't back there?" he inquired hooking a thumb over his shoulder.

"He's in a segregated unit further down," the guard answered.

"Segregated?"

"Not like blacks from whites," the guard quipped. "Solitary confinement. Some inmates have to be separated. They're too violent and mean."

"That's like a prison within the prison," Shell said.

"Maybe so. Never thought about it like that. Not all of 'em are dangerous.

19

Some are in protective custody. They got drug debts, been threatened. Some are sex offenders. They on everybody's blacklist."

"My grandson's not a sex offender," Shell protested defensively. "He's got no drug debts. Never used a drug in his life. He's not violent. I know about prisons. Why is he in solitary confinement?"

"They don't tell us," the guard responded.

"Who's they."

"Warden. Sometimes they suicidal."

Shell didn't respond.

The guard pulled a large ring of keys from his side pocket, jingling them as if the sound conveyed authority. He selected one and slipped it effortlessly into a lock the size of a man's wallet on a thick metal door, the lock clicking with an oiled certitude. The guard stepped into the room and flipped on the light, motioned for Shell to follow.

"You have a seat. I'll bring inmate Ferguson to you."

Taking in the musty smell, Shell looked around. Every prison has one: a long counter with a flexi-glass partition, chairs either side of the partition, a small opening in the glass for talking, like they'd had at Parchman and the prison in Matamoros, like in the movies and on television. Instead, he saw what looked like an office, or a room trying to be an office, perhaps was at one time. A gray metal desk and beside the desk, a dark green filing cabinet, no labels on the drawers. Next to the filing cabinet, tall metal shelving with nothing on the shelves. Scattered around the room, three metal folding chairs. Bare walls, concrete blocks painted the same putrid mustard color.

Beneath fluorescent lights that buzzed off and on, Shell sat and waited. Somewhere in the room a clock was ticking with an unhurried sound. *Like prison clocks all over the world.*

He thought. About what he would say. How he would say it. What he would not say. The questions he would be asked. The answers he would not have. The ones he would and dreaded telling. If Shell's son, the boy's father, was alive this would be his job. But Cal's mother and father were killed in a car wreck. Cal was supposed to have gone with them to Memphis to see a Cardinals baseball game. He was a freshman at Millsaps, a Methodist college in Jackson, the state capital. A young lady had asked him to be her date at a sorority dance. Her name was Sally DuBard. Her father was the governor. She had saved his life, Cal would always believe. He would always believe the Lord had a hand in it. Two months after his parents' funeral, he knelt at the altar of the small United Methodist Church in Rome, Mississippi, Sally kneeling beside him, and made his commitment.

Shell Ferguson had been in tough situations before. He had been in a Mexican-standoff in a Mexican prison and lived to tell about it. He had hitchhiked the length of that colorful and passionate country in search of long lost Confederado kin. He had barely escaped a hanging when his great-great aunt stepped onto the balcony of her hacienda manse and stopped it with him atop the horse, the rope around his neck. He had left what he had strived so hard to find in that country and, in various conveyances, hitchhiked back home to Athen, the love of his life. He had faced her powerful father, the same man who let him sit in prison for a crime he didn't commit, the same man who brought news to him in that same prison, news that knocked every atom out of him except the ones keeping his heart and lungs working. He would never forget the day, the moment.

He was twenty-one years old. The state penitentiary at Parchman was a huge twenty-thousand acre farm surrounded by large privately-owned plantations. It was divided into twenty-three camps, each self-enclosed and independent with cage buildings where the prisoners stayed when they were not in the fields. Long barrack-like twin brick wings were enclosed by fifteen-foot fences of reinforced steel mesh, the tops sloping inward on metal supports bracing three strands of barbed-wire. At that time, forty-five hundred prisoners, most of them black, worked in the fields or hog units from sunrise until sunset with Saturday afternoon and Sunday off when they could rest and have visitors. The prison was an extremely lucrative business whose purpose was not to rehabilitate but to produce high revenue for the constantly observing legislature. In other words, it was a massive plantation operated by slave labor. To the warden and sergeants who ran the prison and supervised its prisoners, and the succession of governors who condoned it; the Civil War never happened.

Shell was at Camp 20, the trustee, honor camp. The camp sergeant called him off a cotton-picking detail. He was waiting by the side of a field road and saw Mr. Pat coming and did not like the look on his face. He did not like the slow, plodding gait of a man who always walked fast with wide strides. He did not like the look in his eyes as he approached him. All of a sudden, Shell's heart tumbled, and he had this empty feeling in the pit of his stomach. Something in Mr. Pat's advancing eyes told him this was the midnight knock on the door coming, the telegram delivered in the dead of night. He did not like what he heard when the man opened his mouth.

"There was a car accident," Mr. Pat said without preamble. "Your mama and daddy were in it."

Shell recalled he couldn't say anything, kept waiting for the rest, for the present tense, "All of 'em are still alive." But all he heard then, reverberating through his head over the years was, "It was fatal. No one survived." And he was two more years in that prison carrying around with him that heavy sadness.

He was still trying to get his thoughts together, what to say. The clock he couldn't see seemed to click louder, faster, as clocks usually do when time is running out. Regardless of what he said, how he said it, the pain would boomerang. He'd leave carrying more than he unloaded.

CHAPTER 2

Shell heard chains rattling, and the door opened. The guard entered with his grandson. He had not seen Cal in a week, since the last day of court. In his navy-blue suit and seated beside his attorney, he appeared calm. The judge told him to rise for the verdict. He stood, his head up, his look confident.

Then the foreman stood and read the verdict.

In a handful of days, the grandson Shell saw now had aged. His head had been shaved, and he looked thin and gaunt and hollow-eyed. He was wearing a shapeless orange jumpsuit and white velcro sneakers with no socks; his hands cuffed behind him; he appeared armless.

The guard moved Cal forward to seat him in one of the folding chairs and the word stenciled across the back of his jumpsuit slammed Shell's eyes. If they would add three letters, they'd have it right: CONVICTION. Shell thought of all the people of faith in the Bible wrongly jailed, but the thought brought small comfort.

"I'll be standing outside," the guard said. "I'll knock when time's up. You got fi'teen minutes."

Cal spoke first. "Granddad!"

Shell couldn't speak. He scooted his chair so he was directly across from his grandson then rose, leaned over and put his arms around him, pulled his head into the crook of his shoulder, held it there a moment, then released it and returned to his chair.

"Granddad, you don't look good," Cal said. "I'm going to be all right. I'm innocent. At least they put me in a prison close to my family."

Shell felt the muscles in his face tighten, his lower lip quiver. He clenched his eyes. Waiting any longer would be cruel, for both of them. He took a deep breath, cleared his throat. "Cal—" His voice trembled, stumbled. He swallowed. "This is hard," his words coming from the back of his throat, his voice cracking.

"What, Granddad?" Cal said scooting forward, cuff chains rattling against the back of his chair.

Shell felt the shudder first in his legs. He raised the one propped across his knee and planted it firmly on the concrete floor as if the movement and change of posture would stabilize him, but the tremor continued. It moved through his waist and into his chest, up his back and along his arms. He felt his head bobbing, saw his hands shaking.

Cal saw them, too. "Granddad, are you all right? Your hands are shaking, and you're white as a sheet."

He leaned forward. "No, Son, I'm not all right," he managed, squeezing those few words that felt like the book of his life through his throat.

"What's wrong?"

Lips still quivering, he mumbled calmly, and with finality, "They're gone."

"Who's gone, Granddad?"

"Sally and Big Mama." He couldn't tell him the rest.

"I just saw them last week," Cal said with a stunned look of disbelief. "Where'd they go?"

Shell drove his eyes into his grandson's, into that horrified expression. It was the only way. Don't be brutal but to the point, quick, clean like a sword plunged and withdrawn, as little bloodshed as possible. "They're dead," he said, then waited in the silence, the kind left after a bomb explodes. He watched his grandson flinch, his eyes close shut, and in that same second widen, his hard black pupils tighten to pinpoints, his face recoil as though struck, his mouth drop and his body jerk backward, handcuffs rattling with the sudden impact, sitting there in that stricken armless posture like a man just impaled by cold steel.

Shell didn't know what to do or to say next, except, "Son, I know it's heartbreaking. It's had me ..."

Cutting him off, Cal jumped up, let out loud wails, "Nooooo, Nooooo," began whipping his head around, beating his cuffed fists against his back, "Nooooo, Nooooo," in the violent rattle of chains screaming over and over, "No! No! No!"

Shell sprang up and grabbed him, held him, pulled him closer pinning his arms and hands.

The guard opened the door and looked in. "What's wrong?"

"It's okay!" Shell said loudly, glancing over his shoulder, trying to contain his own emotions. "I had to break some bad news. Give us time."

"It don't look okay," the guard questioned stepping into the room.

Shell waved him back. "His family died. Let him grieve."

The guard nodded, eased back through the door, and softly closed it.

For long minutes they stood, Shell's arms around his sobbing grandson, the explosion of grief and panic simmering to small, audible gasps into his shoulder as he did as a child when his dog was killed. Shell tried to speak and choked. The two stood weeping together. He hadn't followed his plan. He hadn't told him the worst part. He'd have to plunge the sword again. "Shelley's gone, too."

Cal let out a deep moan. "Not Shelley, oh no, God, no, not Shelley."

Like a puppet whose strings have been cut, Cal's body collapsed and slipped through Shell's arms to the floor. Shell bent down, checked his pulse. He slid an arm beneath his knees, the other under his back and heaved him up on his side onto the desk. Cal's body was lifeless, the tormented expression still on his face. Shell checked his pulse again. *He's fainted is all,* he said to himself. He looked at the door then back at his grandson. He knew if he alerted the guard, they would send a medical team and they'd take him away. He might not be allowed to go with them.

Shell waited. A clear plastic bottle with some water still in it was on the desk. He pulled his handkerchief from his hip pocket, unscrewed the cap on the bottle, splashed some water onto his handkerchief and placed the wet cloth on Cal's forehead. Again, checked his pulse. His heart was still beating. His body curled on its side, Cal opened one eye, then another and blinked. He tried to sit up.

Shell placed a hand on his chest. "Lie still."

"What happened?"

"You fainted."

Cal blinked again, rapidly, as though at a bright light.

Shell stepped over and flipped the wall switch. "That better?"

"Yes, but ...." He began crying again, tears streaming over his temples onto the desktop.

Shell leaned over and, again, wrapped his arms around him, shaking and weeping and whispering as he did, "I'm sorry, Son, I had to tell you. I'm so sorry," his own tears falling onto the table, mingling with those of his grandson.

"How?" Cal asked numbly, the question screwing his face into a tortured grimace.

"A fire."

"Where?"

"The parsonage. They hadn't moved out. They were all asleep."

"Big Mama, too!" he cried.

Shell nodded. "She was there helping them pack. They'd waited for the verdict, hoping it would be different."

"Oh, Granddad." He looked up." "Why? Why?"

"Volunteer fire department chief said it was faulty wiring."

"But the house passed insurance specs."

"I'm going to look into it," Shell said. "Something's not right."

Cal's sobbing slowed to whimpers. "When's the funeral?"

"There was a memorial service this morning at the church, eleven o'clock. Sally's parents and their friends were there, folks from the church. My pastor at the Rome church conducted the service. A private graveside service followed."

"Where was she buried?" he asked tears still tracking his cheeks. "We made a pact we'd be buried together," his voice choppy, gulping.

"The DuBards knew about that agreement and respectfully agreed for her remains to be interred in our family plot on the place."

"Remains?" he cried, his face plowed with pain.

Shell placed a gentle hand on his shoulder. "I'm sorry, Cal. Her body is buried beneath a double tombstone with both your names on it."

As long as he lived, Shell Ferguson would never forget this moment. His grandson sobbing, curled up like a fetus, face collapsed and devastated, hands cuffed behind his back. He would have sold his soul to comfort him. He would have swapped his heart and lungs for helpful words, but all that came out of his mouth was, "You've got to pull yourself together. Any second, the guard's gonna open the door."

"I don't care," Cal's choking voice sounding far away. "I don't care."

"The warden knows what happened. A chaplain's coming."

"I don't want a chaplain. I just wanna die."

Shell leaned over and looked into his grandson's eyes and shook him. "I understand, Son. Believe me, I understand. There's a difference between wanting to die and doing it. Are you suicidal?"

Cal looked up at him with heavy red eyes and said nothing.

Shell shook him again. "Answer my question."

"No!"

"I'm not convinced. We're all going to make mistakes in this world, but suicide's not one of 'em." He lifted Cal's chin with a finger. "You understand?"

He dipped his head slightly.

"Three innocent people are dead. This world doesn't need another. I don't need another."

"Who needs a convicted felon?

"Listen to me." Shell shook him again, harder. "God needs you. You need you. You are convicted, but not of a crime. Don't forget you're a minister. And don't let anyone in prison see you cry. That's like blood for sharks."

Cal struggled to sit up. Shell put a hand under his back and leveraged him to an upright position, so he was sitting on the desk, his legs dangling, the same pained expression on his face.

"I'll be back Sunday week. No visitation this Sunday, it's a holiday weekend, limited staff."

"How could you come today?" Cal whimpered.

The knob on the door behind them turned.

"The warden made an exception," Shell said. "Take courage. You're going to get through this," and with the back of his hand tapped him gently on his chest.

The door opened, and the guard stepped in.

"What happened?" the guard asked flipping on the light.

"He fainted," Shell said. "I laid him on the desk."

"All right," the guard said matter-of-factly. "I gave you a little more time. Gotta take him back."

Cal nodded and scooted off the desk. The guard nudged him toward the door.

Shell laid a hand on his grandson's shoulder. "Don't do anything rash.

Keep the faith."

Shell waited in the room for the guard to return. "How often do you check on him?"

"Every thirty minutes," the guard said. "Who'd he lose?"

"His wife and daughter."

The guard's eyes widened, and he sighed deeply. "My, my. That's some heavy loss. How'd it happen?"

"House fire."

"I'm real sorry, Mr. Ferguson," the guard said sincerely. "That the Methodist parsonage at Bethel?"

Shell nodded.

"I read about it in the *Sunflower News*, but didn't connect the deaths with inmate Ferguson."

"He may need more than a thirty-minute check," Shell said.

"If he's suicidal," the guard said, "they put him on suicide watch."

"What does that involve?"

"He's moved to the medical unit. A guard sits at the door with a constant eye on him. Nurses check on him every fifteen minutes."

"That sounds a bit much," Shell said. "He said he wasn't suicidal, but I didn't like the way he said it."

"He's not in my pod," the guard said. "Mine's 'cross the hall. But, Mr. Ferguson, I'll see he's looked after best I can."

Shell gave a nod of thanks and looked away at the blank wall painted the color he hated. Where he'd grown up, on a large farm not far from the prison, a pod was a husk, a hull, something to be shucked and discarded. *They got it right* he thought.

"I'll take you back to check-in," the guard said.

"Thank you."

They were waiting at one of the gates and Shell asked, "What's your name?"

"Durasmus."

"Durasmus," he murmured. "Interesting name. What's your last name?"

"That is my last name," he said with dignity. "First name's Fain."

Fain, Shell mused. He'd heard that name before. Where? *Fain*. It'd come to him later. "Who're you named for?"

"Got no idea. Mexican inmate said Durasmus meant tough, as in durable."

"Mexican? You got Mexicans in here?"

"Latinos. Quite a few. This facility's got near four thousand inmates, all from states out west."

"How come my grandson's mixed in with 'em?"

"Part of this facility is a county jail. Your grandson was moved from there to segregation."

"Why?" Shell asked reflexively.

"Like I said, I don't know why he was moved."

Shell followed the guard named Durasmus back through the series of gates, through the foyer and checkpoint to the double door exit.

Shell stood in the doorway held open for him by the guard and turned around. "Much obliged, Mr. Durasmus for your assistance and courtesies," and he turned to leave.

"If I'm not mistaken, Mr. Ferguson," the guard Durasmus said, his tone rueful, "There were three people died in that fire. Your grandson have any other family?"

The question spun Shell around. "Yessir. His grandmama, my wife," he said, his voice grim and solemn as he tipped his hat and proceeded to the gates where he'd have to punch more buttons again and wait again before he was again back in that other world, the word *again* resonating like a summary of all that had gone before in his life.

He gathered himself slowly and carefully into the truck cab, groaning as he slid behind the wheel and let himself down into the seat. For a while, he couldn't do anything. He couldn't reach the steering column and put in the key and turn it. He just sat there looking at the huge complex, at the large sign that said REHABILITATION CENTER thinking, *They can call it what they want but it's a prison.*

Driving away, he couldn't quit looking at it, kept glancing through the rearview mirror at the huge structures diminishing with distance, dwindling to the slots he'd earlier only guessed at clamped between sky and earth like blades of a vise, one bright and one dark.

His tough mission accomplished, the day stretched ahead of him with greater void. His eyes swept again across the same dark land, and he thought of the empty house he would enter again, a hollow silence that ambushed him when he opened the door and crossed the threshold, rooms full of memories that only made them feel emptier.

The thought brought to mind a discussion he'd had with Athen, God rest her soul. All of his life he had been called Jo Shelby. He had liked the name, or had grown to like it. But Athen had told him the times had changed, that being named for Confederate General J. O. Shelby put him out of step. He needed to change it.

"How?" he had asked.

"Drop the 'Jo' she had said. "Besides, that's a girl's name. Shelby sounds more like a man's."

He didn't like "Shelby." That was the name of a one-horse town in the Delta not far from where he lived as well as a penal farm near Memphis.

She had countered with "Shell," spelled it for him and said it came from the Hebrew name Michael in the Bible. Besides that, she had said, "Shell is something that protects."

He thought of the other meaning that had started his thinking down this track: Empty. He thought, too, of a variation on the name he had never before considered. Until now. Dropping the S.

He wondered, after today, his birthday of all days, how he'd make it, how people went on when there was little, if anything, to go on for. He'd never take his own life but wished something or someone would. Then he saw a make-shift tilted cross in a field beside a deserted shack and recalled a movie he'd seen with his father at the picture show in Drew. He didn't recall the title. But he remembered a farmer, the actor, maybe Van Heflin, coming home from hunting and finding his family butchered by outlaws and how the farmer dug the graves for each, knelt over each, said a prayer, then walked into the house, strapped on his gun, mounted his horse, and rode off.

Fain! That name again, he thought as it came to him...*I fain would take my stand.* "Beneath the cross of Jesus," he murmured to himself, recalling the line from the old hymn. You only meet people like this in the Delta.

CHAPTER 3

The guard returned Cal to his cell, inserted a key the size of a small wrench into the lock, pulled open the thick steel door for Cal to enter, clanged it shut behind him, then uncuffed him through the food portal. Cal stood, his freed hands still behind him. For a moment he felt unable to move, frozen to the spot, wondering what in his life was left, how he could go on, what move he could make, then fell to his knees, bit his tongue to keep from crying, and began pounding his fists on the concrete floor.

Long minutes later, he stopped, picked himself up. He stepped to the small stainless steel sink to turn on the faucet to rinse his face and looked at himself in the stainless steel mirror above the sink. At his shaved head. At his bleary red eyes sunken and deep, the fine bones of his cheeks and jaw showing sharp beneath his skin. At his upper torso once athletic now wasted down to bones. Since his arrest in May, he had lost over fifty pounds. He turned on the faucet, let the water run awhile as if wondering why he had turned it on, then cupped his hands under the slow thin stream, splashed his face, and dried it.

He laid down on his bunk. He was pulling the woolen blanket over his head and heard a knock on his door, a single rap. He got up and peered through the small square window in the door. It was the guard who had taken him to his grandfather.

"I came back to check on you," the guard said speaking through the doorjamb.

Cal had quickly learned that in solitary confinement you communicated through the crack between the door and the door frame. He moved to the crevice to respond, but the word he wanted to say was half-swallowed and lost in his throat until he pushed it out. "Thanks."

"Are you suicidal?" the guard asked. "Look at me in the window."

Cal moved his face to the window and shook his head he was not.

"That's not good enough," the guard said.

"No!" Cal said louder, speaking through the crack again.

"Sorry 'bout your family," the guard said somberly. "That's a tough one."

The knot forming in Cal's throat became so oppressive it was difficult for him to breath. Warmth rushed to his eyes. "Thank you," a forced whisper all he could manage. He bit his tongue again.

The guard continued. "I lost a daughter some years back, right here in this very prison, the year it opened." He cleared his throat. "Thought I'd die before I got over it."

The words hit Cal like something heavy thrown into a stream reversing its flow. "And you're still working here," he said reflexively, his pastoral voice aroused.

"Wadn't working here then. She was a guard. Raped and assaulted."

"She had family?" Cal asked sympathetically.

"Yessir. Two sons and a daughter. The sons live with me. My surviving daughter is married and works in this prison."

"That has to be hard," Cal empathized, "working where it happened."

"Harder not to," the guard said. "She was a good guard. I was in law enforcement in Drew. The prison needed a replacement for her. I don't work this pod, but the one across the hall. If you need something, ask for guard Durasmus. You sure you gonna be okay?"

"Yessir."

When he was sure the guard Durasmus had left, the sound of his footsteps fading, Cal lay on the lower bunk again and wrapped the blanket around him. The story he had heard was helpful, hearing of another's pain usually is. But his returned and, like a heavy wave, rolled back over him. He felt alone and hollow, ripped apart from the inside out. He buried his head in his pillow and cried, softly at first then wretched uncontrollably, fisting the pillow over his mouth to muffle his sobs. He knew what his granddad had told him was true. Crybabies in the world are scorned. In prison, they're detested.

He had not lied to the guard Durasmus. He was not suicidal. But he didn't want to live. He felt old, and he had already lived his life and could now lay down and die. He could still see and still breathe, but he was in a grave. Missing only were words of interment.

He cried himself to the point of nausea and lay a long time with his cheek resting on his clenched hand. Through streams of tears running across his face, he stared at the wall across from the bunk, at bits of Scotch tape on it. Photos of loved ones had been there. He was going to put up Sally and Shelley's pictures. Sally had been his hope.

They had had their problems. She had become pregnant their senior year in college, and the next year they moved to Atlanta where he attended seminary. Those three years were the best in their marriage. He was winning awards for his sermons. Classmates were calling him "Bishop." A plum appointment awaited him back in Mississippi, he was told. He was on a roll. Sally was excited.

Then she found herself with a three-year-old daughter suddenly confined to the duties of a preacher's wife in a whistle-stop town called Bethel, in the Delta of all places, and in the poorest county in the state. They lived on a meager salary and in a parsonage with little furniture. Few were the visits to her parents. Her father had won a second term as governor. She had resented spending every single weekend at the church and had threatened to leave him if he didn't spend more time at home with their daughter.

But following his conviction, she changed. She believed he was innocent. Her commitment to him and their marriage surged anew. When she had seen him last at the county seat jail in Indianola, she had said all their issues were in the past. She would visit him regularly, write to him daily, pray for him constantly. Now she was gone though not the heavy weight of her name he felt like a phantom limb, a palpable absence where she no longer was. He smothered his face in his pillow and sobbed again.

When he finally stopped, he lay in a dim cell of dead air, the crushing images of family, the last time he had seen them, a hopeless nostalgia spinning through his head. Shelley beaming after he had tucked her into bed and she had said her prayers and said, "I love you, Daddy." Big Mama, his grandmother's nickname, at visitation in the county seat jail, her hair up, face set and eyes glaring: "We'll prove your innocence, Cal. Don't give up." Sally standing behind her, grim-faced: "I'll see you in the new prison. I love you. Keep the faith!"

Keep the faith.

What faith, he thought, that vocabulary near bankrupt, one word left—*Gone.* Everything—wife, daughter, career—*Gone.*

He lay there wondering if his heart was not broken enough for death to take him. Suddenly it began pounding. He broke into a cold sweat. His hands shook. A tremor swept his body. Breathing quickened in short gasps, as though a huge weight sat on his chest. He was smothering, a vise of invisible walls closing in. He couldn't get enough air. "I'm dying." he murmured to himself and crossed his hands over his chest as if they could jumpstart his heart should it stop. The room began to spin, everything in it a whirling blur. He felt himself sucked into a vacuum, free fall out of control; chamber by chamber his heart shutting down. A bolt of terror shot him upright. Dread of impending doom washed over him. This is it. He began breathing deeply, gulping air. Minutes passed. The walls receded. The room stopped turning. His heart slowed. His breathing relaxed. Walls, toilet, sink, mirror—as though spun from the gray blur—dropped into place. As suddenly as the attack began, it ceased. He lay back in cold sheets soaked with sweat. A slight tremor fluttering in his hands soon vanished. He lay still, waiting. Minutes passed. He was still conscious. He was still breathing. He had not died. He could hear iron gates opening and closing nearby, but none closing on him. Whatever had hit him, had let him live.

He had been near death, on the brink, he was sure. Heart galloping, breath escaping, mind fading. Then it stopped. A long time he lay thinking, assessing, what to call it, at least give it a name. He had seen nothing that caused the attack. Had heard nothing. He had been taught to fear nothing. Nothing! Inside was nothing. Outside, nothing. Ahead of him ... nothing.

He did have his granddad, but he was old and would probably die while he served his twenty-year sentence with no parole. His grandad's attorney, a Mr. Sparks, had begun an appeal but that would take two years or longer. His father-in-law, the governor, had said he might be able to speed it along. Even if his conviction was reversed and he was exonerated, his world was gone, blown to smithereens. The lonely aloneness—he used to could tell them apart—was smothering, hung on him like a disease. He guessed that was what caused the attack, invisible walls closing in on him. They surely would again.

He continued lying there, waiting for something to seep into the void, something that would push back on the walls. But all he felt was something oozing from his innards, inflating his lungs, climbing his throat.

He turned so he faced the wall, his back to the rest of his small cloistered world and began sobbing again, ramming his fist into the wall, "Why? Why?" he cried with each blow, over and over, pounding his knuckles into the gritty concrete until he saw his blood running down his wrist, onto his forearm, and then he quit, letting his arm wilt to his side.

He lay there a long time, with his fist throbbing. He flexed his fingers. They hurt, but they weren't broken. He wrapped his hand in a fold of the blanket, twisted it several times to hide the stain.

He'd been lying there a while and thought he heard a voice.

Hey, you!

A husky whisper. It didn't come from the door but higher up. *Am I hearing things?* He pushed back the blanket and sat up. He cocked an ear and heard a light tapping sound. Someone was at his window. But the sound was higher up.

Again, louder. "Hey, you in 208."

It was a voice, coming from somewhere above him. He looked up. All he saw was a small square vent high up the wall over the sink. He stood so he was closer to it.

He hesitated. "Yes?" he responded. Then ventured, "Who are you?"

"I'm in the next cell. Stand on the sink. Speak into the duct vent. We can talk without shouting."

He didn't feel like exerting the energy, but he had nothing to lose. He wasn't going anywhere. He placed one foot on the commode, another on the sink and pushed himself up, so he stood straddling the sink and facing the vent. "I'm here," he said.

"That's good!" the voice replied. "I can hear you better. Thank you."

It was an articulate, older voice, slightly hoarse. The accent was not local, not from the South, a hint of Hispanic. A caring tone. Whether he could trust it, Cal didn't know. "Won't we get into trouble doing this?" he questioned.

"The guards and nurses will just tell you to get down," the voice said. "Sometimes you're docked points, but it doesn't happen often, creates more paperwork for the guards. They're just concerned we might try hanging ourselves."

"You couldn't hang anything in here," Cal said trying to adjust his feet and steady his balance on the sink.

"Believe me, it's been done," the voice countered. "Twice in the past five years. The prison's being sued now for one of them."

"Why're you telling me this?"

"I heard you hitting the wall."

"I was mad," Cal said.

"I've been there," the voice said with emotion and cleared his throat again. "I understand. What's your story?"

A nervous silence.

"You still there?" the voice asked.

"Yeah," Cal murmured.

"What are you mad about?"

The request stuck in Cal's throat. He choked. "I can't talk about it now." He wanted to leave the vent. He was talking to a voice without a name, without a face. He moved one foot to step down.

"I'm sorry," the voice said. "We can talk later, when you feel like it."

A patient voice. Besides his granddad's and the guard Durasmus, it might be the only caring voice he would hear. He replanted his foot. He swallowed a few times, took a deep breath. "I just learned I lost my wife and daughter and grandmother."

Through the vent, a gasp. "Oh... my... God!" the voice sorrowful and grave, emotional. "I am so sorry. I will pray for you."

Jammed with emotion, Cal's throat closed again. He was about to cry again. He could bite his tongue again, but it bled the last time. He couldn't speak. He kept swallowing. "Thank you," he finally muddled on.

Another long silence. Cal thought again of stepping down. He'd emptied his heart. His legs were shaking. What else could he say? He didn't know a name, but talking helped. Moses didn't know God's name, and he kept talking to him. "I don't know your name," he said into the mesh vent.

"It's Chris."

"Mine's Cal."

"Sorry to meet you like this, Cal. And sorry to have to stop, but the guards will start the count soon. Better hop down. I'm praying for you. Let's talk more, when the count is finished. Keep the faith," and he tapped three times on the vent screen signing off.

"Yes, later," Cal responded and returned the taps, his thoughts on the man's last words, keep the faith. They were Sally's last words to him. His granddad, before leaving, had said them, too. They didn't sound strange coming from them, but they did coming from a prisoner, and he wondered more about the inmate named Chris.

He climbed down and stood facing his cell door and waited to be counted. There were twenty cells in a pod, ten on the bottom tier and ten on the top. On the second tier of the pod, in cell number 208, he was one of the last to be counted. He had been transferred, for reasons he did not know, to the facility from the county seat jail in Indianola, to a county jail in the private prison the previous Monday, and on that same day moved into the segregation unit. He had quickly learned the count schedule: every three hours from six o'clock in the morning until six in the evening, then every two hours until six the next morning and the routine repeated. Counts were taken to ensure all inmates were in their place. The clock on the pod wall said three.

Standing and waiting, he thought about what had happened. The voice. And the blessing—a vent.

CHAPTER 4

Beneath a thin sun, Shell continued driving across the cold land. He couldn't get Cal off his mind. The encounter had left both of them trembling with misery. He hoped the prison folks kept their word. He couldn't handle another loss, and he'd have to wait ten days to see him again, an eternity for both of them.

Driving through the lifeless fields, shotgun shanties and boarded service stations flashing by, he thought back to the prison, one scene in particular that caught his attention—the large room with rows of bunks. It was only a glimpse because the guard was pressing him to move on, but he wouldn't forget the bright shower stalls and toilets lining one wall, wide-screen televisions hanging from the ceiling. Near the door, an ice machine. He wouldn't forget the library (law library at that), exercise equipment, basketball courts, a lined baseball field.

Nobody's ever escaped from this facility. Who'd want to? A lot of folks in the Delta, locked in its poverty, would want to escape into a place with three hot meals a day, free clothing and shelter. They'd be glad to swap places. *One man's prison is another man's freedom, or was it the other way around* he thought reflecting on the Delta, that wild, disorderly tangle of power and prejudice, of people trapped by wealth and poverty, pedigree and blood and his grandson innocently snarled in that raveled knot.

He was headed home to Rome, a small village twenty miles due east of the prison. What will I do there? He wondered, aware more than ever of the house's size, its long halls, its rooms filled with nothing but furniture. It's silence. He could sit on the glassed-in patio where he and Athen would sit. She reading her library book and he with the paper, drinks on the table between them. Occasionally, they'd look up at a thicket of willows around an oxbow lake, at empty fields stretching to a line of distant trees and beyond until it all disappeared in the dusk gliding through the trees. Now and then they'd look at each other, a held gaze that said more than their circulating thoughts.

He could ramble around in the house's fourteen rooms, ambushed at every turn. The pot roast smells from her last meal still lingered in the kitchen. The fragrance of her face powder and body lotion still sweetened their bathroom. He'd have to change the sheets and pillowcases, her smells still there, too. The house was still and quiet, empty, yet still full of her. Still. He thought about the word and its meanings: unmoving, inanimate. Amazing how one small word can describe a house, a life, a culture. Still. He thought again of his grandson. *At least, he can see the walls around him.*

He thought how suddenly life can turn, everything, it seemed, erased. How people in the wake of tragedy, reeling from heartbreak, feel trapped by the only thing that stood between them and death: time. He'd been down that road. There was another side to that coin. However dim and bleak, he had a future. He wasn't going back to that porch and sit and wait for it to come to him. If Abraham could jump-start his life at seventy-five, he could his own at seventy-nine. He had to start somewhere.

The ruined parsonage was in Bethel, twenty miles south of Rome. The small community consisted of the United Methodist Bethel Chapel, a convenience store with a cafe, several large grain silos, an abandoned cotton gin and a few homes widely scattered around a fork of two state highways— the north-south Randolph Road and the Drew-Marigold east-west route. Locals referred to the area between those perimeters as the "Bethel Triangle," some of the richest farmland in the Mississippi Delta and a history as rich, or poor, depending upon one's perspective.

In the distance, the white steeple appeared, rising slender and simple against the afternoon sky. He had been there earlier in the day for the memorial service. The burden had fallen upon him to make the arrangements. He had questioned his judgment about holding the service at the church, with the parsonage ruins next door in glaring sight and concluded the church, the setting, was appropriate. He'd also questioned about having the service on Thanksgiving Day. No one that day felt very thankful. But they were people of faith.

He pulled his pickup into the parsonage drive and shut the motor. All he could see was the geometrical outline of an ash heap, gloss on the charred bits of wood reflecting in the sunlight. He sat there awhile and thought.

Cal and Sally had moved into the parsonage in mid-June of 2011. Cal had graduated from seminary, and the conference had appointed him to the church. Shell was on the Board of Trustees of the Rome Methodist church and knew parsonages required smoke alarms. He also knew there were two in the Bethel parsonage, one in the kitchen and one in Cal and Sally's bedroom. Cal said the house had passed electrical inspection. The fire chief said faulty wiring caused the fire, that the structure was old and only needed a spark. The fire chief also said the two smoke alarms were found in the rubble, batteries charred but intact.

Shell sat a while longer, considered other options. Lightning could have struck it but there had been no storm that evening, only a drizzle the night before. Sally or Athen could have struck a match or turned on a stove or heater, but the fire began, reports had said, around two in the morning. No one would have been up at that time. And the outside temperature had been warmer than normal.

He got out of the truck, ignoring the dinging telling him he'd left the door open. He took a few steps toward the ruins, his hand moving along the truck's hood as though he needed a stabilizer. At the front of the truck, he stood looking at the rubble, his hand still anchored to the hood. The bodies of Sally and Athen had been removed, but the air was filled with their presence. The place, so the morning news had said, was totally incinerated by the time fire trucks from Drew and Marigold arrived, another later from Ruleville. First responder medical teams said the bodies were burned beyond recognition. Shell was glad he was not there when they had been removed. Folks who were said the women's bodies had to be placed "very carefully" in plastic bags.

His granddaughter's body was never found. The reasons provided were not satisfying. The team of first responders who searched for the bodies said the six-year-old child was small. Due to the intense heat, the roof collapsing over her body, she was completely reduced to ashes. When questioned about any bones that might have belonged to the child, they responded that, sadly, none were found. It seemed inconceivable to Shell that nothing of the child remained, not even the gold necklace he gave her last Christmas that she never removed except to bathe. Not even her teeth. Teeth survive anything.

To bring some comfort, the recovery team said all three were dead before they burned, suffocated, asphyxiated by the smoke.

He continued standing, gazing at the charred ruins, at the blackened tomb. Shelley's incinerated body was still there. Did he really want to do this, poke around in his great-granddaughter's ashes?

He turned, stepped back to the cab and got in. He blinked once at the site then turned on the ignition and backed out.

CHAPTER 5

Following the count, the chaplain came. He was a black man, tall and lean, gray-headed, trimmed gray beard, distinguished-looking. Black-framed glasses dangled on a colorful cord from his neck. He identified himself as Chaplain Lee. In a gentle voice and low, pleasing tones, he spoke consoling words. "I know I can say nothing to ease your pain. But I can pray for you, and I am in the facility daily. Ask for me, and I will come," his voice soft and persuasive.

"Thank you, Chaplain Lee," Cal responded to the kind words magnified by the unkind environs. He wanted to say more, tell him that he, too, was a minister but felt uneasy. Voices traveled in the chambered pod and, unless you were speaking through a vent, echoed like a whisper in a canyon. He stood looking through the small square window at the man looking back at him.

Chaplain Lee wrote something on a pad. He tore off the sheet, bent down, and slipped it beneath the door. Cal squatted down, picked it up, and read the brief message: God bless you, Reverend Ferguson. *He already knew.* Cal rose to thank him again but the face was gone, the man's footsteps fading. Through the window, Cal watched him as he descended the steps and crossed the open area to the exit, continued watching him as he pushed the exit button. Cal watched him wait a long time before the buzzer sounded and Central Control unlocked the steel door for him.

Cal felt drained and tired. He laid down on his bunk and wrapped the blanket around him again. He turned on his side and looked through the cell's narrow view of the outside world, the mid-afternoon sun glaring brightly through the barbed-wire coils and chain-link fence where small birds flitted freely, and he closed his eyes.

His sleep ripped away and he raised his hands toward the top bunk as though it was a dark lid and he was awakening in a grave. At first, he didn't know where he was, then saw the bloodied wall, the stained blanket, and sheet beneath it. The knot his mind had become, slowly, strand by taut strand, began unraveling and he recalled the conversation with the man in the next cell. Piecing the dialogue together, he almost wept again.

The throbbing in his hand had stopped. He lay motionless on the bunk, and shut his eyes and his mind, for a moment, emptied. He could almost believe that his conviction had not happened, that he had simply dreamed it. That his life was on a good track. He thought of the good times, intimate moments with Sally, the warmth of her body against his. He thought of playing Shelley's favorite game, hide-and-go-seek, with her. Sunday lunches at Big Mama's. The special recognition of his work, the sermons he enjoyed crafting, the bright future ahead. Then the dull throbbing in his hand returned.

Hours passed in a long, gray daze. He lay listening to the new sounds of his new life. Bellowing voices. Snoring. Buzzers going off, doors unlocking, opening and clanging shut. Keys jingling. Heavy footsteps, guards in jackboots that echoed in the pod. Inmates yelling at guards, at each other. Sounds that never stopped.

One was puzzling. The first time he'd heard it, his first day, he had thought it was rain rattling against the window, but it wasn't raining. He would hear the noise for a while, it would stop for hours then start again, an irregular pecking sound, like someone on a typewriter. But who would have a typewriter in solitary confinement? The sound seemed to come through the wall. Maybe it was in the wall, a trapped critter, perhaps a cricket or cicada. He knocked on the wall, and the sound stopped. Then it started again. He slapped the wall again, and it stopped. He gave up and decided the critter would eventually die.

"Hey, Cal."

The voice again from the vent. Chris was his name. Cal didn't feel like climbing back onto the sink. It required energy and a balancing act. But the man was nice and he'd felt better after the first visit. He threw back the sheet and blanket, pushed himself from the bunk and carefully, slowly, scaled the sink, as though he was climbing a cliff with few footholds. "Yes."

"You okay?"

"Yeah. Why?

"You were hitting the wall again."

"I heard something in the wall," Cal said.

"Weird sounds in these walls," Chris replied. "By the way, Cal, what's your last name?"

"Ferguson."

"Old family name?" Chris inquired.

"Very old, all the way back to the first Scottish monarch Angus MacFergus, sixth century. And yours?"

"Cruz," Chris responded.

"Old family?"

"You might say that," Chris said, his voice solemn. "Cruz is Spanish for cross."

Silence, Cal unsure how to respond.

Chris picked up the thread. Where're you from, Cal Ferguson?"

"Rome."

"That's a hike from here."

"Rome down the road," Cal said.

"Gotcha!"

"And you?" Cal asked.

"San Jose."

"San Jose? There's not a San Jose, Mississippi."

"California!"

"But this prison's in Mississippi!" Cal remarked astonished.

"This is a private prison," Chris said. "It's run by SRAA."

"What's SRAA?"

"Social Rehabilitation Agency of America. They're headquartered somewhere up north. All of the prisoners in here, except for the county jail, are from western states—California, Arizona, New Mexico, Nevada, Idaho. SRAA owns fifty other private prisons."

"That's a lot of private jails," Cal said amazed. He'd never heard of private prisons.

"There are private jails all over the country owned by other corporations. It's big money. Crime pays," Chris said angrily.

"What's wrong with the state prisons?" Cal asked.

"Overcrowded," said Chris. "Here's the deal. Private prison corporations spend millions lobbying legislatures to be tough on crime, especially drugs. Criminal count goes up."

"Surely, not that much," Cal said disbelievingly.

"Go figure. In the early eighties, the U S. prison population was four hundred thousand. Today, due mostly to drug convictions, it's in the millions."

"Unbelievable!"

"Believe it. Ten years ago, only five private prisons in the country. Now, over a hundred."

Over the course of the conversation, Cal's feet had slipped on the sink ledge, and he had to reposition them. There had to be a better way to talk to your next door neighbor.

"I've been here three days," Cal said, "In segregation, can you ever talk without having to stand on a sink. Do you ever eat together?"

"No eating together, my man. As you've seen, trays come through the food portal. That's it. There are showers and rec time," Chris added. "You've seen the five shower cages along the pod wall. You can visit with other inmates if you're showering at the same time. Have you been?"

"No," Cal said.

"Taking a shower is an ordeal," Chris informed. "You have to be handcuffed through the portal, led by two guards to a shower stall, placed in the cage, cage door locked, cuffs removed through the shower portal, your clothes passed through the portal, and all of that before they turn on the water."

"*They* turn it on?"

"No knobs," Chris said. "The guards turn it on. If they remember. Some don't care. They put you in and walk off. If they're having a good day, the water will be warm. If you're lucky, they'll remember to turn it off. If you're even luckier, they'll remember to come and get you. I've stood in a shower cage for several hours."

"With the water on?"

"With the water on. After your shower, the whole process is reversed. It's an ordeal for the guards as well. They don't like taking inmates to the showers. A lot of the inmates don't like it either."

"I take it rec is recreation," Cal said.

"You got it. Inmates in solitary can't play basketball or baseball. We can't be on a team, around other people. That's why we're called segregated. But they've got wire cages out back. You been yet?"

"Nope. Didn't know about them."

"The guards cuff us, lead us out a back door at the end of the long hall they walked us down to get us here, then put us, one by one, each to a cage, then remove the cuffs."

"What can you do in a wire cage you can't do in here?"

"Not much," Chris said. "Hang on the wire links, breathe in some fresh air, chat through the wire with the inmate in the next cage. Maybe some exercise: pushups, jogging around the cage. An hour of standing, hanging on wire mesh, talking, and exercising. That's about it, guards holding cameras on you constantly."

"Cameras?" Cal questioned surprised. "You can't go anywhere."

"The chainlink. Inmates work the wire loose and make weapons, shanks. That's also why there's no cardboard cylinder in the toilet paper rolls. Shanks can be fashioned from them."

"My God!" Cal exclaimed.

"I almost forgot," Chris said. "Another way of communicating with other inmates is fishing."

"Does the prison have a pond?"

Chris chuckled. "No pond. Inmates put a message inside a flattened milk carton, attach a long string to the carton, and propel it under the door across the floor. Someone else snares the carton with their carton and reels it in. If you'll notice, there's a two-inch gap between the bottom of the cell door and floor. Inmates can do a lot with two inches."

"I take it fishing is a no-no."

"Correct. With or without a license," Chris added with another chuckle. "But the guards tolerate it. They're even amused by it."

"Do you have a cellmate?" Cal probed speaking softly. He'd seen other guards enter the pod.

"Negative. I'm in protective custody. That's the reason I'm in segregation."

"Protected from what?" Cal pursued.

"From whom," Chris corrected, his voice dropping to a deep whisper.

"They said I snitched. But I've never ratted on anyone."

"Who is they?" Cal pressed.

"The guards and other prisoners."

"I don't understand."

"Neither do I. It was all so innocent. I was in general population just down the hall from us. On certain days, the guards handed out sugar packets for our coffee. On an off day, I saw the box of sugar packets, reached in, got one, and immediately guards were all over me."

"For taking a sugar packet?"

"It wasn't sugar in the packet, Cal. It was crystal meth. I had stepped into a drug deal."

"I may have stepped into one myself," Cal said under his breath.

"What was that?" Chris responded.

"Nothing. Go on. You stepped into a drug deal, and the guards were giving them to the inmates?"

"You got it," Chris said. "Guards get this job to make real money, not ten dollars an hour. Female guards give sex for privileges, favors, and money."

"Sex! In here?"

"Don't be naive, Cal. Whatever happens in the free world, happens in prison. Two halves of the same real world."

"But how can they have sex? Cameras are everywhere."

"Trust me, Cal. They find ways," Chris remarked. "Anyway, back to my story. I was cuffed and whisked away and, to protect me, and possibly someone else, the warden put me in solitary. The gang the meth was for are after my hide. They'd probably kill me if they could get their hands on me. That wouldn't look good for the warden."

"But it's terrible you got put in solitary," Cal said.

"Not so bad," Chris said. "Solitary has its upside. My cell is my sanctuary. I'm alive. I'm alone. I don't have to deal with the crazies in general population. I can do my thing and don't have to worry about others looking over my shoulder."

"And you're protected."

"It's not foolproof," Chris replied. "I have to keep an eye out. The gang can plant a member in segregation. Sometimes gang members in the free world with no police record hire on as guards and really do some damage."

"But gang members are prisoners. They've got no control," Cal surmised.

"They control in weird ways. Some cause fights just to get transferred to segregation to get to their targets. The ones with cell phones have been known to call in hit orders from a shot caller outside and vice versa."

"Shot caller?"

"A gang leader who calls the shots. We have them in this prison."

There was a pause, Cal pondering. "What's the downside?"

"I get lonely. In solitary, you live in a world where you know only yourself, and sometimes you don't know that. Mighty glad they put you in the cell next to me. It's been vacant for months."

A commotion came from down below. Men wearing suits and a lady in a dress and heels entering the pod.

"The brass," Chris said lowering his voice.

"Brass?"

"Later, Bro. Get down!"

CHAPTER 6

Driving back over the same road, twice in the same day, seeing again the same bleak and barren land, the emptiness of the house weighing heavier and heavier upon him so that when he inserted the key into the front door lock, he couldn't turn it. He stood there looking at it, asking himself whether, if he turned it, he was unlocking or locking something. He couldn't stand there forever. It was late afternoon, approaching dusk, the hardest time of day for him. Some called it the "sundowner's syndrome." It used to represent the end of a day of hard work, the shades of the night bringing on a new one. Now he feared the sleepless dark.

He returned to his truck and stood beside it, felt the heat from the motor still warm from the drive. He could sleep in the cab and risk dying from carbon monoxide, that thought spiraling into the early twilight. He decided instead to walk to the mailbox. He knew there'd be no mail on Thanksgiving Day, but did he remember getting it the day before? The box was empty. "I thought I had," he mumbled to himself, eyes scanning the fields. He wished it was February, disking time, when he had something to do. Winter was hard enough for farmers waiting for planting time to kick in again.

He walked back to the truck, leaned against the front grill and, arms folded, stared at the house, at the sheer whiteness of it. He recalled on summer days when the sun was high and bright, how his eyes ached, looking at the white clapboard structure. At the tall white round pillars, the long white porch that wrapped around the side, the white outbuildings, white barn. Athen liked the color white, said it gave the place a classic, clean look. White drapes were in the bedrooms. The kitchen and bathroom were white— white tile, white fixtures, white appliances, and white curtains. On the beds were white sheets and white bedspread. *Aye damn, you make change hard*, the thought almost whispered as if she could hear. The only room not white was the great room, where he had stood his ground. It was a man's room, he had argued, and needed the colors of hunting and the land.

He focused again on the front door (it was white, too), the key still in it, the ruby red fob Athen had platted dangling, the only color, like a spot of blood, he could see. The last time he'd seen Athen walk through that door in her precise and graceful stride, she was wearing a pair of black boots and blue jeans and white blouse, her hair tied back with a red bandana. She was leaving to go to the parsonage to help Sally pack and, after she had kissed him, looked back over her shoulder and said to him in her low and husky voice, "See you tomorrow, Dear." That was three days ago and, as if tomorrow had never come, he was seeing her more than ever, the quiet beauty of her face with its broad brow and arched eyes, the simple way she did her hair and the simple but stylish way she wore her clothes, the classic (that word again) beauty she was.

He walked back to the door, took a deep breath, turned the key in the lock, opened it, and stepped inside to that slightly musty smell of home, and closed the door.

Facing him, as he entered the great room, was the blackened craw of the stone fireplace that covered the back wall of the high-ceilinged space. A fire would be nice, he thought. He'd fought Athen tooth and toe-nail against gas logs. In her wisdom, she'd said, "There'll come a time we won't be able to build a fire." He wished he had listened to her. But he liked a live fire, loved the art of making one, prided himself on using one match to start it, no paper or starter log. Before her death, he had brought in some wood and stacked it in the leather log holder on the hearth. Yet he didn't feel like building a fire. He didn't have the energy.

He flipped on the overhead light. Reluctantly, he climbed the stairs to the master bedroom, quickly undressed and put on his red flannel pajamas, then removed them and put on another pair that had been given to him by Cal as a Christmas present and never worn.

He got a pillow and blanket that were not white from one of the guest rooms and brought them downstairs. He rumbled around in the kitchen for something to eat. He settled on peanut butter and crackers and a glass of milk. Tomorrow, he told himself, he'd go to Piggly Wiggly and get some food, probably frozen dinners.

He tried watching an old western. They always made him feel good, especially the upbeat music. He got part way into *Shane* and turned it off when a family's house burned while they were attending a funeral. He lay there a while longer and thought about Cal in prison and how he could change places with him and not know the difference. Except the space would be smaller.

He turned off the lights and lay on the couch listening to the ticking of the empty house and thinking. And thinking. He kept tossing and turning, images of Athen and Sally and Shelley and the blackened ashes and ruins flashing in his mind. *I turned and ran* he thought. *They needed me, and I ran.* He'd never run from anything in his life.

Before dawn, he flung the blanket onto the floor and got up. He may have some bad nights ahead of him, but he wouldn't go through another like this one. He put on his khaki pants and shirt which he'd brought down with his bedding. He pulled on his socks and brogans. He slipped into his hunting coat and put on a Cleveland Indians billed cap. He had been an Indians fan since 1954 when they lost the World Series in four straight games, the year, too, he was released from Parchman.

Dawns were always better for him than dusks, and there was nothing like the Delta at dawn, nothing like it anywhere. That first flush of light on a horizon straight as if God had laid down a ruler and drawn it. The first shafts shooting upward from behind it like a bomb going off on the other side of the world, firing the clouds jonquil and pink and orange until the whole eastern sky seemed on fire. Then that first cusp of light, old as time, bright as a welder's arc bulging into the fading dark. Its rays streaking across the flatness and you seeing them before anybody else in the world, before they struck beaches or ocean waves or touched the tops of the great mountains, because there was nothing in between to stop them as they raced that straight and true across the earth, that pure and unobstructed and undefiled.

As he drove, the endless changing colors above detracted from the endless drab surrounding him, and he felt slightly... What did he feel? He wasn't sure what it was he felt. It wasn't joy, and it wasn't happiness. It wasn't despair and it wasn't anguish. It was a cut above the latter and a far piece to the other. He guessed a ray of hope had touched him and he thanked the

Lord for the Delta dawn.

He drove on.

He pulled into the parsonage drive and cut the motor. He sat a moment reviewing the scene, then opened the door, got out, and slammed it.

He circled the house once, then again, finding nothing, telling himself he couldn't go too slowly, anything might be a piece that solved the mystery.

He walked to the front of the house and crossed where the porch would have been, his feet crunching loudly on the loose slag. The air smelled of ashes and smoke, the aroma of fire and carbon. Half-buried in cinders was a metal rod. It was heavy, probably steel. He wasn't sure what it had been attached to. He picked it up and shook off the rubbish. *It might come in handy.*

He moved a little farther and stopped. He was standing in what had been the living room. He used the rod to probe the debris, an eerie feeling passing through him that he might be stirring Shelley's ashes. He continued rummaging with his rod, flipping charred bits of wood, wondering again what he might find. He poked through crusted ashes, tapped on blackened rubble. He wasn't sure what he was looking for. He didn't investigate fires. He'd heard that experts could find the point of flame ignition and always wondered how they could do that as he poked around the razed ruins.

He entered where the kitchen would've been. He had been in it before a few times and recalled the placement of some items. The clustered shards of dishes and brittle-rusted cans, gray-smoked bits of broken bottles. He avoided the bedrooms. He couldn't go there. The fire wouldn't have started there.

The sun was well up, traffic picking up on the county road, people slowing, gawking. He decided he'd done enough, all he could do. He didn't know if the church office was open the day after Thanksgiving, but he didn't want to be there if it was and Sadie Doom, if she was still the church secretary, see him and question what he was doing there.

CHAPTER 7

November 29 Saturday

For forty-eight hours, the prison had been on lock-down. The pod had been noticeably quieter. Cal asked one of the guards and got a one-word response: audit.

Mid-afternoon Saturday, he heard pecking and clambered up to the vent.

"Whose brass?" the first words out of his mouth.

"Corporate," Chris said. "Upper management. There's usually a lockdown when they come."

"A guard said it was due to an audit."

"You bet," responded Chris. "Staff fears audits like plagues, especially the warden. If the brass finds errors, heads roll. Recently, a nurse was fired for giving a candy mint to an inmate."

"What's wrong with that?"

"Mints are contraband."

Silence, Cal absorbing the new information. Then, "Where were we?"

"I'd told you why I'm in segregation," Chris said. "What's your reason?"

"Manslaughter."

"That's not enough to put you in seg," Chris said. "There're guys in here for less. What's the real reason?"

"I don't know. Maybe they think I'm suicidal. But I'm not. I've told them I'm not."

"Everybody's suicidal at first," Chris said. "Who'd you kill?"

"A county supervisor. Except I didn't do it."

"I believe you. But that shouldn't be a security issue."

"Then my house burned right after the jury's verdict..." He choked. He opened his lips. Nothing came out.

"I understand," Chris said empathetically.

Finally, he swallowed and managed, "I told you—"

"No need to explain, Cal. You told me about your losses. I don't know what to say, man. I feel your pain."

"I hope you can't," Cal replied.

More silence, awkward, uneasy.

"Did you have enemies?" Chris asked.

"I upset some people. I was the pastor of a Methodist church. It had been an old established white congregation. The three years I was there we integrated blacks into the church membership, admitted a Palestinian Arab couple, several gays"

"You had enemies!"

A buzzer sounded. Below, a pod door opened and closed. Cal bent down and looked through the door window to see if a guard had entered the pod, but it was one of the nurses making rounds. He raised up and spoke again through the vent. "My granddad's looking into the fire."

"You could help him in here," Chris suggested.

"I don't see how."

"A prison is a rumor mill, its grapevine's more compact and alive than in the free world. Keep your ears open. Inmates talk."

"You're the only inmate I know," Cal said.

"You just got here," Chris reminded him. "You'll meet others. Don't forget about the guards. They know the local scoop. They gab more than the inmates."

"But can I believe what I hear?"

"Let me put it to you like this, Cal. In the free world, two plus two equals four. In prison, it might equal three which means you have to figure what to add to correct the math. Or, it might equal five, which means you have to compute what to subtract to get it right. Ironically, that's why most prisoners are here. They can add and subtract, but they want to do it their way. The longer you're here, the more you learn how to sort out the crap from the truth, learn the difference between a prisoner and an inmate."

"I thought they were the same."

"Big difference," Cal said. "An inmate is one who plans to get out someday and will follow the rules, do the math right; a prisoner doesn't care, this is his life. Tell me your story, man. I might be able to help you."

Should he tell this stranger his story?

"You still there?" Chris asked.

"I'm thinking," Cal responded.

"About what?"

Another pause. "About two plus two."

Chris laughed. "Believe me, I totally understand. The world's full of two-faced people. No rush. There's no hurry in here. The only people who hurry are on the outside. The real prison's not in *here* but out *there*," Chris said, "if you get my drift. We can wait. Blessed are those who wait for the Lord. The spirit moves where it will."

The spirit moves where it will. "Jesus said that," Cal said surprised. "You read the Bible."

"Constantly. God's word is the path out of any prison, in here or out there."

His words caught Cal off guard, and he almost lost his balance. More and more, the man was raising his curiosity. "Trust is a two-way street. Tell me your story."

"Dude, you drive a tough bargain. If we have enough time," Chris said lowering his voice. "We don't need to be talking through the vent when the guards make rounds."

"Thanks for the heads up."

"My story may be in serial form."

"I like serials," Cal said, and for the first time since he had been incarcerated, felt distracted.

Chris began with his teenage years, his first arrest at age fifteen for petty theft to support a cocaine habit. He told of subsequent years, imprisonment almost every year until he was twenty-one, all robbery convictions to support his drug habit. He described how he never used a weapon but simulated a gun telling convenience store clerks he would shoot them if they didn't give him the cash. "In my late thirties, I used a real gun, one I'd stolen. I robbed a branch bank in Pasadena, California, and was immediately arrested. I never shot or hurt anyone. I drew a twenty-year sentence for armed robbery."

"Obviously, at some point, your life took a turn," Cal said.

"A big turn. While I was in rehab ninety days at San Quentin, I met a man who was serving a life sentence for cocaine trafficking. He had had a clean record, no history of violence, weapons, or previous incarceration. I'd done more and drew a lesser sentence. I was impressed with this man's serenity, how he moved day to day with a sense of hope and balance. He educated himself and built a career while in prison. I felt I had something to learn from him."

"You got time to tell me what you learned, or is that the next chapter?" Cal asked hearing movement in the pod.

"I looked," Chris said. "No guards, yet. Where was I?"

"What you learned."

"I began studying the Bible, and I learned that darkness is sacred ground, that God meets us in our helplessness and dark nights of the soul and will lead us through them. I began praying and developing prison-based intercessory prayer groups."

"Prison-based?"

"I type newsletters and send them out to churches and groups around the country and the world. I tell them about God's good word for them."

"So that's it!" Cal murmured.

"What?" Chris exclaimed.

"The typewriter explains the pecking sounds."

"Is it a nuisance?"

"Not now that I know."

Chris continued. "The warden, when he moved me to solitary, knew about my newsletters, good publicity for him and the prison. He allowed me to keep my typewriter. Family and friends on the outside keep me supplied with paper and typing ribbons."

"I thought it was an insect or something trapped in the walls."

"If we're not careful, my friend, we're the ones who feel trapped. It all depends on attitude."

"You're a philosopher, Chris."

"Perhaps. Philosophers think a lot. Prisoners think a lot. Now! Your story."

Cal thought about it, impressed with this man he couldn't see.

"You already know I'm a minister," he began.

The sound of doors opening and closing, footsteps. Cal stepped onto the lower shelf beside the sink, looked out and pulled himself back up to the vent. "It'll have to wait."

"I heard them, too. Next time. God bless, Cal."

"You, too." He hopped down, jack-knifed into his bunk, then came the rap on the door.

"You okay in there?" a loud, unfamiliar voice shouted.

Cal gave a thumbs up.

"I need to see your face," the guard shouted again.

Cal turned over and looked up.

"All right," the guard said satisfied then moved on.

After balancing himself on the lip of a sink for a long time, Cal was tired and sleepy. He laid on the bunk, shifted his hips and gazed again through the window. Beyond the garbled skeins of chain-link and barbed wire, a large field stretched into a line of trees. In the Delta, a line of trees usually meant a creek or river. He was looking west. The line of trees had to be the Sunflower River. The irony struck him. He was imprisoned on land he'd hunted on in his teens before it was posted. He knew beyond the Sunflower was the Mississippi River levee, beyond the levee was the river and beyond the Mississippi was .... His eyelids grew heavy and closed.

CHAPTER 8

December 1 Monday

It was dark in the cell when Cal opened his eyes, only meager reflected light from the outside security and indoor pod lights that burned twenty-four seven. A loud buzzer had signaled the three a.m. count.

Each time he awakened in the cool empty solitude, smells of body odor, feces, urine, and flatulence assaulted his nose as his vision reconstructed the world around him, his eyes colliding first with the black steel bunk overhead before the rest of his small new world fell into place.

He had been there a week, but it seemed like years. In that brief skin of time, you'd think he'd know where he was when he woke up. When he got out in twenty years, would his senses have to readjust all over again, prison life so stamped upon them. In his world of sheltered grief and solitary anger, did it even matter where he was when he woke up, as long as he woke up? He kept hoping each time he went to sleep he would awaken and, like a fever breaking, the pain would go away. But each time he awakened, he was slammed anew by grief, by memories powering up from the darkness within. He kept waiting to hear the sound of his soul. But nothing came from that dark night.

He waited until a guard came to his window, shined a light on his face to verify his presence. After his count, he pulled the sheet over his head and returned to sleep only to be awakened again by loud clattering. He knew that sound. Guards pushing food tray trolleys. A large rectangular slot at the bottom of the door dropped open with a loud clang. A tray of food slid through the opening. "Breakfast!" a voice barked.

"What time is it?" Cal asked irritated. Breakfast was usually after the six o'clock count.

"Five o'clock."

"I'm not hungry," he growled from his bunk.

"Take it, Ferguson," a female guard's high-pitched rude voice squawked.

"I don't want it."

"Get off your ass and take it or I'm dropping it."

He had more energy to get up and take it than clean it up. He pushed himself out of the bunk, slipped his feet into flip-flops, and took the tray. The food flap clanged shut and was bolted.

He took the tray to his bunk, balanced it on his knees and surveyed the fare. A slab of scrambled eggs. Two slices of charred bacon. A small container of oatmeal that looked congealed. Two pieces of burned toast. A small carton of milk and a plastic cup of cold coffee. Nothing looked good. He felt a sick lurch in his stomach. He didn't feel like eating breakfast. He set the tray on the floor and curled back up on the bunk, pulled the covers over him. His feet stayed cold. He had been told the air conditioning ran continuously, even in winter, the temperature kept constant at 68 degrees. The only heat was in the administrative offices. He guessed that was one of the reasons he'd been requisitioned a pocketless fleece jacket his first day. Inmates stayed warm by wrapping up in their blankets, wearing the fleece jackets, or both.

It was Monday morning December first. He glanced at a small calendar he was allowed to have then plopped his head back onto his pillow and again stared at the bunk above him and thought, ran the numbers: *twenty more years, 7,293 days to go.* The writer of Proverbs had said, "Without a vision, the people perish." Sometimes he closed his eyes hoping for one. But none came. Nothing came.

Except for the visits from his granddad, the chaplain, the guard Durasmus, and his conversations with Chris, he existed in a vacuum. No former church members had visited him. One, Mrs. Turbyville, brought some chocolate-chip cookies. They were broken into pieces by the time they came to him, guards at checkpoint helping themselves and making sure nothing was inside of them. He tried to shift the negatives to the edges of his mind. But they kept flying back to his core, like iron shavings to a magnet. If he could get rid of the magnet...that thought dangling unsolved.

His second day, Durasmus had completed a form for him requesting writing paper and a pen, any books allowed. So far, none of his requests had been filled. He wondered now why he had requested paper and pen. He didn't have anyone to write to except his granddad, and he could see him once a week.

At regular intervals, nurses came and checked on him. They asked the same questions: How are you? How is your sleep? Your appetite? Do you have any thoughts of harming or killing yourself? So they'd move on, he responded in monosyllables. They didn't seem to know why he was there or what had happened to him. None offered condolences. Like the guards, they didn't seem to care. They were doing their job. He was in a prison smack in the middle of the poorest county in the state, maybe the nation, seventy-five percent of the population was black and most of the rest, was poor whites. This may be the only job some of them had ever had, the only paycheck they had ever seen.

Not all of the staff was like that. Durasmus was different. He came at least once daily and sometimes more. The first few times, he'd tap on the window, motion for Cal to come to the door and each time ask him, in a whisper through the jamb, if he had any thoughts of hurting himself and each time Cal whispered an emphatic, "No." Durasmus would give a thumbs up, and Cal would respond in kind. Durasmus would leave, and each time Cal would watch him descend the steel gridded steps and cross the common area. As far as Cal could tell, Durasmus saw no one else in the pod and was keeping his word to his granddad.

Cal's breakfast tray still lay on the floor by his bed. If he had been home, he would be eating breakfast with Sally and Shelley. That was how their day began. Then he would take Shelley to school, return to the church for morning devotion, swing by the area hospitals to check on the sick, and back at the church to prepare the Wednesday prayer meeting message. Mid-afternoon, he would pick up Shelley and take her by the Kream Kup for a cone of custard. He would take her home, then return to the church, enter the sanctuary, kneel at the chancel rail, and pray for half an hour. Next, he would turn in the outline for Sunday's service to Mrs. Doom, the church secretary, so she could get the bulletins printed on Saturday.

That's why he was in prison. He had left the sanctuary and driven by Mrs. Doom's house to drop off an envelope, information on a newborn that needed to get into the Sunday bulletin. How many people did he know who had been in the right place doing the right thing at the right time and suddenly were in the wrong place at the wrong time? His anger boiled up again.

He kicked the food tray and sent it sailing, dollops of scrambled eggs and oatmeal flying against the wall and onto the floor. A flip-flop landed in the sink. His big toe throbbed with pain and he sat on his bunk holding it.

A female guard, the same who'd delivered his food, knocked on his window. "What happened?"

"I dropped the tray," he said.

"On your toe?"

He nodded.

"I guess you dropped your flip-flop in the sink, too, huh?"

He didn't respond.

She shouted angrily. "Have it cleaned up by the time I come back, you hear?"

He looked up at the window and shook his head he would. He was still holding his toe when she left. He tried standing on it. Not broken. No bleeding. No skin broken. "That was stupid," he mumbled to himself. He sat back down on the bunk and looked at the mess he'd made and thought. How could he one minute have the energy to throw a temper fit and the next, in the aftermath, feel it leaving him like air escaping a punctured tire?

For several minutes, he sat there pondering the paradox, then recalled something a psychology professor had said in seminary: "You can't be mad and depressed at the same time." Cal looked again at the mess. He thought about what the guard had said and decided he'd better clean it up while he was still mad at her. Maybe the nourishment he needed was not food. He needed anger. He needed to get mad more often, at something or somebody. Based upon the short time he'd been there, he shouldn't have much trouble.

"Hey, Cal!" Chris calling through the vent.

Cal climbed up. Before he could say anything—

"What's going on over there?" Chris asked.

"I got into it with a guard about the food and tossed a tray."

"It's part of the racket."

"Sorry I disturbed you," Cal reacted.

"Not that racket, the private prison racket. SRAA gets paid a set fee by states to incarcerate their excess prisoners. To make an extra buck, brass cuts corners with the food."

"That's why it tastes like mush," Cal griped.

"It is mush," Chris quipped. "The cooks are inmates. They get paid a few cents an hour which brings up another profit angle. States don't tell corporations like SRAA where they can keep their prisoners. So, the companies house them where the cost of living is lower, a la your Mississippi Delta, not California, Arizona, Idaho, Nevada, etcetera, etcetera."

"But it costs to transport them," Cal said intrigued.

"Ah," Chris breathed into the vent. "SRAA has its own travel agency: buses, vans, airplanes."

A brief pause, Cal mulling. "So you don't have visitation. Your family's thousands of miles away."

"You got it, my man. My wife and two children won't see me until my time is up, another eight years. They don't have the money or means to travel to Mississippi for visitation. I could kick up a ruckus. The prison might send me back to California, add more time to my sentence. It's a catch-22."

The comment about family ambushed Cal, and he couldn't respond. He swallowed and finally said, "I know about catch-22."

"That's what I mean by 'racket,'" Chris continued his voice agitated. "Prisoners ripped from their families, transported hundreds of miles. The state saves a buck, SRAA makes a buck, over a billion last year."

Cal couldn't believe what he was hearing. "How do you know all this stuff?"

"Libraries," Chris said in a calmer voice. "When I was in general population, I had access to the prison and law libraries."

A buzzer sounded. Nine o'clock count.

"Catch you later, Bro," Chris said, and they tapped off.

CHAPTER 9

December 2 Tuesday

For several days, the parsonage fire continued nagging Shell. Cal had said the house had passed inspection. There had to be more to the combustion than faulty wiring, a house burning like that. Maybe he missed something in the ruins. Or something not in the ruins.

He made another early morning trip back to the site. He gave the rubble another thorough reconnaissance, then crossed where the back door would have been and into the backyard. Ahead was a privet hedge, beyond it vacant fields that would be disked come early spring. Between him and the privet hedge were scattered peach and apple trees planted decades ago by an elderly couple who had built the house. Shell breathed in the sweet aroma of rotting fruit, the only good smell in the air.

In a corner of the backyard, shrouded in Johnson grass and ragweed, lay a heap of cypress boards, the remains of a shed. A bird was tweeting a one-note somewhere behind him, another answering. A slight breeze moved the grass.

He headed for the shed, poked and pried around the boards. Nothing. Brushing back weeds and tall grass with his rod, he worked his way to the rear of the collapsed heap. He turned to make his way back to the ruins, and something caught the tail of his eye, an object in the privet hedge behind the fallen shed. He stepped closer. It was a large can. The letters on it said Kerosene. He didn't dare touch or move it. He leaned close to it and smelled. The odor was fresh.

"I'll be," he whispered to himself.

He squeezed through the hedge around the can, careful not to dislodge it, and stood facing empty acreage. He looked down, his eyes scouring the ground. Between the hedge and the fields, he saw a print, probably a boot.

The soil had hardened after a light rain on Monday, the day before the fire. And so had the prints. He saw another, then another, others beyond it, paralleling sets leading straight ahead. *There were two of them,* he surmised. By the lighter impression of one set, they probably belonged to a smaller man, then he thought again. *It could've been a woman.* He followed the boot prints until he came to a turn-around, a field road running perpendicular to it.

"My, my," he muttered to himself. Tire tracks. He bent down and studied the treads. Mud tire, by the tread pattern, Mohawks, same as on his pickup. But he'd never driven on the crop road behind the parsonage. There was no way to trace the tires. Every tire store sold Mohawks. Then he looked closer and saw something different. In the center of the left rear tire track was a perfect circle. Maybe a gravel rock. More likely a roofing tack lodged in the tread. He followed the track, the mark repeating itself at regular intervals.

The tracks indicated the pickup came from the west, turned around and headed back in that direction, where the field road connected with a two-lane blacktop that terminated in the small town of Merigold and Highway 61. From there, it was anybody's guess where it went.

He pondered his next move. He didn't dare report this to the local authorities. For all he knew, they were the fox guarding the chicken coop, part of the same ignorance and incompetence running the county. The sheriff's department either refused or simply didn't order a formal investigation regarding the cause of the fire. And it drew its funds from the county supervisors. And a county supervisor, the county supervisor of this district, was the one his grandson had been falsely accused and convicted of killing.

He removed his cell phone from his shirt pocket. Athen had taught him how to take photos with it. He focused the lens on the tire tracks, especially the left rear, and footprints and took pictures of each then wheeled to catch their relationship to the hedge and the ruins. With that same view, he snapped a picture of the kerosene can in the hedge, then took some close up shots.

He finished taking photos and stood looking at the ruins, his thinking threading the possibilities. He'd heard of a Bermuda Triangle in the Atlantic where airplanes and ships disappeared. The Bethel Triangle, as the locals referred to it, might give the Bermuda a run for its money. It was one of the most insubordinate and rebellious areas in the county, perhaps the state. In the '60's and earlier, it was a center of Klan activity. Civil rights activists, black and white, had entered the area never to be heard from again. Federal agents in search of the missing met similar dooms. The conflict of those years died down, but the region remained a hotbed of recalcitrants and malcontents. Cal had integrated a white church with blacks along with a couple of Christian Arabs from Palestine. Maybe some old remnant of the Klan torched the parsonage. All of this, he knew, was speculation.

Of one thing he felt assured.

The ruins needed a yellow tape around them. "Crime scene, do not enter," he whispered to himself.

CHAPTER 10

December 7 Sunday

The guard Durasmus brought his grandson to him. Shell and Cal sat facing each other in the same room amid the same bare walls the same nauseous yellow color Shell detested. The same insect-like buzzing of the fluorescent bulbs. The same damp, lonely concrete smell of the room. Cal sat in the same place on the same metal chair in the same position, his hands cuffed behind him. Shell decided same was a word he needed to get used to.

Cal had not shaved, creating a dark quality to his lower face. His eyes looked weak and hollow, his skin pale as paper and he appeared thinner in the oversized jumpsuit.

Leaning forward and putting his elbows on his knees, Shell spoke first. "It's been over a week. Are you all right?"

"I don't know."

"Do you feel okay?"

"Maybe. I'm burned out crying."

"Feelings can change by the minute the first few days," Shell advised.

"The second, too," Cal said. "They may have stopped. There's not much left."

Shell could see the anger and frustration in the tight, bunched muscles of his grandson's neck. He scooted his chair closer, their knees almost touching.

"Are you sleeping?" Shell asked.

"Some, more than at first."

"Eating?"

"The food is horrible," he complained.

"Some people live to eat," Shell said. "You've lost a lot of weight, look thin as a rail. You've gotta eat to live, understand?"

"Yessir. Just not sure why I'm living," his voice crumbling with self-pity.

"I understand," Shell said. "I'd feel the same if I was living in this hole."

"Why am I here?" he complained nodding toward the floor. "They call it segregation, but it's solitary confinement. I'm not suicidal. Nurses check on me regularly. I've told them I'm not."

"I plan to speak with the warden about it," Shell said.

"When?"

"Got an appointment this Wednesday." He was tired of looking at Cal in cuffs, his arms wrenched behind his back. He raised a finger. "Just a minute." He stood and rapped his knuckles on the door.

The guard opened the door.

"Mr. Durasmus, sir. It's painful enough what's happened to my boy, to both of us, and more painful having to look at him like he's armless."

"I understand," Durasmus said. "But all inmates in the segregation units have to be cuffed when they leave their cell. Regulations."

Shell looked at him. "I understand the letter of the law. There's something called the spirit of the law. There's something called compassion. You can lock the door. He's not going anywhere."

"All right," Durasmus said sympathetically. "I guess it cain't hurt nothing." He unsnapped the large ring of keys from his wide belt, picked one, moved behind Cal, and unlocked the handcuffs. "But I'll have to put 'em back on before he leaves."

"Not a problem," Shell acknowledged.

The guard departed. Shell sat again on the metal folding chair facing Cal who sat rubbing his wrists. Leaning back, Shell saw two bright spots in his eyes where the overhead light shined.

"That's better, Granddad. Thank you."

"We need to whisper," Shell said his eyes scanning the room, the upper corners. "You never know who might be listening in."

"Granddad, you're being paranoid."

"I've been in prisons before. Eyes and ears are everywhere." He leaned in closer. "I've got some questions." He looked back over his shoulder at the small square window in the door. "I've gone back to the parsonage several times and looked around. Somethings not right about the fire." He'd already decided not to tell him about the photos he'd taken.

"There was no reason for it," Cal said angrily, hunched over, hands dangling between his knees.

"The timing bothers me, coming only a few days after the trial ended. Then the sloppiness, ineptitude a better word, of the investigation. Not just of the fire but of Ty Doom's murder. After all, Doom was a county supervisor, a power figure. The sheriff's department dragged its feet. The prosecution's case was based upon circumstantial evidence."

"Circumstantial?" Cal blurted.

Shell snapped a finger over his lips and thumbed over his shoulder at the door.

Cal lowered his voice. "They had no evidence. His wife was the church secretary. That was all she was."

Shell thought before he replied. Sadie Beatrice Doom was a looker, hot to trot, *fast*, some had said. Cal and Sally had been having problems; her resentment at her confining role, his long pastoral hours. But his grandson was not the type to have an affair. He was committed to his marriage. "I know," he agreed, "And I believe you. But it didn't help when she testified on the witness stand, under oath, that she'd been having an affair with you." Shell recalled that, too, how she sat all prim and proper in the witness box, long blonde hair pulled up in a bun, telling it with no emotion, no inflection in her voice, looking straight ahead at nothing, like a robot, as if she'd been programmed.

"That didn't prove I killed her husband," Cal exclaimed. He was becoming agitated, moving to the edge of his chair, legs pumping up and down. "Good God! I'm twenty years younger than Sadie Doom. She was having an affair, all right, but it wasn't with me. She lied to protect *her* lover or someone else. Makes me wonder if *she* didn't shoot Doom herself."

"All I'm saying is that her testimony didn't help you," Shell repeated, his voice even, calm, "And your prints on the gun didn't either," he added wishing he hadn't been so blunt. "Sorry, Son, I know you're still reeling from all that's happened, but your innocence is at stake. I'm trying to get to things that'll help you."

"I understand. But we've been over what didn't help me. I was framed."

"I think you were, too. Her lie on the stand was a coverup," Shell responded. "It came across staged. But the prosecutor made a big deal about the prints, blowing them up on an overhead projector for the whole courtroom to see, a fingerprint expert on the stand explaining them."

"I didn't even own a gun," Cal grimaced. "The one that killed Doom was his own, a Glock Seventeen, a semi-automatic. I don't even know how to use one. I said that on the stand."

"And the prosecutor came right back, that if you didn't know how to use one why'd you pick it up."

"That's true," Cal agreed. "It was a knee-jerk reaction, I'd heard something. The gun was fired at close range. They didn't check me for powder burns," his voice rising again.

"That brings us full circle to the inept investigators," Shell said. "Think back to that afternoon when you went to the Doom house. Had you been in the house before?"

"Only once. I testified to that. I'd gone there the first day I arrived on the charge to introduce Sally and me and Shelley to Mrs. Doom because she was the church secretary. The District Superintendent, Brother Hammingtree, said that after going to the parsonage, that should be my next stop."

"How long were you there?" Shell asked.

"About fifteen minutes."

"Do you recall much about the house, what you did while you were there?"

"I don't understand these questions, Granddad. I feel like I'm on the witness stand again."

"You'll understand," Shell advised. "It all has to do with proving your innocence. I have questions that were not asked when you were on the stand. Bear with me."

Cal sighed and gave a reluctant nod. "Her husband was not at home. I rang the doorbell. Mrs. Doom invited us in, that's how I always addressed her, 'Mrs. Doom.' We stepped into a foyer, and she directed us to the living room to the left of the foyer. Sally and I sat on one of two brocaded couches, Shelley sat in a chair beside our couch and Mrs.—" He paused and stood. "Mrs. Doom sat across from us on the other couch. Except Shelley didn't sit much. She was up and moving about." He stepped nervously to his left, then his right. "Sally was constantly reprimanding her about picking up items and opening and closing drawers and the glass doors of an old armoire that held a collection of antiques and China flatware." He bent over with extended arms, mimicking her movements. "There was a round coffee table between us. A large mirror hung over the fireplace mantel. I remember because it was in a gold, heavily worked frame and I thought it was going to fall the way—" he raised his arms and swayed them to one side "—it was hanging, tilted away from the wall.

"We introduced ourselves," he continued, "said we were glad to be there, and looking forward to working with her." He retraced his steps to his chair and sat down. "She was cordial and pleasant in a matter-of-fact, business-like way. Sally said we couldn't stay long because we still had a lot to unpack and she wanted to get Shelley in bed early. She really wanted to get Shelley out of that room. Mrs. Doom asked if she could help. We politely declined, and she escorted us to the door."

"When you went the day Doom was shot," Shell continued, "the second time you'd been to the house, three years later, starting with the front porch—No! Starting with when you pulled into the driveway—tell me what you saw."

"I've been over that a hundred times."

"Go over it once more."

"Ty Doom's pickup was in the drive," Cal said.

"Was the garage door up?"

"Yes. But I remember seeing only the pickup. There were some white rockers on the porch and hanging ferns I recalled from the first visit."

"Did you notice anything as you walked toward the porch, anything on the walkway to the steps?"

"I wasn't looking at the walk. I was looking up at the door."

"Why the door and not watching your step?"

"Because it was open," Cal said. "The detective asked that question."

"Perhaps he did about the door, but not the other details. The investigation was careless. What did you see next?"

"I climbed the steps and pushed on the door ... no, I rang the doorbell. No one came, so I pushed the door open further and called out for Mrs. Doom. That's why I'd gone there. It was Friday. There'd been a newborn in the church. I needed her to note it in the Sunday bulletin which she printed on Saturdays. I had the information in an envelope. She was not at the church.

I couldn't reach her on her cell phone, and the phone at her house was busy."

"How long did you wait?" Shell continued.

"Counting the time I pushed the doorbell, and the two times I called her name, not long, less than a minute."

"Then you went in," Shell continued.

"Yes."

"Think again. Anything unusual? On the floor, on a table, couch, chair?"

Cal thought. "The house had a peculiar smell."

"How's that?"

"Like extinguished candles."

"That could have been cordite, gunpowder," Shell said. "Investigators placed the time Doom was shot shortly about the time you said you arrived. They may have missed that one,"

"Missed what?" He turned up empty hands.

"The smell is not in the sheriff's report."

"Granddad, you're sounding like a detective."

"A good one, I hope. Just trust me. Keep going. Officers missed some clues, like the smell. We're looking for something you might recall now that you didn't recall at the sheriff's office that day or on the witness stand, something that might stand out, that didn't fit then but in hindsight, might fit now."

"All right. When I stepped into the foyer, the living room was on the left. I saw the same furniture, arranged the same, the same large mirror over the fireplace. The armoire."

"Anything else? The smallest detail could be huge."

"I remember looking in the living room first and saw the reflection of the other room across from it, the den, and in the reflection, a man's legs stretched across floor."

"Hold on! You could see something on the den floor reflected in the living room mantel mirror."

"Yessir. The way the mirror was hanging out from the wall, it didn't reflect directly across but down, at an angle. Perhaps that's something you could check out, if Mrs. Doom would even let you back in."

"There's a lot I plan to check out, including that mirror, though I'm unsure how important it is. You didn't mention that in the sheriff's report or in court," Shell said. "Did you see anything else in that reflection, or in the living room. Perhaps there's something else about that room, anything that appeared out of order, unusual. Hear anything, smell anything else?" He leaned over and with a forefinger lifted Cal's chin, drew his eyes into his. "Anything?"

His grandson took a deep breath. His eyes became fixed, and vertical crevices appeared between them as he struggled to remember, then he closed them. He tilted his head back as though his thoughts shifted in that direction, back to that past. For a long minute, he held that posture, then his head came forward, and he opened his eyes. "Nothing."

"So, what did you do next?" Shell asked.

"I crossed the foyer to the den and saw Ty Doom lying face up. He was bleeding in his upper chest and abdomen."

"In your testimony, you said there was a gun on the floor. Specifically, where was the gun?"

"It was lying near, almost touching Doom's right hand."

"You didn't say this in court."

"I wasn't asked."

"In court, you did say you heard something and picked up the gun."

"That's true," Cal said with exasperation. "I acted on instinct. I wasn't thinking about legal repercussions. Let me think a minute."

"Take your time," Shell encouraged him. "And relax. I read somewhere recently that memory improves when you relax. I'm not a prosecutor going after you on the witness stand. I'm your grandfather."

Cal put his shaved head in his hands, ran his hands across it as though smoothening hair that wasn't there. "I did pick up the gun, but not right away. I checked his pulse. It was weak, but he was still alive. When I touched his wrist, he opened his eyes and looked at me. His mouth moved as though he was struggling to talk to me and that's when I heard something in the next room, or I thought it was the next room, and I picked up the gun, turned, and looked around." He paused. His eyes grew wide. "Damn! I can't believe I forgot that."

"Forgot what?" Shell said edging closer.

"The drawers in that room were open, things scattered about. Perhaps I didn't think much about it. Now I recall something else about the living room from the first time I was there with Sally and Shelley. That's when Shelley was wondering around the room, opening and closing drawers and Sally was fussing at her." He paused.

"Go on," Shell said rolling a hand.

"Funny how memory works, thinking about Shelley triggered that recall."

"Lots of things about trauma get buried then surface later," Shell said.

"Maybe so. I said Mrs. Doom was an immaculate housekeeper, everything in its place. But the drawers in that room were open, too, papers scattered on the floor beneath them. I'm sorry, Granddad, I didn't remember that."

"Don't apologize," Shell gently admonished him. "That was in the sheriff department's report. Best I can recall, nobody asked you these questions in court and probably didn't at the county jail."

"No sir, they didn't. This is all new to me."

"It's a very important detail." Shell reached over and laid a hand on his shoulder. "You're doing good, Son, real good. Keep going. You said his lips moved. Did he say anything?"

"No sir. He was trying to push himself up. At that point, the only thought I had was to get help. I'd left my cell phone in my car and ran to get it."

"What did you do with the gun?"

"I laid it back on the floor."

"Where on the floor?"

"I don't remember exactly but near where I picked it up."

"What did you do next?"

"I picked up the envelope I had dropped, and ran to the car to get my cell phone to call 911."

"Did you know Doom was alive when the ambulance got there?"

"No. I wasn't even in the house when the ambulance arrived. I was allowed to leave but ordered by the Sheriff's deputies to be available for further questioning and not to leave the county."

"Well, he was alive when the paramedics reached him," Shell said. "That's public record. It was in the news that he died on the way to the hospital."

Cal looked sadly into Shell's eyes. "Granddad, I guess all of this somehow makes sense to you."

Shell looked over his shoulder again at the door. "It's a fact you didn't kill Ty Doom," he said in a hushed, breathy voice. "Intentional or not, it's also a fact that the investigation was sloppy and shortsighted. It's another fact that nothing was taken from the home, so the ransacking you saw was for something else, not money or jewelry but something possibly more precious, or incriminating."

"What something else could that be?" Cal asked softly.

"That, Cal, is the biggest piece of this puzzle. For whatever reason, somebody was after something Ty Doom had. That something could be the key to this crime."

"You said you'd gone back to the parsonage ruins and that something was not right," Cal remarked as if wanting to change the subject.

Shell had thought long and hard about what to tell Cal about his exploration of the ruins, the kerosene can, the boot prints. "It was no accident," was all he needed to say.

"But who could have done it?" Cal asked vexed.

"Why—not who—is the first question. If we find out 'why,' we'll find out 'who.'"

"My ministry was controversial," Cal remarked. "A lot of people didn't like what I was doing."

"That's not grounds for burning a parsonage and killing three innocent people. This was the work of pure evil." He leaned into his grandson and whispered. "I'm seeing the governor tomorrow. Keep the faith."

Cal leaned back and seemed to relax, a faint smile crossing his face. "Those were Sally's last words to me."

Shell looked at his watch. "Our time is about up. Anything I can get for you?"

"The guard Durasmus has been looking after me. He said I could get paper and pen, toiletries and necessities from the commissary. He brought a form and filled it out for me. I had requested a pen and paper, but never got them."

"They said nothing to me about a commissary. Never mind," he flipped his hand. "That's prisons for you."

"I also asked for some books, any books."

"What kind of books?"

"I don't care. I've reached a point where I feel like reading. Some on psychology might help me deal with all that's happened."

Shell recalled, even as a small boy, how Cal loved to read, devoured every book in the house. "I'll look into it. Do you know what today is?"

"Yes. It's Sunday."

"It's December seventh, Pearl Harbor Day. It was a terrible day in the history of our nation but the beginning of something good."

"What?"

"The beginning of the end of an evil empire."

Durasmus opened the door and signaled their time was up. Shell hugged Cal before Durasmus cuffed him and took him from the room. Shell stood in the doorway and watched as his grandson was led down the long hall.

CHAPTER 11

December 8 Monday

Shell sat uncomfortably in a deep leather chair made for bigger people. It was Monday morning toward the end of the noon hour, and there was no one else in the plush waiting area. Gilt-framed portraits of recent governors surrounded the room. He had lived through their administrations, and some before whose pictures hung elsewhere.

In a prison system corrupt as Mafia politics, governors doled out warden positions. Shell knew all about that process, the politics involved. He was allowed to sit in prison six years for a crime he didn't commit because a governor's pal didn't want him dating the pal's daughter. That governor and that warden and that father were long gone. He thought about that as he sat there, how every hour returns to its beginning, every moment, over and over, is relived. How life strangely and tragically repeats itself, how it can follow an incredulous pattern.

He had last seen the governor at Thanksgiving at the memorial service. The occasion was solemn and sad. Shell found a private moment to tell the governor's wife Dimple she was in his prayers. She broke down. Family members rushed to comfort her, and he wished he had left well enough alone. The only comments between him and the governor were brief condolences, both too emotional to say more.

On this occasion, he was unsure, and anxious, about the governor's reception of him. After all, his daughter would be alive if she hadn't married Shell's grandson. Athen might be alive, too, for that matter. You can't start blaming circumstances for all that goes wrong in life. Otherwise, the universe would unravel. Then he quickly recalled it was circumstance, itself, that had landed him in prison, not once but twice, and now his grandson.

Behind a massive desk across from him, an attractive young receptionist answered phone calls. The way she dispensed with each caller, he considered it a small miracle he was there. He knew how the system worked. Even if his grandson was the governor's son-in-law, he knew he couldn't just drop in. He had called the governor's office the Monday after Thanksgiving, unsure anyone would be there due to the holidays. A young lady answered. Before he could identify himself, she said emphatically that, due to a death in the family, new appointments were impossible until the first of the year. Shell identified himself and she said, somewhat in exasperation and with less contrived formality, that she would, "move heaven and earth and work you in next Monday, one o'clock." She asked the reason for the visit. He told her it was personal and she remarked she understood.

In a large mirror behind the receptionist, he could see his reflection. The thought occurred to him he was wearing the same suit he had worn at the governor's mansion for the wedding between his grandson and the governor's daughter and to the recent memorial service. He could afford a wardrobe, but he had owned this one suit for fifty years. It still fit him, one of the few things in his life that hadn't changed. He glanced down at his feet, at the navy blue socks and plain black shoes. Six days of the week he wore boots and on Sundays these lace-ups, but removed them when he came home from church and pulled the boots back on. A planter didn't get Sundays off, some need on the land always beckoning.

He looked at the clock. One thirty. He didn't expect the governor to be on time and others had entered the vestibule, signed in with the receptionist and taken seats, each eyeing him curiously. He returned equal curious looks thinking, *Are they ahead of me?* One was an older woman, nicely dressed, with a satchel crammed full of papers. Two men in suits were together and sat at the back of the waiting area. He guessed the woman would go before him, that she was part of the "heaven and earth" the young receptionist had tried, unsuccessfully, to move.

He heard footsteps. They grew louder. The portly tubby-chinned governor entered with a springy step, sawing his arms as though they facilitated movement, red suspenders blinking as his coat flared. Bouncing on his large head were long waves of theatrical silver hair that he combed back with his fingers when they fell down on his forehead. Close behind him was his usual detail, two uniformed highway patrolmen wearing Smoky hats.

The governor stopped at the desk, murmured something to the receptionist. She answered in a whisper, but Shell heard his name. The governor said something back to her, then wheeled and strode over to him.

"Mr. Ferguson," he said too loudly, with an air of rigid formality and flashing a bright mechanical smile, "Good to see you."

Shell stood. "The same here, Governor DuBard," and they shook hands.

The governor looked at the lady with the fat briefcase. "Miss Goodman, it's good to see you, too," he said, his voice slightly dropping with a forced and disinterested politeness. "I know your appointment," he glanced at the large clock on the wall, "was at 1:30 and I'm running late, important luncheon. I need to see this gentlemen about a matter, won't take long."

He never acknowledged the two men as he motioned Shell to follow him past the receptionist and into a cavernous carpeted office with a desk larger than the receptionist's. On the wall behind the desk was the seal of the Great State of Mississippi framed by the U. S. and state flags, a couple of photos beside the American flag of the governor shaking hands with the two Bush Presidents. The room smelled of leather and cigars.

Palming a hand to one of two blue club chairs in front of the desk, "Please sit down, Shell," the governor said, as though addressing him formally in the lobby was an apology to those waiting. "How are you?" he asked in an artificial, patronizing manner as he maneuvered around the desk. He picked up a small box of polished walnut that had brass hinges and a brass clasp. He flipped open the lid and offered Shell a cigar. "They're from Cuba, illegal as hell. We're not supposed to smoke in the capitol," he winked and flashed a self-satisfying smile, "but as governor, I do have some prerogatives."

"No thanks, Governor," Shell said. "Nothing against your cigars. I don't smoke."

The governor lifted one for himself. From his vest, he removed a small splitter and clipped the end of the cigar, returned the splitter to its pocket. He twirled the cigar once between his fingers as he lowered himself into a tall executive leather wingback. Still holding the cigar between thumb and forefinger, as though it was something to occupy his hands, he hunched forward. His face turned suddenly humorless and grave, his lips compressed as though he were pondering.

Here it comes, Shell thought.

"Shell, I shared my condolences with you at the memorial service. But from one broken heart to another, I offer them again with an abundance of sorrow and grief."

Shell nodded. "I understand, Governor. My condolences are reciprocal and as burdened with sorrow."

The governor leaned back in the chair, his posture erect, chin high and lit the cigar, watched rings of smoke float upward as though he had created something to behold. Shell had seen the governor smoke during the wedding festivities and noted the way the man cocked a cigar between his teeth and exhaled the smoke as if the mannerisms reflected his flamboyance and enjoyment in everything he did. That was several years ago, and little about the man had changed.

After another puff, the governor leaned forward and brought a hand down onto the desktop with a clap. "I'm sure you're here about Cal," he said, turning his attention back to Shell. "I've joined in the legal steps for an appeal. I think you know that. There's nothing more I can say or do at this point. As you can see," he palmed a hand toward the closed door, "I've got a busy afternoon." The tip of the cigar jutted from the center of his mouth, the position undisturbed as he spoke.

Shell recalled the first time he had met the governor, his first impression of the man, how his mouth barely moved when he spoke, the words unshaped when he said them, bubbling over his lips in a mumbled drawl like pea soup at a slow boil. Now a cigar was positioned in the center of his lips and understanding him was a tad more difficult.

"I understand, Governor, and am grateful for your limited time," Shell remarked, his hands folded in his lap, his eyes leveled straight into the puffy eyes across from him. "But I'm not here about Cal. I'm here about the fire."

"Terrible tragedy," the governor said, his voice emotional, at the edge of breaking, a noticeable tremor in his hands.

"Not so sure it was a tragedy," Shell said flatly.

The governor's thick eyebrows jumped, and he looked at Shell critically. "Not a tragedy? To lose a family in a fire like that." He leaned across the table and his eyes teared, his voice shook. "My God, Shell, if that's not a tragedy, I don't know what is."

"It's my understanding, Your Honor," Shell softly offered, "that a tragedy's due to personal flaw or happenstance. That fire was perpetrated by intentional evil. It didn't just happen."

"Well," the governor said, his face solemn again, his voice a little ruminative. "It was accidental, due to faulty wiring in the attic."

Shell recollected then where he'd seen a man speaking without moving his lips. On television, a ventriloquist working a puppet. He leaned forward and countered. "That's what the newspapers said, and the newspapers said it because the volunteer fire chief, who conducted a sloppy investigation, said it. But the parsonage had passed a recent safety review and met all specs."

"I haven't seen the final inspection report," the governor said, "but that was an old wood-frame house."

Shell slipped his hand inside his coat pocket and pulled out the photos he'd had printed from his cell phone at Walmart. He stood and, like a hand of cards, palmed the photos onto the desktop before the governor's curious eyes. "Maybe these will help."

With a thick finger, the governor parted the photos, scrutinizing each as he spread them out. He looked up at Shell. His face appeared to collapse and fold into its grooves. "Where'd you get these?" he asked laying his cigar in the ashtray.

"I took 'em."

The governor looked up with a wrinkled brow, "When?"

"Tuesday, December second, five days after the fire."

Anchoring a finger on the close-up of the gas can, the governor pushed the others around on the desktop, sorting them, aligning them in his mind, like a small child attempting to assemble a jigsaw.

Shell pointed to the photo of the kerosene can in the bush. "There's no reason for that can to be there. The parsonage didn't have a kerosene stove. Cal and Sally owned no kerosene lamps. No grass burning had been ordered by the county. No reason!" he concluded slapping his thigh.

The governor nodded without looking up as he continued moving the photos into a sequence that appeared logical to him, Shell observing the moth-like flutter in his hands. The governor looked up again. He pushed himself back from the desk, lifted one hand and delicately pinched the bridge of his nose between his forefinger and thumb, then stood, wheeled and, hands clasped behind his back, gazed out the window over the top of his high-backed chair with a sigh, as though he needed a break from the scenes on his desk. Clenched hands dropped to his side, and he remained standing there in the awkward silence, his back to Shell. One hand opened, moved slowly to his face, then came down. When he turned back around, his eyes were moist and pink.

"I left the can in the bushes," Shell said filling the uncomfortable quiet, trying to help him out. "That's a crime scene, and it's evidence."

"Did you touch it?"

Shell had heard that question before. That was the reason he had gone to prison the first time. He had been to the picture show in Drew and stopped by Wang's grocery to get a bottle of pop and a candy bar before heading home and had heard something in the alley that ran between the picture show and the Chinaman's store, like the sound of a dog growling. There was no street-light on the corner of Wang's. He had walked half-way into the alley and had seen nothing. Then his eyes had begun adjusting, and he saw a man lying face-down. He had thought the man was drunk and stepped closer, into something wet. He had seen there was a cut on the man's head and blood gushing from it. Kneeling down to get a closer look, he had put his hand on the ground to steady himself, and it came down on a piece of pipe.

"No sir. I leaned over and smelled the opening. The scent was fresh. As you can see, the can appears to be new."

The governor stroked his chin and looked up at him. "You ever been in law enforcement, Shell?"

"No sir. Let's just say I've been around the block."

"I believe that trip around the block was in nineteen forty-eight."

"Yessir. That's when it began. How'd you know?"

"Sally told me and her mother, said Cal had shared some old Drew newspaper clippings with her. I wasn't even born then."

"When were you born?"

"Nineteen fifty-four."

"That's the year I got out," Shell said.

The governor raised his eyebrows but did not respond. He returned to his chair, sank into it with a low groan, then leaned forward and spread his arms on the desk, so they cupped the pictures. He looked down at them. He picked up the one of the burned house, tears welling up. "Of course, this is all conjecture," he said, his voice suddenly throaty and unstable, struggling. "But..." he reached over and pushed a button on a large desk phone.

"Yes, Governor?" a female voice responded immediately through the speaker.

"Miss Pettigrew, get the Director of the Mississippi Bureau of Investigation on the line for me. It's urgent."

"Yes, Governor."

He turned to Shell and said, "This could be a game changer, Shell. Who do you suspect?" He picked up the cigar.

Shell shifted to the edge of his seat. "I'm not sure, Governor. My grandson had stirred up a hornet's nest in the community. The three years he'd been pastor. He integrated the church."

"Shell, integration has been around since the Civil Rights Act, nineteen sixty-four. The Klan has all but faded."

"With all due respects, Your Honor, it's a new day," Shell submitted. "New issues. New faces of racism."

Holding his cigar carefully in order not to drop the long ash that had grown, the governor blew a puff of blue smoke from the side of his mouth. "Believe me, Shell, how well I know. That Tea Party crowd almost sunk my reelection bid. If it hadn't been for moderate blacks supporting me, I'd have lost."

Shell recalled the election, the dirty tactics, the resurfacing of old racial issues.

The phone rang.

The governor returned the cigar to its tray, thumping the long ash, and answered it. "Yes, Director."

Shell listened as the governor provided the director of the MBI some background on the situation, then, "I've got some photographs Mr. Ferguson, the grandfather of Cal Ferguson, took of the place after the fire," the governor said into the phone. "Once you see them I believe you'll agree, that fire that took my daughter and granddaughter's lives..." he paused to throttle his emotions, "deserves a more thorough investigation."

Shell could hear a muted voice of agreement through the receiver.

The governor hung up the phone and looked at Shell. "You got a duplicate set of these?" he asked pointing at the photographs.

"Yessir. I put 'em in my safe at home."

"That's good. In case we lose track of these. Anything can happen these days in bureaucracy."

"Speaking of track, Governor, "I presume you saw the photos of the truck tracks in the crop road behind the privet hedge."

The governor leaned over the photos, scanned them one more time and anchored a finger on one. "I see it here."

"Those tracks are mud tires."

"Look like regular tire tracks to me."

"By the grid design, they're Mohawks. I'm sure whoever investigates will see that. Not sure how it could help. They're popular tires. I've got 'em on my truck. But one of 'em," he leaned over and pointed, "this one here, has a mark in the tread, probably a gravel rock or shingle tack."

"I see," the governor remarked and looked up at Shell. "You sure you didn't round that proverbial block more than once?" and he smiled.

"Yessir, the year you were born, in Mexico, but that's a story for another time."

"I heard that tale, too," the governor said and winked. He picked up his cigar and stood, a signal the meeting was over.

"There's one other thing, Governor. Christmas is coming. I'd like to have Cal home with me during the holidays. He's all the kin I've got left, and I'm all he's got."

The governor's face turned grave. "Shell, I have the power to grant pardons, not leaves. That's in the hands of the prison system and the parole board. I'd encourage you to check with them." He raised a finger. "But I appointed them, so I'll see what I can do. You'd think the governor of the State of Mississippi had some power. In reality, I'm a captive of power." He walked from behind his desk. "You see all these trappings surrounding me," palming the hand holding the cigar left and right. "You know why they call them trappings? Because a man of power is trapped in that power, that's why." He leaned against the front of the desk, arms wrapped around his sides. "I'm at the mercy, beck and call of every lobbyist, glee club, college president, you name 'em. I've got the legislature to contend with, the bureaus, the departments of this and that," rotating his hands left and right, "and then I've got the Secretaries of State and Treasury, the Public Service and Highway Commissioners, and if all that's not enough, I've got the law and the Attorney General fighting me tooth and toenail. Oh, yes, and the press, the media. Everything I do is scrutinized, seen beneath a microscope. Makes you wonder how anything gets done, here or in Washington. You know the original meaning of the word 'trappings'?"

Shell stood looking at him, bemused at the lecture, and shook his head he did not.

"It's a ceremonial harness for a horse," the governor said and took a puff from his cigar.

"I never thought about it like that, Governor. I had one final request."

"Yes, what is it?" he asked off-handily.

"You mentioned you had the power to pardon and—"

"But it's too soon, Shell," the governor said with an open, blunt face. "Believe me, I've thought about it. Your grandson's not the only person stuck innocently between a rock and a hard place. Again, I can do a few things in this world, in this state. But if I pardoned Cal now, I'd be skewered by all those folks I've just named. It wouldn't look good for him or for me. It's all about timing."

Shell thanked him and shook his hand and turned to leave, the comment hanging in his mind. *It's all about timing.*

"By the way, Shell, how is Cal?"

"He's better, he's going to make it. He's innocent."

"I believe he is, too. I deeply appreciate what you've shared with me today. God bless," and the governor palmed a gallant hand toward the door and sent him on with a pat on the back and a wave.

Outside the governor's office, beneath the domed rotunda and amid all of the marble and stained glass, Shell stopped. *It's all about timing.*

CHAPTER 12

December 9 Tuesday

Early on a Tuesday morning, after he had been in solitary two weeks, a guard asked Cal if he wanted a shower. He certainly needed one. He had sponge bathed in his sink a few times, but he could smell himself.

Cuffed and wearing only briefs and flip-flops, two guards he had not seen before brought him down the steps to the shower cages. Of the five wire mesh compartments, only the middle one was occupied, an inmate washing and whistling, oblivious to Cal and the guards. His face looked familiar, one Cal had seen among those herded back and forth each day past his window. Except for Chris, he knew no names, but saw many faces. The guards, he thought, would put him in an end stall to keep them apart. But one of the guards opened a chain-link door next to the occupied cage. Maybe they could watch them better together than apart, he reasoned.

Once Cal was inside, the mesh door clanged shut. The portal dropped open, and his cuffs were removed. He was instructed to remove his briefs and pass them through the portal; then it was slammed shut and bolted. Within seconds, a spray of cold water hit him, and he jumped. Chris had told him the guards turned on the showers. He looked around.

"Where's the soap?" he said aloud but to no one in particular.

"It's in the tray on the side," the inmate showering next to him responded, interrupting the tune he was whistling as he continued lathering himself.

The voice sounded familiar. Cal turned and observed the man. He was short and portly, balding with gray hair at the temples. In his fifties, Cal guessed. The man pivoted, and Cal saw a cross tattooed over his heart and beside the cross, interlocking semi-circles, the fish symbol of primitive Christianity.

The inmate stopped whistling and lathering and looked at Cal. He stepped closer to the mesh partition separating them and in a lowered voice said, "Cal?"

"Yes," Cal replied softly. "Chris?"

"You got it," Chris said pointing at his mouth and casting warning eyes at the double-tiered rows of cells and the curious faces observing them through the small windows. "If we speak quietly, they can't hear us," Chris said nodding at the cells. "The showers muffle our voices."

"Why is no one else showering?" Cal asked. "There's usually five at a time."

"They probably didn't want to go through the hassle, all the cuffing and uncuffing and re-cuffing," Chris said. "They'd prefer to sponge bathe in their sinks. I told you about the two-inch gap beneath each cell door. For water to drain."

"That's one way," Cal remarked. "That's what I've been doing."

"But nothing beats a shower," Chris countered. "It's a baptizing," he grinned. "Attitude, Cal!" he said, wrapping his knuckles for emphasis against the wire partition. "Imprisonment is all about attitude."

The cold water had warmed. Cal picked up the small bar of soap that was down to a slither.

"You owe me one," Chris said in a low voice.

"What?"

"Your story."

"Here?" Cal exclaimed pointing at the floor.

"It's safer," Chris said and looked around him. "This way it's in the open. The guards have left, gone to other pods to take inmates to showers. They may not come back for another hour."

Cal was standing stark naked about to bare his soul to a man he'd just laid eyes upon, in a prison shower stall, water pouring over him and inmates looking on. He began soaping himself, pondering if he should do this. If so, how much he should tell.

Chris had just soaped his face and quickly turned it toward the shower spray and rinsed it. A towel hung over the shower, but he ignored it and wiped water from his eyes with his fingers and heels of his hands and said, facing Cal, "Speak, your servant heareth," and he smiled.

Cal began with his family. His father managed a large plantation. His mother taught high school. Both died, killed in a car accident while he was in college. Shortly after, he felt a call to preach. He began telling about his seminary experience in Atlanta and—.

"Whoa, Bro. You can't broad-brush conversion," Chris interrupted.

Cal looked up at the myriad faces pressed against the cell windows, eyes trying to see what they couldn't hear, then he peered into eyes he could only see through wire netting. "It was not a conversion experience like yours. I was already a Christian. I think it was an accumulation of things. I had spiritual nurturing, an education, good examples—my parents were caring people. My grandparents have been a mainstay. I felt led to do something other than farm."

"In other words," Chris said, "you didn't need to screw up like me to see the light."

They were eyeball to eyeball, feeling each other's breath, only the webbed partition separating them.

Cal continued. "I need to back up. Before seminary, I attended a liberal arts college in Jackson, the state capitol, and met Sally DuBard, the governor's daughter. We were married our junior year. Sally became pregnant." For some reason, he wasn't sure why, he left out how a date with Sally saved his life.

"I imagine a governor's daughter marrying a preacher caused a stir."

Cal nodded. "That was part of it. The governor—he's still governor—is a Republican. My family's Democrat. In today's political climate, that 'stir,' as you called it, was difficult for everyone in both families. I was in seminary three years, and my first appointment was back where I grew up. You know the rest."

"A prophet is not without honor—"

"But in his own country," Cal interrupted completing the biblical quote. "That's what I said to the bishop. But he had his mind made up. He's a black bishop, a product of the Civil Rights era. He said the Bethel Triangle 'had issues,' needed a preacher there who understood its people and those issues."

Chris squinted and leveled a finger at him. "You the man."

"Not behind bars."

"You the man," Chris said again, emphatically, his finger still pointing.

The pod door opened and banged shut.

"It's just a nurse making her rounds." Chris said. "She'll check on us on her way out."

They continued bathing. Chris continued whistling, a tune Cal didn't recognize.

Suddenly, a commotion erupted on the upper tier. The nurse was shouting at someone in the next to last cell, two removed from Cal's.

"Get those privacy screens down, or I'm calling security," she yelled.

"Go 'way, bitch," a voice shouted.

"Aw right," she barked yanking her radio from her belt and raising it to her mouth. "Nurse Hardin. Security. Pod eighteen, cell two ten. Inmates got privacy screens up, non-responsive to orders, cussing."

Cal looked at Chris. "Privacy screens? You can't get more private than solitary."

"Inmates hang sheets between the john and the bunks," Chris said. "They're a big issue. The warden has outlawed them. Let me put it this way, a lot goes on behind privacy screens, especially if there're two inmates in the cell."

"What do they hang them on?" Chris asked. "Cords are outlawed, too."

"They are. But inmates have a way of getting cords."

"How?"

"Bribe guards. Laundry bags. G-strings on their shorts. In prison, where there's a will, there's a way. And there's lots of will."

"If they'd had as much will outside, they wouldn't be inside," Cal commented as two guards rushed into the pod and scrambled up the steps.

"This is going to get interesting," Chris said lowering his voice.

The pod door clanged open. A column of guards in full riot gear with batons and riot shields, hands on shoulders, one behind the other and marching in loud syncopated cadence, tromped into the pod and up the stairs.

"Special effects," Chris continued. "To intimidate and compel them to exit peacefully."

"And if they don't?"

"You'll witness your first forced cell extraction and oleoresin capsicum, hopefully your last."

"Oleo what?

"Oleorisin Capsicum. OC gas or Pepper Spray. The guards'll shoot it through the food portal, then storm the cell. You'll live with that spray for days. It causes tears and pain in your eyes and throat, not to mention possible temporary blindness. Get your wash rag. Be prepared to cover your face," Chris said snatching his from the shower head.

Cal looked around, saw a washcloth hanging limply from the soap dish and grabbed it.

"I smell alcohol," the lead guard shouted to the others in tandem behind him.

Cal looked at Chris. "Alcohol?"

"Yep. Pruno."

"From prune juice?"

Chris chuckled. "That may be the origin of the word," Chris said. "Pruno is a prison wine made from hoarded fruits, ketchup, sugar, milk, and crumbled bread. Bread provides yeast for fermentation. The fermenting pulp is concealed in a towel or sock, then placed in a plastic bag. Hot water is added. Voila."

"But fermentation takes time," Cal said astonished. "The cells are checked regularly."

"The cells are constructed, as I'm sure you've noticed, of concrete blocks," Chris said. "Using sharp instruments—for example, throw away razors inserted in toothbrush handles—inmates dig out the mortar joints, slip socks, towels, even cell phones, into the crevice then cover it with toothpaste the color of the mortar. Sometimes paper is used. Paper is from wood. Wet it, and it hardens."

"Cell phones?" Cal exclaimed.

"The latest are thin and fit snuggly," Chris said. "Some are as small as a watch. Ironically, they're called 'cell' phones," and he smiled.

Cal slapped a hand against his forehead.

Chris seemed to delight in teaching his new student. "The guards would have to check every mortar joint in the cell. They don't have time." He grinned and pointed at the cells. "Inmates are the only ones with time."

The pounding on cell door 210 grew louder. Its two occupants began shouting something unintelligible, over and over.

"By the way," Chris added. "Those chants you hear mean the cellmates are probably gang members sending messages to others in the pod."

"I never thought of gangs in prisons," Cal said.

"They're here, everywhere," Chris said making a wide gesture with his hand. "And not just in prisons. They're all over the country, especially the West. When inmates are transported here from those states, like a virus, the gangs come with them."

"You make it sound like fraternities,"

Chris snapped a finger at him. "You got it."

"Are you in a gang?" Cal asked.

"Was. Got out."

"How'd you get out?"

"It wasn't easy. That's one of the reasons I'm in seg."

The rancor above them was growing louder.

"They sound drunk," Cal commented focusing his attention back on the disturbance.

"The ruckus may be a ruse," Chris said. "To get them transferred to another pod closer to their gang members. Sometimes it's reversed: inmates in general population stage fights to get thrown into solitary, for the same reason, to be near their gang buddies. There are other reasons I've told you about."

"Shot callers."

"Yes. Here's the thing. Somebody in the hole owes a drug debt or snitched. Sometimes the hit on them comes from a shot caller outside of the prison. Like I said, gangs are everywhere."

The lead guard unbolted the food portal of cell 210, and it fell with a loud clang. The guard behind him began pushing a rectangular prod on a long pole through the portal, ramming it in and out.

"The prod," Chris explained before Cal could ask, "pushes the inmates away from the door so the guards can inject the pepper spray without getting knifed or sprayed. Inmates have a way of getting their own pepper spray, not to mention concoctions of urine and feces."

The prodding ceased.

"Now!" Chris said clapping his washrag over his mouth and nose.

Cal followed suit.

The lead guard began spraying through the portal. More loud chants, like cheers, erupted from the cell. Bangs on the door, like gunshots, grew louder. The cell door was forced open. Gas masks on, shields in front, batons raised, guards plunged through the doorway.

Cal looked over at Chris who was shaking his head.

"Unnecessary," Chris uttered. Then in a lower voice, "Fascist mentality. They should've let them sober up."

Amid the struggle and raucous noise, the chants of the two inmates continued. More nurses and guards had drifted into the pod, along with office staff to witness the spectacle. It took six guards to drag each inmate, kicking and screaming chants, down the steps and across the pod.

"Get ready!" Chris cautioned, "They're headed for the showers."

Hands cuffed behind them, screaming and coughing, the two rioters were thrown into shower cages, one into the stall next to Cal, the man's skull banging against the wire mesh, his body collapsing onto the floor, his head bleeding.

Cal kept the washrag clamped to his mouth and nose, but his eyes were beginning to burn and water. He noticed Chris had raised his face toward the shower head.

Cal observed the inmate in the stall next to him. The man lay doubled up on the floor. Water, tainted red from his bloodied head and face, flowed over his shoulders and twisted body that was covered with tattoos, including his domed skull. Cal could only guess the story they told. *It must be a long one*, he thought. The other man in the first stall was on his knees coughing, his face toward the shower head. Sporadically, they continued screaming their defiant chants. Guards aligned outside the showers stood watching, coughing, and rubbing their eyes.

Cal looked at Chris, who was preoccupied with rinsing his eyes under the shower.

"Get your face under the shower, Bro," Chris admonished him.

Cal lifted his face to the shower and let the water run over his eyes, opening and closing them for relief from the pain. The washcloth over his nose and mouth had helped, but pepper spray had seeped through. The burning sensation went deep into his throat and chest and made him cough.

Coughing brought no relief, but the water on his face helped his eyes. Others in the pod who had come to observe, along with the inmates in the cells, were coughing. It seemed as if the air within the pod was consumed with incessant spasms of hacking.

One by one, the onlookers began leaving, but inmates in the cells had no outlet. Some were cursing and banging on their doors for relief, the vapors of the spray penetrating their cells. The whole pod smelled of chili peppers. It was a scene Cal would never forget.

Amid the din of coughing and shouting and banging, Cal heard a sound from the inmate in the adjacent stall and looked down at him, at his expressionless scarred face and felt his wild red eyes on him.

The man's jagged mouth opened. "You in 208," he said, his voice with a taint of razor in it.

Cal nodded and looked at Chris who was listening, a serious look suddenly on his face.

"Ferguson?" the man inquired.

Chris lurched toward the screen. "Don't answer!" he whispered.

But Cal had already nodded again. He saw the exasperated look on Chris' face and shrugged as if to say, *It's too late.*

"Don't talk to him," Chris whispered louder.

The inmate said nothing, just continued looking at Cal, his rapid eyes deliberate, calculating.

The pod grew quieter. Cell 210 had been thoroughly searched and cleaned. Everyone had left the pod except the guards watching the two extracted inmates in the shower cages and Cal and Chris and the other inmates looking on, coughing behind their steel doors. A guard turned knobs outside the shower cages, and the water stopped. Cal and Chris were cuffed, removed from the stalls and taken to their cells, the cuffing procedure reversed, the doors closed and locked.

How did the man know his name, Cal wondered. Since he had been there, he'd spoken only to Chris, the guards and nurses when they came by with their clipboards. Then again, his name was on the ID card in the clear plastic slot beside his cell door. Anyone walking by could see it. But the inmate was in cell 210, at the top of the stairs. He would never have been led by his door.

CHAPTER 13

December 9 Tuesday

Several hours passed. Aside from the usual noises—gates and doors clanging open and shut, the pod television blaring, inmates yelling at each other—all was relatively quiet again. Guards turned on large fans to clear the air but pepper spray, once dispensed, is hard to dispel. Even after the lunch trolleys rattled by, Cal could hear sporadic coughing throughout the pod. Occasionally, he would have a spell.

He waited until afternoon, before the three o'clock count, to check in with Chris. He climbed onto the sink and tapped on the vent. He didn't have to wait.

"You made it," Chris said his voice low. A guard was seated at the pod desk but focused on completing reports. "But you misstepped."

"The inmate in the shower?"

"Yep!"

"Why?" Cal asked.

"Too much information. He's in a gang."

"How'd you know?"

"The tattoo on his scalp," Chris said. "Didn't you see it?"

"He had tattoos all over his body."

"This one was distinct. A crown atop a cross superimposed over the letter N."

"I did see that, but I thought it meant he was Christian."

"Pseudo-Christian."

"I don't get it," Cal said.

"A crown and cross over the letter N is the symbol for Aryan Nations. Ever heard of it?"

"No."

"It's a domestic terror network, a militia anti-government movement. It spun out of Christian Identity which was the first nationwide terrorist network."

"I've heard of Christian Identity. It's neo-Nazi, anti-black and anti-Jewish."

"Exactly," Chris confirmed. "Like Ayran Nations, the goal of Christian Identity is to overthrow the U. S. government and replace it with a white racist state. It's prominent in California, Nevada, Idaho, and also in the South. The name's a misnomer. Has nothing to do with the Christian faith. I could bore you with some history."

"Bore me! I've got time."

"That's good, Cal. Your sense of humor is showing."

"Glad to know I still have some."

Chris continued. "Aryans invoke the image of the SS trooper envisioned by Hitler to be destined to rule the world. Groups like the KKK identify with Ayran Nations."

"Don't bore me with the KKK. Too close to home."

"Fair enough," Chris said. "But before I'm through, it may get closer. Aryan Nations, like Christian Identity, interprets the Constitution literally, as in legal fundamentalism. They say it's being eroded. Citizens must organize, stock weapons, rise up. They crown the cross and hide behind it."

"That's scary," Cal said. "And the guy knew my name."

"I don't know that he did," Chris conjectured. "I heard him say it, but with a question. You confirmed."

"He caught me off guard," Cal said defensively.

"Being caught off guard, Cal, is not good in the free world. And perilous in prison. Regardless, he knew it. Had a reason for knowing it."

"Which was?"

"He was on a mission, making a courtesy call to make sure."

"I don't like the sound of this," Cal said alarmed. "What reason would he have?"

"I don't know. Perhaps he was identifying a target. Prison grapevine says he was in a fight yesterday, probably staged it to get put into seg. Which suggests he got your name from someone else in the prison, or from outside."

"But why?" Cal, asked again feeling a strange anxiety building within.

"Have no clue," Chris said. "It's strange. You haven't been here long enough to make any enemies."

"I don't do dope. I don't belong to a gang."

"I know. For an inmate, you're clean as a whistle. Unless...."

"Unless what?" Cal questioned nervously.

Silence.

"Unless what?" Cal repeated, his voice rising.

"Unless he's connected somehow to why you're in here."

"I don't see how," Cal said. "He's from out west."

"That's a fact!" Chris exclaimed. "Fact two: He's Aryan Nations, and they're all over the country."

Another pause.

"What will happen to him and the other guy in cell two ten?" Cal asked.

"Security'll split them up, transfer the inmate who made the pruno to another pod, leave the new guy, the one who staged the fight. Which brings us back to square one."

"Brings us back to he's two cells from me," Cal said concerned.

On that last word, they heard a chair scoot below and then footsteps on the stairs.

"Signing off," Chris said. "Be on guard, pun intended."

Cal clambered down from the sink and onto his bunk.

There was a loud rap on his door, a guard's face in the window. "Get up Ferguson. Come to the door."

He got up and walked to the door. This was a guard he didn't know.

"I seen you from down there," he said his hard flat eyes glaring through the small window. "What you doing standing on the sink?"

Cal's brain scrambled for a response. "Just checking the mirror. I thought it was broken."

"Bullshit," the deep voice boomed. "Next time we catch you up there you're gettin' pointed. You understand."

"Yessir," he responded.

He returned to his bunk and laid down. *Be on guard.* "So much for being clean as a whistle," he whispered to himself and eventually drifted off to sleep.

CHAPTER 14

December 10 Wednesday

After passing routinely through the outer gates and checkpoint, a short, stout female guard who walked with an exaggerated swagger ushered Shell through a door that said ADMINISTRATIVE OFFICES. The guard introduced him to a tall, regal black lady who was wearing a turquoise sweater beneath a navy blue coat, ropes of hair dyed red piled on her head. She looked him straight in the eye with a manly handshake and briskly introduced herself as, "Compton, the warden's secretary." No misses or miss. Just Compton.

He sat in her small office observing her munch on popcorn and watch a small television. By the muffled dialogue, it was a court show. He never watched them and figured people who did watched wrestling too.

On a small table beside his chair, a magazine lay open, and the title of an article caught his eye: "The Case Against Solitary Confinement." He glanced at the secretary who was still glued to her television. He picked up the magazine and checked the cover: PRIVATE PRISON NEWS BULLETIN.

Shell glanced at the secretary again, who seemed oblivious to his presence, and began reading. Eighty thousand prisoners in the United States were being held in solitary confinement the article began, many for minor infractions. He read on about the high cost to taxpayers, the impracticality, and immorality of the practice then his eyes slammed into—"Psychological harm and suicide rates are higher in solitary confinement, and the longer prisoners remain, the more their mental abilities suffer, the more they cannot function normally."

That was enough. No need to read further. He glanced again at the secretary absorbed in her television show and wondered who had sat in the chair before him and left the magazine open to that article, much less had taken the time to read it. Surely not a prison employee. They would've closed it. He returned the journal to the table and left it open as he had found it.

A lady emerged from the warden's office, a face Shell vaguely recalled. She had short black hair and was smartly dressed in a dark pants suit and heels. She was wearing large hooped earrings and sunglasses, appearing to look neither left nor right but straight ahead. She exited with a slight sway and her legs scissored across the room in smooth, sharp strides. Her rhythmic heel clicks faded away after the door closed behind her.

The secretary jumped at a loud buzzer, and a gruff male voice over an intercom said, "Send Mr. Ferguson in!"

The warden was on the phone as Shell was ushered in by the secretary who pointed to a chair for him. Shell took a seat and waited. Around the walls of the large office were photos of uniformed men and women shaking hands with the warden and framed mottos and slogans. Directly behind the warden and between two windows was a large red-framed cork board with what appeared to be carelessly thumb-tacked notices. In the center of the board, surrounded by the notices, was the print-out of a large collection of small individual photos arranged in groups. The caption at the top said SOCIAL CLUBS. Apparently, this was an assortment of local civic organizations, like Kiwanis and Rotary, that worked with or helped in the prison. Shell counted five groups of photos. They resembled trees, or had that shape, a single photograph at the top of each group, two below that, then three and so on until the faces spread across the bottom. The photos were small, and Shell could not make them out except all appeared to be males. Considering they were in the center of the board that was behind the warden's desk, they must be important, he thought.

But not as important as another. On a wall by itself, surrounded by plaques with large gold seals, was a larger framed collection of photographs, men in business suits, their names on brass plates. Large stenciled letters above the casing said SOCIAL REHABILITATION AGENCY OF AMERICA. Shell figured he was looking at the who's who of the company, surprised to see the picture and name at the top: G. Byron DuBard, Governor, State of Mississippi. This was a private prison. But somewhere in the scheme of things, the governor carried some weight. He still appointed the warden, or the warden got his job through channels that went through the governor's office. Not the current governor but, according to what the guard Durasmus had told him, the one before him.

Below the governor's picture was a blank frame. The title beneath it said Commissioner, Department of Corrections. Shell recalled a black man named Epps had held the position for years but had been recently charged with corruption, kickbacks for awarding contracts to prisons. The current governor, lieutenant governor at the time, was not involved but probably knew about it. Besides his comments about being basically powerless, Governor DuBard impressed Shell as having an odd presence of mind, or naiveness, that allowed him to move in lofty circles and see only the good and nothing of evildoing or corruption. The next photographs and names, Shell didn't know—CEO and ASSISTANT CEO, Social Rehabilitation Agency of America—his eyes tracking down the tree of power to the last on the totem pole, the man seated across from him: WARDEN, John W. Culpepper.

The clean-shaven fifty-ish looking face in the picture looked younger and leaner than the warden seated behind the desk. He was a bulky bear of a man with a ragged iron-gray beard, matching hair and thick eyebrows that met at the bridge of his nose. His eyes were heavy-lidded and bloodshot, deep pouches beneath them and he had the purplish nose of an alcoholic. He resembled a western movie actor of Shell's youth, one he couldn't name right off. The warden's face looked mad, an expression Shell had come to surmise went with the job.

"Good morning, Mr. Ferguson," the warden said, his voice gruff with a little bark to it after hanging up the phone and without looking at him. He stood ponderously and had to push his chair to the wall behind him for his stomach to clear the desk. He wore a wrinkled white shirt open at the collar revealing curls of chest hair, the sleeves rolled to his elbows. His hair was disheveled, as though he had just arisen from sleep. His face had a disreputable quality about it. Nothing about this man suggested warden. He looked more like someone trying to recover from a Saturday night drunk. He could have been a bondsman from some small Delta town or a two-bit detective from one of the river towns. The guard Durasmus had said he was from Tunica. Shell felt the probing appraisal of the man's eyes upon him. He pumped Shell's hand up and down and squeezed hard.

"Mr. Ferguson, what can I do for you?" the warden said in the same rough voice Shell had heard over the intercom, the deep scratchy quality of someone who routinely smoked. He spoke revealing graveled tobacco-stained teeth and, for the first time, Shell noted the man's lower lip bulging with a tuck of snuff, and he recalled the name of the movie actor. He couldn't remember his last name, but the first was Gabby. *About right*, he thought.

"I'm here about my grandson, Calvin Ferguson," Shell replied.

"I suspected," the warden said. "He's been here a short time. Good inmate. No complaints from him."

"Around Thanksgiving, I spoke to your secretary about him, about recent events."

"Yes, yes," he said, flipping a hand as though at a pest, his eyes crinkling slyly at the corners. "She did mention he'd had some deaths in his family," making the remark with no show of emotion.

Some deaths in his family, Shell thought, appalled at the man's lack of sensitivity. "Warden, he lost his wife and daughter two days before Thanksgiving."

The warden's face turned red, and he looked down then mumbled, "Seems like I do recall Diane, my secretary, saying something, too, about a grandmother."

Shell breathed in deeply. "Yes sir. That was my wife."

Suddenly, the warden dropped a large paper clip in his hands he'd been nervously rotating and tried to look at Shell, but his restless eyes veered off to something on the wall. "Mr. Ferguson, my sincerest condolences. I did not know."

"I don't take it personally, Warden," Shell said grimly. "When I alerted the prison of my grandson's situation and possible mental state, I had no idea he'd be put in solitary confinement."

The warden turned his gaze on him, and in his eyes, Shell saw a color he didn't like. "We call it segregation," the warden said curtly. "He also killed a county supervisor—"

"Alleged," Shell interrupted crisply.

"But convicted," the warden quickly countered. "I took him out of the county jail in this facility and—"

"And you put him in solitary confinement," Shell said tartly, interrupting again, aware his anger was rising. If he hadn't read the article in the lobby, he might be in a better frame of mind.

The warden sat up stiff and straight. His gaze slid away then back on Shell. "Protective custody," he reframed sharply with cold measuring eyes.

Ok, so now it's called protective custody, Shell thought. He sensed the warden knew what he was going to say next. "Protected from what?"

The warden looked up from under his brows, and not pleasantly. "From who, Mr. Ferguson. Ty Doom was as close as it gets to a godfather in these parts. His murder blew a hole in a gravity feed of political handouts. In fact, this prison sits on land formerly owned by him, all one hundred and forty acres. Your grandson," he went on in his raspy voice, "is at risk. And not just from others but from himself. He suffered a terrible loss, and we can keep a better eye on him in the segregated unit. If you'll recall, that's the reason you called me back before Thanksgiving, and I made a special allowance for you to see him on a holiday when we have reduced staff." He picked up the paperclip and began rotating it again.

"With all due respects, Warden Culpepper," he said addressing the man for the first time by his name, "I was concerned about his mental state, but the main reason I wanted to see him was to break the tragic news before he heard it elsewhere."

"I understand," the warden said. "If it makes you feel any better, he's denied being suicidal to our guards and nurses, who check on him several times daily, and our prison psychologist. Nonetheless, I still believe he merits protection, at least for the foreseeable future."

Shell Ferguson knew Ty Doom was a powerful man, a male queen bee, that when he was shot and killed the bullets blew holes in his hive and set off a buzzing confusion across an intricate network of power and patronage. Homeowners wouldn't get their roads graveled or drives graded in the spring. Potholes wouldn't get filled, and fallen trees wouldn't be pulled away. Pinkus Little and a host of others wouldn't get their Christmas hams. Hundreds with patronage jobs would be looking for work. It was one thing for a man of Ty Doom's magnitude and power to die naturally. Life would go on. But it seemed a stretch that Ty Doom's murder was the reason his grandson was in protective custody. There had to be other reasons.

Shell decided to shift gears. He pulled out his billfold, opened it, tweezed out a $100 bill and laid it on the warden's desk. "That oughta get my grandson's account started. No one told him or me until recently that he could have an account and make requisitions to it from the prison commissary."

The warden picked up the bill, flattened it on his desk blotter as if the gesture gave it legitimacy, wrote something on a yellow sticky note and put it on the bill. "My apologies, Mr. Ferguson. An oversight. Technically, your grandson's a county prisoner. I'll see our prison accountant gets this and your grandson's account is opened. My secretary will give you a receipt on your way out."

Shell thought about the best way to frame his next request. "He'd like some books to read."

"We got tons of books here for inmates," the warden responded, wiping a droll of snuff from his lower lip. He leaned to the side and spat a long brownish spurt, presumably into a cuspidor.

"He would like to have some books on psychology."

"He can have books, but not books on psychology," replied the warden, his eyes grave. "Books on psychology are simply not good for our inmates. They don't need to be figuring out what makes 'em tick. They're here to serve time for a crime they committed, and that will reform them in ways no psychology book can," he finished with a contemptuous smile.

Shell was startled at the warden's response. He couldn't believe the man thought psychology books were bad for anyone who wanted to better himself. "Warden, do you examine every book that comes into your prison?"

"Every frickin' one," he snapped in a voice that was hoarse and came from deep in his chest, glaring at Shell as though he'd drawn a line in the sand. "I check everything, even magazines. I don't want anything in here that'll give these inmates ideas," he concluded with a self-justified air, and a wolfish grin that Shell wanted to backslap into oblivion.

Shell considered the irony and thought of the scripture, *You blind guides, who strain out a gnat and swallow a camel.* Little wonder guard Durasmus said cellphones and drugs flow like rivers in this prison. This warden is nitpicking what the inmates can and can't read. Made Shell wonder who was controlling who, the alarming news he'd read in the lobby still percolating in his brain.

The warden pushed himself up, signaling their meeting was over. Shell sighed as he rose and shook the fleshy hand extended to him. He thanked the warden, though he wasn't sure why. The collection of photos dubbed

"Social Clubs" behind the warden snagged his vision. "Warden," he said, pointing at the photos, "I see you get support from the civic groups in the area. I still belong to the Rotary Club in Drew."

The warden glanced over his shoulder. "Oh, those," then back at his visitor. "They're not social clubs as you think of them. They're prison gangs. You may know that all of the inmates in this facility, except those in the county jail, are from other states out west."

Shell nodded he did.

"They bring their gangs with 'em. We know the tree toppers and hierarchy of power," he remarked boastfully.

"Tree toppers?"

"They're the shot-callers," he responded, pointing to the photos along the top as though proud of the production. "I had these flowcharts put together so I could keep an eye on 'em. Otherwise, they're in control, and I'm not, if you get my drift."

Shell didn't mean to smile, it leaked out. "So, you know the names of the gangs and who's who?"

"Yep. It's all in their files before they leave other states," the warden said with restless eyes, nervously walking around his desk as if ready to usher his visitor to the door.

"My, my," Shell muttered reflecting on his time at Parchman. "Gangs have come a long way." He moved to the door and turned, a final question popping into his mind. "Warden, sir?"

"Yes?" The warden shot him a hard, questioning glance.

Shell faced the warden squarely and eyed him sternly. "You look familiar. Where were you before you had this job?"

The warden appeared to swell with pride. "I was the head detective of the Tunica police force."

Shell wasn't sure how the man got this job. Reflecting on the tower of power on the wall of his office, and what he'd said about who owned the land before the private prison, he'd bet the chain of command that led to his getting it rattled with the sound of politics. How else would a detective from Mississippi's casino capital catapult to warden with a single bound, and probably over a number of other suitors to the office who made hefty gubernatorial donations?

Crossing the lobby to the door, that last thought still on his mind, Shell thanked the secretary, waited for her to give him a receipt for the hundred dollars. While he was standing there, the image slid into his mind, like a deer out of the dark at night into headlights, recalling now the face he'd seen leaving the warden's office.

CHAPTER 15

December 12 Thursday

In fact, this prison sits on land formerly owned by him.

After his encounter with the man, Shell wasn't going to take the warden's word about anything he'd said. The Ty Doom Shell knew was buying up land hand-over-fist at bargain prices; expanding his acreage, not selling it. From Bethel, north to the Coahoma County line, east to the Parchman penitentiary boundary and west across the Sunflower into Bolivar County, he had created a veritable fiefdom. So it seemed inconceivable he'd subtract a hundred and forty acres, almost a full square mile, from that fanatical accumulation of property.

Shell Ferguson was no stranger to mysterious deeds and titles. Years ago, over half a century, his persistent probing of documents in the Sunflower County Courthouse, and in Mexico, led to action that returned to him, legally, the plantation that had been his family's dating back before the Civil War. While his great-great grandfather, the rightful owner, had been in Mexico trying to found another South, the plantation had been illegally sold to a carpetbagger named Marshall in 1875 who, in 1912, sold it, illegally again, to Shell's wife's grandfather, a story too long and complicated to even think about telling.

Shell had been in the Coahoma County record room once before. He was in his late-twenties. He'd been hunting on wilderness land beyond the Mississippi River levee and stumbled upon a structure beside an oxbow lake, a spur off the Mississippi River cut off from its source. It seemed an odd place for a yellow school bus. Apparently, it was a hunting camp with a lean-to, evidence of campfires, cigarette butts, beer cans. He had asked around, but no one knew who owned it, the bus or the property. Somebody went to the trouble to haul that bus to the bottom wilderness, probably on a logging trail, and strategically planted it, propped it on concrete blocks, next to an old cutoff and perfect duck hunting site.

He walked through the double glass doors of the Chancery Clerk's office which had been renovated since his visit decades ago. A lady behind the long counter greeted him pleasantly and asked if she could help him.

"I'm looking for a deed," he said. "I've been here before, but it was a long time ago, and things look changed around a bit."

"The documents room is at the end of this counter, to the left."

"Thank you, Ma'am."

He started to leave, but the clerk was not finished. "Do you know the location of the property?" she asked.

"I've got a good idea."

"Well, you'll see the township map on the wall and across from it are the sectional indices. The land deed records are in the large books marked by years."

"Yessum, I can take it from there," he responded, he hoped not curtly, as he turned and headed for the document room before she tried to give him more help he didn't need. He knew the procedure. At the end of the counter he turned and the clerk was eying him with undisguised interest.

The record room was much larger than the one he had recalled. He guessed it should be. In fifty years, a lot of land changes hands, deeds increase.

He immediately saw what appeared to be an updated township map, a bird's eye view of the county, its rivers and roads, and communities, everything gridded into sections. He had no trouble pinpointing the section that was located near his neck of the woods. He pulled out his small spiral notebook, wrote down the township and section number. He went to the sectional indices, obtained the deed number, then went to the Deed record book #1872, page 519, and there it was. "Grantor, Tyson R. Doom, and Grantee, Social Rehabilitation Agency of America."

"Aye damn, the man was telling the truth," he whispered to himself.

Fact or not, the warden's comment shook loose an old memory.

Athen was the football fan in their marriage. She had graduated from Ole Miss and was a big Rebels fan. A few times he had gone to home games in Oxford with her, tail-gated with her friends, visited her sorority. But Shell had never gone to college and the rah-rah folderol, Frankie frat rat rush, and all that hoopla had never appealed to him. Though he'd never attended any Delta State games, he did keep up with their football.

From Clarksdale to Cleveland and the Delta State campus was about an hour's drive. As a member of the Delta Council, a consortium of planters and political leaders in the Delta, Shell had been to the Walter Sillers Coliseum often and knew his way around the campus.

"Is it possible for me to look at some old yearbooks?" he asked the lady behind the front desk at the school's library. She was broad-shouldered and stout looking with short black hair and wore dark-rimmed glasses. A tag above her jacket pocket said, "Librarian." She identified herself as Ms. Butler. She spoke in a deep, almost masculine voice.

"Are you a student here?" she enquired eyeing him suspiciously.

The question caught him off guard. He guessed times had really changed and old folks went to college these days. "I wish I were, Ma'am."

She smiled tightly with thin lips.

"But I am a lifelong member of the Delta Council," and pulled a card from his billfold and showed it to her.

She looked at the card which did verify his membership.

"Mr. Ferguson, we have Delta Council members who have guest privileges at the university. Perhaps you are one."

He shook his head. "No, Ma'am. Afraid not. I don't want to check anything out, just look at a few old yearbooks, see some pictures of folks I know. I'll be happy to pay you," he said still holding his billfold.

"We are really supposed to allow only students, former students or those with guest cards use the library." She paused and looked around. She pulled a small card from a slot in the desk, wrote something on it and handed it to him. "This is a temporary card, Mr. Ferguson. It's good for today."

He thanked her profusely, took the card, and placed it in his shirt pocket next to the spiral notebook.

She told him the yearbooks had been archived and were in the stacks. He enquired what she meant by "stacks" and she told him everything in the library was stacked systematically and that the *Broom* yearbooks were on the third floor. She drew him a map with an arrow pointing to the aisle where he would find the annuals where they arranged in numerical order by years.

He took the elevator to the third floor and followed the arrows. He got turned around and tried to return to the elevator and found himself lost. *He never returned, no he never returned, and his fate is still unlearned.* The lyrics from the past popped into his mind. He couldn't recall the time, maybe late 50's, or the song or musicians, Kingston something. He patted his shirt pocket and whispered, "She gave me a card to get in, I might need one to get out," the song continuing to play in his head until he finally stumbled onto an aisle labeled BROOM.

He ran his finger down the spines, checking off the years. Ty Doom was fifty-five when he was killed. That would have put him at Delta State late '70's early '80's. His moving finger stopped on a 1983 *Broom*. He pulled the volume off the shelf and began turning the pages, flipping past photos of campus buildings, faculty, senior class officers—He wouldn't have been one of those. The senior class photos were arranged alphabetically. He turned quickly to the D's. No Tyson Doom. He checked the Junior Class photos. Not there either.

He replaced the volume on the shelf and, thinking he may not have had his picture taken his junior year, pulled out the 1982 *Broom*. Thumbing past the usual campus and faculty pictures, he came to the Senior Class and began perusing. There were several with the last name beginning with a D, most of them women. No Doom.

Shell ran the math again. Perhaps he was delayed. Dropped out, then got back in. Got expelled or suspended. He knew he was there on that shelf somewhere. He was selected All-Conference guard his senior year. Shell tried again, continued working the years backward. In the 1981 edition, Senior Class section: Davidson, Dickinson,—and there it was—Doom. The picture showed only his face, not the tremendous frame of the man. But the same cold eyes penetrated past the page.

Shell turned toward the back of the annual, to the Sports section and went right to the football section. He saw the picture, Ty Doom in a running pose tucking a ball with the caption Fullback, All-Conference. But what caught his eye was another photo on the same page above his. "I'll be," he whispered to himself, the words echoing through the stacks, a slight chill moving through him.

Shell began flipping pages back to the Senior Class and something in the

Who's Who section snagged his vision, and he stopped. It was not the picture, though she was stunning. Nor was it the caption at the top of the page signifying the honor and title. It was her last name that got his attention. He pulled out the notepad and jotted down the name.

He took the elevator back to the first floor and returned to the front desk.

"Have any luck?" the librarian asked.

"Yes, Ma'am. But I need a little more information." He tore the page from the pad and handed it to her. "Would it be possible for me to get more information on this person?"

The lady looked at the name. "My, my, that was a long time ago."

"Yessum, it was," but he was thinking *is*.

"I'll be happy to get the information for you, but it is public domain," she said. "You could get it over the internet."

He didn't want to tell her that his wife, who did his computer work for him, had recently died. "Mine's not working right now," which was not a lie. Without Athen, it just sat there on her desk in her study, a room he avoided.

"Very well," she said in a cheerful, accommodating tone. "This will just take a minute."

He watched as she sat down and turned the computer screen facing her, placed the note on the desk and began typing. He looked around. A few students sat at tables, books scattered around them, their heads down.

The lady finished typing and hit a button. "I'm printing this for you," she said and in seconds handed him a single sheet.

He stood looking at it in disbelief.

"Is that not what you wanted?" she questioned.

At first, he didn't hear her. Then he looked up, "Yes, yes," he said and looked back down at the page, at the name of her parents, then back up at the librarian. "Indeed, it is. I'm mighty grateful to you." He reached in his shirt pocket and pulled out the card she'd given to him." I don't think I'll need this anymore," gesturing to return it to her, then withdrew his hand. "On second thought, I just might. Again, much obliged," and he tipped his hat and left.

Outside on the steps, he glanced at his watch. He had time.

Over the same highway, he returned to the Coahoma County Courthouse.

"You forget something, Mr. Ferguson?" the same lady behind the long counter asked.

"I hope not," he said. "Need to check on another deed."

"You know the way," she said, but he was already headed toward the record room. This time he wouldn't have to go to all the trouble he did last time which was fifty years ago. He was surprised that seeing the name again tripped his memory and that he still recalled it. But, it was not a name one easily forgets. All he needed was to see if the name on that deed was the same as the name on the sheet of paper just given to him by the librarian, the same as the campus beauty, and the same as the one he saw on that deed fifty years ago. At that time, he had jotted it down, but that scrap of paper was long gone.

He by-passed the Sectional Index. He didn't need to know the history of the deed. All he needed was to see the name. He went straight to the property tax rolls, opened to the S's, flipped several pages toward the end of that section, ran his finger down the page and stopped. "Son of a gun!" His finger anchored on the name, he kept staring at it. "Sure as hell's a small world."

CHAPTER 16

December 14 Sunday

A different guard led Shell down the same long corridor. He was dressed similarly as the other guards but without lapels. His rapid and grunting speech, when he spoke, was near unintelligible. He was grossly obese and walked, it seemed, with effort, the accouterments of power dangling from his belt, jingle-jangling with each step. Observing the man's huge rear sagging from side to side, Shell had a tacky thought he'd keep to himself.

"You look better," Shell said to his grandson after the guard had sat him on a stool with rollers, and left locking the door behind him. The guard was not as accommodating as the guard Durasmus and for twenty dollars uncuffed Cal. They were in a different room down the hall from the last. Same size, same mustard-colored walls. Based upon its contents—eye chart, weight scales, examining table, jars of cotton balls, and tongue depressors— a medical examining room.

"I've had some distractions," Cal said flatly after they had embraced and he sat down with his elbows propped on his parted knees, his forearms hanging loosely between them.

"I've got another," Shell said, "Don't know if it'll help or hurt," quickly wishing he'd dropped the last part.

Cal's eyes twitched. His chest heaved. He straightened up. "What?"

"You first," Shell said. "Your distractions."

"No!" Cal snapped his voice angrily as hard as the walls around them. "You've got this look on your face. I'm not sitting here waiting on more hurt. Give it to me now."

"It might help explain the fire," Shell said attempting to mitigate his opening damage.

"Go on, Granddad," he said rolling his hands anxiously. "Cut to the chase."

"All Right," he acquiesced in a patient voice. "I've gone back over the trial transcript, read it twice. I've winnowed and sifted through every detail of Doom's murder except one—"

"Which is?" Cal interrupted anxiously.

"The envelope."

"Envelope?"

"The one you had the day you went to Doom's house. You stated it had information Sadie needed for the Sunday bulletin. A newborn."

"That's right. I'd forgotten about it."

"What kind of envelope was it?"

"White regular business-size."

"No print on it, like a church return address?"

"Nothing. Plain."

Shell scooted his chair closer. "Where was the envelope when you entered the house? Did you have it in your hand or was it somewhere else?"

Cal thought a moment. "I remember putting it in my coat pocket when I left the church office."

"You don't normally carry something like that in your hand," Shell suggested.

"No sir. I'd be afraid I'd put it down somewhere and forget it. I put it in my inside coat pocket."

"You're fairly certain."

"Positive."

"At the house, you said you dropped it when you picked up the gun."

"I said I dropped it?"

"In our last meeting, you said you picked up the envelope you'd brought, suggesting you'd dropped it. But you never said you dropped it. Did you drop it?" Shell lifted a finger. "Better question: Did you even have it in your hand?"

Cal folded his arms and leaned back, looked at the ceiling, drew a long breath. He had a habit of grinding his molars when in deep thought. The muscles in his jaw stopped moving, and he inclined forward.

"Guess I misspoke, Granddad," he said embarrassed. "Now that I think about it, I never took the envelope out of my coat pocket."

"You didn't misspeak, Cal," Shell said bending toward him and placing a hand on his knee. "You told the truth. You said in court on the witness stand that you picked up the envelope you'd brought only *inferring* you'd dropped it."

The room grew suddenly quiet. Both sat still as statues, eyes locked.

"Granddad, I picked up a different envelope."

"Yes!" Shell said. "Now the million dollar question: What did you do with it?"

"In the excitement, when I went to get my cell phone, I think I laid it on the car seat."

"Was it the same type, white unmarked business-size?"

"Best I can recall. It looked the same. Obviously, I thought it was the same."

"What did you do with it when you got home?" Shell pressed.

"I trashed it. After what had happened, Sadie wouldn't be printing a Sunday bulletin."

"Trashed it at the church office or at home?"

"At home. That's where I went after I was released at the crime scene. I testified to that."

"You were the last one to testify before the jury deliberated but it was the first time you mentioned picking up an envelope. That was Friday. The parsonage burned Tuesday."

"Granddad, how does this relate to the fire?"

"Drawers and cabinets at Doom's were rifled. According to authorities, nothing was taken. Except..."

"That envelope," Cal murmured almost inaudibly, a stunned look on his face. "And I took it."

For a while, no one spoke. Somewhere a clock ticked.

"What in heaven's name could have been in it?" Cal questioned.

"That's the second million dollar question," Shell replied. "And, due respects, it wasn't in heaven's name. It cost us dearly," those words gone before he could retrieve them.

Cal's head dipped. He sniffled. "And I caused it, Granddad. I picked up something that wasn't mine."

Shell reached over, placed a finger under his chin and pulled his face up even with his. "Stop it!" he snapped. "You didn't know it wasn't yours. Besides, it's only a clue, not a conclusion." He turned and glanced at the small door window. With this guard, he didn't know how long he had or if the twenty dollars tacked on more minutes. "You said you'd had some distractions."

"They're not distractions now," Cal remarked, his voice shaky.

"But they were," Shell said firmly. "Talk to me."

Shell listened as his grandson told him for the first time about his new friend named Chris. How they had met and communicated through an air duct vent, Chris' background, his crimes, his conversion and intercessory prayer groups he'd started around the country, the world.

"I've been in prisons before, Son," Shell said skeptically. "I've heard these stories."

"But Chris is for real, Granddad," Cal countered, his voice stronger. "He's a soulmate." Then he told his granddad about the forced cell extraction, the inmate that was thrown into the stall next to him, his tattoo, the gang connection and Shell sat on the edge of his chair taking it all in. "Chris says the gangs have a lot of power."

Shell recalled the flow chart in the warden's office. *Otherwise, they're in control, and I'm not.*

A single rap on the door.

Shell got up and peered through the small window into the dark syrup-colored eyes of the guard. The guard held up five fingers and mouthed five minutes.

Shell flashed a thumbs up and sat back down. "We've got five minutes, the guard said. You said the guy knew your name."

"He said it with a question, and I nodded."

Shell winced and shook his head. "Cal, in prison always let information come to you, not from you."

"Chris said that, too."

"Your friend's sounding better," Shell said. "Did he know the prisoner?"

"He'd never seen him before. He was concerned about the tattoo on his scalp, a cross on a crown over the letter N. He said it was a symbol of Aryan Nations, a domestic terrorist gang. They're all over the country, he said."

"That doesn't tell us anything," Shell said reflecting again on the group of photos he'd seen in the warden's office. "What did your friend think the guy could be up to?"

Cal told him what Chris had said about the staged fight earlier and the inmate possibly being on some kind of mission.

"What kind of mission?" probed Shell.

"Chris didn't know but said it was strange, that I hadn't been there long enough to make enemies."

"Does Chris know why you're here?" Shell followed up.

Cal nodded.

Shell slapped a hand to his head.

"Granddad, I trust this man. I had to tell somebody."

"Okay, okay," Shell said frustrated. "I've been there, done the same to a friend. Maybe this friend—you said he's been here a long time—will pick up on something."

"He said I needed to be cautious."

Shell was already becoming concerned but didn't want to alarm his grandson. "It could be nothing. Regardless, keep your eyes and ears open. Which reminds me. I met with the warden and asked him why you were in solitary."

"Which is?" Cal asked eagerly.

"Protective custody."

"It's not very protective. An inmate I've never seen or known knows my name, stages a fight to get thrown into my pod for unknown reasons. So, why am I in protective custody?"

"Because you," he paused choosing his words more carefully, "allegedly killed a powerful man. The warden is concerned about reprisals, and there's no protective custody unit in the old county jail or in the county prison section of this facility."

Cal threw up his hands. "Give me a break!"

"There may be other reasons," Shell said. "I'll leave you on a couple of positive notes."

"I could use them."

"I met with Governor DuBard last Monday. We talked about the fire. While I was there, he spoke with the director of the Mississippi Bureau of Investigation. There'll be a thorough investigation."

"Is he working on my appeal?"

"Yes. It's moving forward. Another positive. I gave the warden a hundred dollars and opened an account in the prison for you. You can requisition necessities, including writing materials. You can have books but," he wagged a finger in front of his nose, "no psychology books," choosing not to go into the warden's perverted reason.

There was a loud click, and the doorknob turned. "I'll see you in a week. Remember what we talked about," and gave a thumbs up.

Cal nodded understanding as the guard entered to cuff him and take him away. Shell slapped him on the back and said, "Keep the faith."

CHAPTER 17

December 19 Friday

Shell was back in the plush lobby sitting in the same plush leather chair amid the "trappings," as the governor had referred to them, of the office. He had called the governor's office early that morning, and before he could request an appointment, the receptionist had preempted him.

"Mr. Ferguson, I was about to call you. There's been a development. How soon can you get here."

"I can leave now," he'd told her.

There's been a development. The fire investigation? Cal's Christmas pass? A possible parole? He had not expected to hear this soon from the governor. Especially after all the folderol about his limitations of power. Whatever this development, he had some of his own to bring to the table.

This time, he was alone in the cavernous lobby. He'd arrived mid-morning and had been waiting patiently, almost an hour. The receptionist was typing away on her computer, soft rapid pecks that seemed as urgent as her summons to him, her face that serious, her eyes that focused. The only other noise he heard was air whooshing from a vent somewhere above him, and he thought of Cal and his friend, glad his grandson had a vent. The legislature was not in session. The Capitol was quiet.

He kept waiting for the receptionist's phone to ring announcing the governor was ready to see him when the big man himself walked into the lobby. He was coatless. His tie was pulled down, and his shirtsleeves rolled up as though he'd already put in a full day. Shell rose to greet him.

"Come into my office," the governor said matter-of-factly, and Shell followed him through the marble-columned entrance into the inner sanctum that impressed him less this time than the last.

Immediately, Shell noticed the presence of another man, a distinguished

116

face he'd seen before, maybe in the papers or on the news. He was tall and physically compact. His hair was gray and parted down the middle, and he had a prominent nose, thick black brows contrasting the silver hair and deep-set eyes.

"Mr. Ferguson," the governor said, jerking a thumb at the other man in the room, "I'd like you to meet Garland Holifield, Director of the Mississippi Bureau of Investigation."

The director was standing by one of the wingbacks cater-cornered the large desk and extended a hand. "My condolences, Mr. Ferguson. Many thanks for coming," the director said, his handshake firm and genuine, compatible with the voice and eye contact.

Shell nodded slightly acknowledging the expression of sympathy. He also realized he was the only one in the room who was wearing a coat and tie. Both men appeared as though they'd been working furiously through the night. Their faces were tired and grim, and neither had smiled.

"Have a seat, Shell," the governor said motioning glumly to one of the chairs facing his desk. From the somber tone, Shell sensed there was more bad news. The room had that solemn ambiance about it.

The director and Shell sat.

The governor slowly worked his way around the desk to his chair. Leaning forward, shoulders hunched and hands folded prayerfully, Governor DuBard cast a grave look, first at Shell, then the director. "Mr. Ferguson, I've asked the director to join us this morning. You may recall I spoke with him by phone during your last visit, directing him to follow up on the sloppy, and I use that word advisedly, investigation of—" He paused and cleared his throat— "the fire that took my—" and he paused again, his voice cracking, his chin quivering "—our loved ones." He had looked down at his hands when he said it, then suddenly at the ceiling and Shell caught the glimmer of a tear that would have fallen had the man's eyes not averted. He also saw something else he'd never seen before. The man's human side as his face came down and the tear with it he quickly dismissed with a flick of a finger.

"Yessir," Shell confirmed tipping his head toward the director.

"Based upon the photos you took," the governor continued, glancing at the director, "MBI investigators returned to the scene. The director also ordered both corp—" The governor cleared his throat. "—bodies, I mean, the two that could be removed, to be exhumed and someone other than the county coroner conducted the autopsy. Before I turn this meeting over to him, everything we discuss is strictly confidential."

"I understand, Governor," Shell said. "I'm grateful for your trust."

"Don't be grateful to me," the governor responded. "We're indebted to you. You got this ball rolling," then the governor glanced at the director, "Garland, if you will."

"I second the governor's gratitude to you, Mr. Ferguson," the director said. "Without your efforts, we would not be here this morning. Allow me." He stood and walked toward a flip chart on an easel set up for the occasion. He flipped over the first sheet and Shell recognized the floor plan of the parsonage with its carport, driveway and surrounding yard including the privet hedge at the back and the perimeter of the adjacent field. The director lifted a pointer from the easel tray and with it gestured at the diagram.

"This, I'm sure," he began eyeing Shell, "you recognize as the parsonage floor plan and surrounding area."

"Yessir," Shell responded.

Tilted back in his chair, hands folded beneath his chin, the governor quietly observed.

"We have concluded that the fire was the result of arson," the director said. "We've also concluded, based upon several pieces of evidence that are not significant at this point, that the arsonist, or arsonists—there was probably more than one—started the fire from the inside. Wiring in the attic was not involved."

"Kerosene," the governor injected nodding at Shell.

The director ignored the interruption and continued. "As your photos showed, Mr. Ferguson, a large kerosene can was embedded in the privet hedge. We surmise it got caught in the branches when the perpetrators were dashing from the fire which was not only severely hot but also lit up the area."

"Before you go further," Shell interrupted, "were you able to get any prints on the can?"

"No prints. They were probably wearing gloves," the director concluded. "They left the scene we think this way," he added, the pointer tracing an imaginary path from the back door of the house, through the fruit trees, past the shed to the privet hedge where the can was lodged. "Here," he tapped the pointer, "is where they exited the backyard to a waiting vehicle." He paused, as if to allow time for what he'd said to settle in.

"The tire tracks were Mohawk mud tires," Shell said flatly. "There was a feature on the left rear tire tread."

"Correct," the director confirmed. "A fact to keep in mind as others surface." Popping the pointer gently in his palm, the director continued. "All of this, we calculate, happened in seconds, not minutes. This explains why the young child Shelley was not found. She was small and, with the heat of that fire, incinerated." The director dipped his head. "I apologize, gentlemen, for the poor choice of words."

"But her teeth?" Shell spoke up. "Teeth don't burn."

"In ordinary fires, Mr. Ferguson, you are right," the director responded. "The enamel can withstand very high heat." He raised a cautionary finger. "But not all heat. An extremely hot fire, like a crematorium, will consume teeth." The director laid down the pointer and returned to his chair. "That parsonage was an old wood structure, tinder awaiting a match. Add kerosene, and you've got very hot exploding flames."

"I never realized," Shell murmured.

Thumping his knuckles on his desk blotter, the governor blurted out, "Go ahead, Garland. Tell him the rest."

Shell perched on the edge of his chair and braced himself for the *development* he'd been expecting.

The director inhaled as though about to plunge into deep water. "Mr. Ferguson, our forensic examination of the two adult bodies that partially survived the fire revealed both had been shot—"

"Shot!" Shell cried out falling back in his chair.

"—by a Glock seventeen," the director finished his sentence. "The gun that killed Ty Doom, based upon our ballistics, was the same that killed the governor's daughter and your wife. We surmise there was a battle and the two females were shot."

"And the place was torched to cover their murders," injected the governor.

"My God!" Shell exclaimed in disbelief. "Ty Doom, then, was not shot by his own gun."

"Correct!" the director verified. "The ballistics don't match Doom's gun. His gun was fired twice, probably at the real culprit—"

"Or culprits," the governor interrupted again.

"My grandson is innocent," exclaimed Shell breathing excitedly. "He can be freed."

"Mr. Ferguson, we have more work to do before we can release any of this to the press and seek his release," advised the director. "In fact, if we can obtain more evidence, the district attorney may drop the case against your grandson and request his exoneration."

"What more do they need?" Shell questioned still trying to recover from the shocking news."

"We're reinvestigating the Doom house," the director continued. "Agents are there now, even as we speak, going over it with a fine tooth comb, inch by excruciating inch, looking for fingerprints and two bullets lodged somewhere in the house, a door jamb, a wall, the ceiling."

"Or in somebody's anatomy," the governor jumped in.

The director shot the governor an irritated glance. "But we checked with all of the hospitals and medical clinics in the area, including Helena, Arkansas and Memphis, on or around that date. Law enforcement would have been alerted. No medical facility reported treating any gunshot wounds during that time frame. It's been our contention all along," the director eyed the governor, "that whoever was there, probably more than one, was looking for something Ty Doom had that they needed. Officers testified when they arrived at the Doom house, it had the appearance of being searched; drawers open, papers everywhere."

"We're not sure if it was a deal gone bad," the governor surmised. "That Doom wouldn't give 'em what they wanted, there was a struggle or what."

"Perhaps, Doom walked in on them," the director added. "They fired first, and Doom got off two shots before he went down."

"All of this is still at the theoretical stage," the governor commented. "No motive."

Shell had been waiting. "Could it be an envelope?"

"Envelope?" exclaimed the governor and the director in unison.

"Where'd you come up with an envelope?" the governor asked startled.

"I've been thinking about the puzzle, mulling over the pieces," Shell continued. "I was quizzing Cal about everything he saw that day at Doom's house, then this piece came flying into the picture." He told them about the sequence of events involving the envelope in Cal's coat pocket that day he went to the Doom house. "No envelope was mentioned in the sheriff's investigation," Shell said.

"This is true," agreed the director.

The governor added a confirming nod.

"Cal testified he'd picked up an envelope, thinking he'd dropped it. After rethinking, he told me he only thought he'd dropped it. The envelope he brought to give to Sadie Doom containing the birth announcement for the Sunday bulletin was still in his inside coat pocket. Gentlemen," he looked at the governor then the director, "the envelope Cal picked up was not his."

"That fits our theory of a deal gone bad," said the governor.

"If the envelope was the deal," questioned the director. "What happened to it?"

Shell continued. "It was apparent Sadie wouldn't be printing a Sunday bulletin, so Cal said he took it back to the parsonage and trashed it."

"As in garbage," the governor said.

Shell nodded. "Yes."

"But the birth announcement was still in his coat pocket," added the director.

"Yessir," Shell confirmed.

"Let me make sure I've got this right," the governor said. "Cal's picking up an envelope he thought he had dropped did not surface until he was on the witness stand the last day of the trial and a few days before the fire. That means that from May twenty-six of this year, until Friday, November twenty-first, that envelope was a non-issue in this case and quickly developed, almost overnight, into a big one."

"Right, Governor DuBard," Shell affirmed.

"Mr. Ferguson, you're doing a yeoman's job of knitting this case together," the director said, his tone complimentary.

"Don't know about knitting," Shell said "I just kept sifting things around until one wouldn't sift anymore. That was the envelope."

The director appeared amused. "I'd like to borrow your sifter and shake it one more time."

Shell gave him a salute.

"When I first heard about your son-in-law's controversial ministry, the parsonage fire and loss of life," the director said, "I thought hate crime. Then, the details linking the murders with a single weapon, I caught a gut. Could this be domestic terrorism?"

Shell moved to the edge of his chair. "Excuse me, Mr. Director, hate crimes and domestic terrorism sound about the same to me."

"I understand," the director said. "They do for most people. But a hate crime is one targeted against individuals because of race or membership in a social group," he motioned with his left hand. "Domestic terrorism, on the other hand," he opened his right palm, "is acts of violence carried out by groups of two or more U. S. citizens against persons or property for political or social objectives. In this case, there is no common thread of 'hate.' The common thread, at this point," he brought his hands together, "is a weapon, a semi-automatic Glock 17-ten millimeter, short recoil, locked breech, with an effective range of one 150 feet—the type used by domestic terrorist groups and militia. And, it was used in two different locales. That's the gut I caught."

"Another would be that envelope," asserted the governor.

"Possibly," countered the director. "We don't know what was in it."

"Which raises the question about objectives," the governor said, "or motives which could lead us to the murderers. The envelope, if it contained something valuable, and we assume it did, would be one motive. Then, there's the motive behind the motive, the source of its importance, the terrorist group or militia's big objective."

"That's the heart of this case," said the director. "The only real clue we have, at this point, is a semi-automatic Glock 17, plus a thin speculation of militia involvement, and an envelope we have no idea what the hell it contained." He looked at Shell. "I'm afraid, Mr. Ferguson, that, barring anything earth-shattering from the inspection of Doom's house, your sifter will need to keep sifting."

"I'm ready to shake it again," Shell said. "Right now."

The director palmed a hand toward him.

"There's militia in Mississippi," Shell avowed.

"This is true," the director agreed with a serious side-eye cut to the governor that Shell didn't miss. "There are a few cells in northeast Mississippi—the Hatchie Hills and a place called Twenty Mile Bottom; one in Jones County, the southeast part of the state. Another militia group—and there may be more than one—is also located, or I should say operates west of the Mississippi River levee in a two hundred mile oval-sized area with Memphis a rough center. It's been there a few years, their presence basically benign, limited to hunting and war games. Lately, it seems, according to the FBI office in Oxford, the activity of the group has raised some red flags."

"I can raise some more," Shell said. "All due respects, Mr. Director, your office and the FBI may have missed one," and he told of his visit with the warden, the flowchart of photographs, Cal's story of the forced cell extraction, the violent inmate was thrown into the shower next to him. "Cal got a good look at him and the tattoo on his scalp."

"Which was?" the director questioned leaning with interest toward him and rolling his hand for more.

"Cal said it was a cross with a crown over the letter N."

The director's eyes widened.

"That ring a bell, Garland?" the governor asked noting his director's reaction.

"Rings more than a bell," the director responded. "That's the symbol for Aryan Nations, also known as Aryan Brotherhood."

"Cal learned from another inmate," Shell said, "that this Aryan Nations came from, or was kin to, something called Christian Identity."

"That inmate," the director said pointing his finger at Shell, "is well-informed."

"Well, inform me," the governor said annoyed. "Who the hell are we talking about?"

"Sorry, Governor," the director apologized. "Aryan Nations is a militia domestic terrorist organization that sprang from a similar, but broader white supremest movement called Christian Identity."

"I was in lock step with you up to this point about the militia, Garland," the governor said. "But I've never heard of 'em."

"You have, Your Honor," the director corrected. "Timothy McVeigh, the Oklahoma City bomber, was a member of Christian Identity."

The governor's eyes expanded, his face reddened.

The director continued, addressing the governor. "I'm sure you recall the Ruby Ridge debacle in Idaho."

"I do," replied the governor.

"That was Aryan Nations." The director said. "Aryan Nations and Christian Identity are both white supremacist, anti-Semitic religious groups. They are also fiercely anti-government and have amassed a significant arsenal of automatic and semi-automatic weapons. Aryan Nations usually works in sync with its members, and it's assumed that Christian Identity intertwines through their network." He pointed at the US flag beside the governor. "Their common goal is to bring down the government. In other words, they are basically two peas in a pod. Their members meet in churches and wear robes. Sound familiar to anyone?"

"Okay, Garland, I get the picture." remarked the governor. "The Klan is still alive."

"They are, Your Honor," confirmed the director. "Splinter groups from the KKK belong to Christian Identity and Aryan Nations. Both have been branded by the FBI as major terrorist threats. They are homegrown and a bigger threat to our country than the ones overseas. Since nine eleven, almost twice as many Americans have been killed by white supremacists and anti-government fanatics than by radical Muslims."

"Does the FBI identify the militia operating beyond the levee?" inquired the governor.

"Not at this point," the director responded. "But, Mr. Ferguson, through his grandson and recent events in his prison pod, has added another clue that puts us closer."

Sitting there listening, Shell Ferguson had been taking all of this in and did not like what he was hearing. Something else was cycling through his mind. He felt a growing tightness within, winding from his gut to his throat so that the utterance of the word "pod" sprung a coiled spring. "Gentlemen!" he said rising partly from his chair and raising a finger. He was trying to keep his voice neutral but addressed them louder than he meant. "First of all, the prison in Sunflower County is not far from the levee. And second," another finger popped up, his voice rising, "my innocent grandson is in solitary confinement for purposes of protective custody in that prison that's infested with gangs and one of the terrorists we're talking about two doors down from him."

"I understand your concerns, Mr. Ferguson," empathized the director, "I must speak candidly."

"By all means!" Shell exclaimed fiercely with glaring eyes, rapping a knuckle on the governor's desk. He couldn't believe he'd been so direct with the Director of the Mississippi Bureau of Investigation.

"Mr. Ferguson," the director said grimly. "You were asked to come today for several reasons. You are helping us and the FBI break this case, and you're doing it with remarkable sleuthing, better than some on my own staff. And," he paused and glanced at the governor as if he needed permission to proceed, "the FBI has reason to believe that something big is developing beyond the levee. I wish I could tell you more, but I cannot."

"I'm familiar with that territory," Shell said. "I've hunted over it most of my life. Perhaps I can help."

"Perhaps," the director said. "I'm not at liberty to provide any details."

"Whatever or whoever it is, Mr. Director," Shell replied testily, "massacred my family, framed my grandson and put him in harm's way."

"And your grandson, Mr. Ferguson," the director said somberly, "is another reason you're here. He may be the key to more than just the murders of Ty Doom and your loved ones."

Shell felt the mood of the room shift. He could feel it in the silence, the weight of the words that seemed heavier rolling off the tongue of the director.

"He may be a flashpoint," said the director. "If he is, from what we know now, the perpetrators need to get what they think he has which could flush them into the open."

"Or, Cal will wind up in greater danger," Shell said.

"Shell, he's in solitary confinement, protective custody," emphasized the governor.

"It's not very protective," Shell recoiled, "the enemy is two cells from him."

"Gentlemen, let's keep this in perspective," said the director. "They think your grandson has something valuable, how valuable we don't know. Being in solitary confinement, in a strange way, protects him."

The tension in the room was thick. Shell was doing all he could to contain himself. "You just hit on it, Mr. Director, and we've been missing it."

"What?" both said.

"He's in protective custody, all right," Shell continued. "We all agree on that. But, is he being protected from somebody?" He paused. "Or, for somebody?"

The director and the governor exchanged blank looks and said nothing. The room was still. Typing and muted voices could be heard in the lobby. A siren sounded a few blocks away. In the silence, Shell could feel the implication sinking in.

The director rubbed his chin contemplatively. The governor sat tapping the tips of his fingers together as if in nervous prayer.

The governor spoke first, looking at Shell over prayerful hands. "Did the warden provide any additional information to you about this situation with your grandson?"

"A couple of things, one you may know. First, he said the land the prison sat on originally belonged to Ty Doom."

"That's true," the governor confirmed. "Doom sold the land to the private prison company. No reason to believe the sale was inappropriate at the time. My predecessor recommended the appointment of the warden, but the warden is formally hired by the prison company. No objections were raised. There was no indications of impropriety."

"At the time," the director echoed. "But, with the Corrections Commissioner under indictment for taking kickbacks and with this new information today, it merits reassessment. You said *two* things, Mr. Ferguson."

"The other wasn't something the warden said," Shell said. "While I was waiting, a smartly dressed woman came out of his office. At first, I didn't recognize her with the short black hair. That woman, gentlemen, was Sadie Beatrice Doom."

The governor gave the director a low-brow look. "What reason would Sadie Doom have for being in the warden's office?" he asked.

Shell raised a finger. "What reason would she have for being there in disguise, hair shortened and dyed black or wearing a wig."

"Not sure I understand about the hair," said the director.

"Sadie Beatrice Doom has long blond hair, or did," Shell injected.

"Interesting," the director said eying the governor.

"Gentlemen, if I might proceed?" Shell said with a raised palm.

Both nodded approval.

"When the warden told me the land the prison was on was sold to the private prison company by Ty Doom, I smelled something that didn't smell good. I'd heard the name Ty Doom long before he became a supervisor. I mean, the name Doom is not one that flits into and out of your mind but hangs around. After circulating some through my head, I recalled where I'd first heard it." He turned sideways in his chair, so he could swivel between the governor and the director. "To make sure—at 79 years old, my memory's a tad less than it used to be—I did some checking." He told them about his visit to the Delta State University library and review of old *Broom* annuals. "And there it was," he exclaimed, "year nineteen hundred and eighty-one, in the senior football player section, a photo of Ty Doom, alias T.D., played wide receiver, broke school records, selected All-Conference."

"Mr. Ferguson, sir, all due respects," the director said slightly annoyed, "the fact Ty Doom played football at Delta State doesn't tell us much. Where are you going with this?"

"I'm just about there," Shell advised. "On that same page, two rows up was the picture of another player, all-conference fullback," leaning forward and tapping his finger on the desk as though on the picture itself. "Any takers on his name?"

The director shrugged.

"John Culpepper," the governor said.

"Bingo!" Shell said bringing his hand down with a clap onto the desk. "They grew up in each other's pockets. It was alleged Sadie Doom was having an affair," Shell continued. "She stated on the stand, under oath, it was with my grandson. He denies it. There was not one shred of evidence presented that he was having an affair with his secretary, or anybody else for that matter. All of that is based upon speculation, not even circumstantial speculation, if there's such a thing. And there was another picture in that same yearbook. The Maid of Cotton for that year. The name? Sadie Beatrice Swift," and he threw his hands into the air. "Sadie Bea Doom's presence in the warden's office suggests she and the warden had been long connected. I think, gentleman," he concluded looking at one then the other, "when she testified she was protecting somebody. I know that's speculation, but it's highly suggestive."

"Who would she be protecting?" the director asked dismissively with open palms. "She may or may not have a relationship with the warden. She could have been returning something to him her husband had borrowed or even taking him memorabilia since they were old friends. She could have been there for reasons we have no knowledge."

Shell again: "Then why was she in disguise? I guess that's what we don't know and are waiting to find out from this tangle of clues. Somebody, or bodies, out there somewhere in the Delta thinks my grandson possesses something of value. That something will protect him, and we are waiting for that flashpoint when he draws them from the shadows into the light, and if that happens or doesn't happen, I am not one for waiting for that moment when they discover what they thought he knew is long gone. That, gentlemen, is the flashpoint that bothers me," and he clapped his hand again on the desk, his body twisted, so he was looking eye to eye with the director.

"Your observation about Ms. Doom being in the warden's office and attempts to hide her identity along with your comments are speculative. But they do raise questions," the director said to him.

"Mr. Director," Shell addressed him matter-of-factly, "you are a logical person. Since you uttered your first words, I've been impressed with your logical approach to this case, or cases. When you have more time to think about it," he turned to the governor, "and you, too, Governor DuBard, I believe a logic will surface that Cal Ferguson for a reason, not just some reason, was placed in solitary confinement and that hovering around that reason is the reason Sadie Bea Doom, the widow of Ty Doom, was observed exiting from the office of the one person, who had the power and authority to put Cal into solitary confinement. There you are. Go figure. Now you have two motives for Doom's murder. And there may be another."

The meeting adjourned with the understanding Shell would be kept informed and that he, through his incarcerated grandson, would keep the director updated on events within the prison, all of which could help solve the crime in question and possibly uncover something much larger looming out there beyond the levee.

"One way or the other, directly or indirectly," the director said to Shell as he was leaving the office, "You'll hear about any new developments."

Driving home, Shell sensed the governor and the director knew more than they were telling. He did not miss the knowing glances between them and sensed they were feeding him bad information, asking questions they already knew the answer to. Were he and his innocent grandson toys or pawns in a cruel and volatile ploy? That question lingering longer than he wanted as he drove.

CHAPTER 18

December 20 Saturday

Before he was incarcerated, he had been preaching, visiting the sick and shut-ins, marrying couples, baptizing babies, burying the dead. From one end of life's spectrum to the other, he had had a role in helping others find meaning. Now, he was no longer involved in those beginnings and endings for others but outside of all that and faced with finding a different meaning in his own life.

He had recalled something helpful from seminary. One of the older male students, his name was Gus from Georgia, had experienced God's call to the ministry while he was a prisoner of war. The subject of imprisonment had come up, and he had told the pastoral counseling class that one thing had saved him: routine. Class members quickly challenged him. What about faith? What about prayer? What about God? They had helped, he said, but many POWs had faith and prayed, yet died or committed suicide. "They stayed in bed and slept and withered away," Cal recalled him saying that day in class. What had saved Gus was the discipline of routine. Getting out of bed each morning, shaving in cold water with the same rusty razor, brushing his teeth with his fingers, eating a tasteless breakfast. "These rituals, the discipline of routine, are what kept me on track," he had said.

After almost a month in prison, a routine was beginning to develop. Following the morning count at six came the trundling rattle of the breakfast trolley entering the pod. On the second tier toward the end, he was one of the last to be served and had timed the twenty minutes it took the cart to reach his cell, time enough for him to splash bathe himself from the sink, shave, change into his "whites," as the loose-fitting prison outfit was called, and read his Bible.

Following breakfast, a nurse checked on him, asked her rote questions.

Each time, he told her he was not suicidal, had no intentions of hurting himself and each time, she smiled and said, "Have a good day." The psychologist came next and talked to him through the door asking some of the same questions. Cal questioned the reason for the duplications, but the regimented intrusions filled the emptiness, if only briefly. Around nine, the chaplain stopped, slipped devotional materials beneath his door assuring Cal he was praying, "with you and for you." Durasmus checked on him each day at six as he was leaving his shift and always asked about his grandfather.

Since the reprimand from the guard ten days ago, Cal had not spoken with Chris. On his way to exercise or the showers, Chris would look in Cal's window when he was escorted by, but there had been little contact with his new friend. He would hear the typewriter going all hours and knew Chris was cranking out epistles telling of God's mercy and love. Cal was beginning to take showers on a regular basis, in hopes he would be bathing with Chris. But it never happened.

For whatever reason, or reasons, the guards seemed to be keeping him and his friend in the next cell apart. He was also aware the guards were watching him more closely, casting more frequent looks at his cell, making more walk-bys, writing longer notes on the clipboard that hung on a nail beside his door.

Increasing his chances of contact with Chris, Cal had gone to recreation. But he never saw his friend there. Apparently, they were not allowed at the same time. Everything Chris had told him about rec was accurate—the chain-link cages, the guards with cameras constantly on him. Little to do except see the sky, feel fresh air, run around in a 12 X 12 area, do push-ups, hang on the wire, and look at the walls of other buildings.

Chris didn't tell him about the grass, a strip of green turf between the cages and the next building, and stretching the length of a football field to a tall double gate Cal recognized as the one he'd been brought through his first day. He questioned why whoever designed the prison would put inmates where they could see the gate where they were brought in, unless it was part of the punishment. Give them a vision of the exit with no means to reach it. Each time, he was led into one of the recreation cages and his cuffs released, his eyes slid quickly along the turf to the gate. He had run the hundred yard dash in high school. He was thinner now, down to one hundred twenty pounds from one hundred sixty-five since his arrest in May. He could probably do it again, if he could break loose. Each time, the idea ballooned in his thoughts, it flattened. He might be able to make it to the gate but not over the coils of barbed wire atop it. Whoever had built this prison had made it escape proof. Over and over the guards had reminded him, as if to say, "Don't ever try." Maybe it was a psychological thing, pounded into your head so you would passively accept it.

Patiently, he waited for opportunities to climb to the vent. From his cell window, he watched the guards, tracked their movements, shift changes, faces with the shifts. He learned their voices, the sounds and the booted cadence of their footsteps. Their idiosyncrasies. Their habits.

One of those habits, in particular, was interesting. Guards on the late shifts wadded paper napkins and placed them between the locks and doorjambs on the pod door and the rear exit. Central Control had limited staff on the late shifts. It took longer for doors to open, an inconvenience for guards in a hurry to slip out and take a smoke break through the rear exit that led to the rec cages.

Day by day, ever so slowly it seemed, he was adjusting. He was also living his routine to keep his sleep pattern consistent, so he could dream. At this point, his life belonged to and needed his dreams.

As a pastor, many in his congregation, especially the older members, told him that evenings, sundowns, were the most difficult time of day for them. But for him, mornings were the hardest. Releasing a dream, opening his eyes, the realization he was in a cell starting the day over again. He wanted to stay in his bunk, return to sleep and catch the last dream. It mattered not if it was good or bad, comforting or threatening. He was in another place. Then he would awaken, sit up, swing his legs over, his feet touch the cold floor, and begin another day.

He'd heard nothing from cell 210 and decided the inmate with the tattoo on his head may not have been Aryan Nations or could have been at one time and converted. Tattoos last forever. Or if he was Aryan Nations, he had another reason for staging a fight to get into the pod. If he had staged a fight, gone to that much effort, surely something would've happened by now. In the days following the forced cell extraction, he had not seen the man cuffed and escorted down and up the stairs. He had not seen him in a shower cage.

For all Cal knew, he may have been moved.

Chris would know, but climbing to the vent was risky. If he got pointed, he feared being moved to another cell or pod away from his friend. At times, the night guard would leave the pod. Cal timed his absences. None longer than ten minutes, most within five. But he was afraid to try. Any guard looking at his door window would see the light partially blocked. Cal had tried to put a positive spin on the predicament. If he was in protective custody, he was protected.

He kept track of the days for his granddad's visits on his wall. The next was tomorrow, Sunday, December 21st. With that anticipation, he laid down, pulled the covers over his head to block out the light and drifted off to sleep.

Later that evening, he was awakened by a faint sound like a muted ping. He'd hear it, *plunk*, then he wouldn't, like a slow, dull erratic drip. Minutes passed. He heard it again, *plunk*. It came from outside his door. He got up, walked to the door and looked out. Nothing. Down below, a guard sat at the pod desk. The television was off. Cal lay back down and waited. It started again, like someone trying to strike a match or start a car with a broken ignition switch. The sound persisted.

He tired of listening and fell asleep and was again awakened, this time by a different sound: *Swish*. He looked down. On the floor just inside the door, he saw a small flattened milk carton tied to a string. Chris had told him about fishing. Cal had not fished. He'd sent nothing to anyone. Perhaps this was a mistake. Wrong address, wrong cell, wrong inmate. He got up, bent over to slide the carton back under the door and saw FERGUSON penciled on the side. He went to the door window and looked out. A white string stretched from his door along the walkway and vanished beneath the door of cell 210. *How could he get it under my door?* Then he saw the railing pole outside his cell. *Richochet.* He looked back down at the carton. Should he open it? He thought about it. He had no idea. No doubt it was for him. No doubt its origin. He popped open the container. A small piece of paper folded twice drifted to the floor. He picked it up and unfolded it, smoothed the wrinkled piece across his palm and one word with a question mark rushed his eyes. He returned the carton to the floor and sat on his bunk, the small scrap of paper trembling in his hands. He sat for a long time looking at the carton, at the note. *Let information come to you, not from you.* He reached down to return the note to the carton and *swoosh*, it was yanked away.

He sat on the bunk, the small scrap fluttering in hands that trembled between his knees. For a long time, he sat looking at the note. He went to the window and looked out. He needed to speak with Chris, but that was not an option. The lone guard below had apparently heard the sounds and adjusted his chair to locate the source, the probable reason for the sudden disappearance of the carton. The inmate was casting and reeling when the guard was distracted.

His options closed, Cal returned to his bunk, the shock still shaking his eyes, ringing in his brain. He would wait for the morning and his granddad.

CHAPTER 19

December 21 Sunday

Shell was back in the medical examining room. He had decided the first room was someone's office and in use on certain Sundays. He had the twenty folded in his hand and gave it to the guard as he brought Cal in, sat him on the same stool, and uncuffed him. The guard left and locked the door behind him.

"How are you?" Shell asked. "You look peaked."

Cal slipped a hand inside his jumpsuit pocket. He removed it holding a small piece of paper folded once and handed it to his granddad.

"What's this?" Shell questioned.

"Open it," he said in low tones, his eyes on the window.

Shell unfolded the paper. His eyes ballooned. "ENVELOPE?" he whispered and turned it over looking for more.

"That's all it says," Cal confirmed.

Shell shook the note in the air as if to dislodge more from it. "How'd you get it?"

"It was cast under my door."

"Cast?"

"Fishing. Propelled beneath my door in a flattened milk carton tied to a string," Cal described.

"Who sent it?"

"The inmate two cells down from me."

"And you kept it."

"I tried to return it, but the carton was yanked away."

Shell stared at the note, not just the note but the mystery behind it.

"It's a question."

"Yep!"

"He's fishing for an answer."

"Yep."

"As in, 'Do you know its whereabouts?' Or, 'Do you know what was in it?' Or, 'Do you have it?'"

"You know those answers," Cal said exasperatedly. "I never opened the envelope. Sally emptied the trash daily."

Shell waved off the comment. "We know that. What matters is what they think. They're gonna act on what they think. They, whoever they are, think you killed Doom, think you heard his last words, think you may know who killed him, and think you know something about that envelope."

"Chris said for an inmate to stage a fight to get into a pod was high risk, a big deal," Cal responded. "If they did it on orders from someone else, it was a bigger deal."

Bigger than Cal knew, Shell thought. On the long drive from the state capitol to home, in the long hours that followed, Shell had thought hard and heavy, sifted through the options and moved them around like chess pieces in his mind. In the precious few minutes he and Cal had together, what should he tell him about his meeting with the governor and the director? What did his grandson not need to know, what did he need to know? Shell had been in prisons before. He knew the tactics guards would take to wrench truth from prisoners. Before a lick was hit, Cal would tell the truth. That was his nature, how he was raised. What he didn't know couldn't be pried out of him. He wouldn't lie to avoid punishment.

Cal didn't need to know the parsonage fire was the result of arson. He didn't need to know that his wife and grandmother were shot before they burned and that his daughter was totally incinerated. He didn't need to know, not now, that the gun used to murder them was the same that killed Ty Doom. He didn't need to know he saw Sadie Bea Doom, in apparent disguise, coming out of the warden's office and all the questions that raised.

Two things Cal did need to know, Shell concluded. That recent evidence established his innocence, which he would save till last and—"It may be a big deal evidenced by this," Shell said holding up the note.

Cal's eyes widened. He took a deep breath. "I got no sleep last night trying not to think about it."

Shell leaned toward him. "You need to think about it. Two days ago, I met with the governor again, this time with the Director of the Mississippi Bureau of Investigation."

Cal sighed again and raised a finger to make a comment.

"Let me finish," Shell pressed leaning closer to his grandson and speaking in a sound almost too low to be a whisper. "The FBI and the MBI have had their eyes on a militia group operating beyond the levee. If they know why, they're not saying. But the envelope," he held up the note again, "ties Doom with Aryan Nations, i.e., a militia group."

"And I'm in the middle," Cal whispered without emotion.

"The governor and the director think you're the key and this," he held up the note again, his voice still low, "confirms it. That's the real reason you're in protective custody. Not protective from someone but for someone."

"Granddad, this doesn't sound good."

Shell glanced back at the window in the door then back at his grandson. "It does, and it doesn't. As long as somebody thinks you've got something they need, you're valuable and protected."

"Until they find out I don't have it."

"That's right."

"So I play this cat and mouse game."

"That's right. But only for so long. Here's the good news I've waited to tell you last," and he told him about the new ballistics report on Doom's murder avoiding mention of the circumstances.

The news shot Cal straight up on the stool. He raised folded hands and whispered, "Thank you, Lord." Running his thumbs against the inside corners of his eyes he wiped away his tears as he continued whispering, "Thank you, Lord. Thank you, Lord."

Shell stood and put an arm around him.

"When can I be released?"

"I don't know," Shell said. "They didn't either when I asked. Something about judicial process."

Cal groaned.

"With the holidays coming up, probably after the first of the year. You want to keep this?" Shell asked holding up the small piece of paper.

"The guard'll frisk me when he takes me back."

"Very well," and Shell slipped it into his coat pocket. "I'll pass it along to the proper folks." Shell said. "And by the way, you're in good company. He forced a smile and patted Cal on the shoulder. "You've got two strong forces with you on this, The FBI and the MBI."

There was a rap on the door, the knob turning.

"I usually get a five minute warning," Shell said. "I'll see you next Sunday, with some luck Christmas Day, only four days away." He drew Cal close and embraced him. "Be careful."

Cal pushed back and smiled faintly. "I'm valuable."

"I was in prison once with something valuable," Shell responded. "Had to give it up to stay alive."

"I have nothing to give up to stay alive."

"Keep 'em thinking you do. Keep 'em fishing. And keep the faith."

The guard came in, cuffed Cal, and led him away. As they were leaving, Shell said, "Merry Christmas!"

Hands cuffed behind him, his body contorted, Cal turned and looked back. "Merry Christmas, Granddad."

CHAPTER 20

December 21 Sunday

The news from his granddad was an answer to prayers. Tonight his dreams would not own him, Cal thought as he lay down on his bunk. Instead, he almost feared sleep, afraid what he had been told was a dream, and he'd awaken to find it gone. He pulled the sheet over his head to block the exterior and pod lights that stayed on all night.

The sound of a series of clicks, like a gun being loaded, woke him. But guns were not allowed on the prison grounds, even by the guards. The cell was dark. He noticed the lights were out in the pod, the security halogens off as well outside. Perhaps there was an overload outage. Or there had been an electrical storm. But he'd heard no thunder, seen no lightning flashes through his narrow window to the world.

He lay still and listened. He heard the clicks again and realized what they were when he heard the steel door groan open and turned his head to see, from meager light somewhere in the pod, a wedge of shadow expanding, a body stepping into the shadow, another behind it.

"Who is it?" he asked in a small voice that resonated through the cell in the dark silence.

No voice responded, but he recognized the sound of the footsteps he heard day in and day out, two sets of them, clomping quickly toward him. Before he could speak again, two shadows grabbed his hands and feet and yanked him from the bunk onto the floor. A body quickly pinned his arms, another stood on his legs.

"What the—" he attempted.

A hand clamped his mouth, another grabbed his throat. He could hear the radios on their belts scratching with static. All he could feel were huge weights on top of him. "Shut up, Ferguson!" a rough nasal voice with bad breath whispered loudly. "You know why we're here."

Cal shook his head back and forth. "No ... I don't!" he mumbled through the sweaty hand that smelled of grease and body odor covering his mouth.

"Where's the envelope?" the one sitting on his arms pressed, momentarily releasing the hand over his mouth.

"What envelope?"

"The one you got at Ty Doom's." A different voice with a thick rural accent.

"I don't know." Fear ripped through his head into his heart. "I thought it was mine," he said, the words squeezing through his throat.

The assailant on top of him slapped him hard, and the one standing over him whispered, "We know better," and swung a baton into one leg, then the other.

Cal tried to push up, but he was pinned to the floor.

A hand still held his throat, but his mouth was free. He knew not to call for help. Maybe they'd believe him and leave him alone.

The one sitting on his hands looked up at the one standing on his legs, then the one standing hit his legs again with the baton, and again pain swept through him like fire, and the hand again clamped his mouth.

"What do you think?" the one sitting asked looking up at the other.

Cal could see the one standing shake his head. "He's lying."

"Fess up!" the one sitting on him said and hit him again in the face, this time with his fist. His ears roared, blood thrumming through them. He tasted copper. "You took the envelope."

"Yes," was all he could manage and both began hitting him. Batons and fists thudded against his face and body, and then the one who'd been sitting on his arms got up, and the guard standing up moved toward the door.

"That's enough for now," the one who'd been sitting on him said. "Give you time to think about it. We'll be back."

"Next time, you tell us," the other drawled, the rural accent again in the truncated syntax.

Cal couldn't respond. His tongue filled his mouth.

They left as quickly as they had entered, locking the cell door behind them. Cal heard their measured boot-heel clicks down the metal steps and across the concrete floor. Moments later, a buzzer and the loud slam of the pod steel door.

He lay on the cell floor face up in the darkness unable to move. His spine felt as though it might crack. There was a coppery taste in his throat, and he could feel blood pooling in his mouth. He knew enough from Boy Scout training to keep his head turned to the side, so he didn't strangle. He ran his tongue around his mouth. No teeth broken that he could tell. His nose was numb, and he couldn't move it without pain. It might be broken. He thought his arms and legs might be broken. At first, they wouldn't move. After a few minutes, little by little, he gained movement in both and was able, carefully and slowly, to turn over, an effort that seemed to take forever.

The lights in the pod were still out, but the ones outside were back on, and from their glow he could see his bunk. It was only a few feet away but seemed further. Using his elbows, he propelled toward it. Getting onto the bunk was another matter. He recalled once jumping into an open moving freight boxcar, which seemed easy at the time. What lay ahead of him, even though the bunk was lower and not moving, would be a challenge. He recalled the movements of that summer day. Raising his right leg and arm and pushing up with his left hand on the floor, he was able to gain purchase of the bunk's edge, enough to tortuously flip himself over onto it, so he was facing up.

He would have to explain the blood on the sheet. If he snitched, he'd be in for more trouble. His granddad had taught him that and Chris had confirmed it. He would just say he fell and knocked his chin on the sink. He didn't know how he'd explain his nose. He reached up and touched it, with two fingers moved it back and forth. It didn't seem broken, the cartilage still intact. He changed his story. He slipped, and his face hit the sink.

His granddad was right. What matters is what they think, and they're gonna act on what they think. Somebody thought he knew something he didn't. He didn't know what that something was. If he did, he might be a free man. Or a dead man. Whatever it was, the envelope or something else, it must be something big for him to get this much attention. A prison hierarchy wouldn't waste its time on a convicted small fry, defrocked minister at that. Whatever he'd walked into that day in his church secretary's house was big.

He was beginning to get the picture his granddad had been trying to draw, why he was in "protective custody." Indirectly, it might have something to do with suicide risk. They wanted him to stay alive all right, for a while at least. They, as best he could tell, were dressed in black. They were guards. Only guards wore the heavy soled boots. Only guards had keys to cells and radios on their belts. They were white. He could tell that blindfolded. They smelled white. He had been around blacks and whites all of his life in the Delta, and he could tell the difference. Not only the way they smelled but in the way their hand's felt, at least the one sitting on his arms. He knew the feel of a black hand and a white hand. Their accents, too, told him something. The one who'd been sitting on him was more educated. The other was redneck uneducated. He thought about the lights going off then coming back on.

Sometimes gang members with no police record hire on as guards. The thought slammed his mind. He was a sitting duck, but for whom. He could not protect himself, had no weapons, didn't know how to make one. He needed to speak with his granddad. But Christmas was four days away. A lot could happen in a prison in four days. In one day. In a handful of minutes, seconds. People serving time didn't measure it. They used it.

A long time, he lay there in pain. He was cold and very thirsty and felt an intolerable desire to sleep. His arms ached where they'd been stretched in the sockets from the man's weight on them. His shins hurt where they'd been battered by a nightstick. His head was pounding. He thought of his wife and daughter, his grandmother, and entertained the thought he wished the men had killed him. At least, he'd be at peace and with his family, that thought leading to another. Escape. What did he have to lose? He made himself comfortable on the side that pained him the least. He closed his eyes and thought. If he wasn't in solitary, but in general population, he'd have a chance. Ideas bloomed and died. None could get him beyond the guards, the barbed wire and the electric fence. But there had to be a way, at least out of the pod.

CHAPTER 21

December 22 Monday

Early morning, Cal was awakened by a pecking sound. Too frantic for a typewriter, nothing deliberate or thoughtful about it. He raised his head slightly and pain shot along his spine. "My back may be broken," he thought to himself. He felt heavy and slow. With effort and gritting his teeth against the pain, he turned his body. The rat-a-tat-tat continued, and he realized it was coming from the vent.

He hit the wall three times to let Chris know he got the message but the tapping continued.

"Damn!" he murmured. He recalled another time after a Friday night football game his senior year. He was the quarterback, got sacked and roughed up, and had to be helped off the field. The next morning his muscles ached, and his head hurt. The doctor said he'd had a concussion. He couldn't get out of bed. His father came into his room and told him he'd been bruised, to make himself get up, start moving. He rolled onto the floor and crawled to the bathroom and pulled himself up at the sink, splashed water in his face, stood, and limped to breakfast. Monday afternoon the team practiced and, against doctor's advice, he was back in the thick of it.

He looked at his watch. Almost five. He'd not heard the breakfast trolley. The lone guard on duty would be doing his paperwork, getting ready for the shift change. What did he have to lose? So what, if he got pointed. His innocence had been established. He was going to be released. He had a window. Go for it.

Pain was in every bone, ligament, and muscle it seemed. He swung first one leg and then the other off the edge of the bunk and rolled over onto the floor. Pushing himself up on his hands and knees he dragged himself to the commode. Using the sink for leverage, he pulled himself onto the seat, sat a few minutes, then maneuvered himself where he could grab a towel rack bolted to the wall and pull himself upright atop the sink. Many minutes later, some of his strength returned and he stood shakily on the rim of the sink and tapped on the vent.

"What happened?" Chris asked. "The lights were out last night. I heard a ruckus over there."

"My dark night of the soul just got darker."

"How so?"

"I was assaulted."

"By whom?" Chris asked, his voice incredulous.

"Guards, I think," Cal said. "Two of 'em. It was dark. I could see the face of the one sitting on me. Not the other, he was standing. They were white. I know that."

"Had to have been guards. Only guards have keys."

"The warden have anything to do with hiring guards?" Cal asked, struggling, his breathing labored.

"Absolutely," Chris replied. "They have to pass his muster. Prison hires new people every week. Warden meets each one personally, then in a group, conducts a workshop for them."

"How do you know?"

"Guards talk."

Cal hesitated. "Just wondered. The lights went out before it happened. Came back on after."

"A confederate in Central Control," Chris said lowering his voice.

"Aren't they screened?"

"I think I told you," Chris began. "Some gang members maintain a clean record, apply for a guard's position, get the job, and are allies to their gang friends in prison. A paid-for ally with access to cells, inmates and a lot more, including Central Control."

"You did tell me. I didn't think it could go that far."

"Whoever assaulted you was probably paid to do it, on top of their prison pay. In other words, it was a hired hit, maybe ordered by a shot caller. What did they want?"

"Something I don't have," and Cal broad-brushed that story. His legs were getting weak and wobbly. "I can't stand here much longer," he groaned.

"I feel like I'm in crosshairs. There's got to be a way out of this."

"Don't think about escape," Chris enjoined. "No one's ever escaped from this prison. It's impossible to get beyond the barbed wire and the electric fence and razor wire. You'd have to have power tools. Some were smuggled in frozen meat a few years back. Even if they hadn't been discovered, inmates would have had to get through the water and sewage tunnels."

Silence.

Chris again. "But the warden is paranoid about a prisoner dying on his watch. If you could come up with a medical problem, you'd get taken to the prison main medical unit. If they didn't treat you, you could sue them, something else the warden is skittish about. The corporation that owns this prison has been sued thousands of times. Not good for the bottom line. Wardens get fired when suits arise."

"Where's the main medical unit?"

"In another part of the prison."

"How do I get there?"

"Here's the thing," Chris began. "You complain. A nurse will come and check on you. You'll be cuffed and taken to Main Med. They'll place you in one of the treatment cells. If they can't treat you, you'll be transported to a hospital in Clarksdale or Memphis."

"I'd still be on somebody's radar."

"Maybe so, but it would throw them off. They'd have to regroup, might buy you time for a different strategy."

He didn't need to say anything about the news from his granddad, new evidence proving his innocence. "I think I've got a serious medical problem now," Cal responded. "May have a broken back."

"Not standing on that sink. Gotta come up with something else."

Another pause.

"You have any medical history, past problems?" Chris inquired.

"Not really. When I was young, I had some seizures, but they stopped in my early teens. I had a concussion playing football."

"Your medical records are in your file. If they're not, then it's your word."

"What's my word?" questioned Cal.

"You had a seizure and fell off the top bunk."

"But I didn't." They were keeping their voices to a swift whisper.

"You wanna get out of here, preacher? The answer's yes. There's a time for truth and a time for shading the truth. They should have your medical records. Your seizure history would be on them. That's standard. If they can't treat you and don't medivac you, they're legally liable."

"But I don't sleep on the top bunk."

"You did last night because you spilled something in your bed. Another story would be you urinated in your sleep, but that would get complicated. We need to finish so you can throw some water on your bunk and lie in the floor, face down. Guard check's in five minutes."

"Thanks."

"Got any toothpaste?" Chris inquired.

"Right below me on the sink."

"Empty the tube into your mouth, then lie on the floor face down. It'll make you sick as hell, throw up."

"Sounds horrible."

"That's the idea. Good luck. If they ask me, I'll tell them I heard you fall. Signing off now," Chris concluded and tapped the vent three times.

Cal lowered himself to the floor, turned on the faucet and scooped handfuls of water onto his sheets and blanket then, moving gingerly and slowly, cleared what few belongings he was allowed to bring with him off the top bunk where he kept them. He swallowed as much toothpaste as he could, felt the nausea rise in him like disturbed sediment. He lay on the floor face down as Chris had suggested. Shortly after, he felt his stomach cave in, explode outward and he tasted sour, acid vomit.

There came a hard rap on the door, and a voice bellowed, "You okay, Ferguson?"

"No!" Cal groaned.

"You look plumb awful. Why're you lying on the floor? What happened?"

"Had a seizure, fell off the top bunk."

CHAPTER 22

December 22 Tuesday

Cal was asleep when two guards entered his hospital room and awakened him. He had been taken to the hospital in a sheriff's cruiser and put in a room at the end of a long hall, one hand cuffed to the bed railing. He immediately doubled up and covered his face with his free hand.

"What's wrong with you?" one of the guards asked.

"Why're you here?" Cal cried.

"Taking you back," the other guard replied gruffly.

The large clock on the wall in the room said a few minutes past two.

"I haven't even been here a day. Why this early in the morning?"

"Warden's orders," said the first guard who was taller and spoke with a kind voice. "So inmates won't see you."

"So they won't get any ideas," chimed in the other.

The warden must be addled, Cal thought. Regardless the time of day, any movement, especially in solitary, arouses inmates. He'd never seen either guard and guessed they'd been pulled from other units.

He was placed in the same sheriff's cruiser, he guessed because he was still a prisoner of the county. He sat in the backseat alone, his hands cuffed behind him, his eyes straight ahead. Long before the cruiser reached them, the halogen lights of the prison glowed like bright clusters in the flat Delta dark, like something from outer space ready to take off.

He had been through the sally gate two other times. When he entered the first time before Thanksgiving and yesterday when he was taken to the hospital. The gate was a double chainlink fastened in the middle by two thick chains and a huge padlock. Each gate section had coiled barbed wire across the top. But he glimpsed something this time he'd not noticed before. Perhaps it was because he wasn't looking for it, had no need on those

147

occasions to even look for anything out of the ordinary. Perhaps it wasn't out of the ordinary with anyone whose life had not been threatened, who was a target for terrorists.

Before he was returned to the pod, he had to sit on the "boss" chair. His mouth and throat were examined. The clothing he'd worn from the hospital was removed from him, and he was given fresh whites t-shirt and drawstring pants, socks. He could keep his slipper shoes. At three a.m. when he entered the pod, the two guards beside him, he saw myriad faces pressed against cell windows, watching.

The guards led him up the steps. At the top, turning to go to his cell, he looked into the muddy yellow, slightly belligerent eyes of the Fisherman in cell 210. Cal stopped and returned the stare before the guards pushed him on, placed him in his cell, and went through the routine of uncuffing him through the food portal. He was returned to the same cell, but it looked different. Items had been rearranged. Things he'd moved from the top to the bottom bunk, to support his story, had been moved back. The marker in his Bible, which he had left in Genesis was in Revelation. His toothbrush, which he kept on the side of the sink, had been removed and placed behind the faucet. The squeezed toothpaste tube was gone. He was certain his cell had been shaken down, searched thoroughly. They didn't find anything because there was nothing to find. Which meant, based upon what his grandfather had said, they'd keep looking. *We'll be back.*

There was something new. On his bottom bunk, a pad of lined notepaper, two short stub pencils on top of it. It had been over a week since his granddad had formally opened his account and Cal had sent another requisition. Was this inefficiency? Was the warden being nice? Or, was someone else?

He knew Chris was aware he was back. He didn't want to attempt contact with him again, not then. He was tired. He had been through a bunch of tests at the hospital. After the tests, a neurologist, who wasted no time, had spoken to him. He was young with small fingers, the tip of a little finger missing, Cal had noted. Tests showed no seizure activity. "But that was a nasty fall," the doctor said. "You're bruised from head to toe. Lucky you landed on your butt," he added as he was leaving his room. "Or, you'd have some serious head trauma." After the doctor and his nurse had left, Cal had seen a clipboard left behind on the stand by his bed. He had leaned over to see what was on it. Everything was in small print except at the bottom where it said DIAGNOSIS. Beside it, MALINGERING. He was sure to hear about that later.

For now, all he wanted to do was sleep. With his whites still on, he laid down on the bottom bunk. He was almost asleep, then the *plunk, plunk* noise started again. His granddad was right. The Fisherman was getting better. On the third try, the flattened carton swished across the floor. He lay there several minutes thinking. *Should I?*

He got up and picked up the carton. He opened it, saw the note, tweezed it out and opened it: JETS?

"Jets?" he whispered. Then again, "Jets!" He sat on the edge of his bunk and thought. Envelope ... jets. Somehow, they were connected. Keep him fishing. He retrieved one of the pencils from the top bunk where he had placed them with the tablet. Don't respond immediately. Don't make him think you're anxious. Let him wait.

He laid back on the bunk, questions circulating through his mind. You couldn't put jets in an envelope. He dozed off. When he awoke, an hour had passed. He amended the note by adding another question mark. He folded the paper and put it back into the carton, pressed it flat, laid it back on the floor and jerked the string once.

The carton disappeared.

Sometime later, he laid down, was almost asleep and a thought, imperceptibly, like something from the tail of his mind, flared on the rim of his consciousness.

CHAPTER 23

December 23 Tuesday

Shell sat at a corner table toward the back of the long pine-paneled restaurant, sconces along the wall. A large black woman with loose sagging arms and wearing a hairnet and grease-stained white T-shirt approached him. She was not a waitress but one of the cooks he had known over the years. "Maxine, the usual."

"Yessir, Mister Shell."

He wanted a beer. He had tried to call the governor yesterday to tell him the latest he'd learned Sunday about the envelope but was told he was out. He had left a message with the receptionist, told her it was urgent and for the governor to call him at his earliest convenience. Then, he'd called her back and asked if she could forward his call to the Director of MBI. She said she could, and tried, then reported he was out as well. "It's the holidays, Mr. Ferguson." He had the governor's personal cell number but had been reluctant to use it and had decided to go through channels first.

Shortly after his phone call attempts, his cell phone rang, but the call wasn't from the governor's office. An FBI agent named Brent Chase said he had been given his name and phone number from the Director of the Mississippi Bureau of Investigation and could they meet. It was urgent the agent had said. Shell had given him the name of a Clarksdale restaurant, The Ranchero. They had agreed upon three o'clock after the lunch crowd had left and before early evening customers began arriving. Shell had begun giving him a description of himself and the agent had interrupted him, "I know who you are." The call had set him on edge. Shell had been sitting there nursing Maxine's cup of black coffee, nervously waiting, wondering, a bundle of emotions pressing from the inside out.

Three o'clock and no agent. Nobody. Shell sat alone in the restaurant, waiting. He got Maxine's attention and ordered another coffee she promptly brought.

"Need anything else, Mister Shell?"

"No thank you, Maxine," he lied. What he needed he couldn't put into words.

Quarter past three by his watch, a tall white male entered the restaurant. He had a memorable face with sharp cheekbones, a beaked nose, and a dapper mustache. He was hatless, had dark, thick hair, and wore a black leather jacket with a dark muffler. He moved with confidence, his sharp eyes sweeping the large dining area like a broom as he made his way toward Shell.

"Mr. Ferguson, Brent Chase," the man said quickly flashing a badge.

Shell rose, they shook hands. The agent pulled out a chair, and they sat. He kept on his coat and muffler, Shell noted, as if to say, This won't take long.

"Sorry, I'm late. You picked a good place," the agent commented. He spoke with an even pleasant voice, and his thick mustache wagged when he spoke. "Wish I could count the times I've eaten here. Better Bar B Q ribs than the Rendevouz in Memphis. Had a beer or two in front of the fireplace but I see it's gone."

"They didn't replace it after the fire a few years back," Shell said, the recollection nicking his emotions.

"Thank you for agreeing to meet with me," Chase said.

"You said it was urgent."

"It is," Chase replied, a grave look on his face.

Maxine approached.

"Coffee, black," Chase said and waited for her to depart before continuing. "I'll get to the point, Mr. Ferguson. Director Holifield informed our field office in Jackson of circumstances surrounding your grandson's parsonage fire, more particularly the ballistics report." He paused as if to retrieve a forgotten thought. "My condolences for your loss."

Shell nodded and looked down into his coffee cup, his hands wrapped around it as though it was an anchor. An emotional flash swept through him. He'd thought the sympathies had stopped. Everyone he knew, had offered them and life was moving on. Unprepared for this one, coming from a total stranger, it caught him off guard. The agent's additional comments didn't help.

"I understand you know about the ballistics report."

Shell nodded, gravely sipping his coffee, replacing the cup unsteadily in the saucer. He grabbed a napkin from the aluminum dispenser on the table and placed it in the saucer to absorb the slosh.

"But there's another ballistics report you may not know about," Chase said seriously. "It came to us yesterday from MBI. They thought it more convenient and practical, for reasons I'll discuss later, that I meet with you and share this latest."

"The director had said he would keep me informed," Shell said.

Maxine walked up, "Your coffee, sir," and set it on the table before Chase and departed. The agent waited a few moments, glanced around and proceeded. "Investigators, warrant in hand, conducted a full sweep of the Doom residence and found two spent bullets, both from his gun. One in a window sill adjacent to the door exiting the den and leading to the rear of the house and the other lodged in the ceiling above that same doorway."

Shell breathed deeply. "That confirms my grandson's innocence."

"It certainly substantiates it," Chase said.

"He needs to be released."

"Mr. Ferguson, I agree. I'm not an attorney, but I know releases of this nature must follow a judicial process."

"Has it started?"

"Director Holifield said he and the governor have the ball rolling," Chase said as he blew across his cup and took a sip.

"It needs to roll fast. My grandson's in a corrupt private prison and in probable danger."

"That's one of the reasons I needed to see you. The FBI is aware of your grandson's precarious status," and he encapsulated information passed along regarding the envelope theory, the inmate with the tattoo in Cal's pod, and suspected gang involvement.

"Let me bring *you* up to date," Shell said. He reached in his coat pocket, retrieved the note Cal had handed to him and laid it on the table in front of the agent. "Cal got this from the inmate with the tattoo."

The agent picked it up, examined it closely. "When did he get it?"

"Three days ago, Saturday. He gave it to me Sunday during my visitation."

The agent said nothing, continued holding the note, looking at it, pondering, flicking a fingernail against his cup. He stopped flicking the nail. "This tends to confirm the envelope theory."

"Any idea what was in it?" Shell pressed.

"Ideas only," he said as he returned the note to the table, glanced around and turned it over. "During the sweep of the Doom's house, agents also discovered some other interesting items including Doom's personal safe in the den beneath the liquor cabinet."

"Strange place for a safe."

"Even stranger, it was in a wine grotto, a cooler, with no racks or wine which increased our suspicion. MBI returned to the judge, laid a premise of probable cause and His Honor issued a second warrant for the safe. Mrs. Doom refused to give agents the combination, so one of their experts cracked it open and *voila*."

"Drugs?"

"Several pounds of cocaine plus other items we didn't find going through desk drawers and personal papers. A folded page from the New York Times and a want ad circled in red ink: "Wanted: turbine jet engines. Will pay fair price." No name on the ad, just a United Kingdom phone number."

"England?" Shell assumed.

"Yes. Manchester. All of this was passed along to us. The number was called. Disconnected, as we expected it might be given the lapse of time."

"Crazy to think Doom would have jet engines."

"Who knows?" Chase said a serious look on his face. "Theft of jet engines is nothing new. In two thousand seven, a jet engine was stolen from the Malaysian Air Force and found in two thousand ten in Uruguay. Two F-five—E jet engines were heisted from Malaysian military, shipped by an individual to Argentina, turned up in Iran."

"Iran means terrorists," Shell said.

"Iran certainly supports and funds terrorism in the mid-East." Chase took a sip from his coffee, looked around and continued. "Jet engines are worth a lot. In each of these episodes, a monetary exchange occurred, but the transactions of the sales and the money trails were never detected or discovered in any bank accounts. No one knew the buyers. In January of two thousand eleven, eight F-sixteen jet engines were stolen from an Israeli air force base, several more the next year. None were recovered or found." He took another slow sip.

Shell was antsy for him to get to the point.

"Now comes the kicker," Chase said. "In two thousand thirteen, last year, two jet engines were stolen from the air force base in Little Rock."

"Little Rock's a hop, skip, and jump from here."

Chase nodded. "I was personally involved in the investigation of that case."

"And?" Shell pushed, drumming his fingers on the table.

"Our number one suspect passed a polygraph test. Months later, we were informed he rigged the test."

"How can you rig a lie detector?"

Chase smiled wryly. "He placed a thumbtack beneath his right big toe, pressed his toe on it when he was answering early questions thus creating a false baseline for truth."

"That should have done it for you."

"We wish. The suspect disappeared, was never found. He's probably in some Latin American country hiding, living high off the hog."

"What about the jet engines?" Shell asked.

Chase shot him a grave look. "Never found, allegedly buried somewhere in the Mississippi Delta."

"That would be two needles in a very big haystack."

"Exactly. There's more. MBI agents found a contact, address, and phone number for an attorney in Colon, Panama. As we speak, our agents are trying to track down the leads, see if the threads connect."

Shell raised a finger. "Maybe, as we speak, your suspect is in that neck of the woods."

"Predictably, Mr. Matlock," Chase said with a slow-spreading ironic smile, "you're one step ahead of me."

Shell grinned briefly at the compliment and said, "Based on all that, my question again: what could've been in the envelope?"

"We've pieced together a possible scenario," Chase continued. "Doom was a militia member. Did you know that?"

"I suspected, but only recently," Shell said.

"He belonged to a militia in northwest Mississippi. Militias network.

Doom becomes aware that the Arkansas Aryan Nations—I understand you're aware of that group—"

Shell nodded.

"—has two jet engines. This is speculative based upon information I can't share. Doom sees the ad—he subscribed to the Times Sunday paper—and makes contact. As I said, turbine engines are not cheap. They are constructed of exotic materials (titanium, Inconel, and the like), are built to exacting tolerance, and leave the factory with a price tag of approximately ten million each," he gestured seesawing his hand. "Value goes down as they age, but they resell anywhere from one to four million, some as high as eight million dollars."

Shell leaned in close and, above a whisper, said, "Why would anyone spend that much money on a used jet engine."

Chase set his cup down and began ticking the reasons off on his fingers: "Jet engines power aircraft, rockets, cruise, and military missiles. They're used for powering generators and water." He kept talking, nailing down the facts. "For natural gas and oil pumps, not to mention industrial gas turbines. Those are just a few," he said running out of fingers and flattened his hands on the table.

"I get your point," Shell said. "But it boils down to money for the Aryan Nations."

"Precisely, domestic terrorist groups need a source of revenue. We've been monitoring the communications between the Arkansas and Mississippi cells. They don't have a very sophisticated code system. They are stockpiling weapons and bomb materials—"

"Excuse my interruption," Shell injected, "as a planter, I know they can come by those—fertilizer, ammonia nitrate, fuel oil—with little trouble or expense."

"True," Chase agreed, then countered. "But if they have big designs, and we have every reason to believe they do, they'll need revenue for explosive grade ammonia nitrate fertilizer, diesel fuel nitro-methane, and the commercially manufactured explosives, Tovex and Primadet," he concluded with crisp logic.

Shell palmed an open hand for him to continue.

"So, on his own, Doom brokers a deal and, after the fact, lets the Arkansas

Aryan Nations cadre in on it. Formally or informally, a contract of sorts is arranged between the two. Both would profit. The Arkansas bunch would get a huge chunk of change and Doom, we conjecture, would receive a finders fee."

"I knew Ty Doom. He'd want more than a finder's fee," Shell said.

"Understood," Chase said stroking his mustache. "Anyway, money was wired to a Panamanian bank from some international location, possibly Manchester, with the understanding the products would be delivered, most likely on a barge down the Mississippi River to New Orleans," he went on, his voice low and toneless. "The one person who would have the means and contacts to move the jet engines—they are huge, weigh a ton and a half each—was Ty Doom, a county supervisor with access to heavy equipment."

"They'd have to go through customs and be transferred to a ship," Shell inserted skeptically.

"Yes. But that port in New Orleans is a sieve for contraband on falsely labeled crates. From there, a tanker transports it to an international port. Regardless, Aryan Nations comes knocking to collect before they'll release the goods to Doom for transport, which is where the envelope comes into play. Doom either reneges, double crosses, or something else happens. Suffice it to say, it was a busted deal."

"Money paid. Goods undelivered," Shell said. "On top of Aryan Nations, you've got a dissatisfied customer somewhere overseas."

"Right, two very angry groups," Chase retorted. "A foreign entity, possibly terrorists, that wants its merchandise, for whatever reason we do not know, and an Aryan Nations outfit, angered over non-payment and the blow to their grand schemes. Tempers flare. The rest is history." He raised his cup and held it as though in suspension. "All of this is circumstantial but, based upon what we know, reasonable circumstantial."

"I know all about circumstantial evidence," Shell said grimly studying the note laying on the table between them as if it was something that might explode. "You said the stolen jet engines were never found."

"Correct. Part of our theory is that they were not buried, as alleged. That Doom allowed the Arkansas bunch, who, more likely than not, stole the engines, to hide them somewhere on his property until the deal was done and he could move them."

"In other words, that militia group still has them."

Chase nodded, "We think so," finally bringing the cup he'd been holding mid-air to his mouth.

"And, if there was a transaction, no one would deliver several million dollars to Doom in an envelope," Shell reasoned.

"We don't think so either," Chase agreed.

"If not the money, the means for getting the money."

Chase pistoled a finger at him. "Right! That's what we think was in the envelope."

"Except, I got one question that's been nagging me."

"Yes?"

"If Doom had been shot and was down, why didn't the intruders, when they had a chance, snatch up the envelope, if it was so valuable?"

"Good question, Mr. Ferguson, one we've asked ourselves. Neither intruder was shot. That leaves one other reason. They were spooked by something, perhaps your grandson's arrival."

"All respects, Agent Chase, there's another reason."

"Which is?"

"A combination of the two you've mentioned. Doom wasn't down, but going down, that's the reason for a bullet in the window sill adjacent the exit and one in the ceiling over that door. Word had it he was a crack shot. In other words, he was down but still holding the gun and firing at that point. Then my grandson drove up. The gun was found at Doom's fingertips."

Chase rapped his knuckles on the table. "The director said you were a crackerjack sleuth. You could probably have a job, if you're interested."

"Not at seventy-nine years old, thank you. I've always wondered, though, why Cal didn't see them leave as he drove up."

"They entered the house through the front door, which is why your grandson found it open, and exited the back of the house and, we believe, crossed a bean field to a pickup parked in a field road."

"Any tire prints?"

"As you know, the initial investigation was done by the sheriff's department," and he rolled his eyes. "So far, that's all we've known. Now this," he pointed at the note, "connects Aryan Nations with the envelope. Our proposed scenario just became less circumstantial."

A commotion at the front of the restaurant caught their attention. A group entering and gathering at the bar. Shell glanced at his watch. Almost four. "Early happy hour crowd," he said to Chase.

The agent nodded and leaned in closer across the table. "Director Holifield said you have hunted in the woods between the levee and the river."

There was no territory within thirty miles of that area Shell did not know—cutoffs, landmark trees, paths, logging trails. He could have led anyone directly to any spot and brought them back. "Every year since I was able to shoot a gun. Except for this year. My hunting partner is incarcerated," the last word sardonically over-articulated, emphasis on each syllable.

Chase pulled a paper napkin from the dispenser, opened and flattened it on the table with his hand and with the same hand pulled a pen from his inside coat pocket. "I didn't bring one of our maps with me, so this'll have to do. I'm not an artist mind you," he said with a slight smile.

Using the pen, the agent deftly sketched an area Shell knew well, dropping in roads, cities, landmarks—hunting lodges, abandoned buildings, river landings—and the Mississippi River snaking south, drawing lines where the river changed course creating oxbows. Chase paused and looked up. "I said I'm not an artist, but I've looked at lots of maps and aerial photographs."

"I'd say!" remarked Shell, amazed at the accuracy of the raw sketch.

"The boundary of our area of interest is somewhere from a line north of Memphis to one south of Helena," he said thumping the point of his pen at a place he'd previously identified as Australia Landing. "Somewhere in this area," he drew a large oval, "our suspected militia is maneuvering. Our latest surveillance says they are near Australia Landing which is directly across the river from Snow Lake and their Arkansas Aryan Nations kin."

"I'm quite familiar with the area, especially Australia Landing. I've launched boats near there duck hunting."

"So, tell me what I left out. Some points of interest are not on the map nor visible in an aerial photograph. We can't fly over it too much and raise suspicions. We certainly can't go in, even with the pretense of hunting. We've given them a leash and waited too long to have them pull up stakes and move their operation to another location, which they're expert at doing."

Shell studied the map, sensing he was being tested. How much should he tell him? Not tell him. "May I borrow your pen."

Chase handed it to him.

"You've got the hunting lodges marked about right," Shell began, "the levee road and its offshoots and Australia Landing, which at one time was a small hamlet of just a few buildings. You left out a large oxbow, so big an eye might miss it looking for something smaller on a map or an aerial. It's called Cessions Towhead. Ever heard of it?"

Chase shook his head. "I've heard of it."

Beginning at the Mississippi River just above Australia Landing, Shell drew a loop, a large earthen bulge that connected at a distance northward with the river. "That loop is an oxbow lake and the area within it is Cessions Towhead. And all of it's in Arkansas. In fact, the state line follows the center of the oxbow cutoff."

"Another reason the Arkansas militia might want the jet engines on Mississippi soil," Chase commented. "Convenient for evading authorities and moving contraband," suggesting again to Shell that he knew more than he was letting on.

Shell then drew a long line from Australia Landing connecting with the Levee Road further north. "This is one of the routes in and out of that area," he said and leaned back assessing what he'd drawn. "I'm sure you know that all land west of the levee is private," Shell said.

"We've tracked down the deeds on some," Chase responded. "Some we couldn't locate."

"Nor could I," Shell said. "Right about there," he dropped a dot south of Cessions Towhead on the Mississippi side, "is an old school bus set on concrete blocks. Obviously, someone who owned that portion of land at one time parked it there. There's a dirt road extending down the levee, and off from it an old logging path and the school bus is at the end of that trail. It sits in a thick stand of timber, the reason you wouldn't see it from an aerial photo."

"Do you know who it belongs to?"

"I'm getting there," Shell said impatiently. "Earlier, you mentioned Doom possibly harboring the two jet engines. Interesting. When I returned from a trip to Mexico—a long story—I started hunting again, picked up where

I'd left off as a teenager, and there was this bus. I tried to find out who owned the land, to get permission to use the bus for a campsite. I asked around. Nobody could tell me. I went to the Coahoma County Courthouse."

"We did the same trying to locate Doom's properties."

Shell raised a finger to continue. "The property in question was not in a name I recognized."

"Swift. Samuel Loden Swift," Chase said interrupting him again.

"That's right. The name it's still under today. Just recently, I checked."

"Except Samuel Swift is deceased and the deed was not transferred to another name," Chase continued, his intrusions wearing thin with Shell.

"You fellers dropped it. I did, too. Then something about the tragedies of May and November, my grandson's conviction and something the warden told me when I met with him, brought the name back up, kept nagging at me. Swift. Swift. I dug a little deeper. Back then there was a Cotton Carnival in Memphis and a Maid of Cotton Pageant. I was on the National Cotton Council. A young lady from Indianola was selected Maid of Cotton. I'd forgotten until I saw her picture in the Delta State 1981 *Broom* annual. A few pages over, in the football sports section, is a photo of John Culpepper, the prison warden where my grandson's incarcerated. The Maid of Cotton's father was Samuel Swift. She, Sadie Beatrice, later married a man, last name Doom. His photo's on that same page with Culpepper's, all of which makes for an interesting triangular affair. For all practical purposes," he shook the pen he was still holding for emphasis, "that land was *de facto* Doom's, but his wife's father's name is still on the deed, and apparently, she's still paying the taxes on it," he concluded returning the pen to Chase.

"That's interesting," Chase said.

"Very!"

"Did you camp at the school bus?" Chase asked.

"Yes sir. Outside, not inside. It appeared abandoned. Some supplies I buried in a cooler last time Cal, and I hunted are probably still there. I sense you going somewhere with all of this. That picture you just drew's not big enough."

Chase reached inside his coat pocket and withdrew a newspaper clipping and laid it beside the note. It was from the Memphis Commercial Appeal with the current date, December 23, 2014. Above a picture of the old

Memphis/Arkansas Bridge and some river barges, the caption read: ISIS THREAT TO MISSISSIPPI RIVER BRIDGE. "The threat was passed along to the FBI before it hit the papers," Chase said. "Now you understand the urgency."

"Yessir," Shell said, then lowered his voice to a conspiratorial whisper. "But the Islamic State is not Aryan Nations."

"Correct! But their objectives are the same. Destruction of the United States federal government," emphasized Chase and pointed his pen at Memphis on the makeshift map. "Knock out the two bridges on the Mississippi here, the old trestle and the new one, and halt river traffic. Take the Army Corps of Engineers months to clear a river a mile wide with a narrow channel."

"That would do some damage."

"I'll say," Chase said. "The Mississippi River services three hundred million tons of cargo annually. Stopping traffic on it halts twenty percent of the country's coal supply, figure ten percent of all U.S. electricity used yearly."

"I had no idea," Shell said shaking his head.

"That's just for starters." He moved the point of his pen further south where he'd printed Helena. "Blow up the two bridges in Memphis and one more at Helena and no telling what it would do to this country's economy."

Shell was shaking his head in disbelief, his eyes still on the map.

"To wrap this up," Chase said, "there are two issues: plans to blow up Mississippi River bridges and two stolen jet engines. The two are different but intertwined. The theft and attempted resale of the jet engines, i.e., the envelope, has led our investigation to the former."

"But at a price," Shell bemoaned.

"Again, Mr. Ferguson. My condolences."

More distracting noise up front. More customers coming in, mingling at the bar. Slight clinks of glasses, coffee cups against saucers.

"This place is gonna start filling up shortly," Shell said.

There was a pause, the agent stroking his mustache, thinking, drumming the pen on the table. "This takes me to another reason I wanted to speak with you."

"I'm waiting for you to run out of 'em," Shell quipped sardonically.

"When do you see your grandson again?"

"Next Sunday. Possibly, Christmas Day. The prison has reduced staff on holidays, but the warden authorized me to see him on Thanksgiving Day. Maybe he will again."

"Shoot for Christmas Day." He paused, stopped drumming the pen. "Even better, Christmas Eve."

"Why Christmas Eve?

"This note and the headline I showed you concern me. That's all I can say."

Shell bolted upright. "Concerns?" he exclaimed, eyeing the man sitting across from him sternly. "My grandson's life may be in danger."

"Probably not as long as they think he knows something."

"'Probably doesn't cut it with me, Agent Chase," Shell said angrily, making a fist and smacking his palm. "He's in there because the law screwed up its investigation. The law can get him out," he continued his voice rising. "You can flash that badge and go in and get him out."

Chase glanced at the empty tables around them, the ones toward the front filling up. "Mr. Ferguson, I understand your frustration," he responded, leaning in closer and lowering his voice. "It's not that simple. We couldn't do that without a warrant, and we'd have to have probable cause for a judge to sign one. Right now all we've got are threads of conjectures, speculations. Furthermore, the FBI showing up at that prison entrance could place your grandson in greater danger not to mention sabotaging months of our investigations. It's a delicate situation. Much hangs in the balance. A scenario looms larger than all of us put together, bigger than the MBI and the FBI, than the state of Mississippi, maybe the entire country. You and your grandson are our pipelines. The FBI is poised to launch a full-scale attack. We're waiting for the right moment. You've moved us one step closer."

"I'm just trying to save my grandson's life," Shell said impatiently.

"You may be saving a lot more." He pointed at the note. "May I keep this?"

"If it'll help."

They were pushing back their chairs to rise.

"When will I see you again?" Shell asked.

"Probably not. Here's a secure phone number where you can reach me. Call me after you speak with your grandson. Twenty-four seven," and he slid a business card across the table. "Hope to hear from you tomorrow. Your grandson is our boots on the ground. Bring him up to speed."

Shell picked up the card and slid it into his shirt pocket. "Speed. That's the word," Shell said, and they shook hands.

Shell let the agent leave first, watched as he made his way through the small crowd at the front. The man could not have walked into a place without attracting attention or walked out of it without leaving a wake of talk.

Shell sat thinking about the load just dumped atop the one he was already carrying. An old advertisement notice with a disconnected phone number in England. A disconnected number with a fictitious attorney in Panama. Millions in a Panamanian bank. A wild bunch sitting on two jets worth the money in that bank. Pieces coming together, but not yet. His grandson in the middle, innocent. But not yet free.

He pulled out his cell phone and dialed the number from memory. A lady answered. He did not recognize the voice. Visitation suspended until after Christmas, she said. Shell identified himself, told her it was an emergency, that the warden had granted him an emergency visit at Thanksgiving. She couldn't authorize any visits, she said, regardless the of nature.

"May I speak with the warden?" he requested.

"The warden is unavailable," she said.

He hung up, sat there thrumming his fingers on the table. He couldn't turn it loose. He called again, a different number for the main office. Again, he identified himself and needed to visit his grandson. It was urgent. A friendlier female gave him the same response. Again, he asked to speak with the warden. The receptionist told him to hold. He held for longer than it should have taken, then she returned and said the warden could not see him today and would not be able to see him until after New Year's. If it was a medical emergency, he could call the Main Medical Unit, so she gave him the direct number.

Shell thought. Did the warden know? Did the warden know that Shell knew he knew? He was ready to bite a chunk out of his cell phone. He was ready to drive to the prison and demand to be seen. He was ready to call 911 and tell them his grandson's life was in danger. He was ready to call the governor's office again. Instead, he signaled for Maxine and ordered a beer.

CHAPTER 24

December 23 Tuesday

Gunshots bolted him from sleep.

A guard banging on the door.

"Git up, lazy ass," the guard bellowed. "Cain't sleep all day."

The food portal banged open. A food tray appeared.

Cal got up and retrieved it.

The guard slammed the portal shut, slid the bolt across it. "Eat your dinner," he ordered.

Cal groaned. He sat on his bunk in his underpants, head forward, rubbing the tips of his fingers across his head staring at the food. He wasn't hungry. A slab of scrambled eggs again. Too much work cutting them up. He slid the tray under the bunk and laid back down.

Later, footsteps. Another loud rap on the door. "Guard!" a gruff voice called out.

More footsteps.

"Unlock this door," the gruff voice commanded. "I'm going in."

"You want him cuffed first, Warden?" the guard asked.

"No!" the warden clipped.

The guard unlocked the door. A large man with a bushy beard stepped into the cell and shut the heavy door behind him.

"Mr. Ferguson!"

Breathing deeply, Cal stood. "Yessir," he responded looking at the face near his, at the mouth in a tight straight line.

"I'm Warden Culpepper. Sit!"

Unnerved, Cal sat back on the edge of the bunk.

"I understand you had a seizure and fell off the top bunk."

"Yessir."

"Don't sleep there again," the warden commanded.

164

"Yessir, I won't."

The warden looked down, his eyes roaming the floor settling on the tray visible beneath the bunk. "You didn't eat your supper. Our food not good?"

"I'm not hungry."

There was a pause, the warden staring stonily at him. "Come clean with me," he said in a lowered voice. "You didn't fall off the bunk."

"Yessir."

"Yessir you did or yessir you didn't?" the warden pressed, his voice pitching.

"I didn't."

Emotionless, arms crossed against his chest, the warden stood there looking down at him, a long speculative look, testing Cal with his eyes. The same look Cal had seen in the judge's eyes before he sentenced him. He was expecting more questions, questions the warden probably knew the answers to.

"I know about your losses," the warden offered, his voice softer, but without emotion.

Cal looked away through the long narrow window on the outside wall.

"You don't need another," the warden added, eyeing him sternly then he reached in his pocket and pulled out something. "I believe you're out of this," the warden said, leaning over and handing him a small tube of Crest toothpaste.

The warden turned to leave, looked back and wagged a thick finger. "Don't try it again," and he opened the door and called for the guard.

He knew the answers Cal thought and laid back on his bunk wishing he'd thanked him for the tablet and pencils. The warden obviously didn't know what Cal knew, that he was getting out and this place was going to be history. Or, was it going to be history before that history had a chance.

Late that evening, after the guard check, he heard again the familiar flat caroming *plunk...plunk...*Again the carton slid beneath his door, and again he got up, opened it, saw the addition: DOOM'S JETS.

Did Doom have jets? If he did, what kind of jets? He assumed the note referenced jet plane but did Doom even fly. The envelope was somehow connected to jets. Was that what was in the envelope? A name? Receipt?

Payment on demand? If not from Doom, someone else?

Cal didn't have answers to any of the questions. But he had a leg up on The Fisherman. He had something The Fisherman wanted. Be coy. Keep the tension between knowing and not knowing. *Let information come to you, not from you.*

Time to throw out my own line. He turned over the note and wrote on the back: WHAT KIND? He refolded the wrinkled scrap of paper, replaced it in the carton and pressed the small box flat again. He yanked the string. The carton snapped away.

He smiled mischievously to himself. He was getting the knack of fishing and thought in amusement, of the two of them, he was the real fisherman? For the first time since he had been led from the courtroom, he was entertained. It could cost him, this cat and mouse game. But it could save him. The idea that having fun could save his life was not exactly enjoyable, but, as the saying goes, it was the only game in town. It was a distraction. As long as it lasted, he was safe.

Long minutes later, a single *plunk* and the carton appeared, this time stopping near his bunk. The Fisherman's precision was close to perfect. Cal removed a square of fresh paper: YOU KNOW.

He sat on the edge of the bunk and thought. He glanced at the calendar he'd taped to the wall. The day was Tuesday, December 23. Two more days and he could see his granddad. Keep fishing. Keep the Fisherman guessing. No telling what else the Fisherman might cast and the hook Cal would cast back. He turned the scrap of paper over and drew a question mark, observing its resemblance to a hook. He replaced the paper in the carton and yanked the string. Nothing. He pulled the string again, and again, nothing. He was about to yank it again when he heard footsteps. No wonder. A guard had entered the pod. He was making his rounds, first the bottom tier, then the top. Outside Cal's cell, he stopped and tapped on the window.

"You okay in there, Ferguson."

"Yessir." He had slid the carton under the bunk, but surely the guard saw the string. Chris had said most of them ignored the fishing, were even humored by it.

The guard moved on to the next window.

Minutes later, Cal heard the pod door close.

Swish! The carton disappeared.

He'd no sooner laid back down and pulled the covers over him and, *swish*, it reappeared. He got up and opened it. Another fresh note, three words rushing his eyes: ANSWER OR DIE.

He kept the note and yanked the string.

The carton disappeared.

PART II

CHAPTER 25

December 24 Christmas Eve

Shell sat in the great room gazing out the tall windows that faced west.

Outside, it was dusk, that nostalgic purple shade. Only a glow of evening left in the sky, colors turning gray, trees becoming silhouettes. Staring at the pink crease where shade and night met, he could still see the bayou, the mists ghosting up from it and the fields beyond.

He closed his eyes, and it was Christmas Eve a year ago—everyone gathered around the dining table, later around the tree, opening gifts, singing Christmas carols. On Christmas Eve, Cal and Sally and Shelley slept in the "big house," as Shelley called it. Shelley was always gleefully and excitedly off to bed early. The adults sat around the fireplace where a large fire breathed and crackled warmth and enjoyed a cup of eggnog, told stories about the past, dreamed of new ones to come.

The great room was the largest room in the house, a simple room furnished in heavy oak and leather, the only room not defined by Athen's more delicate tastes. In one corner near the long stone hearth, was an enormous armoire filled with family pictures. Hanging randomly on the walls were shadowboxes displaying artifacts of family history, prints, and some of Athen's water-colors. At each end of the mantel were antique books Athen had purchased on a trip to Scotland she had taken by herself. Between them hung a large painting of a clipper ship. Shell liked it because it might be the closest he would ever come to seeing one of the great oceans.

Despite the room's memories, it was the safest place for Shell in the house. The larger the room, it seemed, the easier it was to enter and tolerate. He went to the kitchen only when necessary, stayed only as long as needed. Their bedroom and adjoining bath smothered him. Sheets and pillowcases were discarded, given to the Salvation Army. Women from the church came and removed Athen's perfumes and hairsprays, soaps and shampoos. But the fragrances lingered. Every room smelled of her. He slept in the guest bedroom and used a different bathroom. He moved his clothes and toiletries. He could not enter the room he and Athen together had painted and decorated for their granddaughter. Just walking by it, not even looking in, choked him up. He had not touched it, or anything in it, since Shelley's death. When the women from the church came to help with Athen's clothes and items, he told them that room was off limits, that he wanted to leave it exactly as Athen had left it for Shelley's next visit. Walking by these rooms, through the corridors of the house, he felt the memories stacking up like kindling for a fire and guessed that one day that's all the house would be useful for.

Sitting alone in the great room, Shell felt blessed about one thing. His grandson was innocent, and he reflected on his visit with Agent Chase and all that had been entrusted to him. There would be a new trial or no trial if the district attorney, with evidence in hand, dropped the charges and Cal was exonerated. Or, the governor would pardon him. He wasn't sure how all that worked legally. The sifter of fate had left him his grandson, and for now, he was grateful for his life.

Thinking of Cal reminded him. He needed to call Agent Chase and tell him he would not be able to contact his grandson until after the holidays. He still had the card in his shirt pocket and pulled it out. He dialed the number. It rang several times then a message popped up—*I can't talk now.* Chase had said call him twenty-four seven. Shell drew the phone closer to his eyes and dialed the number again. Same message. He would try again later.

At first, he had decided not to build a fire, too much effort for just one person to enjoy. Then, he had decided he would. He was lonely, and a fire was like having company in the room. He had decided, initially, not to put up the tree. Same reasons. But Athen would want one. With all of its lights and ornaments, a tree, though not the same as a fire in the fireplace, would add a different comfort to the room. It would also trigger memories, infuse the air with sadness. Athen won. He dragged the box with the artificial tree from the garage closet and assembled it, then went limb to limb fluffing the branches as Athen always did, tracking down the burned out lights. Where he failed, she always succeeded. He sat looking at a Christmas tree with lights at the top and around the bottom but darkness in between. He could never find the disconnect or burned out bulb, whichever it was. One more time, he thought he would try, Athen guiding him.

He got up, was jiggling a string of lights that suddenly came on when the house phone rang. The landline rarely rang. When it did, the person on the other end, usually had a foreign accent he had trouble understanding or was selling something. Athen was more patient with them. Most people knew to call him on his cell phone.

He stood back from the tree, and the string of lights lit up, and he picked up the phone on the table beside his lounge chair. "Hello!"

"This mister Shell Ferguson?" the voice said.

"Shell Ferguson," he responded, "Who's this? What do you want?"

"The name's Charlie Goforth, and I don't want anything," the voice responded in reciprocal shortness. "But I got something you may be looking for."

"I doubt you do, but what is it?"

"It's not a what but a who, a little girl who says you're her granddaddy."

The receiver slipped from Shell's hand, and he caught it before it hit the tabletop and raised it back to his ear.

"Can you hear me okay?" the man questioned.

"Yes." He'd heard him, but wasn't getting his hopes up. It could be a crank caller.

"I said my huntin' buddy and me picked up this little girl who says you're her granddaddy."

"What's her name," Shell asked, his breath coming in rapid bursts, the receiver shaking in his hand, blood pressure heating up his face.

"What's your name, Hon?" he heard the man say.

Then, a child's weak voice, as though traveling from a million miles away. "Shelley."

Can't be, can't be, that thought a mantra flying back and forth behind his eyes. "How'd you know to call me?"

"She gave us this phone number. She knew it by heart."

And, by damn, she did. Her grandmother had had her memorize it in case she ever needed them after Cal was arrested. "Is she all right?"

"She looks like she's been through a reaper, arms and face scratched up pretty good, clothes torn. Only got socks on her feet. She don't say much, looks scared. One other thing, mister Ferguson, we called you instead of 911. We don't wanna get involved, if you git my drift."

Did he ever. The failure of local government was one of the reasons all of this had happened. "That's good. Where are you?"

"We're on State Highway One, between Alligator and Deeson, just out of Round Lake, close to where it intersects with Highway four forty-four."

"Know exactly where you are." He knew the place all right. From Round Lake was an access road to the levee he and Cal used when hunting. The intersection was almost a straight shot from Rome, about twenty or so miles. No idea who the men were except they sounded white and were hunters.

"That's where we picked her up. She was walking south, said she could direct us to you if she knew where she was, bless her heart. We don't mind bringin' her to you," the man continued, "if we knew where you was."

She was headed the right direction, he thought. "I'll come to you."

"Mighty fine. We'll stay put. She's a sweet thing. Got her feet in front of the heater now."

"Thank you, sir. See you in half an hour or less," and hung up.

He grabbed his coat and keys and cell phone, then it hit him. He didn't ask the guy his number, then remembered it would be on his house phone caller ID window. He went back, wrote it down on a pad near the phone and crammed it into his pants pocket. The fire in the fireplace had burned down some, and the screen was up. Going out the door, he turned off the Christmas tree lights, then flipped them back on. It was an artificial tree, and Shelley would light up when she saw it. He hoped.

The night air was crisp and cool, the sky aswarm with stars. He wasn't sure how bats out of hell flew, but that night he was kin to them in every way but species and blood. Tunneling through the darkness, the truck's speedometer rested on eighty, and the roadside speed limit signs he passed said fifty-five. He didn't care. He had never seen a constable or county deputy on that stretch of lonely road, always lonelier in the winter. Tonight, they were all at home with family. To be safe, he reached over and flipped on his emergency flasher. If someone did see him, maybe they'd think he was making a mad rush to the hospital and leave him alone.

He slowed as he came to the intersection of State Highway 32 and State

Highway 1. He turned right and headed north. There was no traffic on the road, but he slowed going through Deeson, a small hamlet of scattered houses and what was left of a store. The Mississippi River levee was on his left. On his right, dark flat land.

The smooth straight road was deserted. Ahead, about a mile past Deeson, was the Highway 444 intersection. All the time he was driving, Shell Ferguson was wondering was this really happening, would she really be there where the men said? Others knew of his private investigation. Endless questions raced through his mind. Had they passed the word along to the wrong people? Was this some sort of trick, was he being lured into some kind of trap? If it really was Shelley, would he have to pay something to get her back, was there a catch? Where had she been and how had she been treated, had she been injured, molested? Was she sick? Will she need to see a doctor? Who should he call next? Cal first, it was his daughter? The governor, it was his granddaughter, too? The director? Should he take her with him to the prison and let her daddy see her for real or was that a bad idea? Did Cal need to be briefed beforehand? It was also risky. Too much information for the Aryan Nations gang might put Cal in a worse predicament. He was thinking about what he should do next. Take her home and let her get a bath and some clean clothes her grandmother always kept for her. Or to a hospital? He decided he'd cross those bridges when he got to them. He opened his glove compartment and pulled out his pistol, just in case, and he drove on.

He neared the intersection and slowed. His emergency flashers were still on. They might identify him. He'd forgotten to tell the man the model and make of his truck. He could call and tell them, but not while he's driving and he didn't want to stop. Shelley would see it and tell them.

There was no stop sign at the intersection, but he stopped, scanned left and right. Nothing. No traffic behind or ahead of him. Nothing he could see that was parked. He was about to pass the intersection and drive further north when lights appeared on the levee side of the road. It was a red pickup pulled off the road and parked, lights on, motor running.

He maneuvered behind the truck. All he could see in the truck cab was two heads. A man emerged from the truck. He was tall and broad-shouldered with a long bushy beard and walked with a slight limp. Shell put his hand on his pistol and rolled down the window.

173

The man approached him. "You mister Ferguson?"

"Yessir."

"It's him," he yelled back to the other man in the truck.

The other man got out and behind him, tumbling from the cab, came Shelley.

Shell took a deep breath. A chill passed through him. He opened the truck door and got out. "I'm much obliged to you," he said with a shaky voice and began walking toward his granddaughter. Little arms flailing the night air and thin legs churning, she ran towards him squealing, "Big Daddy! Big Daddy!" slamming into his legs with a force that almost knocked him down.

The man had described her right. Scampering through the headlights, Shell glimpsed the thin body, tattered shirt, and disheveled hair. He picked her up and held her, smelled the body odor and saw the sunken eyes and scratches on her face. She began crying, punching tears in her sockets with her little fists. Great gulps of happiness shook her shoulders, her entire body and all he could think to say was, "Everything's all right, Hon. Everything's all right," his body shaking against hers. A hundred questions stacked up in his head but they could wait. He wouldn't forget them. Whatever had happened to her, wherever she had been, for now, she was in his arms. She was safe.

For a long time, between the two stopped vehicles, in his headlights he held her, the two men stood looking on, helpless at the moment, but smiling. One of them, Shell noticed, closed his eyes and rubbed them with his thumb and forefinger.

Shelley's sobs turned to sniffles. She leaned away from him, blotted her eyes with her tiny palms. "I'm okay, Big Daddy," she murmured bravely. "I'm okay."

She had always called her great-grandmother, "Big Mama," and him "Big Daddy."

"I know you are, Shelley. Let me talk to these two men." He put her down and asked the men their names and contact information which they readily provided, and he jotted down in the spiral notebook he always kept in his shirt pocket. They turned and were walking back to their truck.

He called out to them. "Gentlemen, we thank you."

"Thank you, mister men," Shelley called out, her voice hoarse and raspy and, holding her granddaddy's hand, waved to them with the other.

"Happy to be of help," one of the men said, casting an it-was-nothing flip of his hand.

"Merry Christmas," the other called back as they simultaneously opened the truck doors and got in.

Shelley, still waving, returned the holiday greeting, "Merry Christmas, mister men."

As the truck pulled away, Shelley was still waving, "Thank you, mister men," she called out again.

Shell curved his arm around his granddaughter's shoulders and walked her to the driver's door and opened it for her. She scrambled up and into the other seat as if nothing had happened, and she was ready, one more time, for another adventure with Big Daddy in his pickup.

"Are you really okay, Punkin?" Shell asked, then noticed, shining in the overhead cab light, the necklace he had given to her.

"Yes, Big Daddy. I'm with you now."

CHAPTER 26

As he did each day at six o'clock before clocking out, Durasmus came by to check on him.

"When is visitation?" Cal asked.

"Not any," the old guard said.

"But it's Christmas Eve."

"Holiday. Limited staff," Durasmus responded in his usual terse fashion.

"My granddad came on Thanksgiving," Cal said.

"Special permission. Next visitation's this Sunday."

Cal groaned.

Sensing his desperation, Durasmus responded, "Anything I can get for you?"

Oh yes! A 24 hour pass. A phone. A gun. Knife-proof vest. Can of pepper spray. "I wish," his only response.

"See you day after t'morrow. Off Christmas Day."

"Thank you, Durasmus," Cal responded weakly.

He lay on his bunk thinking, assessing. Twenty-four hours had past since he had received the threatening note and left the Fisherman empty-handed. It was Christmas Eve. Skeletal staff. Perfect time for trouble. He had grown overly cautious about the guards. The ones who beat him were from another unit. But they rotated. No telling what early morning visits he might get. *We'll be back.* They probably wouldn't kill him. They thought he knew too much. Then the note—*answer or die.*

He could hear Chris on his typewriter furiously pecking. Christmas Eve. Perfect time for the opposite of trouble. Peace. Goodwill. Chris doing his part. No need to interrupt him. No need to speak with him anyway. Chris couldn't help him with this decision.

He had a plan. It was full grown in his head. In his mind, it was a perfect plan. In his mind, he'd discovered a secret seam, a hidden fissure in the otherwise perfect seal. In his mind, it would work. In the real world, it was imperfect, out to the far end, the edge of wildness. It might work. *Answer or die.* Any plan, far-fetched or not, beat no plan.

The scheme had been percolating, bits and pieces accumulating. It hadn't begun to fall into place until the early morning he had returned from the hospital and had noticed a weak link in the prison's otherwise tight security. He had wondered why others hadn't noticed it. He had wondered why Chris hadn't mentioned it. Chris, who seemed to know everything, who missed nothing.

He had bet hundreds of inmates had lain awake at night planning escapes. Figuring. Refiguring. Hitting dead ends and starting over. He had bet they'd thought of using blankets thrown over the barbed wire and wire cutters with insulated handles to cut through the electric fence and razor wire. He had bet they'd probably thought of digging tunnels and the utensils they'd use, eventually discarding that idea. The only places they could secretly penetrate the concrete floor were in the lower segregation cells and, barring an intricate conspiracy, inmates in segregation were rotated too often to make any substantial progress.

In their secret machinations, inmates had surely thought of the two service entrances. One for grocery trucks, inmate transportation buses, ambulances, and emergency vehicles, trash removal. The other, a corrugated vertical metal sliding door. The first entrance was the double chainlink gate on the north side of the compound near the main prison entrance. The second portal was near the outer service gate. For security reasons, the times the portals were open were never divulged. Inmates being transported to other prisons were never given advance notice. Inmates who worked in the kitchen never knew delivery times. But, what he had noticed did not depend upon either gate being open.

The prison compound comprised ten two-story buildings, lettered alphabetically, all connected by halls and some by outside fenced sidewalks. Surrounding all of that were double chain-link fences thirty feet apart, barbed wire coils along the bottom and top of each followed by horizontal barbed wire strands topped by electrical razor wire. Signs along the outer fence said DANGER: HIGH VOLTAGE.

But engineers made mistakes. Auto designers committed construction flaws, omitted a minuscule emission part. Surgeons skipped steps, cut corners, missed stitches. Someone in the state capital or corrections commissioner's office—an architect or security expert—had overlooked something. Above and below the outside service gate were the usual barbed wire coils topped by razor wire. But, they did not run continuously. There was a gap. The gate was a double gate. Sections swung open and closed from the middle where double chains and a large padlock secured them. At the top of the double gate, where there was no wire, coiled or razor, was an opening, a space wide enough for a thin person to thread. Beyond that to the tree line a hundred yards away, if one could get that far, was the Sunflower River. If they could make it past the Sunflower, next was the Mississippi River levee and beyond that the "Mighty Muddy."

Cal did not know why he had been attracted to stories about great prison escapes. Perhaps, it was because he had grown up near a penitentiary and had heard all of the stories about breaks there. Perhaps, it was because of old late night movies he had seen based upon true stories. *Papillon* starring Steve McQueen and Dustin Hoffman was one. *The Great Escape* with James Garner and Steve McQueen was another. Somewhere, he could not recall the source, he had read about the famous escape from Alcatraz by three inmates. Authorities presumed they drowned in the San Francisco Bay but their bodies were never found.

He did not know, or understand, why he was fascinated by these stories of convicted criminals, why he found himself pulling for them, for their success. Unless, it was because most of them were innocent or their punishment did not fit the crime and his heart went out to them. Or unless, early on in life, growing up in Mississippi near the state prison, he had developed a sense of social injustice and his empathy for the downtrodden and outcast and imprisoned had spread from that pivotal core of his life. Or perhaps, the fascination sprang from Bible stories he had read in his youth— Joseph, Moses, Samson, Daniel. Then, there were Jeremiah, John the Baptist, Paul. And, of course, Jesus himself. He did know one thing. He'd had no inkling his fascination with prisoners and prison escapes would come into play later in his life; that he would become obsessed with a gap one foot wide, how to get to it, and through it.

He had often reflected on the more notorious escapes that were successful and how they were pulled off. He recalled an item he had read about something the great escape artist Houdini had said, that the secret to opening a lock was from the inside. Cal had often wondered what Houdini meant by, "from the inside," and had given it a lot of thought. It could refer to the inside of a lock, but could also mean something else. A lock could be symbolic of prison and to escape from prison means knowing the combination of the prison. The movements within the facility. The who, what, when, and where. Not just the physical walls and how to break, bore, or crash through them. "From the inside," could also mean from inside of one's head. Thinking. He had nothing to do day in and day out but think, think, and think some more. He reflected on the theological implications. One's salvation, spiritual freedom, was from the inside out. The more he thought about Houdini's comment, the more he focused on the who, what, when, and where. But mostly about when and where—timing, distance, and speed.

Timing was simple. He had kept a daily count of guards. The number was always the same for his pod: two. Always the same in the hallway: two. Chris had told him there were always two in Central Control, except on the night shift when there was only one. He had timed the guard shift changes: at six in the morning, six in the evening. They worked twelve hours with no breaks. On the downside of their shift, they were tired, bored, and sleepy.

Along comes Christmas Eve. Prison half-staffed. Only one guard in Central Control scanning the cameras. Only one in the hall, one in the pod. The last time Cal had looked, the one in the pod was sitting behind the desk, his head down as if asleep. Both guards were near the end of their shifts, asleep or near asleep. Another plus for Christmas Eve—a waxing new moon. Darkness over the land.

Conspiratorial darkness in the prison.

Assessing distance was easy. He had measured the paces from his cell, down the steps to the pod door, and from the pod door to the outside exit which led to the exercise cages. The distance from the exercise cages to the service gate he'd guessed to be fifty yards.

Distance plus speed was not as easy. All doors were opened electronically from Central Control. A button had to be pushed and a guard in Central Control, viewing the door through a surveillance camera screen, pushed another button. There was a loud buzz, and the door opened. At least this was what he had observed and how Chris had described the operation to him. Chris had also told him that the guards in Central Control would get busy or lazy and take their time opening doors, particularly on the night shift and on holidays with only one guard in the control tower. Guards grew resentful, having to wait for doors to open when they had duties to perform or wanted to sneak a smoke break through the outside exit to the exercise cages. As Cal had observed, they jammed the door locks with wadded paper towels. When he was returned from the hospital, Cal had seen paper towels in the hall exit door to the outside exercise cages. The pod door was also jammed. Details falling into place, almost as though he had a confederate.

He had estimated how long it would take him to get to the pod door, then the time from the pod door to the outside exit, removing the wads so the doors locked behind him and could only be re-opened by the one guard in Central Control who was tired and sleepy. Cal had been a sprinter on the track team in high school and had estimated the time it would take him to get from his cell down the steps to the pod door then the back exit door. Once outside, he had a straight shot to the service gate. He had estimated the time he could get from the first exercise cage to the service gate. What he had not figured then was the time it would take him to scale the double gate, slip through the gap at the top, jump to the ground on the other side and make it to the tree line and river before security recovered and scrambled to the alarms and spotlights.

On the track team in high school, he had also been a high jumper and pole vaulter. He recalled an incident from his adolescence. It was Halloween. He was walking down Main Street in Drew with three male friends. Some local thugs Cal knew, the Ruthvens, approached them and Cal whispered to his friends, "Let me handle this." A conversation ensued between him and the leader of the gang, a large pimpled-face brute named Eugene. All seemed to be going well. Cal was with his mother when she had taken food to the Ruthven home, a shack in the boondocks, one Christmas. Pleasantries were passed, and the Ruthvens strolled on down the street. To Cal's astonishment, one of his friends had lit a cherry bomb and tossed it near the Ruthvens. Cal didn't wait for their reaction. He tore off in the other direction. The Ruthvens were in hard chase and gaining. Cal ducked into an alley and headed for one of the two cotton gins in town, the one that was fenced. He came to a high double mesh gate with a bar across the middle. He didn't think twice. With a running leap his left foot landed on the middle bar, he grabbed the top bar, pushed off from the middle bar and propelled over the top, landing on both feet, his friends stuck on the other side, the Ruthvens breathing down their necks.

The outer service fence at the prison was about the same height as the fence he had vaulted over that Halloween. It had a middle bar. Once over that gate, it was a hundred yards to the Sunflower River, the moonless dark on his side.

Another plus, a big one. The surprise factor. With no escapes ever from the prison, none would be expected. From American history, he recalled an early morning surprise that might have saved the Revolution. Washington's Christmas attack on the Hessians at Trenton.

Putting a prison posse together on Christmas Eve would take a while. The prison was under-staffed. Guards leaving their post to pursue him would create a security risk, a big deal with the brass. Getting reinforcements would take hours.

There were obstacles. He was still sore from the assault, but he had been exercising and was otherwise in good physical shape. Outside it was cold, and he'd be in his orange short-sleeved jumpsuit. But he could wear his dark fleece jacket. It would keep him warm and blot half the bright color. Once to the river, he could slap mud on his pants.

That was another barrier, crossing the Sunflower. He was eighteen the last time he and his dad and granddad hunted along the river, but the area hadn't changed that much in ten years. Upstream, the Sunflower was shallow. He could wade across. If he didn't freeze to death in the process. The nearest bridge was several miles downstream. But, he knew the river. He had hunted up and down the Sunflower all of his life. He had hunted all kinds of game—doves, quail, squirrels, rabbits, turkey, deer. Mostly, he'd hunted ducks. From Clarksdale to Indianola, he and his father, when he was alive, and grandfather had traversed the river in his grandfather's small boat. Cal had known every beaver dam, every sand and gravel beach; where the river widened and where it narrowed. And it was narrow upstream near the prison. If he could make it across the river, he had another plan. A prophet may be without honor in his own home, but he knows the lay of its land.

The biggest obstacle was getting past his two assailants. When the guards were preoccupied, he had practiced climbing to his perch above the sink, timed his speed. He was surprised how easily the stainless steel mirror above the sink detached from the wall. It slotted over a single screw and was heavier than he'd imagined. At night, when the guards were out or distracted, he'd practiced the drill—climbing onto the sink, removing the mirror, holding and balancing with it.

There was only one security guard on duty in the pod, and his head was on his desk. Only one guard in the long hallway. Only one in Central Control. Three hours till their shift ended. They were sleepy and tired. The two doors to his freedom, jammed with paper towels. The security cameras would be on, but doubtfully watched that time of night and, if history repeated itself, all the lights would be out, the security screens in Central Control black. He glanced at his watch: three thirty. Next count, six o'clock. The timing was right. Only one thing missing.

We'll be back.

CHAPTER 27

Shell stared at the illuminated macadam, the white lines scrolling beneath his headlights, and thought. Occasionally, he'd glimpse Shelley sitting on the passenger side, her profile like something jagged cut from the backdrop of rolling dark outside. She had seen him return the gun to the glove compartment and flinched when she saw it but said nothing.

He thought of reasons she was where she had been. They could have been holding her for a ransom. But no notes had been received. Unless the ransom they wanted was the contents of the envelope. Further down the road, it hit him: hostage shield. He shivered at the thought. One thing was sure. Suddenly, she'd become the key to the case.

He wanted to ask her questions, but they might upset her. The answers might upset him as well. All she had said when she got in the truck cab was, "Big Daddy, they are mean people." He continued driving in the uneasy silence thinking about what he should say, hoping she'd say something and give him an opening but she remained silent. He didn't know what she had seen, what she knew about her mother and grandmother. There was no telling what she had seen that night, no telling what had happened to her afterward. No telling. One thing for sure. There was one long story behind it, one, in her own time when she was ready, she would tell.

"Shelley, you okay?" he attempted.

She jerked her head up and down.

"Big Daddy needs to make sure. I'm taking you to the hospital."

"Okay," she said and continued looking straight ahead at the darkness and the highway spooling beneath the truck's headlights. After a few minutes, "They won't hurt me will they?" she said in a soft cautious voice, her eyes still straight ahead.

"No, Hon. They won't hurt you. They'll just make you stick out your tongue and look in your ears like Dr. Winkler does." He knew he was not telling her everything. After they heard the story, the emergency room staff would look other places. He glanced at her again, at the cuts along her arms and across her face. "They'll make those scratches feel better."

"They don't hurt anymore," she whispered, as though speaking to herself.

"But they need doctoring. Then I'll take you back to Big Daddy's, get you a warm bath, put some warm pajamas on you and tuck you into bed." He swallowed a lump in his throat when he said it. He couldn't say he'd take her home. He couldn't say he'd take her back to her mama's or to her daddy. There was little else he could say except what he'd said.

He knew he'd have to contact the authorities, but that wouldn't be the sheriff's department which had bungled the whole thing to begin with. He would call the governor and have him alert the director. Or, agent Chase, make him aware of this development.

Besides taking her to the hospital and notifying grandparents, the next thing he needed to do was a catch-22. Her father needed to know she was alive. But, taking her to the prison might put her father in greater danger. The question was moot until next Sunday. *Take it one step at a time*, he thought as they crossed a long bridge.

At the Clarksdale hospital, one of the triage nurses in the emergency room motioned them to her desk. Shelley sitting beside him, Shell stated his granddaughter had been abducted and held for almost a month by strange people beyond the levee. He kept placing his hand on her head and stroking her hair as he spoke trying to keep his comments to the nurse brief.

"Are the police aware of this?" the nurse questioned.

"Not yet," he said. "Governor DuBard—she's his granddaughter, too— and the Director of the Mississippi Bureau of Investigation are aware of this situation. She was presumed—" he paused, considering the words he should use. "She was presumed lost in a fire," he finally said.

Shelley tucked her chin and began softly crying. He put his arm around her and struggled to maintain his own emotions.

The triage nurse did not help. "Oh, I remember. That was the parsonage fire at Bethel," she blurted.

"Yessum. I'm afraid so. Now if you wouldn't mind moving this along. I just want her examined before too much time goes by, if you understand."

"I do," she said with a single embarrassed nod. "You know we must report this."

"I understand," he acknowledged. "The authorities who need to know will know soon enough."

"But I still—"

"Yessum. If you'd call the local police station and not the sheriff's department, that would be helpful. On second thought, the Department of Human Services has a hotline."

"Yes, we have the number."

"Considering the circumstances, that would be even better."

"No problem," she said and began asking questions: name, age, place of birth...social security number?

"I don't know it," Shell said.

Shelley looked up and gave the nurse her social security number.

Shell and the nurse looked at her with equal amazement.

"How did you know that?" he asked her.

"Big Mama taught it to me," she said meekly, embarrassed with the sudden attention.

"The same game you played to memorize our house phone number," he said.

Shelley nodded shyly.

The nurse asked a few more questions.

Then: "Does she have any insurance?"

"She did," Shell replied. "It was under her father, but I think he lost it. I'd rather not go into details," glancing down at Shelley. "I'll be responsible for payment."

The nurse rose and stretched out a hand to Shelley. "Come along with me, Sugar."

Shelley was simpering when she took the nurse's hand and was led away.

If it hadn't been a place he knew as though it was part of his heart, Shell would have followed his granddaughter to make sure she returned to him. But he sat there and watched her disappear into one of the curtained rooms.

He knew what he needed to do next but was unsure how to do it. He pulled his cell phone from his jacket pocket. Athen had programmed all of the important numbers he called with any regularity. He paused. He needed privacy. No one was in the emergency waiting room. Folks too caught up with holiday merriment with lit up trees and gifts and eggnog. Eggnog. Wrecks. Fights. Knifings. Drug deals gone bad. Any second somebody barreling through the door.

He stepped outside and hit the buttons Athen had taught him, that loss again slicing through him like cold steel. The phone began ringing. He looked at his watch. Almost seven thirty. The governor was probably in the mansion with family gathered around, sharing presents, no idea the best one was ringing in his pocket.

"Hell-lo!" the governor finally answered, his voice cheery as if he'd been into the eggnog himself.

"Governor, Shell Ferguson."

"Yessir. I'm in the middle of family Christmas tree right now. Can it wait?"

"I'll let you make that call. I've got—"

"Let me call you back—"

"—I've got Shelley in the hospital emergency room in Clarksdale."

"What!" he blurted into the phone.

"I've got Shelley. She's alive."

An incredible silence.

"My God!" The rough voice on the other end of the line quavered. "My God. Where...how?"

"Some hunters found her walking down State Highway One. One of 'em had the presence of mind to call me."

"How'd they know to call you?"

"Shelley. Athen had had her memorize the house number. She was scratched up pretty good. I drove her straight to the hospital."

"Where had she been, for Christ's sake?" the governor said almost shouting into the phone.

"She's got a story to tell but you and the director or somebody besides me might need to be present when she tells it. I've got a hunch it's going to blow this case wide open."

"You taking her to your place?"

"Yes!"

"We'll be right up."

"That's fine. I'm sure she'd love to see her other grandparents. But she'll probably be asleep before you get here. She's wore out, eyes barely open."

"We'll come in the morning, first thing. Dimple won't believe this."

"I'm still trying to," Shell said. "One other thing."

"Yes?"

"Not my place to tell you what to do, Governor, but need to keep it under wraps as much as we can. Word gets out that she's alive might stir up her captors."

"Captors?"

"She said she was with some mean people, her words. I didn't press."

"That was prudent."

"I'm concerned about Cal. He's more in danger now than ever when word gets out where she was and where she is. It's all tied together."

"Yes, it certainly is," the governor responded. "I'll notify the director immediately. It's Christmas Eve, but he's got staff on duty."

"Thank you, Governor." He almost said 'Byron' but, out of respect for his office had never called the man by his first name, even if he was an in-law.

"Hug Shelley for us, Shell. Tell her we love her."

He agreed he would, and they hung up.

He clapped his phone shut then opened it again. He put in again the numbers for agent Chase. It rang longer this time raising his hopes, then the same message. "The man said call twenty-four seven," he mumbled angrily to himself, anxiety sinking in. That lifeline might not be available.

He reentered the emergency room lobby. He was still by himself in the expansive area, chairs aligned in rows and around the walls. Some outdated magazines lay on a table beside the chair where he sat. He picked up one to flip through it and the triage nurse returned with Shelley under her arm.

Shell rose to meet them and immediately noticed something different. Shelley had on shoes.

The nurse noticed him eyeing them. "We rummaged through our clothes closet where we keep items that are left behind by patients and found this Mary Jane pair. It's a little bigger than her size, but the straps hold them on."

"We're grateful to you," he said. "Aren't we Shelley?"

Her small head bobbed up and down, and he noticed, too, that her matted hair had been combed.

"Except for being scratched up, slightly anemic, having a cold, and being sleepy, she's fine," the nurse said. "We did a thorough checkup," she continued, emphasizing thorough with a sharp glance to Shell. "No indication of abuse. Department of Human Services might consider neglect charges for whoever had her."

"I'm much obliged," he responded as he pulled Shelley to his side and draped an arm around her shoulder. He wanted to say they'd get charged with more than neglect. "How much do I owe you,?" he asked pulling out his billfold.

She handed him a sheet of paper. "Take this to the nurse at checkout, and she will tell you, Mr. Ferguson. That is your last name isn't it?"

"Yessum," he answered.

"You'd said earlier that that was her last name, too."

"Is that a problem?"

"No sir, it's just that we ..." she paused. "Let's just say that we've seen more than the usual number of Fergusons here within the past 24 hours."

"Who might that be?" he inquired pulling Shelley closer to him.

"We're not allowed to say, HIPPA regulations."

"HIPPA?" he exclaimed.

"The Privacy Act."

"Oh, I understand," he said wishing he could tell her more about privacy, the invasions of private lives that tear families apart and put innocent people behind bars. "We appreciate your help. All due respects, I hope I don't have to come back."

"We hope you don't either, Mr. Ferguson," she said with a faint empathic smile and waved at Shelley.

CHAPTER 28

The drive from the Clarksdale hospital to Shell's house was about twenty minutes. Shelley sat quietly peering trance-like straight ahead into the dark until they turned into the driveway and she saw the Christmas tree lights and let out a shriek of joy.

Shell thought how perfect the tree looked through the sashes, surrounded by warm yellowish light. A scene Athen had always enjoyed returning to after holiday visits.

"Santa Claus is coming tonight," she said gleefully clapping her hands.

Shell groaned inwardly. There was nothing under the tree for her. "We can't go in the front door," he said. "We don't want Santa to see us in case he's coming down the chimney," then recalled the fire he'd had going. It would have burned to ashes by now.

They entered the house through a side door that led to the kitchen, so he could get her something to eat. While she ate, he would scramble to find something to go under the tree. He knew Athen had bought a few things before she died. He had vague ideas where they might be.

"Sit on that stool, Hon, while I fix you something to eat. What would you like?"

"A peanut butter and jelly sandwich," she said as she clambered onto the stool at the kitchen counter, positioning herself with tiny fists on its shiny granite surface as though clasping an invisible knife and fork.

Since Athen's death, Shell had been learning his way around the kitchen, a room he usually just passed through. He found a jar of peanut butter in the pantry, located a jar of jelly in the side door of the refrigerator and what remained of a loaf of bread in the bread box. He began making the sandwich, questioning if that was what she really needed. But it would do. "Sweet milk?" he asked.

She nodded.

He put the sandwich on a plate, poured a glass of milk, and set them in front of her. "Now, you sit there and eat while Big Daddy tends to some business."

"Don't leave me," her small voice gasped.

"Big Daddy's not leaving you. He has to go upstairs, but he'll be right back."

"Can I go with you?" she asked, clutching the sandwich with her tiny hands, a smear of jelly on her cheeks.

"Big Daddy needs to make sure everything is all right for Santa Claus. You surely don't want him to see you. Just stay put. I'll be right up those stairs," and he pointed to the railing she could see through the open kitchen door.

"I don't want to sleep up there in my room. I want to sleep where you and Big Mama sleep."

Her comment caught him off guard. "You certainly can sleep in the room with me. I'll be right back," and he darted through the kitchen door and up the stairs before she could think of another reason to detain him.

At the top of the stairs, from the corner of his eye through a front room window, he caught a sweep of headlights. The governor could not have gotten here that fast. The deer hunters would not have followed him. The triage nurse had told him she'd contact the local police or Department of Human Services. But, this was no official vehicle, too big for that. He dashed to the window, looked out, then bounded back down the stairs, taking them two at a time, and into the kitchen.

"Come on, Shelley," he said almost shouting, grabbing her off the stool with one arm and heading for the back door.

"Where're we going,?" she cried out still holding onto the sandwich.

"Tell you later," he said breathing heavily. Rushing through the utility room, he heard the front door open and male voices. He had not locked the door behind him when he and Shelley had entered.

Behind his house were open fields that stretched to the state penitentiary at Parchman. Across them, he raced as fast as his 79 year old legs could take him toward the bright halogen lights surrounding the penitentiary compound, holding Shelley on his bad hip until he could hold her no longer and put her down. "Run, Shelley! Fast! Toward those lights," he shouted glancing back at the house, at two men emerging from the back door running toward them.

She was yards ahead of him, her small legs churning. "Why are we running, Big Daddy?" she questioned looking back over her shoulder.

"Bad men," he managed, breathing gulps of air. Several hundred acres of his property abutted the property of the state penitentiary. Day and night, guards constantly circled its periphery. At that fenceless boundary was help. He didn't know who was chasing them, but they were not friendly, and Shelley was probably who they were after. She knew too much.

"Are they the mean men?" she shouted looking back at Shell. She was slightly ahead of him, her tiny arms sawing the cold night air.

"I don't know, Hon, just keep running. I'm right behind you." His breath ragged in his chest, his lungs hurting.

"Where're we going?"

"Toward those bright lights you see yonder." He could hear heavy footsteps clomping behind him, gaining. He had seen only two men in the truck. He was afraid to turn around and look, fearful he'd stumble and fall. His heart was heaving in his chest, his breath coming in short puffs. He'd heard of how life and death situations pulled adrenalin from nowhere and shot it through a person's body giving them miraculous strength. Something was surging through him, its source the small figure running ahead of him. He would die for her and thought perhaps that was what he should do, turn around and confront the pursuers. If he did, Shelley would be alone and not know what to do when she reached the prison. He ran on, his heart pounding, his legs rubber against the hard ground.

The nearer they came to the prison lights ahead of them, the brighter they shone, and the more the footfalls behind them fell away. Other lights came into view, headlights rounding a corner of the prison compound. Shell chanced a glance over his shoulder. No one was behind them. Their pursuers had seen the headlights, too. But, he didn't let up. "Shelley, stop at the road and wait for me," he called to her. She was further ahead of him and didn't hear and hadn't seen the headlights. There was no fence around the penitentiary, and she wouldn't know to stop. If she crossed the road, she'd be in another field that belonged to the prison. If she kept going, she'd come to one of the camps, single level dormitory style structures that housed prisoners, most of them trustees.

But, she came to the road, stopped, and looked around, waited for him.

"What do we do now, Big Daddy?" she questioned in a perturbed pseudo-adult voice, hands on her hips.

He had to catch his breath before he answered. "Big Daddy's not ... used ... to running ... like that." He bent over and put his hands on his knees, for his heart and lungs a chance to catch up to his brain so they'd work together. "We wait for that pickup ... coming yonder." He pointed behind her at the approaching headlights.

She turned to see, then grabbed him around the legs. "Who ... who's that?"

"Don't worry, Hon. They're good men." He knew many of the penitentiary guards. Some had worked on his plantation before they decided to quit the long hours required for growing cotton and soybeans. He doubted he would know these two guards working a night shift on Christmas Eve. They could be new recruits.

The truck slowed, and the driver dimmed the lights, probably because Shelley had both hands cupped shading her eyes. A black man on the passenger side leaned his head out the window. "What are you doing out here in the middle of nowhere on Christmas Eve, Mister Shell?"

In the glare of lights, Shell couldn't see the two men, but he recognized this voice. Moses Malone, once his foreman. "I might ask you the same question, Malone, a man of your seniority riding a guard truck on Christmas Eve."

"Meet my driver, Roosevelt. Worked for Jack Stevens."

Jack Stevens owned the plantation next to Shell's, and he'd recalled Stevens mentioning Roosevelt, something about a run in with Ty Doom, Ty crossing a corner of his land with a tractor-trailer bed hauling heavy equipment. Shell had thought no more about it. Now, he wondered what was on the trailer bed.

"Glad to meet you, Roosevelt. How long've you been working for the prison?" Shell asked.

"Not long, about a year," Roosevelt responded.

Shell had questions, but they could wait.

Malone got out on the passenger side, left the door open and walked toward them. "Why I'm out here tonight is a long story. Cameras on the lights spotted you and the young lady," he nodded at Shelley, "running toward us. Two men chasing you. You all right?"

"That's another long story," Shell responded.

"Bad men were after us," Shelley injected impatiently.

"Malone, you recall the parsonage fire back in early November."

Malone nodded.

"My granddaughter's been missing. Hunters found her tonight between Alligator and Deeson and kept her for me. We'd just arrived home when a wide-bodied white pickup, raised cab type, came barreling into the drive. We high-tailed it."

Malone pulled his radio from his shoulder strap and clicked it on. "Malone MSP. APB. White pickup, wide-bodied, elevated cab, headed on ... ," he looked at Shell.

"Highway Thirty-two," Shell said. "Headed west."

Malone flipped on his radio again. "Probable Route 32 ... headed toward the river."

"Deeson and Alligator," Shell said, then added, "Levee Road."

Malone speaking again into his radio. "Source says probable destination Deeson or Alligator, Levee road."

Immediately, a male voice returned the message. "Got it MSP. Alerting Shelby police." The male voice barked again. "ID occupants, allegations."

"Two white males," Malone responded. "Kidnapping."

The radio went silent.

"Hop in the truck, Mister Shell," Malone directed, his voice alarmed. "Look!" he shouted pointing toward the house.

"My God!" Shell exclaimed.

Shelley looked and began crying.

Malone ushered them into the truck, entered behind them and closed the door. Shelley crawled into Shell's lap.

Roosevelt turned into the fields and headed straight for the house, gaining speed toward the bright throbbing turbulence.

Malone began barking emergency calls into his radio. "MSP ... add probable arson to kidnapping. Call nine eleven. Ferguson house in Rome on fire."

"Will do, over and out," a voice answered.

Shell couldn't believe his eyes, flames licking along the edges of the roof, sparks shuddering upward and dying in the blackness overhead, dark smoke billowing into the night.

Shelley put her hands over her eyes. "I can't look, Big Daddy."

He knew. This would be the second fire she had seen in as many months. With all she'd been through, she was relatively calm, bless her heart.

By the time they arrived, the interior of the house was lit up, windows shattering, beams popping, shingles splintering and flying about, embers rising in almost festive designs, tall flames curling and bursting through the roof, smoke expelled through windows as though breathed by a monster, it seemed so inhuman and hellish, Shell thought. Nearby trees caught and flared like giant candles. He had not expected the wind from the rapidly moving fire, the runaway train sound it made.

In the distant dark, sirens screamed. No fire department would save this house was all Shell could think. It was old, built in the early nineteen hundreds and constructed, except for the stone fireplace, completely of wood. Everything he owned in it, gone. He tried not to cry and put his arms around Shelley who was sobbing. He tried to think of something good. The good flooding his mind was that no one would die in this fire. Another good thing, all be it twisted, he wouldn't have to enter the place alone again. He wouldn't have to sit and be ambushed by the memories again, by the smells. And by the white again.

Watching the house disintegrate, he knew, even at his age, he'd build again. Probably not as big a house, and not in the same place, not on the same old ashes. But, he would build a place for himself and Cal and Shelley. Something that embraced the memories of their pasts, yet freed them from it. That one he'd have to think about, how you free yourself from heartbreak yet stay linked to the parts you love. Perhaps that was something God sorted out for you.

Shielding her eyes with her small hands, Shelley looked up at him. "Big Daddy, my peanut butter and jelly sandwich."

Out of the mouths of babes, the thought spinning from the noel night like a guiding star. He palmed a hand gently over her head and looked into glistening eyes where tears hung. "Thank you, Shelley."

"What for?" she whimpered back.

"For reminding me." Of course, she didn't understand so he followed up. "I'll just bet we can find you another sandwich tonight. Maybe Santa Claus will bring it."

She smiled and blinked, and the tears shook loose. He pulled a handkerchief from his hip pocket. He was about to wipe her eyes, but she took it from him and did it herself, then handed it back. He held on to it. He might need it next.

"I'm sure sorry about this, Mister Shell," Malone groaned.

"It's a shame," added Roosevelt. "And on Christmas Eve."

"A good thing happened on Christmas Eve," Shell said and hugged Shelley.

Malone looked down at her. "It sure 'nough did."

"Yessir, yessir," Roosevelt murmured.

A flashing red light appeared down the road and Shell recognized the Rome Volunteer Fire Department truck, pickups trailing behind it, some arriving from the other direction. He and Shelley sat in the cab of the truck while Malone and Roosevelt got out and ran to help.

"Big Daddy, where will we sleep tonight?"

"Punkin, you know what night it is."

"Christmas Eve," she blurted.

"And what do we celebrate on Christmas Eve?"

There was a brief silence. He could feel her little wheels turning.

Then: "Baby Jesus was borned."

"And where was he born?"

"In a manger, Big Daddy," she said in a scolding pseudo-adult voice tired of the questions.

"And we will find a place to stay tonight."

"Even if it's a manger," she retorted, and snuggled closer to him as the flames from the house began dying under the sprays of water from the fire hoses spread over the lawn.

"We can stay in Little House over there," he said pointing at the guest house, but everybody called it Little House. "Nobody's in it." The small house behind the big house had previously been the foreman's home. It was the house Shell grew up in when his father was the foreman of the then Patrick

Plantation, all of that a history he didn't mind remembering, a piece of his past that started the ball of his life rolling. He and the wealthy planter's daughter fell in love, and one thing led to another. Over the years, other foremen and their families had lived in the small house. Malone may have been the last. Shell and Athen had had it remodeled and renovated for guests.

Shelley nodded but said nothing.

"Big Daddy lived in that house once," Shell said.

"In Little House?" she said pointing to the low slung structure with the long front porch.

"That's right."

"How old were you?"

"I was your age."

She spun around in his lap and looked up at him. "But that's your house on fire."

He was unsure how to respond. The story was too long for adult minds much less a child's. "I just grew up and moved into the big house. You'll grow up and someday live in a big house." He wished he hadn't said big house making it sound overly important but the choice of words probably didn't matter to her.

"Big Daddy, it doesn't have to be a big house. Mommy and Daddy didn't live in a big house."

She'd stunned him again. "That's right, Punkin. Any house will do. Tonight it's probably going to be Little House."

Another fire truck, red lights throbbing, pulled into the yard, the name Tutwiler Fire Department on the side. Tutwiler was a small community just north of Rome. It not only had its own fire department but of the thirteen officers on its police force, one was a bona fide detective he wished had been involved in this investigation. But Tutwiler was in a different county.

Shell and Shelley sat in the warm truck watching firemen yell and dash and scurry as the fire died under their water cannons. All they could see that was left were the stone fireplace, the chimney, and a bare frame rising above glowing ashes and collapsed burning timbers.

Malone and Roosevelt walked back to the truck and got in.

"I wouldn't have thought it moments ago, Mister Shell, but I think the frame of the house may have been saved."

"Some of the floor, too," Roosevelt chimed in.

"But it'll need to be torn down," Shell said sadly.

"We can stay in Little House," Shelley contributed.

"You can stay at our house on the prison grounds," Malone offered.

"Thank you much, Malone, but the foreman's house was good enough for you and your family. It's good enough for us."

"If I recall, Mister Shell, you grew up in that house," Malone said.

"You recall right, Malone," Shell replied. "I have a key with me." He pulled a ring of keys from his pocket. "The heat works and Athen always kept sheets on the beds, just in case."

"Just in case pretty much says it all," Malone said. "Can we help with anything? I radioed the prison, and the security captain put another truck on the rounds."

"Nope, but thanks," Shell responded. "Me and my sidekick here," he hugged Shelley, "have got it all under control." Then, he caught Shelley's eyes cutting on him. "If you have any peanut butter and jelly and bread, Shelley would be mighty grateful. She lost her sandwich in the scramble."

Malone smiled. "I can take you to my place and have the missus fix her one, or we can bring it to you."

"Thank Imogene for us, but if you could kindly bring it to the house, that would be appreciated."

"Thank you, mister man," Shelley said softly.

"There is one more thing," Shell said. "What about the truck. Any reports?"

"Nothing!"

"We'd've heard," Roosevelt spoke up. "Perhaps they went another way."

"Perhaps," Shell agreed. "Evil is a slippery beast."

"They may still be out there," Malone surmised.

"I doubt it," Shell questioned. "You guys spooked 'em."

"You think you're safe in that small house?" asked Roosevelt.

"I think so. There's a twelve gauge Remington shotgun in the house. Cal used it when he'd stay over for dove hunts. I've got a Beretta in the truck, if it's still there." The two men came and went so quickly he wondered if they would've taken time to break into the truck much less bust open the glove compartment. He had had the presence of mind to lock the truck.

"The bad men have guns," Shelley interrupted.

"Thank you, Shelley," Shell responded patting her shoulder, then returned to his explanation. "Athen always kept the place road-ready in case of any emergency. Like you recalled, Malone, I grew up in that house. Might as well live some of my final years there."

"I figure we'll see you in a new place," Roosevelt predicted.

"I like Little House," Shelley joined in as though now she'd become one of the group.

Everyone laughed.

Shell opened the door and got out.

"Need a flashlight?" Malone asked.

Shell pulled out his iPhone and turned on the flashlight. "Besides making phone calls, that's another thing Athen taught me about this gadget."

"We'll be back with the peanut butter and jelly sandwich," Malone said as Shell closed the door. "I wish you'd come with us. I'm concerned about you and your granddaughter staying in that house," he said pointing at the small house near the pecan orchard.

"Bye-bye, mister men," Shelley said waving as the truck pulled away.

They turned to face the big house, what was left of it, and the cleanup operation by the two fire departments. While he was sitting in Malone's truck watching, Shell had thought ahead about the questions he'd be asked, about how the fire started and why he left, discussions Shelley's ears didn't need to hear. This didn't involve her. Then again it did. He had a ready response: "My granddaughter and I have had a long hard day. Come by tomorrow."

He placed an arm around Shelley's shoulder and together they walked toward the small house, the beam of his cellphone flashlight bouncing ahead of them. The last person who had lived there was the man who brought them, the same who would return with a peanut butter and jelly sandwich, and he pondered that irony, that his former foreman, now prison guard, had been their savior.

Little House was dark. The porch creaked when they stepped upon it. Shell withdrew his key ring, fumbled through several keys and stopped on one, Shelley eyeing the operation with profound interest. He opened the door, and a wave of musty, smoky air washed over them. The smoke from the big house had filtered through the crevices. He ushered Shelley in and turned on a light, found the thermostat and turned on the heat. It might take a while, but the air would circulate and be fresh again and pondered that small parable of life.

Next, he went to a small cabinet on the wall in the living area. He pulled out his key ring again, unlocked the tall narrow doors and removed a twelve-gauge shotgun along with a small box of shells.

"Big Daddy, there's lots of those bad men," Shelley said in an advising tone.

"I know, Hon." He contemplated the gun and shells then put them back. "I don't think they'll bother us tonight. They've got a lot of good men after them."

A truck pulled into the drive startling him. He reached for the gun and shells and was fumbling to open the box when a voice called out.

"Mister Shell, it's me, Malone. Got the young lady's sandwich."

Shell put the shell box down and watched the smile crease Shelley's face.

She beat him to the door and opened it. He'd forgotten to lock it behind them and reprimanded himself. He needed to be more careful, think more clearly.

"Thank you, mister man," Shelley shouted with glee and took the sandwich handed to her through the door.

"Don't mention it, Young Lady. The missus was glad to make it."

"Thank you, Malone," Shell added. "And Imogene, too, again."

"Glad to do it," Malone responded. "I'll check back with you tomorrow."

Shelley sat on a stool at the kitchen counter and began eating her sandwich as though there had been no life-threatening interruption. He got a glass from the cabinet and poured her some water.

"I know you like sweet milk with your sandwich, but this is the best I can do."

She glanced up at him. "That's okay, Big Daddy."

Contemplating the shotgun again on the counter, he waited for her to finish the sandwich. He turned off the living room light and led Shelley back to the bedroom where his father and mother had slept, where he had come running when frightened in the middle of the night. Athen had always kept the place ready for guests. They had cleaned her up at the hospital, so a bath could wait. There was a set of pajamas for him in the dresser but none for Shelley. He found a man's white shirt folded in one of the drawers and told her to go into the bathroom and put it on. She emerged looking like something dangling from the shirt. He rolled up the sleeves for her.

"There. Now crawl into bed."

"Aren't we going to say our prayers first?" she said.

"Sure. Would you like to say them?"

She nodded, and he followed her on his knees with folded hands and listened.

"Dear God, bless little baby Jesus who was borned tonight and bless Big Daddy. Bless Big Mama and my mommy in heaven. And, dear God, bless my daddy where he is in the place that will make him better. In Jesus name, Amen."

CHAPTER 29

Shell couldn't sleep. His mind was gridlock, thoughts sailing in, none going out. He felt trapped by forces beyond his control. His home was gone, mysteriously torched, probably by terrorists. They may still be lurking out there, his thoughts swinging again to the twelve-gauge he'd left on the kitchen counter. There would be a meeting he dreaded with the county investigation team. The governor and his wife were coming. He needed to contact the insurance company but couldn't recall its name. Then, there was Cal, the evidence in his favor for his exoneration, but that was going to take time. The governor might have an update, and on his next visit to the prison Shell could bring Cal up to date. Next visit? It couldn't be tomorrow. What was tomorrow? He'd almost forgotten. Christmas Day. He'd try for Sunday and hope the prison was back to full staff.

He didn't want to awaken Shelley and didn't need to lie there staring into the dark. His mind flashed again to the gun. Carefully, he pulled back the covers, swung his legs over the side of the bed and quietly got up. He closed the door to the bedroom behind him and tiptoed in his sock feet down the short hall into the living room which opened into a small kitchen and dining area and turned on the light over the sink. He picked up the box of shotgun shells and read the print. Number 9 shot. If he hit anybody, it wouldn't kill them, but it would knock them down, stop them. He opened the box and removed three shells, pressed two into the magazine, slid the handguard and shucked one into the chamber. He saw the safety was off and flipped it on hoping he wouldn't need to flip it back.

He turned off the light.

He sat on the couch facing the front door and windows, the shotgun across his thighs. The big house was gone. In its place, beneath the glare of security lights, was a mound of dark ash and twisted timbers, curls of smoke still climbing into the air. All that remained was the fireplace and chimney.

He sat staring at all that was left of his home as if he could not accept it was gone. Except for the clothes he wore and items in Little House, all of his cherished possessions—family photo albums, Athen's keepsakes, his clothes and gun collection, cherished memorabilia from his Mexican family—were gone. But he had his granddaughter and his son. He had himself. With those thoughts, he murmured a prayer of thanks.

Christmas morn was a few hours away, and there was no tree, no presents for Shelley beneath it. Regardless where they were in this world, regardless of the circumstances, children should get presents on Christmas morning.

The bedroom where Shelley slept was on one end of the house, a walk-in utility room on the other. He didn't need to disturb her. He hoped she was sleeping soundly with fairies and sugar plums dancing in her dreams and no more ghouls and demons. No telling what was in the utility room. It was worth a look see.

Taking the gun with him, he pushed up from the couch and walked lightly to the utility room. Athen always had it neatly arranged, everything in place. An assortment of mops and brooms, a sweeper and a dustpan hung aligned along the back wall. Shelving along one side of the large walk-in room was filled with blankets and linen and extra pillows. In one corner, a vacuum cleaner that probably hadn't been used in a while, since the last guests. That would have been May of last year when the governor and Mrs. DuBard came for Shelley's first-grade graduation, before the hiatus at the Doom house. Athen had insisted they stay in the guest house. The two highway patrolmen who had accompanied the governor and his wife she put up in rooms in the big house. She'd already prepared the rooms. It was hard for the governor to say no.

In the corner opposite the vacuum cleaner, Shell saw a large box he vaguely recalled. It was the box the vacuum cleaner came in. He opened the top flaps and peered inside. Then he remembered what he was supposed to remember. Athen had purchased the toys from the Salvation Army in Clarksdale for Shelley and other children when they visited with their parents. Inside were a variety—Lego toys, small cars, a miniature plastic typewriter, segments of train tracks and a locomotive with cars and a caboose. He thought of dumping everything onto the floor, but that would make a racket. One by one, he pulled the items from the large box until he was near the bottom then angled the box, so the rest slid quietly onto the floor. Among the toys, one he didn't see when peering into the box, was a dollhouse and a small box complete with furnishings and miniature dolls. He smiled at the house. It was not a replica, but it would do. He'd tell Shelley Santa Claus brought her the house to replace the one that burned. He doubted she'd ever seen the dollhouse. She and her parents had only stayed in Little House once. On most visits, they stayed in the big house.

That accomplished, Christmas morning was not Christmas without a tree. No way he'd go outside, leave Shelley alone, and look for a conifer. He thought. He looked around the utility room, the hallway to the back door where some coats and hats hung on pegs. Nothing came to mind. He looked again at the mops and brooms, how he might tripod them to resemble a tree, hang makeshift ornaments from them, then a thought hit him. He walked back into the living room. There it was in a far corner, almost lost between the drawn drapes and a sideboard. A ficus tree, a gift to him and Athen by a friend who had stayed one night in the house on his way to the coast and dropped it off as a thank you gift on his way back. It was only four feet tall, but Shelley wouldn't care about its size.

For decorations, he rummaged through the kitchen drawers. He found some uneven lengths of red and green cloth strips that were used once for God only knew what, then realized they were knitted strands that had unraveled from an old pot holder. Athen didn't throw away anything. In the same drawer was a small bowl of colored rubber bands that had been wrapped around the weekly paper and saved. Next to them, in an old Peabody Hotel ashtray, were paperclips and beside the ashtray a small plastic spool of Scotch tape. In another drawer, sandwiched between kitchen towels, he noticed some white paper napkins with clusters of red candles in the center and at the corners. They had been used for somebody's birthday and tucked back for another. *Thank you, Athen.* A pair of scissors in a large jar on the counter filled with an odd assortment of knives and wooden spoons rounded out his cache.

He retrieved the shotgun from the closet he'd almost forgotten leaning against the door jamb and moved the ficus tree near the couch. He sat again on the couch, laid the gun beside him, and spread before him on the oval coffee table the variety of odds and ends he'd collected. By pinching two rubber bands together and securing them with paper clips, he constructed clusters of dangling squiggles he attached to the limbs of the ficus tree. With the scissors, he cut the centers and corners from the paper napkins and, using the Scotch tape, dropped them from alternating limbs of the tree. The pieces of red and green cloth he cut into smaller lengths and tied them to the branch ends of the tree.

When he finished, he placed the tree in front of one of the windows. He leaned back and observed his creation and thought it was resourceful and ingenious, even if he said so himself. It was not a Christmas tree, not in the traditional sense. But it was a decorated tree, and it was Christmas morning. It would do. Shelley wouldn't care. She also wouldn't care if her gifts were not wrapped, but a Christmas tree without a wrapped gift beneath it is not a Christmas tree.

He assessed the scraps of his endeavor laying on the table. He thought about what he could wrap and what he couldn't. He couldn't wrap the dollhouse. He could wrap the small box which held its dolls and accouterments. He could wrap the locomotive and cars and caboose separately, six more wrapped gifts he counted he could place beneath the tree. There were four small cars. He wasn't sure Shelley was into cars, but he'd wrap them anyway. With his bright ideas, he had to come up with wrapping paper and eyed several of the napkins left over. They were for a birthday, not Christmas, but it was someone's birthday. Shelley had established that fact. And candles were used at Christmas.

Carefully, he wrapped the smaller items in the paper napkins, secured them with tape, flipped up one of the napkin corners to resemble a bow. He centered the dollhouse beneath the tree and hooked the train tracks together, so they encircled the tree and the house. Shelley would have fun putting the cars on the track and hooking them together. He placed the gifts in a semi-circle around the house.

Again, he sat back, took a deep breath, and assessed his creation. He thought how God must have felt on that sixth day. God, whoever or whatever God was, held at bay, imprisoned eternally by the chaos, the deep, then breaking out, creating life. A special warmth filled Shell, spread throughout his body, rose into his cheeks and around his misting eyes. You can do some things when you put your mind to it, even if it seems your mind is locked and has no place to go.

The gridlock in his head was gone, magically reversed it seemed. This time by forces within his control. He could think only of the lights in a little girl's eyes when she awoke on Christmas morn' and saw, despite the hell she'd been through, that there was a tree and gifts for her and that famous line came to him. *Yes, Virginia, there is a Santa Claus.*

CHAPTER 30

Christmas Morning, Around 3:30

It began.

The perimeter lights went out. Seconds later, the pod lights. Near total darkness. Overlooking one thing, the mastermind behind this ruse—darkness cuts both ways.

Cal listened. He had waited for them, sounds he knew instinctively, boot steps entering, crossing the pod, deliberate and unhurried. By their resonance, only a pair. Was he blessed? Or cursed? Only one person to do the job? Had the stakes gone up? Down?

The air in the cell turned to sludge. His mouth was dry standing on the sink waiting, holding the heavy mirror, breathing air pumped by a heart not his own. He'd not expected his plan to unroll so fast—the key in the lock turning, the cell door opening, pouncing from the sink onto the guard, the guard collapsing beneath him, the mirror gonging on the guard's head. Cal's feet pushing off his back and dashing down the steps and through the first door; pulling the paper wad, door locking behind him; through the second door, pulling that wad; dashing past the rec cages, removing his fleece jacket as he ran, tying it around his waist; fence coming up, leaping, arms and legs dreamlike and light, left foot hitting the mid bar, his body powered upward, hands gripping wire, pulling him to the fence top, to the gap. Breathless, one hand clutching the top bar, he pulled the jacket from his waist and shoved it through the gap. Lights still off. No alarms. Working against time. Everything in one movement, nothing piecemeal, slipping his body into the gap, left arm first, left leg, right hand on the frame bar, stomach sucked in, pulling on the bar, squeezing, all at the same time. Then—something holding him back, shirt snagged. Barbed wire scratching his back. He tried but couldn't reach it. He jumped, cloth tearing, soft rip. Still no lights. Grabbing his jacket and heading into the darkness, toward trees stamped against the night, dark fields stretching either side.

Midway to the trees, the lights came on. Then, the alarms. He stumbled and fell, his heart slamming side to side like a wild bell clapper, hammering in his ears; his breath short as if he'd run a great distance and he'd only run fifty yards. He picked himself up, kept running, energy pulsing through him like a good burn, as if the boundaries of his world had dissolved, the landscape before him limitless. But he knew better, he was running for his life.

He dashed into the hedgerow and slipped on his jacket. Breathing darkness, sawing his arms through dense brush, slapping at branches and dodging trees by sense of feel, clothing catching on brambles and briars, feet snaring and tripping on vines and roots, he uttered, "They oughta put this around prisons instead of barbed wire." Falling, getting up; falling getting up, he kept clawing the tangled foliage until his hands grabbed empty air and he almost plunged headfirst into the Sunflower he heard gurgiling beneath him.

He looked behind him. Prison lights twinkling through the leafage. He could hear the alarms, muted by the distance and his heart beating like a drum in his ears. But no dogs barking. Not yet.

He knew where he was. The Sunflower River meandered due south, and after a few miles State Highway 32 bridged it. He shook off the thought. By the time he reached the bridge, all eyes would be on it. His granddad's place was not far away. Fresh clothes, food, and money were tempting. Another bad idea. He recalled prison outbreaks at Parchman and a few posses he and his dad because their land abutted the penal farm, had been invited to join. Cal knew prison authorities immediately contacted county officials where the escapee's home was located and placed surveillance on the property. In some cases, neighbors were alerted, told to contact local authorities if they cited a fugitive.

Stay on plan, he told himself. The Mississippi River levee was ten miles away. Due west one mile beyond it was Cessions Towhead. Cessions Towhead was a hook-shaped area surrounded by an oxbow lake. On the south side of the lake was an old school bus with a lean-to. Several years ago, his granddad, who had discovered the bus in his twenties, had taken him and his dad to it on a duck hunt. The bus was rusticated and rundown, vacant with no sign of recent habitation. It looked so dilapidated and vermin-infested, most hunters probably avoided it. The kind of place someone running from the law might hole up, his granddad had once remarked.

The last time they had used the camp, almost a year to the day, behind the bus, his granddad, always one for being proactive, had buried an Igloo chest of supplies—canned stew and and pork 'n beans, tins of Vienna sausage and sardines, bottles of water, matches, and toilet paper. To remember where he had buried it, his granddad took out his hunting knife and scratched a letter T after BUS and laughed, "Nobody but us'll know that T stands for treasure."

To get to Cessions Towhead, his granddad always followed State Highway 444 until it T-boned at Highway 1, turned right and went a short distance to the community of Round Lake, turned left there onto Sandy Ridge Road which became a gravel road leading up onto the levee. His grandad then followed the levee road for a short distance and descended the other side. Cal worked the geometry. If he was correct, and if he went on a straight trajectory due west, he would eventually run into Cessions Towhead.

Growing up, Cal had hunted all over this part of the Delta, criss-crossed it in every direction imaginable. In the early mornings, they'd hunt ducks, turkey, squirrel and deer; mid-morning, run rabbits; mid-afternoon, they'd shift to quail and finish off the day at dove roosts. He knew the state and county and crop roads; the rivers and creeks and bayous. He knew the hunting tracks and turkey crossings, the logging trails and fire lanes. He knew where the bridges were, where they weren't. He knew where the fallen timbers, sandbars and gravel washes were. He knew all of this as though it was tattooed on the back of his hand. What he didn't know was how to see the back of his hand in the dark.

Through creepers and vines, spider webs and briars, he moved among the lacerating underbrush making his way downstream looking for a place to cross. Another quarter mile, just above the bridge, the Hushpuckena River joined the Sunflower, and it would be impossible to cross without wading through water waist-high. In the darkness, fallen timbers appeared as pencil lines in a matted lattice of brush. Most were broken, half submerged. He knew some fell across the river. He'd seen them duck hunting. Once, he and his dad had heaved two together so they could walk across, but that was below the bridge. He needed to find one soon, now.

He kept on, his ears alert for dogs barking. If anyone at the under-staffed prison had the presence of mind to get the bloodhounds out of the kennel and put them on his trail, he was doomed. In the prison, the guards had no guns, only pepper spray canisters. But they were given guns, scoped rifles, when going after escapees. Once across the river, he didn't have to worry about the dogs, at least for the time being. He had to worry about humans seeing him. He tracked closer to the bank and began scooping up soft mud and slapping it on his pants, spreading it around his waist. For extra measure, he smeared some across his forehead and on his cheeks, the back of his neck.

Beneath the clear cold starry night, he kept working his way south. There were fallen trees across the river in this area. He saw several angling from the water, none completely spanning it. He looked up and remembered. A tornado had ripped through here last year, stripping the trees, rearranging the land. Against the lesser dark of sky, he could see trees snapped mid-trunk, tops dangling like the broken necks of birds.

He was looking up at the tortured tableau when his foot caught something hard, and he tripped. He pulled himself up. His hands felt and followed something round and long that drew them toward the river. In the dark, it was a long slash. His dad had said similar pipes they'd encountered hunting were PVC tubes for utility lines, but his granddad said they were irrigation pipes. No matter what this one was, it was his ticket across the Sunflower.

He maneuvered down the bank, wrapped his legs around the pipe and began to shimmy across as he and his dad and granddad had done, their guns lashed through their belts across their waists. Halfway across, he heard them. The dogs. They sounded distant. They would come to the pipe and stop. He kept scooting, his feet and bare hands inching him along on the cold pipe.

Once across, he continued clawing through the thick underbrush, thrashing his way out of the hedgerow to get his bearings. He was in a barren crop field, distant lights to his left and right. Isolated houses, field shacks, children about to awaken and see what Santa brought. Overhead, stars sharp in the wintry sky.

He knew to continue west. He was cold but warming as he ran over the uneven terrain, ankles twisting on dirt clods, at times stumbling. He almost fell over an irrigation pivot he didn't see protruding from the ground. If someone took a video of him, they'd think he was drunk, the unsteady gait and erratic lurches. The dark new moon night helped him now but wouldn't when he neared towns and highways. He'd stand out like a ... fugitive.

Ahead, a tree line arcing north. The Hushpuckena. When his dad and granddad found no ducks on the Sunflower, they'd beach the boat and trek across fields to the Hushpuckena. He followed the tree line north staying in the fields where he moved more freely and made better time distancing himself from the prison property.

Ahead, lights. The hamlet of Hushpuckena, a small cluster of trashy house trailers and an abandoned store and gas station. Nearing its outskirts, he reentered the hedgerow and tracked close to the river's bank. Returning to thick brush and brambles, his momentum slowed. But he was camouflaged. The Hushpuckena River crossed Federal Highway 61. Despite less traffic on Christmas Eve, he had concerns about crossing the four-lane thoroughfare. Then it dawned on him. If he stayed along the bank, he wouldn't have to cross the highway. He could go under it.

Past the village of Hushpuckena, the river turned north again. Near State Highway 444 it narrowed, and he crossed it again, this time using a sandbar and gravel bed. Moving across the sandy bottom, his feet and ankles burned from the cold water's frigid bite. But if the dogs were able to get this far, they'd be stumped again. *Thank you, Lord, for rivers.*

He guessed the time was about five o'clock. He had escaped the prison after three. Sunrise was after seven. Another hour of darkness before the sun's first blush. In the flat Delta, once the big bright ball pierced the horizon, it laid down daylight fast.

CHAPTER 31

Christmas Morning

Shell awoke confused, his eyes on a strange ceiling. He smelled smoke and the night's events washed over him. He looked at the clock by the bed. Almost six. What time had he gone to bed? He guessed two, maybe three.

He flopped his arm over the bundle curled next to him, and Shelley mumbled something unintelligible. He got up and patted her. "You keep sleeping, Hon, Big Daddy's going to get up and see if he can find some coffee."

She lifted her head from her pillow, muttered something again he couldn't understand, and plopped her head back onto the pillow.

He scanned the room for his pants then realized he'd slept in them. His shirt, too. He felt for the shotgun on the floor beside the bed. Still there. He picked it up and walked down the hallway to the living room. The sight of the tree and gifts stopped him. If he lived to be a hundred and became senile and demented, that image would be the last beat in his brain, then decided it would be the next to last. The last pulse before he flat-lined would be Shelley's gleeful reaction. He would let her sleep. She'd had a long day and night and, he feared, an even longer twenty-four hours ahead of her.

He went to one of the front windows, pulled back the drapes he had drawn before he went to bed and looked out, at the chimney beneath the security lights, ghost-like in wreaths of smoke a slight breeze lifted northward. Malone was not wrong, at the time, when he said the structure would survive. It eventually collapsed under the water pressure from the firehoses. There was not even a shell of the house. It had burned down to a nest of quaking embers, red sparks still rising and shuddering and disappearing in the last dark before dawn. When a place dies, he thought, a lot of life and memories go with it.

His truck was still parked in the main drive where he'd left it. While

Shelley was asleep, this was a good time to check on the pistol. Quietly, he opened the front door, shotgun in hand and eased the door to behind him. The smell of the smoke was still strong. He walked past the remnant of what was once a beautiful stately home of his ancestors, wondering if the place or the family was cursed.

He headed to his truck and behind it noted the imprint of tracks on the concrete drive. He shined his flashlight on them. Mud tires. Mohawk. The identical aberration in the left rear tread. "Well, I'll be damned," he murmured to himself. "The bastards!" Then, "The sorry bastards."

He unlocked the passenger door. The truck had taken a lot of water, but inside it was dry. He opened the glove compartment. The holstered Beretta 92 was there, an extra clip beside it. He stood in the open door looking at the gun. Another gun might frighten Shelley. Should he leave it or take it? It had a seventeen-round clip in the magazine and one to boot. Take it. They might come back. He removed the gun and the clip from the small compartment, locked it, shut and locked the door. He pushed the gun into his waist and dropped the extra clip in his pants pocket.

Walking back to Little House, passing the smoldering ruins, something large and square and black lodged at a tilting angle in the smoking ruins caught his eye. He swung his light on it. The safe. Records. Ten grand emergency cash. Fire insurance policy. The photocopies of the burned parsonage. If he could open it. He knew the combination by heart. He'd try later. He needed to get back inside in case Shelley woke up.

He stepped onto the porch, the loose boards creaking beneath his feet. He reentered the house and peeked into the bedroom. Shelley was still asleep. He slipped the handgun into the top drawer of the nightstand along with the clip and returned to the kitchen.

"Now that coffee," he whispered to himself.

CHAPTER 32

For two hours he had been on the run, slogging westward through dark woods, crashing through willows, across fallow fields, his breaths coming in ragged gasps, tucking his hands under his arms for warmth. He stumbled onto a gravel road he didn't immediately recall. Until he saw two silhouetted structures, an old silo and shack where he and his dad and granddad had stopped once to eat their sack lunches. The top was gone from the silo, and the shack was leaning near collapse. He didn't know how tired he was until he stopped. *Stop and rest.* The tempting thought flying into his mind and out as fast. *Keep going.* He could see light at the end of the tunnel, if the tracks didn't run out. And they would if he stopped. If he stopped, he'd fall asleep.

Further along the graveled crop road, more abandoned silos and sheds. On his left, an open field; on his right, a hedgerow and the soft rushing sound of water. The Hushpuckena? He'd already crossed it. He didn't know this creek, if it was a creek, the strange harmonics. Had he gone astray, veered north or south? Was he lost? Was his mind playing tricks on him? Surely, he would know a creek near a road he'd hunted along. He looked at the sky, at that chart of the heavens he had learned from his youth. Speaking from the night, the Little Dipper's Pole Star said he was still headed west. He stayed on the gravel road, hugging the hedgerow.

A loud clattering exploded overhead and stopped his heart. Helicopter. He'd been spotted. Then all was quiet; a still universe. Only doves roused from their roost. He released his hand from its clamp on his heart and breathed relief.

He veered from the road into an open field. He was making good time on the road, but feared rousing other creatures of the night lurking in the hedgerows, along the creeks and bayous. Except for the silos and shacks and occasional irrigation equipment, charcoal cows, no other objects on that dark landscape resembled residences or barns or equipment sheds and he questioned again his location. Again, he looked at the sky and stayed his course.

His feet were aching from running over the lumpy turf and his mouth dry from constantly sucking in and expelling air like a fish out of water, but he was not hungry. He was being nourished by two nutrients. He had always preached fear and hope were opposites, that hope trumped fear. Never in his wildest theology had he envisioned them working together. But, on this Christmas Day, they were in sync.

He didn't know how long, it seemed an eternity, he'd been running across the choppy land with no signs of human life, no sign of a highway ahead, no lights either side or in front of him. Then, like a blur, amber lights appeared in the south. The small town of Deeson. Soon after, to the south and north, about a mile apart, halogen security lights. Homes. Outbuildings. Equidistant between them, a small copse of trees. If the emerging lights were not enough illumination for someone on the run, the first blush of dawn was bulging on the horizon.

He knew now exactly where he was. Highway 1 was straight ahead, the levee just beyond it. If he'd gotten his geometry right, once on the levee it was straight shot downhill and another mile to the school bus. The problem was getting across Highway 1 undetected. At least, it was double- not four-lane. The other problem, where to wait until the way cleared for him to cross. He couldn't just stand on the shoulder like a hitchhiker. By now, an APB was out. Law enforcement had been alerted. Anyone with a radio tuned to a local station, early morning disc jockey coming on, would hear the bulletin. In the shawl of night, dawn around the corner, he headed for the copse.

CHAPTER 33

The other grandparents were supposed to arrive mid-morning. He could at least have coffee ready for them. Athen kept the guest house stocked with staples for visitors and family when they came. He had not seen any on the shelves in the utility room. There's got to be coffee somewhere, he thought to himself checking the cabinets either side of the sink and below it.

Reaching for the cabinet above the refrigerator, he heard a commotion outside, vehicles pulling up. He grabbed the shotgun, flipped off the safety and rushed to a front window. Beneath one of the security lights, two highway patrol cars sat in the driveway parked beside his pickup. He looked at his watch. 6:30 a.m. The governor had told him morning, but not this early. The sun was not even up. He again noted the burned ruins, and it hit him. He'd forgotten to call and tell the governor about the fire.

He flipped the safety back on and propped the gun against the window molding. The headlights of the two patrol cars were still on. He stepped onto the porch into their beams and beneath the porch light which had been left on all night and made a sweeping all clear wave with his hand, a gesture to ease concerns.

The headlights shut off. The governor and Mrs. DuBard emerged from the backseat of the first car. A man in a dark suit unfolded from the passenger side of the second. Shell did not recognize him. He was tall and gangly with high shoulders.

"Is Shelley all right?" the governor shouted.

"She's fine, asleep inside," Shell said thumbing over his shoulder.

"Sorry we came so early," the governor said loudly, "But, Dimple was hell-bent to be here before Shelley woke up and put some presents out for her."

"That's mighty thoughtful of you, Mrs. DuBard," Shell said. "It's not much, but I jury-rigged a tree and found some toys and wrapped some presents to put under it."

She seemed not to hear him. Frozen in place and clutching a large shopping bag, she stood transfixed gazing at the smoking ashes, a look of stunned fright on her face. Shell almost didn't recognize her. She was a slim attractive woman in her late fifties with exceptional smooth skin for her age, shoulder length blond hair and makeup that was usually model perfect. The disheveled woman he saw looked thrown together.

"What the hell happened?" the governor bellowed.

"Night riders!" Shell said. "But we're safe," he rushed to assure them. "Shelley handled it well," he said lowering his voice, the hint not picked up by the governor.

"Night riders?" the governor yelled as he and Mrs. DuBard began stepping on the circular stones that led from the drive to the house, followed by the man in the suit and two highway patrolmen in full uniform, Smokey hats and all.

Shell stepped to the edge of the porch to greet them.

"I'm so sorry about your house, Mr. Ferguson," Mrs. DuBard offered, obviously distraught over the scene.

"This is terrible, Shell," the governor added.

"After I brought Shelley home last night, two men drove up. We barely got out. They torched the place."

The governor stopped at the front step, the retinue halting behind him. Mrs. DuBard appeared to tire from holding her bag, and the man in the suit behind her was anxiously tapping his foot as if he felt time was being wasted. The two patrolmen were statues, legs spread, arms folded, faces expressionless.

"And, you stayed here?" the governor questioned skeptically nodding at the house.

"Yessir." Shell went on to describe in greater detail, the governor and his entourage still standing at the steps, the events of the evening, how he and Shelley fled through the back door and across the fields toward the penitentiary, the two prison guards who came to their aid and probably saved their lives. "The house was beyond saving by the time the fire departments arrived," he concluded.

"Those guards should be commended," the governor remarked with authority turning to the man in the suit: "Be sure and get their names."

The man gave an affirming nod.

The governor turned to face Shell, then pivoted again to the man in the suit. "Cavenaugh, that fire needs to be investigated along with everything else on your plate. Whoever torched it is probably tied in with the other reason you're here."

The man he called Cavenaugh gave a thumbs up. He had an intelligent face and short-cropped blond hair. The name had not surfaced in any of Shell's discussions with the governor and the director. Perhaps he's an investigator, Shell thought, the only one they could round up on Christmas Day, then remembered. "Excuse me, but I believe Merry Christmas is in order," he said to everyone through a forced smile.

Mrs. DuBard returned a faint smile, and the governor stepped onto the porch and shook Shell's hand. "Shell, a Merry Christmas to you, too. I don't think anyone would question that the 'merry' could have been merrier. I don't know how you can be so magnanimous with all the hell you've been through."

Releasing the governor's hand, Shell responded. "With all due respects, Governor, given the history, it can't get much merrier with our granddaughter back safe," the words no sooner out of his mouth than a loud, prolonged squeal from inside the house split the early morning air startling everyone, including the two patrolmen who instinctively reached for their guns.

"Speaking of which," Shell said, "Shelley's awake and has just seen the Christmas tree and gifts Santa brought. She'll squeal again when she sees yours," he said to Mrs. DuBard. "Y'all come in," and he opened the door and motioned the group forward.

Shelley was an image of sheer joy examining the items beneath the decorated fica bush. When her other grandparents entered from the porch, she jumped and squealed again, ran and embraced them. Reflecting on his seeing her for the first time, Shell dabbed a tear from his eye. *It's like a resurrection*, he had thought then.

Everyone was eyeing the converted ficus bush and improvised gifts with impressive wonder. The governor began a remark directed at Shell to the effect it was a job well done, and Mrs. DuBard stopped him with a reprimanding glare, quickly stating that the gifts she'd brought had been left by Santa at the governor's mansion. Her message was clear to all adults in the room. This is a child's moment. Don't mess it up.

Her comment didn't keep the governor, who was standing near Shell, from bending his ear and whispering, "Thank God for Pilot. They're open twenty-four seven. You'd be amazed at all the kids' toys in that place."

While Shelley continued gleefully exploring her gifts, the governor, as though waiting for an appropriate moment, crooked a finger at Shell and motioned him toward the hallway. Shell was reluctant to leave the memorable scene playing out beneath the tree, but the grave look in the eyes behind the beckoning finger suggested otherwise, and he followed the governor down the hall to the bedroom.

"I apologize, Governor, for the mess back here. It's not been a typical night."

The governor waved off the comment. "You've had one helluva night and may not know."

"Know what?"

"Cal escaped."

"No!" Shell exclaimed, the shock sucking breath from him.

The governor put a finger to his lips and pointed down the hall.

Shell lowered his voice. "How? That prison was escape proof."

"I don't know," the governor responded.

"When did it happen?"

"Apparently, early this morning. I got the call around four from Cavanaugh Bowen, the investigator who came with us, who got the call from Department of Corrections. My apologies, in all the commotion I neglected to introduce him. Besides being one of the director's key associates, he's been working on the Doom case and another connected to it, one you and I have discussed. Some pieces may be falling into place. Big pieces I can't comment on, at least not now."

"Any word on Cal's whereabouts?"

"They said he headed west."

"That all?"

"The dogs lost his scent at the Sunflower River," the governor continued. "They were taking the dogs to work the other side. That was a couple of hours ago. No word since."

Shell thought. Cal had hunted that land, knew it by heart. If he continued due west, he knew he'd cross the Hushpuckena. If he crossed the Hushpuckena, the levee was next. He had more than a hunch where Cal was headed, where anyone on the run would be headed if they were seeking refuge in a wilderness with knowledge of a buried cache of supplies: Cessions Towhead. For now, he'd keep that to himself.

The governor continued. "When Shelley has finished with her gifts, Mr. Bowen needs to ask her some questions. Do you think she's up to it?"

"She's calmer than I am."

"We can play it by ear," the governor said above a whisper. "Bowen works well with children."

"She works well with adults," Shell quipped. "So well it's a little unnerving at times. She's done remarkably well for what she's been through. I had her checked at the hospital to make sure she was okay, had not been molested."

The governor gave a thumbs up.

They returned to the living room where Mr. Bowen was on the floor with Shelley. He had helped her connect the train cars, and she was pulling them around the tracks going, "Choo choo, Choo choo..." Through the window, Shell could see the two patrolmen on the porch smoking. Mrs. DuBard stood in the kitchen with that ramrod posture pouring coffee into cups she'd also found.

"I located the coffee pot and coffee," she said cheerily.

"Thank you, Mrs. DuBard," Shell offered. He knew her name was Dimple, but he'd never felt comfortable on a first name basis with the first lady. "I was looking for the coffee when you drove up."

"You remember, we stay'd here for little one's first-grade graduation. I may not be the first lady in everything, but I remember where a coffee pot and coffee are." A slight pause, "I also brought breakfast. There was a McDonald's at Pilot, and I picked up a fruit and maple oatmeal for Shelley—"

"Yummy," Shelley shouted on hearing the comment, then quickly returned her attention to her train and interaction with her new friend she called "Mister B."

"—and for the big people," Mrs. Dubard continued, "Egg McMuffins, biscuits, and orange juice."

Shelley shifted her attention from the train to the typewriter, banging on the keys, dinging the carriage back and forth and then turned to the dollhouse. She stopped there long enough to eat her breakfast, fitted in with the others around the small kitchen table, then jumped down and returned to the dollhouse.

The two patrolmen had entered the house and turned on the television with the sound down and began watching ESPN. Shell, the governor, and Mrs. DuBard sat and observed Shelley and Investigator Bowen interact on the floor with the toys.

Shell anxiously awaited for the upward spiral of Shelley's Christmas morning enthusiasm to wind down. He noticed the governor tapping his foot and Inspector Bowen checking his watch. No one wanted to interrupt, but Shell saw a window.

With the friendly help of Inspector Bowen, whom Shelley had decided to call Mr. B, Shelley had furnished the small house and aligned four dolls on the floor in front of her. She was in the process of populating the rooms of the miniature residence.

Shell got up and knelt beside her. "Shelley, who is that you're putting into your house?" he questioned.

Investigator Bowen pushed back to observe. Responding to a gesture from the governor, the patrolmen turned off the television and turned their attention to events on the other side of the room.

Holding the tiny female doll between her thumb and forefinger, eyeing it closely, she said, "Big Mama," and she deftly placed the doll in the kitchen.

"And this man here," Shell added, pointing at another doll beside her, "Who is he?"

She made a small fist around the doll, smiled big and pointed at him. "That's you, Big Daddy."

Shell waited while she placed the male doll in the kitchen beside the doll she'd named "Big Mama." When she had finished, she picked up another male doll. "And who is this?" he asked.

She examined the doll carefully, turned it around a few times close to her eyes. "That's my daddy," and she put him in a bedroom.

Shell had intended to move the play along and was not prepared for the emotion her comments triggered. The profound quiet in the room suggested others were not prepared as well. He needed to finish what he'd started. There was one other doll left, a female. Shell was poised to inquire about it and Shelley, sensing his intent, said, "And this one is my mama." She placed the doll in the bedroom with her father, then removed it. She thought a moment then reached in and removed the one from the kitchen she'd said was Big Mama and placed it beside the one she'd designated as "my mama." She then placed the two figures beneath the tree. "My mama and Big Mama have a new home. They're in heaven."

Shell could hear Mrs. DuBard sniffling behind him and, from the corner of his eye, glimpsed the governor wiping his eyes. But, he had one more question before he stopped the play turned drama. "Shelley, there are some other people over here," he said pointing away from the house. "Who are they?"

"They are bad people," she said angrily and, with a sweep of her hand, scattered them.

CHAPTER 34

Ducking a fierce shuck of briar, Cal plunged into the thicket, and a dog began barking. Another joined in. He froze. They couldn't be prison dogs. The sounds came from the house on his left, not behind him. In the dark, he couldn't see a stick. He waited. The yelps grew louder. For a better view of the house, he pulled back a cluster of vines that smelled like honeysuckle. No lights on. Yet. *Cross the road. Get across the road* his brain hammered to his legs. He kept on, crashing through the brake, branches and saplings whipping past him until they were no more and he stood on the edge of the copse looking at the highway fifty feet away. No need to worry about farmers out and about early. It was Christmas morning. There should be fewer big trucks and traffic on the highway. Most folks would be at home.

A northbound eighteen wheeler suddenly roared past spreading ground tremors. Its taillights faded, then southbound headlights appeared. They seemed far away. The Delta flatness distorted distance perception. The vehicle could be closer. It could turn off before it reached him. He ran other options. The barking grew louder, and he heard the dogs crashing through the brush behind him. He looked back at the house. A light had come on. The lights on the highway were still headed in his direction, but the way was clear. "It's now or never," he whispered to himself and dashed across the double-lane, through a canebrake on the other side and into an open field, running for his life toward the levee. The dogs were still barking but fading. They'd been trained not to cross the road, or the lights he thought farther away were approaching and spooked them. He'd dodged that bullet. There were times in life when the pluses and minuses canceled out each other and kept a person on track.

The Mississippi River levee was constructed of compacted soil and clay and rivaled in length and height of the Great Wall of China. In spring and summer, the color of its sodded flank was green. In the pre-dawn December gunmetal light, it was a long dark wall. He scampered across the short distance to its base and continued running full tilt up the grassy slope, his shoes sinking softly into the turf. Mounting the last pitch of the long climb, a flurry of shadows stopped him. Deer. He'd forgotten they grazed along the grassy slopes. There'll be more on the other side, he thought and began assessing the dangers ahead.

He had forgotten about traffic on the levee. A well-maintained single-lane gravel road stretching from Memphis to New Orleans was used by the Army Corps of Engineers, farmers, and hunters. He'd seen no lights, but hunters could enter the road at several points and without warning. He knew turkey and small game seasons had closed. But, deer season with dogs began December 24th. *That was yesterday. Dogs.* He'd have to deal with them again. Hunters, too. They'd be on the levee road and in the rich hunting lands, up in tree stands waiting for anything that moved. Some rode horses behind the dogs. Be his luck to escape from a maximum security prison only to end up shot by a trigger-happy kid trying to bag his first buck. And he was headed to a hunting camp. He hadn't thought that far ahead. Plan A unraveling by the second. No plan B. Maybe one would come to him on the fly. He'd gotten this far on a wing and a prayer.

He recalled the days of his youth, the thrill of standing atop the Mississippi River levee. On one side the rich cultivated Delta fanning in every direction straight to the horizon. On the other, a jungle-thick markless wilderness of wild boars and panthers and alligators. Everything this time was reversed. Behind him, dangers. Ahead, a sanctuary.

Peering east, he saw no lights. The light he had seen in the house was off. Someone just checking on their dogs. He had seen no one. He heard a rooster crowing somewhere below, but nothing else, no dogs. There was a burning in his chest, in his throat. Burrs and beggar's lice stuck to his socks and pants leg, briars on his coat. His legs had been cramping, and he kept having to stop to rub them.

The breaking half-light of dawn had a calming effect on him, and he thought of one positive among all the negatives. No mosquitoes or snakes. Anyone considering escape from a Delta prison, had to do it after first frost.

He knew where he stood was the closest point on the levee to the river a mile away. He knew this portion of the levee bulged into an S with the shape of the river and that he was standing in the middle of that S, on its down slant. He knew near that point was the imprint of a road, one he and his grandfather had taken that led to Cessions Towhead. He squatted on his haunches and waited. The long reach of dawn spread farther across the sky, and he saw, not far from him, two ruts angling down the levee. Through a light fog, he descended the dirt trail.

Behind the levee, it was still dark, only a hint of dawn. At the bottom of the dirt trail was the old cattle gate he recalled that had no fence. He asked his granddad why someone would put up a gate without a fence. His granddad said at one time there might have been a fence and it deteriorated. Or, he mulled the conundrum, it might have been placed there to mark the pathway, so it could be seen from atop the levee. That was the more logical reason.

Cal stepped around the gate, and a high sharp bark stopped him. He took a couple of steps and heard it again, the bark this time like a tear in the air drawn out into a scream. "Fox," he murmured, the whispered word riding his frosty breath. A red fox warning of danger. He'd heard the eerie screech often when hunting. This one came from the south of him. He was headed west. He waited longer, then continued on, the fox apparently satisfied. He didn't hear it again.

He was following fresh truck tracks superimposed it seemed over larger tracks he could not decipher. Probably deer hunters on the first day of the season. He needed to be careful, keep his ears alert. That would be his luck, hunters see his orange jumpsuit and arrest or shoot him. Then it hit him. That's the color they wore to avoid being mistaken for a deer and accidentally shot. The story he would tell fell into his lap. If caught, he was deer hunting, fell into a creek, lost his gun. He rehearsed it. Better not get caught.

The school bus was a mile away. There were two ways to get to it. Take the truck path, a straight shot to Australia Landing, then hike a few hundred yards to where the bus rested on the banks of the Cessions Towhead oxbow. Or, at a dead sycamore he and his granddad used as a landmark, take a right fork that looped in a wide semi-circle to the front of the bus. His granddad had surmised the second path had been created by whoever brought the bus in and, after disuse, the tracks faded.

Crouching, Cal moved slowly, heels down first, eyes peering left and right for the little he could see in the grainy light, the fog thicker in the bottom and the dawn, not yet cresting the levee wall behind him. The tracks led through a long dark corridor, a palisade of trees shrouded in mists. The silence was eerie.

Given the holiday and new moon darkness, it was doubtful anyone along the route he had taken had sighted him and called authorities. But it was not impossible. A light had come on in the house facing Highway 1. Then, there were the prison dogs. He had crossed two rivers. At the Sunflower, the guards would have taken the dogs to the other side and picked up his scent where he got off the pipe. They would have more trouble following his scent at the Hushpuckena and problems again at Highway 1. For now, fragile darkness, thanks to the levee wall, prevailed. He was safe. On that hopeful thought, he continued farther into the dense river wilderness, a world of its own, his raised eyes following the receding hem of the night over the treetops, squinting up into dark branches backlit by gray sky, scanning for the ghostly pale sycamore.

CHAPTER 35

"Shelley, what do you remember about the place where you were?" Mr. B asked softly as he placed a doll in the miniature house. He had removed his coat and rolled up the sleeves of his white shirt and was laying on his side, his head propped on an elbow. She sat on her knees across from him, the dollhouse between them.

She glanced around the room, relishing the adult attention she was getting—Big Daddy, her other grandparents and the inspector. The two patrolmen had adjourned to the rockers on the porch.

"It was on a river, " she said meekly as though telling a secret.

"Tell me about the river, Shelley," Mr. B prodded. "Was it big, little?"

She moved her head from side to side, her small forehead furrowed with deliberation. "It was different," she responded.

"How was it different?" Mr. B asked.

"It was a river, and it wasn't," she said throwing open her hands, a look of dismay on her face. "It didn't move. It just sat there."

Cutoff, Shell thought.

"Shelley, tell us about the river that didn't move,"

She picked up one of the male dolls she had knocked down, brought it close to her face as if it might provide an answer, then set it back onto the floor. "It had boats on it."

"Can you describe ... " Mr. B started and checked himself, "Tell me about the boats. Were they big, little?" he asked, obviously trying to keep his questions open-ended.

She spread her arms wide. "Big."

"Were there people in the big boats?"

"No. There were boxes. Men were putting big boxes in them."

Shell's anxiety jumped a notch. He recalled what the headline agent Chase had shown him; terrorists blowing up bridges.

"How many people were there at this place?" Mr. B asked after a brief pause, allowing her time to move a doll.

"Sometimes lots, sometimes not lots."

"In other words, you'd see a few people, then at other times you'd see a lot of people," Mr. B verified.

She nodded. "Mostly not a lot, except last night."

"There were a lot last night," he validated.

"Yessir."

"Shelley, could you hear them talk?" Mr. B asked.

She nodded again, shifting her posture, so she was sitting cross-legged, leaning forward and listening.

"Do you remember anything they said?"

She thought a moment. "Some things."

"What were some of those things?" Mr. B pressed.

"I heard the word 'money' a lot."

Bowen rolled his finger for more.

"And 'little girl,' and, oh yes, x something. I can't say it."

"Explosive," Shell interrupted louder than he meant.

"Yes, Big Daddy," she exclaimed bright-eyed with discovery.

The governor leaned forward from his chair. "Did any of these people hurt you?"

"No Granddaddy. Aunt Gracie wouldn't let them."

"Who was Aunt Gracie?" the governor injected.

"She took care of me. She didn't have a gun."

"Did other people have guns?" Mr. B resumed his interrogation.

She looked down at the dolls on the floor she had scattered. "Everybody except Aunt Gracie did."

"Shelley, did they shoot the guns?" Mr. B followed up.

Her eyes opened wide. "Yessir," her head pumping up and down. "They shot them at each other."

Mystified, Bowen sat up. "Did they hurt each other?"

"No sir. They shot colors."

"Wargames," the governor injected parenthetically.

The inspector nodded and added. "They also shoot real ammo."

The comment was insensitive, Shell thought as he observed Shelley, her head down and eyes watering. The governor must have thought so, too, as he opened his mouth and, out of character, closed it.

The investigator continued. "Shelley, did you see anyone you recognized, anyone you had seen before?"

This time, the governor couldn't resist. Casting a hard look at his MBI agent, he intervened. "Shelley, Hon, you don't have to answer that if it's too upsetting."

Her head was still down, her eyes scanning the dispersed dolls as if for distraction. "I want to, Granddaddy," she said with a fierce look. "I saw the men who shot my mama and Big Mama. They were mean to them." She became animated and stood up as if to act out what she'd seen. "They grabbed my mama, like this," she said angrily, making a circle in the air with her fists, the movement pitching her slightly forward. "Big Mama hit one of them with a lamp, and they shot her with a gun. Mama broke loose from them, and one of them shot her." She stopped and sat down, breathing heavily as though she had fought the battle herself.

There was a long silence. Everyone else in the room knew the rest of the story. She didn't need to go further. The governor and Mrs. DuBard were both visibly shaken. Shell fought back tears, his thoughts, too, on her father, where he might be, if he was still on the run or captured. Radios were in the patrol cars. The inspector or patrolmen on the porch could find out. Why hadn't he thought of that? He'd ask when Bowen finished with Shelley.

Mr. B leaned in close to Shelley, a cautious look on his face. "Shelley, did both of the men have guns, or did they just one have a gun?

She held up a finger. "One."

"Thank you, Shelley," Mr. B said, "You're a sweetheart, a very brave sweetheart," and with that turned toward the governor.

"Your Honor, should we take a break?"

"Shelley," the governor said, "Do you want to stop for a while and rest?"

She looked at the tree, the toys around it. "Grandaddy, when we're through, can I play?"

"You surely can," the governor responded with a tight smile.

"Okay. Then let's don't stop," the indication she didn't want her play interrupted.

Mr. B shifted his posture on the floor, the expression on his face suggesting he needed a break if no one else did. "Shelley, tell me about the place where you stayed by the river."

Shelley screwed up her face and pinched her nose. "It stinked."

"Shelley, when you say 'it'" Mr. B probed further, "What was 'it'?"

"Where I was," she responded.

"What was it like, the place where you were that smelled bad," the inspector gently pressed, attempting to break the six-year-old's circular logic.

"Well ...." She tilted her head to one side and placed a finger on her cheek, a gesture mimicking deep thought. "Like my school bus."

Shell almost came out of his chair. The governor and the investigator didn't know it was Cessions Towhead. They were asking too many questions. Maybe agent Chase hadn't passed that information along to MBI. Cal was heading toward a hornet's nest. Shell tried to remain calm and listen as she answered questions about the school bus. But, his face was hot and his heart hammering in his chest.

"Shelley," Mr. B leaned in closer to her, "was it yellow like your school bus?"

She nodded it was.

"Was there more than a school bus at this place?"

She gave another single nod.

"What else?"

She steepled her hands. "Tents."

"What kind of tents?" Mr. B pursued, Shell increasingly uncomfortable with the investigator's dogged persistence.

She glanced up at Shell. "Like the kind I camped out in with Big Daddy and Big Mama one time."

Shell had almost forgotten. That was two years ago. Shelley was four years old. Cal and Sally were attending the church's annual conference, and Shelley had stayed two nights with them and two with the grandparents in Jackson. He had pitched the big camping tent he and Athen had used touring the country the summer before. They had cooked hotdogs and roasted marshmallow over a fire he had built.

"How many tents were there, Shelley?" Mr. B continued.

"Lots," she exclaimed, again spreading her arms.

"Bowen, ask her the size of the tents," the governor injected.

"I'm getting there, Your Honor," he said casting another annoyed look at his boss.

Shelley looked up at her grandfather. "There were two big ones, Granddaddy."

Ask her what was in the big ones, Shell thought, impatiently about to ask her himself.

"Shelley, could you see inside the big tents?" Mr. B continued.

"I didn't have to look inside, I could see outside."

Bowen glanced back at the governor. "The flaps were up."

"Must be," said the governor agreeing.

"Shelley, what was in the big tents?" Mr. B continued.

"Under one was big boxes."

"How big?" Mr. B pressed.

She stood, raised her hand over her head. "As big as me."

"Were these the ones people were putting in the boats?"

"Yessir. But there was lots of 'em."

"What was under the other tent?"

"It was a bigger tent."

"Could you see what was in it," Mr. B persisted.

"Yessir. There was two of them," she said.

"What did they look like?" Mr. B kept on.

She sat back down and thought, her forehead wrinkled with effort. She looked around as if searching for something to help her answer the question. Bewildered, she threw up her hands. "I don't know how to say it."

Inspector Bowen glanced up at the governor, then Shell as if looking for help. The governor rolled a hand for him to continue.

Flipping a page on his notepad, Mr. B said, "Shelley, I'll bet you like to draw."

She grinned broadly. "Yessir," and she glanced up at Shell. "Big Mama taught me."

Shell recalled those nights Shelley would stay with them and, Athen, an artist in her own right, would get on the floor with her sketch pad and Shelley watched as she outlined familiar objects—horse, car, house, tree. Then Shelley would try, her grandmother carefully guiding her hand. One night, when Athen couldn't find her brushes, she chewed the ends of wooden kitchen matches. Side by side, the two swabbed them through the colors on Athen's palette and painted. Over time, Shelley's copies of her grandmother's drawings became clearer and sharper, the water-coloring more controlled and within the lines. Shell looked on proudly as Inspector Bowen handed the pad with his pen to Shelley.

"Mister B, do you have a pencil?"

He looked in his coat pocket. "I'm afraid a pen is all I have."

Heads turned, eyes scoping. Mrs. DuBard found a pencil by the telephone in the kitchen and handed it to her.

"Thank you, Grandmama."

Mr. B continued. "Shelley, draw me a picture of what you saw under the big tent without the boxes."

She put the pad in her lap.

"Shelley, you can come to the table and draw," Mrs. DuBard offered.

"That's okay, Grandmama. I can draw sitting down."

With everyone else, Shell was leaning in close to observe. He'd forgotten she was left-handed as she manipulated the pencil between her thumb and fingers and began slowly drawing, stopping and reviewing, flipping the pencil and erasing, starting again, occasionally moving one hand to the side of her head to push her hair away from her eyes. With intense focus, she drew two arcs. She leaned back then forward then, after a lengthy pause, connected the arcs. She did the same in the space beside that drawing, drew two arcs, then connected them. For several minutes, she scrutinized her work, a look on her face that something was not right. She flipped the pencil in her hand and erased the point at one end, repeated the procedure on the other figure so that both, side by side, had a pointed front and blunted end. She looked up briefly at Mr. B, held up the pencil, and said, "They look like a pencil, but they're fat," and handed the pad back to him along with the pencil.

Everyone was leaning in, looking, trying to decipher the art work.

"Looks like two blimps, to me," the governor said.

"Huh?" Shelley reacted.

"Big balloons in the sky," her grandaddy DuBard clarified his comment.

The "Huh" still shaping her mouth, she looked around at the others.

"She wouldn't know what that is," said the inspector then stated he needed to take a break and stepped outside onto the porch. Through one of the windows, Shell could see him making a phone call, a short call, and he was back inside.

The governor took another stab. "The camp being next to the river, more logically it would be two submarines, all be it, small ones."

His wife smothered a chuckle with her hand.

Well," he exclaimed testily, "Dimple, can you do better?"

Sheepishly, she shrugged her shoulders.

Everyone seemed stumped.

Everyone, except Shell Ferguson who was beside himself. He wasn't sure until she erased the rear points, flattening them, and decisions forked in his mind. He could inform the trigger-happy governor or call agent Chase or both which would place Cal in a crossfire.

Or...

Don't even think it.

But he thought it again.

He needed an excuse. Thoughts raced. The ruined scene out the window tripped a wire. He stood up. "You folks carry on with Shelley. I've got to call my insurance agent about the fire."

He went to the bedroom and simulated a call to his agent, loud enough to be overheard: "Meet you where?" Pause. "When?" Pause. "Right now?" Pause. "Be right there."

He lifted his hunting coat from the trunk at the foot of the bed where he had laid it the night before and put it on. He stepped to the night table, opened the top drawer and retrieved the Beretta. He unholstered the gun and slipped it into the coat's side flap pocket and deposited the clip in the other matching pocket. He returned the holster to the drawer. He glanced in a closet mirror. The pockets bulged slightly but not enough to raise any questions. He returned to the living room. "Sorry to have to leave you but my agent wants me to come to Clarksdale and meet with him about the fire."

"On Christmas Day?" Mrs. DuBard exclaimed dismayed.

"Yessum. He said with any fire the sooner, the better." He didn't make that up on the fly. If the parsonage fire had been assessed sooner, there would've been a different outcome.

Shelley's hand shot up. "Can I go with you?"

"No, Punkin. You stay here with your granddaddy and grandmama DuBard and Mr. B and the two officers," he nodded toward the porch where the two state troopers were smoking. "You'll be safe. Enjoy your presents. I shouldn't be long." He knew he was lying.

"Before you go, Mr. Ferguson," Inspector Bowen said, "I have just one more question for her."

Anxiously, Shell stopped at the door.

"Shelley, everyone in this room would like to know how you were able to run away from this place."

"Oh! That's easy," she said bringing her small hands together in a single soft clap. "I asked Aunt Gracie to play hide-n-seek with me."

"And?" Mr. B questioned.

She threw up her hands in a V and grinned. "I won," she exclaimed, her voice light and playful.

While everyone else was awash with amazement, Shell was out the door. He acknowledged the troopers and quick-stepped to his truck. If he could only reach Cal before he got to the others. Or they got to him. He glanced at the fuel gauge, the needle pushing EMPTY. He could get there.

The question was getting back.

CHAPTER 36

Dawn breaking, first blade of light crests the levee, striking the sycamore bone pale amid ink-black slashes of trees and tangle of shadows. Cal had been following deep cleated tracks made by wheels larger than a normal size pickup. He imagined someone had driven a caterpillar or backhoe into the bottom. Someone building a lodge. Army Corps of Engineers constructing a berm.

At the sycamore, he stopped.

Morning light fell through the bare tree branches shattering the sky.

A scent of fear in the air, in the sounds he heard. A flock of sparrows flushed up from the brush startled him. A slight wind scuttled across the woodland floor rattling dead leaves, making empty scraping sounds. Dead grass around him thrashed softly. Then a noise like someone scraping a fingernail across a blackboard, a high mad squeal. He stopped paralyzed. Wild boar. They ran out of breath quickly but their razor tusks, if they got to you before you shimmied up a tree, could take off a leg. Or a bottom panther's caterwaul. Then he heard clucking and breathed easier. Turkey.

At the fork, he could go straight or turn right. The tracks took a sharp right. He pondered his decision, which way to go, his objective the bus, the cooler behind it. He turned right.

About a half mile from the sycamore, before the trail curved toward the oxbow and the bus, he stopped, his tongue licking dryly at the corners of his mouth. He couldn't tell if the rattle of whispers he was hearing was his own raspy breathing, his pants brushing together, steps crunching, scraping of leaves in the slight breeze. Or something else.

Something else.

Muted mumbles.

Frogs maybe or turkeys gobbling.

He continued along the wide tracks more visible in the developing light.

More disturbing. Was the school bus still there? Had it been carted off? Demolished? Had the ground around it been scraped and leveled for new construction, that worse case scenario coming to mind along with another. The cooler gone. What would he do then?

He clenched his teeth to still them. He wasn't sure if they'd begun chattering because he had stopped running and the morning chill was taking over. Or he feared what he was about to find.

He continued on, slowing to a creep, one foot in front of another, trying not to make any noise in the dry twigs and leaves. The sounds grew louder, less jumbled, breaking into distinct phonics and he knew then he was hearing the rising and falling cadence of human voices.

Deer hunters he thought. But deer hunters, before the first glimmers of dawn, would already be on their stands. They wouldn't be talking. Behind some scrubby oak and small brush, he dropped to his hands and knees, then flattened on his belly and began crawling on the cold ground. No one could see him. And he couldn't see them. He smelled wood smoke but saw no fire.

Farther along the trail, the voices became clearer, accents discernible. Had he heard them before? He listened, to voices he didn't recognize. To what they were saying. If they're not hunters, what were they talking about so excitedly, because there seemed an urgency to their rural jabber?

He raised up slightly. One hand, one knee at a time, he inched closer.

The trail began to arc.

Mid-way into the trail's curve, flickering through the misty veiled light and black paling of trees, he saw the fires, several of them. He was close enough to see the sparks soaring upward through the overhead limbs and hear the burning wood popping and crackling.

Cautiously, slowly pushing himself along on his elbows, he listened, hoping their talk covered any noises he made. A couple of squirrels made a sudden racket leaping between two trees. Not far from him, a blackbird landed and strutted, rustled its feathers then flew away.

He inched closer.

CHAPTER 37

Shell Ferguson knew the prison mindset. He knew the twenty-four seven plotting that went on. He knew all about escape routes, contingency plans, backups. He'd been there. And he had more than an inkling the route his grandson would take. Cal knew the lay of the land, the memorized geography of his youth. He had hunted it since he was a boy. He would know to steer clear the main roads. He would know to thread his way through the canebrake and foliage along the bayou and creek banks. Orange jumpsuit or not, he would know to travel at night in the new moon dark and hole up from dawn to dusk. He would know all these things, but he would also know there'd be a posse with a pack of bloodhounds breathing down his neck. He would know how far he was from the levee, work that calculus which might cancel out holing up somewhere. It might mean not stopping but staying on the run, following the bayous and rivers and crop roads and field trails. Regardless of the options, Shell knew the boy's destination. Question was, could he get to him before he stumbled into a revolution brewing at Cessions Towhead.

He pulled out onto the Baltzer-Rome Road that ran east and west, then immediately turned right onto the Clay Ridge Road, the route he always took to the prison to see Cal. Approaching the southern perimeter of the posted prison property, he turned left onto a dirt crop road. The road ran due west parallel the Coahoma-Sunflower County line for a few miles, dog-legged through a maze of fields, abandoned silos and shacks before making a southward loop rejoining the Baltzer-Rome Road and, via a network of county roads, to the small hamlet of Hushpuckena.

Hushpuckenna was due south of Duncan where he would turn left onto Highway 444, a short straight shot to the levee. If he had guessed right, he was on Cal's tail, maybe a stride ahead. He glanced at his hands gripping the wheel, at a vein that throbbed then stared out at the unchanging scenery in the foggy drab Christmas dawn.

Driving fast would eat up more gas, but he didn't have a second to waste. He was hoping Cal had not made it to the levee. He would have to cross two ankle- and knee-deep rivers, two highways, one of them four-lane, not to mention the new moon pitch dark, feeling his way around marshy bodies of water and through dense hedgerows and the creeks they lined. If that was not enough, there were open fields and farmhouses, dogs.

Maybe, he'll get caught, that thought briefly crossing Shell's mind. Chances of that on Christmas Day, slim to none. People too preoccupied. Unless the prison bloodhounds picked up his scent. Crossing two rivers and highways would slow that down. If he escaped early morning,—fingers counting on the steering wheel—Shell might beat him to the levee. Cal would recognize his truck on the levee. Then, he thought of what was brewing beyond the levee. In all of the confusion over Shelley's return, the governor and investigator's arrival, he'd not thought to pull either or both aside and tell them of his visit with the FBI agent two days before. Probably just as well. If the MBI didn't know what an FBI agent had shared with him, there must be a reason. The governor liked the spotlight, and the last thing the FBI needed was media exposure.

He tried Chase's cell number again and the same message flashed on the screen.

He was nearing where Highway 444 T-boned with Highway 1. In the distance, like a long gray wall, loomed the levee. Left and right across the dreary plow-ribbed fields he scanned. No sign of Cal. Wearing orange, unless he somehow changed clothes, he'd be easy to spot. Maybe he'd already been captured. But by who, the prison gang or the other outlaw gang? A horrifying thought, he was trapped on Cessions Towhead and caught by the militia. Worse than that, the negatives piling up, he was executed by the radical mob that killed their wives. Nothing worse than that. He drove on.

He encountered little traffic, no official vehicles in search of an escapee. At 441 he turned right, still no sign of Cal on or atop the levee slopes. No sign of anyone, which was a good thing, he thought, as he came to the intersection and turned right onto Highway 1. Less than a mile up the road, at Round Lake, he would take a left onto a gravel levee access road. Did he want to do that, put his white truck in full view on the levee road? Or park on this side, hike up the levee and down to the school bus? Approaching the turn, he ran the options through the hopper. He wouldn't stand out. There'd be other trucks, hunters. Time was everything. He needed to get as close as he could to the school bus, be prepared to hightail it out, hopefully with Cal. He could park at the dead sycamore tree. He patted the gun in his pocket.

The gravel road came up sooner than he'd expected and he turned. On the left was a farmhouse, nothing stirring except some chickens outside. At the foot of the levee, he shifted into second gear and climbed the incline, gravel pinging the undercarriage.

Atop the levee, Shell questioned again if Cal was ahead of him or behind him? From the glove compartment he pulled a pair of binoculars he kept there for overseeing crop work and spotting deer and wild prey. From north to south he panned. The clouds were scattered and high and still. The only movement, was a lone semi going south on Highway 1. A few cattle moping in a pasture below. No sign of orange, not a flicker. He hoped Cal was behind him. Sooner or later, he'd have to cross the levee. Unless he already had.

Shell decided to drive on. He had nothing to lose. And everything to lose.

He guided the pickup onto the narrow dirt road angling down the river side of the levee. He steered around the fenceless cattle gate and stopped. Overhead, crows were making a cawing racket in the tree branches.

Mid-point between the levee and Cessions Towhead, the sycamore was about a half-mile away. Should he drive that far? He thought for a minute, considered the two options and continued in the truck tracks toward the sycamore. If he ran into trouble, he could drive out faster than he could run to it parked at the gate. If he got into a shootout, he'd rather have the truck nearby.

He drove on, slowly, cautiously, puzzled over the two sets of tracks he was following. One was normal pickup size superimposed on another with wide, deep treads. Maybe heavy equipment. Maybe to clear land for lodge construction. Or for moving something heavy and he thought of Shelley's drawings and the discussion with agent Chase. They are huge, weigh a ton and a half each.

In the distance, like lightning frozen in a web of black limbs, the old sycamore came into view, always easy to spot in winter, its bare ashen limbs giving the sky a cracked appearance. The tree had always fascinated him. He had wondered why it was dead. Sycamores lived forever. They loved moisture and certainly had plenty beyond the levee. Perhaps it was swamp-rotted, or killed by a disease or lightning struck, or some unnatural freakish twist of nature. The tree looked like a bleached arthritic claw rising from the wilderness dark.

He continued toward the sycamore. Atop the tree, like a lone sentinel, a crow crouched. He stopped at the tree and turned the truck around, so it was headed back toward the levee. He pressed the door to quietly and locked it with his key fob, The crow pushed off and with slow strokes of its wings, was gone. Don't need to announce myself. He stood still and listened. The crow cawing. Further away, a low rumbling, a barge's throaty diesels straining upriver.

He scanned the ground. Cal would've been wearing his velcro sneakers—flat soles, no heels. He would've known to stop where the trail forked at the sycamore and turn right. He would've known that if he went straight, he would've ended up by Australia Landing, near the reentry of the Cessions Towhead oxbow loop into the Mississippi.

Shell kept scouring the ground, his eyes sweeping back and forth. He was about to move forward, then saw, inside the left large tire track, impressed over its raised tread, a right shoe print. *Didn't think to look inside the tracks.* A stride away, another, then another, his eyes sliding further up the trajectory, observing the same pattern in continued succession. He placed his size eleven boot beside the print. The owner of the shoe wore one size below. Cal wore a size ten. "Damn!" the exasperated whisper flying from his mouth into the chill air like something ripped.

In the right truck track, faint in the dust, a small print, sock foot, several in sequence pointing the opposite direction toward the levee. It had to be. Bless her heart.

CHAPTER 38

Through the gloom of canebrake and dormant wood and shadow, the first thing Cal saw was the oxbow, some ducks skimming the surface, quacking. The voices he'd been hearing were louder. He smelled coffee and caught a whiff of frying bacon. Then the sun came smoking up through the mist over the levee behind him, the moving edge of the levee's receding shadow falling lower, a dark blade sliding incrementally, revealing the world in new light.

He blinked. He blinked again. Not at the school bus he was used to seeing. But at a village of camouflaged tents and lean-tos scattered through trees where kerosene lamps hung. At a huge Confederate flag hanging from a tall pine pole. At men in camouflage sitting around fires, rifles slung over their soldiers, clusters of three and four wheelers scattered about. Deer hunters he thought at first. Maybe they'll leave. But these were not deer hunters. They were not leaving. He might be in for a long wait. If he could last that long. He was thirsty and weak, exhausted, maneuvering on adrenalin.

Through the ragged edge of trees in the fog-lifting dawn, beyond an assortment of clothes on a line between two tents, like humped beasts crouching. He almost didn't see them—a large tow wrecker and flat bedded truck and several wide-bodied pickups, one with a raised cab. That explains the tracks. He sensed he'd come upon a rough, wild bunch, bad toughs, as his eyes swept more of the startling scene.

Sitting low in the still waters of the oxbow, partially hidden by the school bus, he saw several large pontoon boats—five he could count—canopied with camouflage tarp and brush. Adjacent the school bus were two big camouflage tents, side flaps up. From the tent nearest the bus, men were carrying large crates and loading them onto the pontoons. The crates had labels he couldn't decipher, not from where he lay fifty yards away. He couldn't imagine the contents of the crates and why they were being loaded onto pontoon boats in an oxbow that emptied into the Mississippi. Cargo perhaps for a barge

240

rendezvous destined further down the river. But, why not at Australia Landing near the mouth of the river? And why all the camouflage? All the guns? Had he stumbled onto the prep stage of an assault? But, against what? Whom?

As long as he laid low and on the tire path behind underbrush, he could not be seen or heard. Unless someone came over the levee. Time was not on his side. The prison guards knew how to work the hounds. Sooner or later, by trial and error, the dogs would pick up his scent, that thought sending a chill through him. He would hear them coming, but he was boxed in. Unless, he could make it to the cutoff and swim to the Arkansas side, that plan not realistic.

His attention was drawn to the other larger tent, twice the size of the first one. Its front and side flaps were up. A partial view suggested two large objects. Crawling closer, the objects slid into clearer view. A chill ran through him. He'd never seen one not attached to the wing of a plane. But there they were, two of them. Jet engines. His heart raced.

He stopped crawling. He had gone as far as he could. Ahead, near the trail, was a campfire he'd not seen. Around it were three people sitting side by side, their backs to him. The two on the outside were tall and broad-shouldered; the one in the middle short and slender. They were talking. He could see the pale puffs of their speech but couldn't make out what they were saying. The two on the outside sounded gruff and raspy. The middle voice didn't fit. It had an inflection pitched higher, with an edge. It sounded familiar. He turned an ear, held his breath. A branch blocked his view, and he shifted to his right. The voice wore a floppy camouflage hat, blonde hair curling beneath its brim. It was a woman. The man on her right turned to say something to her. Cal thought he'd seen him. She turned to respond and the two profiles Cal glimpsed grabbed his throat.

No wonder she lied.

CHAPTER 39

Shell continued following the tracks. In the distance, to his right, in pale-slatted gray light coming through the bare trees, he could still see the levee. Shouldn't be any traffic on it this time of Christmas Day, he thought. Deer hunters already in the woods. But there was the prison posse. He'd been on posses before, helped the penitentiary search for escapees—they often crossed his fields—and its dogs eventually, after some dead ends, found their man. Only a matter of time before dogs locked onto Cal's scent and Shell would hear them howling, leaping over the levee. He needed to find Cal first before he stumbled into a hornet's nest at Cessions Towhead.

In the long reach of the morning behind the levee, all was quiet, a massive silence, like dawn before battle. Every few steps he'd stop, listen. Too quiet. He could hear his held breath. He could hear his eyelids blink. Squirrels he had heard splashing among the leaves were silent. The barge he had heard earlier had moved on. Sparrows and titmice and chickadees he had heard chittering and seen flitting in and out of the brush had vanished. The only sound, dead grass rasping dryly in a breeze that was picking up, blowing toward the river. The only sign of life, a hawk high overhead drifting on a thermal. He wished he could be that hawk, see what it saw. The bus. The activity. Cal. He thought of his cell phone. What if Chase returned his call. He pulled it out and thumbed it on vibrate, closing that door.

He couldn't move too fast. A twig or fallen limb stepped on would snap like a firecracker. It was that quiet, the woods that loud. For years, he had hunted in them and never known them to be this dry. Normally, it rained in the Delta in November and December, long, slow, steady rains. He hadn't checked lately, but the last rain he recalled was before Thanksgiving, before the parsonage fire. He caught the faint smell of woodsmoke and hoped it was a campfire, one well protected. This brush and timber would go up in a flash.

He would be hunting in these woods today if not for circumstances. Then, the thought occurred to him. He was hunting all right. For something wilder than wild game. Wilder than a nightmare. It may be the most important hunt of his life, maybe his last. He pondered the peril. An old man and his young grandson he needed to reach and rescue, a fight that might start before the good guys could get to it, if that was still the plan he'd last heard from agent Chase.

The sun was rising higher, rapidly burning away the ground-hugging mist, warming the air. He could see more clearly. Others could see him better, too. At least he was wearing dark clothes. He checked the gun in his coat pocket. The safety was on. The spare clip was snug in the other pocket. Thirty-four rounds. He hoped he didn't need any. Besides this handgun, the only other pistol he had ever owned was a Navy Colt which he had swapped with a warden for his freedom from a Mexican prison in Matamoros. In his entire life, he had never shot at anyone, only used the Beretta for target practice. He thought about why he was where he was and all that had happened over the past year. The good book said, "Thou shalt not kill." In less than a heartbeat, he could kill the scumbags who killed his wife and daughter-in-law and ruined his grandson's life. He could use all thirty-four shots and not waste a one. At his age, he was still a good shot.

He neared the bus and began to hear a patter of voices, garbled and indistinguishable, all talking at once it seemed. He crept closer along the trail. He saw the bus. He saw the two large tents next to it. He saw camouflage tents and shelters scattered through the woods as far back as he could see and pontoons on the cutoff lake behind the bus. He saw the antique flag that belonged in a museum, men dressed in camouflage moving large crates onto the boats. He shifted further to his right to see what was under the other large tent and what he saw caught his breath. *Shelley got it right.*

He moved further along the track, a sharp eye out for Cal's orange jumpsuit. They'd had a signal they used to locate each other in the woods. It was the call of the Barred or Hoot Owl—*who who who-whooo, who who who-whooo*. With a wry smile, Shell's father had said the sound was *who cooks for you, who cooks for you.* There were Barred Owls all through these woods. To distinguish their call, he and Cal added an extra who ... *who who who who-whooo ... who who who who-whooo.* He hadn't used the signal in a long time, but he knew the pitch. It required little from his vocal cords, more from his lungs. He cupped his hands around his mouth to soften the sound—*who who who who-whooo ... who who who who-whooo.*

CHAPTER 40

Who who who who-whooo. Who who who who-whooo. The sounds came haunting from the wilderness quiet. It couldn't be, Cal thought. Or could it? Would his granddad have known of his escape? Probably not. But the call came again—*who who who who-ooo...who who who who-ooo.* It came from behind him, not far away.

Scurrying around, most in the camp didn't notice. Except the trio seated around the fire. Cal ducked lower as they turned their heads. The man on the left stood up, turned and looked. Cal was sure now. He was one of the guards who'd assaulted him, the one who sat on him and hit him. No wonder there was just one. He'd never forget that hatchet face, the hatchet-mind with it. The man on the right turned and looked into the woods, confirming the profile Cal had seen moments before.

The guard sat back down, flipped a hand at the other two as if to say it's just a hoot owl.

Cal heard the call again. It came from up the trail toward the levee. He looked back at the three sitting, talking. Answering the call this close might draw more attention. But, if it was his granddad, he needed to respond. It had to be him. No Barred Owl would have made that sound. Nobody else would've used it. Cal turned, faced east, cupped his hands around his mouth and softly echoed the call.

This time, the guard stood up, said something to Sadie Doom and the warden, and pointed. They turned and looked. The guard took a step into the brush, then another sweeping back briars and brambles with his rifle barrel. Cal could hear him coming. He froze. He didn't dare move. He was trapped. Damned if he did and damned if he didn't. Dead if he'd stayed in the prison, dead on the run. Death was the magnate pulling him through life. His executioners were yards away. He didn't have a prayer, but prayed one anyway, for a distraction. For anything.

CHAPTER 41

Shell heard the call. It came from nearby, ahead of him. He continued along the truck path. Entering the bend where it arced, he saw, thirty yards ahead, Cal crouched behind a bush, a man in camouflage whacking back underbrush headed toward him. Behind the man, two others in camouflage with floppy hats sat before a fire. They appeared to be detached from activity around the bus and disinterested in the man's movement. None could see Cal. Not yet.

The next thought came in a flash. The wind brisker, still blowing toward the river. The area was a tinderbox. With all the campfires, he was surprised the woods were not already ablaze. A small collection of leafy debris nearby caught his eye. He pulled out a Bic, flicked it, held the flame and thought. *Do I want to do this?* Dynamite in the area, some nearby, enough to blow all of them to kingdom come. Bad idea. He shut the flame and returned the lighter to his pocket. He looked around, saw nothing he might use for a diversion. Except himself.

The man was getting closer to Cal. Shell saw the rifle he was using to beat back the underbrush. He reached in his coat pocket and pulled out the Beretta. He kneeled, popped off the safety, propped an elbow on one knee and stiff-armed, his finger on the trigger, aimed. The first shot needed to count. Whether it did or didn't would incite the entire camp—a hundred or so he'd estimated. In the seconds that followed, they wouldn't know the source. By the time they figured out what was going on, he and Cal could beat a retreat to the truck and make it over the levee. The pickup had at least enough gas to do that. Struggling to keep his arm still, his aim steady, feeling the trigger curl lightly beneath his finger, he waited.

Suddenly, the man stopped. He yanked off his floppy hat and looked up.

Shell heard a noise. A moth fluttering in his ear? The sound grew louder. The gun still aimed, Shell strained to see what the man, stopped in his tracks and head tilted back, was trying to see. The whop-whopping grew louder.

Then, in the northern sky, a glittering speck, its whirling metallic blades strobing the sun's early morning level rays.

Shell was unsure what to make of the helicopter, whether it was passing over or stopping. The man still in his gun sight seemed equally puzzled, gazing up at it, his comrades doing the same. Shell shot a quick glimpse at them, his eyes back on his target, then the double-take, the faces. He lost his stance and almost dropped the gun. "I'll be damned," he murmured to himself. He wanted to shoot both of them.

While the man was hightailing it back to Sadie and the warden, legs leaping over the brush, the copter was circling, hovering, lowering, pivoting. Shell saw what the others had seen, the letters on the side of the copter—FBI. Everyone heard what came next. A voice from the copter loudspeaker: "This is the FBI. You are surrounded. Stack your weapons. Surrender. Hands on your head. You will not be harmed. Again, you will not be harmed." A few seconds later, the announcement was repeated, again and again at intervals.

Shell flipped the safety on but kept the gun in his hand. He called out to Cal, but Cal couldn't hear him. A second copter had joined the first, the noise deafening. He gave up trying to get his grandson's attention and made a beeline for him.

Shell placed a hand on his shoulder. Startled, Cal spun around, and mid-swing of his fist cried out, "Granddad!"

CHAPTER 42

The camp was astir. Men exploding from tents, assessing the sky, running helter-skelter with rifles, tossing gear clanging into truck beds, cranking pontoon motors. Automatic rifle fire pinging, ricocheting off the copters, guns firing from the copters. From the north, a rumble of traffic.

"FBI's comin' in on the Australia Landing road," Shell said, and he thought of the map he had drawn for agent Chase, questioned if that was his voice he'd heard over the loudspeaker. No wonder he didn't answer his phone.

"Look!," Cal whispered loudly pointing at a flotilla of gun-turreted US Coast Guard boats rounding Cessions Towhead where the oxbow joined the Mississippi.

Shell saw the warden and Sadie and the other man running toward them with rifles. "We've got to get out of here" he said. "Truck's around the bend."

They headed up the trail.

"Halt!" the warden yelled. "Or we'll shoot."

They continued running.

The sycamore and pickup came into view. They picked up speed, Shell was huffing and puffing with pain flaring in his hip. Cal saw him limping and put an arm around his waist. It was a race to the truck before they were fired upon. They jumped into the cab and slammed the doors.

"I've got enough gas to get us out of here," Shell shouted to Cal, as he started the truck.

"Out of here works," Cal shouted back, his head down watching his granddad slumped in his seat gunning the motor like a race driver, hands stiff-armed on the steering wheel.

In the rearview, Shell saw the three who were chasing them rounding the bend, rifles shouldered. One shot blew out the rear window. Another Cal's side mirror. Bullets pinging and ricocheting, glass shattering around them, the gate a quarter mile away.

CHAPTER 43

Shell fishtailed around the gate and floored the accelerator. Tires spun, caught traction, and up the incline they sped, sailing as though airborne, bouncing onto the levee road.

It seemed they had crossed a boundary from one world into another, the sky behind them crumbling in destruction; the one ahead bright and calm. They could hear explosions and the roar of motors in the distance, but no one had followed them, not yet, Shell thought, nervously glancing in the rearview.

They descended the levee and Shell eased his foot off the accelerator. Approaching Highway 1 all seemed normal for a Christmas morning. Except the wind whistling through the rear window where it had been blown out and shattered glass all over and around them. He shuddered to think what would have happened if the FBI had been an hour later. Bridges were blown up. Cars sailing into the river. People killed, drowned. River traffic at a stand still.

At the intersection of Sandy Ridge Road and Highway 1, Shell stopped, hooked his seatbelt into place. He'd forgotten in the hectic rush. Cal followed suit. They turned right onto the state highway paralleling the levee, near the place where Shell had picked up Shelley, as good a place as any to break the news to Cal. He might go into shock, but the only way sometimes to break good news is the same as breaking bad news.

"Cal, Shelley did not die in the parsonage fire. She's alive."

Cal's head snapped around, a stunned jaw-dropping look on his face. "What!"

"Shelley didn't die in the fire. She was found alive last night."

"Oh ... my ... God!" he exclaimed covering his face with his hands half-laughing, half weeping. "My God!"

"I felt the same but I need your head up, eyes alert. No telling who might be behind us." He kept expecting a white wide-bodied pickup with a raised cab to come barreling over the levee.

Cal lowered his hands and looked at his grandfather, tears streaming down his cheeks. "Where is she?" he said, his eyes glistening. A chip of glass hung briefly to one cheek then fell.

"She's at Little House with the DuBards."

"The DuBards?" Cal blurted eyes still wide.

"They drove up from Jackson," Shell responded, his eyes on the rearview. "She's okay,"

"How'd she get to Little House?"

Shell jerked a thumb over his shoulder. "She escaped from back there." They were coming up on the 444 intersection. "It was about here two hunters found her walking south in her sock feet," Shell said and told how one of them called the house phone, that Shelley had been taught to memorize the number by her grandmother. "I can't imagine if she'd still been there and you stumbling onto her, the mess that would've caused."

Cal remarked. "It's miraculous these people spared her."

"They needed her," Shell said. "She was a shield. If she hadn't escaped, she might be dead. If we'd been caught back there, we'd have taken her place."

Exasperated Cal asked, "How'd you know I escaped?"

"Governor DuBard," Shell answered. "Mississippi Department of Investigation had been notified. An MBI investigator was with the governor."

"You knew I'd head for Cessions Towhead."

Eyes on the road, Shell nodded. "Yep. The cooler. Supplies. I imagine you're famished, not to mention thirsty."

He nodded. "I'm more tired than hungry or thirsty."

"You can rest soon. There's a bottle of water in the compartment. Help yourself."

Cal opened the compartment between them, retrieved the bottle, screwed off the cap and took several long swallows. "Granddad, you were right. As long as they thought I knew something, I was valuable." He told him about the succession of notes about jets. "I played it out as long as I could. When I couldn't dodge anymore, I was a dead duck." He told him about the beating in prison, the trip to the hospital, the threats. "I knew another assault was coming and I probably wouldn't live through it. The man with the warden and Sadie was one of the guards who beat me."

"So you were the other Ferguson at the hospital," Shell said.

"I don't understand."

Shell told him about taking Shelley there and the nurse's comments about several Fergusons.

"Shelley was okay?" Cal asked.

"Except for a slight cold and some scratches."

"I can't imagine what she's been through," Cal said.

"How'd you get out?" Shell asked. "The place was supposed to be foolproof."

"It's complicated, a long story," and, for the first time, a tremulous smile.

Shell was intrigued but didn't probe. He'd hear the rest later. There was no traffic on 444. For a while, they rode and said nothing, Shell's eyes scanning the flat landscape for a posse with bloodhounds.

Cal broke the silence. "Shelley alive! I can't believe it," he said with emotion. "Just can't believe it. Thank you, Lord," and continued mumbling that mantra.

"She's one tough, brave little girl," Shell said. "If it hadn't been for her, we wouldn't be having this discussion. You wouldn't be in this truck." He cast a grave look at his grandson. "You might not even be here, period," and he told about the MBI inspector, his questioning of Shelley, what she'd told him and his probable alert to the FBI. "Unwittingly, she pulled the trigger on the terrorists' plans. She escaped. They couldn't get her back or kill her. They had to move."

Another stretch of silence. The emotional impact of what was happening, both seemed at a loss for talk. Shell leaned over, turned on the radio, got a local station from Clarksdale playing Christmas music, let it play a while, then turned it off.

"Why'd you turn it off?" quipped Cal.

For a second, Shell didn't answer. He wasn't sure himself. "Thought I might get some news. Those thugs back there were going to blow up something big."

"I think those crates they were putting onto pontoons, did you see them?—"

Shell nodded.

"—were explosives. And the two jet engines." He was animated now leaning in towards his granddad, "No telling what they were going to use them for."

"They were poker chips for bigger game," Shell said, and he related what agent Chase had said about the history of the jet engines, their theft, the ad in the New York Times and the Central American connection. "Doom brokered a deal, in the millions, between Aryan Nations and probable foreign terrorists. The Arkansas bunch came to collect. Doom reneged. You stumbled in on that deal gone bad," he concluded.

"Granddad?" Cal said exasperated and confused, "How do you know all of this?"

"Let's just say the FBI and I have become friends. They think I'm Matlock," he said turning and grinning. "Joking aside, the FBI came to me via the governor's office based upon my independent investigations. By the way, in addition to the other information their agent provided to me, a recent ballistics report confirms your innocence," and he updated Cal on the two spent bullets found in Doom's residence.

"Oh ... my!" he reacted. "What I can't get over was Sadie Doom in there among them."

"That's one I finally figured out," Shell mused.

"It's a little clearer now why she lied on the witness stand."

"She didn't lie just to protect someone," Shell offered, "but something much bigger."

"Aryan Nations?"

"Yes, that, but something even bigger. A movement. Christian Identity. A domestic terror network. I think she was the Queen Bee of this cell and using her church job as a cover. Just like Aryan Nations hiding behind a cross topped by a crown, like Christian Identity behind that religious label. I'll bet if you peeled back the onion skin of her life, you'd come across thick layers of racism, anti-Semitism, and white supremacy. May I have a swig of that water?" Cal handed the bottle to him, he took a long swallow, eyes on the road, and handed it back. "You'd find that her father was a founding member of the all-white Citizens Council, that he was involved in the Klan. I did some research. Sadie's father, Samuel Swift, was arrested once for simple assault against a civil rights worker. Blacks boycotted his business in Indianola. He had to close it down. Add all that up and top it off with the fact she was a looker and seductive. The jet engines of note were on her father's land. I checked into it. The deed was in his name, never transferred to his daughter. Everything you saw at that camp could be traced back to Sadie Beatrice Doom. She was one angry human being. This was payback time."

"But I thought Ty Doom was the kingpin."

"She used him, too. She used his friendships. He and the warden went all the way back to football days at Delta State. The prison you were in is on land once owned by Doom. He sold it to the state and used his influence to get his friend, John Culpepper, appointed warden. That gave him a base camp for terrorists. Sadie was probably behind all of that, too."

"So it was the warden Sadie was having the affair with," Cal said astonished.

"That's my read."

"And he double-crossed Doom."

"Or Doom double-crossed him," Shell said. "He discovered that his wife was having an affair with his good friend, that triangle dating back to college days. And those jet engines were at the center of it." Shell went on to tell him what the FBI agent had shared with him about the discoveries at Doom's house in his safe and in the wine cooler.

"Looking back, that might explain the lack of followup on the parsonage fire and the bungled investigation surrounding my conviction," Cal said.

Shell raised a finger. "And the reason you were transferred from the county jail to the prison county jail unit, then into a segregated unit on the false premise you might be suicidal and needed protective custody."

"They could keep a better eye on me," Cal said.

"Absolutely," Shell exclaimed.

They were coming up to the intersection and the route home. Time had rushed along, speeded up and was now slowing down as though unnoticed. Shell removed the gun from his coat pocket, the clip from the other. "Better put these back in the glove compartment," then withdrew them. "On second thought, maybe not," and he returned them to his coat pockets. "This crowd never gives up. They keep coming back."

The truck barreled on, Shell nervously eyeing the gas gauge, needle quivering on empty.

"I need to give you a heads up," Shell said a little wearily, his voice grave. "The place is not gonna look the same."

"How's that?"

"The house is gone," Shell said.

"Gone?"

"Burned to the ground."

"How?"

Shell flipped his head back. "The thugs back there. They got eyes and ears everywhere. Somehow, somehow mind you, they learned Shelley was with me at the big house. We barely got out. That's why she's at Little House. It's what's left."

Groaning, Cal bent over and again covered his face in his hands. When he raised up, he was smiling. "Like father, like daughter," he said.

Shell returned the smile. "Never thought about it till now, both of you escaping at the same time. She is going to be very excited to see you."

After a pause, "What does she know?" Cal asked.

"Her mother told her you were in a place that made people better."

He thought. "Some it does. Some it doesn't. One for sure it did."

"Your friend, Chris."

"Yes."

Shell gave him a second head's up. "The MBI investigator is at Little House along with two highway patrolmen. The investigator knows about your innocence. The two patrolmen may not. To them, you're an escaped fugitive. What do you want me to do? I can take you to another place until things die down."

"No!" he almost shouted. "I want to see my daughter. If they arrest me, they arrest me."

CHAPTER 44

To avoid shocking everyone, Shell called ahead to the governor to inform the gathering at Little House that he was a few miles away and had Cal with him.

"You what!" the governor shouted into the phone, loud enough for Cal to hear.

Shell repeated.

"How the hell!"

"Hell is what we've just come through," Shell said. "Can't go into it now, but you might tell Shelley that Santa Claus has a big surprise for her."

"Great news, Shell, great news. I'll tell her," and they hung up.

"My father-in-law is a touch bombastic," Cal said.

"A touch," Shell agreed.

As they neared, Cal saw the ruins of the mansion. "Oh, Granddad," he whispered, almost inaudibly. "Oh my!" he uttered louder, then saw Shelley on the Little House porch, a retinue gathered around her as though for a photo op and he began pinching his nose, fighting the tears.

The driveway was a good hundred yards off when the truck began sputtering.

"We're outta gas," Cal said.

"Yep," Shell said as they coasted and he turned into the drive. "How's that for timing."

Cal didn't respond. Shelley was running toward the truck, "Daddy, Daddy," beaming and crying at the same time.

Cal jumped out. A flood of emotion propelled him toward his daughter who slammed into his legs with a force that rocked him on his heels. Scooping her off her feet, he swung her around, kissing her cheeks and hair. "Shelley! Shelley!" He held her at arm's length to see her better, the bright smile, the tears, as close as he would ever come to seeing pure joy, then pulled her close again.

"Mommy's not here," she said, and he almost lost it, clutched her tighter as if to smother the sobs erupting deep within.

"I know," he whispered into her ear. "But she's still with us."

Everyone watched quietly. Shell was concerned about the reaction of the two patrolmen seeing Cal in his orange prison garb, if they would rush to arrest him and slap cuffs on him.

Cal put Shelley down. She grabbed his hand, and they walked to the house, his orange jumpsuit bright in the morning sun. Shell introduced him to Inspector Bowen and to the two highway patrol escorts whose names he'd forgotten, but the governor readily supplied. The officers, in the dark about events, felt awkward and cautious. Instead of shaking hands, they nodded, heels of their hands on their guns.

The governor stepped forward and embraced Cal and said, "You've been through a lot."

"Hope it's about to stop," Cal said softly.

"Soon," the governor said. "We can talk later."

Mrs. DuBard stepped forward and gave Cal a hug whispering in his ear, "We've never lost faith in you," and he shook slightly, almost wept again.

"That means a lot," was all he could manage, the multiple times he'd almost lost faith in himself flashing across his mind.

Inside, the mood was celebratory, not just for the return of Cal but another drama being played out miles away beyond the levee. Shelley kept pulling on her dad's hand, steering him toward the door and inside where she began showing him all the nice things Santa Claus brought to her.

"Yes, Hon, Santa Claus knows you are very special," shifting grateful eyes at his granddad.

Dimple DuBard asked Cal if he wanted some breakfast, that she'd brought Egg McMuffins and biscuits.

"I'm famished, Miss Dimple," he replied. "That would be wonderful."

"I've also got some orange juice," she added.

Cal gave her a thumbs up.

The two patrolmen seemed in a quandary what to do about the escaped prisoner in their presence, but Inspector Bowen mouthed it's okay, and they stepped outside.

Shelley pulled her father down to the floor beside the tree and began showing him the dollhouse and her other gifts, her voice as gleeful as if nothing bad had ever happened in her young life. *Except ye become as a child.* Shell stood there taking it all in, all the blessings that, at this moment, eclipsed all that had been lost. He thought about that, how the word "all" threaded his thoughts when not long before the word "nothing" had summed it up.

Shell took the opportunity to pull the governor and Mr. Bowen aside. They stepped out onto the porch. The patrolmen were leaning against their patrol car smoking. Shell recapped for them what had happened, what he'd discovered over the levee, the war camp, the arrival of the FBI and at that point looked at Bowen. "When Shelley was being questioned, and you stepped outside—" He left the sentence unfinished.

Bowen nodded but said nothing.

"Well, it saved the day," Shell said.

"Shelley and your grandson saved the day, Mr. Ferguson," Bowen responded. "You were in that mix as well. Agent Chase updated MBI on what you'd shared with him. Shelley confirmed what had been passed along to us."

"Would you believe it? Sadie Doom, the queen bee of this outfit, was there with the warden." Shell exclaimed.

The governor and Bowen exchanged glances. "I'd believe," the governor said knowingly.

Dismayed, Shell said, "You been holding out on me."

"We weren't certain," Bowen said, "Only suspected, based upon information you and your grandson were feeding to us, her visit to the warden in disguise, putting it all together and it spelled domestic terrorism."

"Inside job," the governor interrupted. "It began to make sense, why Cal was transferred from the county jail in the county seat to the county jail in the prison, then into solitary confinement."

"We figured as much," Shell said.

"We knew, based upon what Cal had told you, that a domestic terrorist group had infiltrated the private prison." Inspector Bowen continued with some annoyance he'd been preempted. "After the arrests are made, and after the interrogations and investigations, it's going to be very revealing to see how far and deep and wide into the body politic the tendrils of that cancer penetrated, a plot, no one would have guessed, whose epicenter was a private prison."

The governor jumped in again. "Those terrorists were the largest gang in that prison. Makes one wonder who was running the prison, the warden or Aryan Nations."

After playing with Shelley on the floor and devouring two Egg McMuffins and a tall glass of orange juice, Cal expressed he wanted to see Sally's grave. "I understand she was buried in the private family cemetery on the property," he said somberly.

"I wanna go. I wanna go," shouted Shelley.

Shell froze. He'd had a marker placed there, next to her mother, her name on it with birth and death dates. "Hon, you need to stay here with grandmama DuBard."

She pouted. "No! I want to see my mama, too."

"I think she's earned it," the governor said, unaware of the other marker.

Shelley clapped.

"It's just not a good idea," said Shell. "I can't go into details."

"I agree with the governor," said Cal swapping glances with his father-in-law.

Shelley clapped again.

Shell started calculating. He could get there ahead of them and remove the small stone or turn it over. He could tell her the truth that he thought she had died in the fire. He could just say nothing and hope she didn't see it, hope she didn't recognize her name. Finally, he said, "OK, let's go," deciding he'd come up with something.

Shelley jumped up beaming and clapped again. Anyone seeing her, Shell thought, would never know she'd been through more hells than most people face in a lifetime.

The family cemetery was in a small copse of cedar trees and a large sycamore a hundred yards from the compound. As word of mouth had passed down over the years, originally it was in the peach orchard behind the house. Athen's grandfather, the first Patrick, bought the place in 1912. He had the graves dug up and moved to the woods some distance from the house, presumably to make room for Little House. The woods were later cleared for more cotton acreage so what remained now was a patch of earth having been plowed around all those years. The gravestones of Shell's mother and father were there, others, too, arranged in the order of their generations. He had once cataloged those generations, worked the arithmetic, the representation in total years lived of all those buried there. Over six hundred, he'd estimated, several hundred more if he counted the ones in Mexico who fled with Confederate General J. O. Shelby and Jefferson Longstreet who died in Cuba with the Rough Riders. When he finished, the sum total surpassed a thousand years, not including his own meager seventy-nine. What remained, what it all came down to, was a square-footage of Delta earth near equal the summation of years. Inscriptions on the tombstones were barely legible, weather-blackened chiseled names and dates, filmed over with moss and lichen, so the ones recently placed stood out.

As they neared the plot, hoping to get there first and pull up and turn down Shelley's stone, Shell walked quickly ahead. But Shelley broke from her father's hand and joined him, still reviewing his options when they reached the small wrought-ironed fenced plot. The sagging gate squeaked as Shell opened it for Shelley and Cal and he followed them, closing the gate behind him.

Cal paused at his Big Mama's grave. Shell observed him as he read the name—Athen Patrick Ferguson—then the dates. Adjacent to it was Sally's grave, a marble, double-tombstone with her name—Sally DuBard Ferguson—and her dates and beside her, his name and his birthdate. He let go of Shelley's hand and knelt, covered his face and Shell watched as Cal's body trembled and shook. Shelley reached down and grabbed her father's hand, knelt beside him patting his back with her other hand. The scene was about all Shell could take. Shelley had not yet seen her small slab. Then—

"That's my name," she shouted pointing at the small white marble upright beside her mother and father's tombstone.

"I'm sorry, Punkin," Shell said awkwardly. "Big Daddy thought you'd died with your mama." He knelt beside her and gathered her close to him. Fighting back tears he said, "We're glad you didn't. Big Daddy just hasn't had time to take it down."

"That's okay, Big Daddy," she said sympathetically. "It's Christmas," her little arms squeezing his waist.

Over her shoulder, he could see Cal folded over Sally's grave, hands covering his face, quietly weeping.

Shell patted Shelley on the shoulder, stood, and looked away toward the distant tree line to hide his emotions. At first, he thought the glint he saw was a spark of sunlight filtering through a tear. He blinked and it was still there, moving, like a light flickering. Then he saw them, three figures carrying rifles emerging from the trees, moving rapidly across the empty fields toward them. Alarm swept through him. "Get down, Hon," he said pushing Shelley so she was sprawled beside her marker. Cal looked up, saw what his granddad saw, and lunged across her.

Shell pulled out the gun still in his jacket pocket and stepped behind the sycamore near the graves. He pushed off the safety and fired three shots into the air to alert those at the house. Shots from the three approaching them rang out. Bullets smacked into the sycamore, thudded into the ground, cracked off tombstones. Shattered chips of marble and bark flew around them. Shelley began bawling, Cal trying to comfort her. Shell kneeled, aimed and began firing, short bursts as he ducked back and forth from behind the tree. The next time he snuck a glance and fired, he saw only two. One down. He'd lost count of the shots and pulled the clip from his coat pocket, laid it on the ground beside him. He looked over at Cal and Shelley peppered with marble and bark fragments. He moved to fire again and heard shots from behind him. Both highway patrolmen, guns raised, were standing at the edge of the peach orchard. He peeked around the tree. Three lifeless clumps lay on the ground in the open field.

"We got 'em," one of the patrolmen shouted.

"I think it's safe now," Shell said to Cal and Shelley. "But let me make sure." He stepped from behind the tree and immediately felt the sting in his leg. He stepped back as the patrolmen fired another volley then began walking slowly toward the three bodies, guns in aim, fire position.

"We'll take it from here," one of the patrolmen yelled.

Shell said nothing but gave a thumbs up, then looked down at Cal and Shelley. "Shelley, everything's okay now."

She looked up whimpering, "Thank you, Big Daddy."

Cal, unconvinced, continued hovering over her.

With the gun at his side, Shell stood, his heart thumping while he breathed the smells of cedar and cordite, musing at the ironies. Their lives had been protected by tombstones, and they were lying across Shelley's grave, beneath it an empty coffin for a child. He wouldn't dig it up. But the marker he would destroy.

Of the three assailants, the warden and the guard were dead. The guard was shot in the chest and the warden through his head, that shot later determined to have come from Shell's Beretta. The only one still alive was Sadie Doom.

Unbeknownst to everyone, investigator Bowen had called ambulances.

"Big Daddy," Shelley said pointing at his leg, "There's blood."

They were walking back to the house.

"It's just a graze," he said. "A scratch. Nothing barbwire hadn't done before."

"I know something about a barbed wire graze," Cal said and showed them the one across his back. Later, he would tell the rest of that story.

CHAPTER 45

Mid-morning, ambulances from Clarksdale arrived, followed by two MBI investigators from Oxford. Sadie Doom was rushed to the Clarksdale hospital then medivacked to The Med in Memphis. She was in critical condition, gunshots to her left leg and one through her neck, the latter thought to be self-inflicted, an unsuccessful suicide attempt. At this point, there was no clear evidence or indication she was directly responsible for, or directly linked to, the parsonage fire and the deaths of Athen and Sally Ferguson and abduction of Shelley. But if she was the queen bee of the domestic terrorist cell, as Shell and others had suspected, she was essential to any investigation, the information she could provide possibly a swap for the lesser sentence she might be offered.

Shell stood and watched as the bodies of the warden and the guard were examined by the MBI duo and EMT medics before bagging and tagging them with instructions they were to be taken to the city morgue in Clarksdale to await identification by next of kin. *If any existed*, Shell reflected. Their guns, AK-47s, were confiscated. No wonder bullets were flying everywhere, he thought. It was a miracle any of them were alive.

On the porch, Shell and Cal were interrogated by Inspector Bowen and the two investigators. They answered basic questions, with the understanding they would be available later for a full recap of the day's events and the aftermath. Bowen told them, "MBI Director Holifield might drive up from Jackson, tomorrow or the day after, depending upon his schedule."

Late morning, Mrs. DuBard ran water for Shelley in the bathroom and gathered her clothes. Shell had found a t-shirt for Shelley to wear until her clothes had been washed and dried. Cal had showered in a utility room where he used to clean up after working in the fields or hunting. Shell had provided him a set of clean clothes and said he was going to burn the prison suit.

They were in the small living room—Shell, Cal, Shelley, the governor, and Mrs. DuBard. Shelley was back on the floor in front of the tree pulling the toy train on the toy tracks going, "Choo Chooo, Choo Chooo."

Amused, Cal was sitting in a chair near her and went, "Who, who, who, who-whooo. Who, who, who who-whooo."

Shell laughed.

"What was all that about?" the governor humorlessly inquired.

"Inside joke," Cal said looking up at him and smiling.

"Those of us on the outside," Mrs. DuBard said, "are intrigued. Tell us more."

Shell provided the backstory on their hunting days, then motioned to Cal who finished the true tale and concluded, "We almost gave too much away and ended up being no 'who.'"

Shell gazed out the window where Inspector Bowen and the two other MBI investigators and two patrolmen were huddled on the porch talking. Bowen had been providing everyone with updates on the action beyond the levee. Ten militia had been killed and several wounded. Two of the ten killed went up with explosives on a pontoon boat shot by one of the Coast Guard cruisers when it refused to stop. Two FBI agents had been wounded, one medevacked to Memphis, the other taken to the Clarksdale hospital. One of the helicopters had been shot down and its passengers were miraculously unscathed. Several of the terrorists surrendered, and were taken to the Lafayette County Detention Center to be interrogated later by the FBI.

The Sunflower County Rehabilitation Center had been notified along with its corporate headquarters. Both were aware of the presence of gangs in the prison, but unaware of the terrorist infiltration and oblivious to Warden Culpepper's involvement. One of the assistant wardens replaced Culpepper. A prison lockdown was immediately imposed by the new acting warden. Thanks to Culpepper's meticulous records, including photos of the gang in his office, Aryan Nations inmates and cell members were rounded up and quickly isolated. An investigation was underway for others employed or incarcerated by the prison, including a thorough review of any in the Aryan Nations prison gang.

The picture emerging, as Bowen described it, was Warden Culpepper's attempt to turn the prison into a breeding ground for domestic terrorism, using the inmates, once they were discharged, as his foot soldiers. A battle plan of sorts was found on the warden in one of his pockets. In addition to the three bridges, other targets included bombing the Lorraine Motel in Memphis where Martin Luther King, Jr. was assassinated and the nearby Civil Rights Museum. Bowen had advised the governor, Shell, and Cal they should not leave the house or grounds until the mop-up of Operation Bridges was complete. All readily agreed.

Around noon, the governor pulled Shell and Cal aside and informed them that he had phoned the head of the parole board. "I told him I was going to issue an official pardon for you before the judicial process was completed for your exoneration."

"Won't the pardon be enough?" Cal asked.

"You need to be exonerated," Shell injected. "I had to go through the same process when the real murderer confessed, and I was released from Parchman. A pardon only means you are forgiven and does not expunge the crime from your record. You committed no crime."

"That is correct," said the governor. "This is one way I can obtain an early release for you."

"Can I stay here, then?" requested Cal.

"Yes," the governor confirmed. "Your release is immediate."

"I'm very grateful to you, Governor," Cal said and embraced him.

Late in the Christmas Day afternoon, just before sunset, Inspector Bowen received an all-clear notice from the FBI. The governor and Mrs. DuBard asked Shelley if she wanted to go home with them to the governor's mansion. She quickly, and emphatically declined, stating, "I'm staying with my Daddy and Big Daddy." They understood and gave hugs and kisses before departing, issuing an invitation for later, for her and for her daddy, to which Shelley nodded but said nothing.

The governor apologized for not staying over stating there was no bed for them there, and he had to return to running a state that was a 24 hour job. Inspector Bowen left with the governor and Mrs. DuBard and drove the highway patrol cruiser they had arrived in, leaving the two patrolmen until a replacement detail arrived to provide security and protection. Due to the wide network of Christian Identity and Aryan Nations, no one could offer absolute certainty that the terrorist cell outside of the prison had been completely eradicated.

Shell and one of the security patrolmen, whose name was Phillip, drove into a convenience store in Rome that stayed open 24/7 and loaded up on pizza, fried chicken, hot dogs and condiments, fresh milk, cereal and soft drinks. He added an extra package of Fig Newtons which he knew was one of Shelley's favorites.

After dinner, comfortable with the relief patrolmen outside, one in the cruiser and one on the porch, Shell and Cal sat on the couch while Shelley continued to amuse herself on the floor in front of the tree with Santa's gifts. Shell observed her head nodding over the train. He nudged Cal's shoulder. "I think she's about ready for bed."

Cal nodded, "I think you're right."

"You two sleep in the master room, I'll take the guest room." He watched his grandson gently sweep Shelley, her eyes almost closed, from the floor up limply into his arms. From the bedroom came the tender goodnight murmurs between father and daughter, sounds Shell imagined were being heard by countless fathers and daughters in countless bedrooms around the world, sounds he was still surprised, and glad, to hear again.

Cal returned and sat beside him, and Shell felt the slight bulge and remembered he still had on his jacket with the gun and clip in the pockets. He hoped he wouldn't need to use it again, but after what they'd been through, he pulled it out and laid it on the table next to him at the end of the couch.

"How many shots did you fire?" Cal inquired gravely.

"Don't know, wasn't counting. Clip holds seventeen." He picked up the gun, checked it. "One left. Then these," and he pointed to the clip.

They sat looking at the makeshift tree and the front windows, the night beyond. Shell could see the movement of a rocker on the porch and the front of the state highway patrol cruiser parked in the drive of the burned house. He needed to remember the safe. He doubted anyone could carry it off, especially with a highway patrol car less than fifty feet from it. He had made a call to his insurance agent and was to meet him at the ruins in the morning. He could check it then. Cal seemed in a deep state of mind just sitting and staring, eyes leveled out at the ficus tree.

"The FBI should be able to identify who killed Sally and Athen," Shell said breaking the silence. "They know the truck and its owner, not to mention fingerprints they lifted at Doom's house." He looked over at Cal.

Cal gave no response, as though his mind was elsewhere.

"Have you thought about what you might do once you're exonerated?" Shell attempted.

After a long delay in answering, Cal said, "I've thought about it. Everything's been swirling around in my mind, like a merry-go-round I need to get off but can't."

"You can when it stops," Shell said. "And it will eventually stop. Time is on your side."

"Time," Cal sighed with a single nod. Then uttered the word again and nodded again. "Time is what I was serving. Now I'm out and still feel like I'm serving it."

"We're all serving time, Son," Shell said. "If you're living, you're serving time. Time is God's other name. No way to get around that big clock."

Cal looked at him. "That should be my line. I'm the preacher."

"Glad you still feel that way. You kept the faith. You survived."

A pause. Cal thinking. Then: "I don't think I survived because I kept the faith, whatever that means. Sounds like protective custody, that if you hang on to it long enough, God will eventually bail you out. I survived because..." He sat there, molars grinding, jaw muscles rippling, rolling his hand as if the movements spun the rest of the thought.

Shell sensed him struggling. "What you're trying to tell me, Cal, is that faith doesn't sit on its haunches and wait, it has legs."

"Granddad, you're amazing," Cal said looking at him with bright eyes.

"Back to my question," Shell said. "What do you plan to do with your new, excuse me, renewed legs?"

"I've been thinking about it," he responded. "First thing is to get an appointment with my District Superintendent and the bishop, get reinstated. They didn't revoke my credentials, only put me on what's called 'Voluntary Location.'"

"Wasn't much voluntary about it."

"I know. Makes it sound like I've still got a say so," Cal said.

"So you'll get a new appointment."

"It'll be new, all right. I'm creating one."

"I don't get it," Shell said puzzled.

"I want to start a church."

"Where?" Shell asked. "Seems they've got plenty, some they need to close, like the one here in Rome. Only get a handful each Sunday. The place is dying."

"In the prison."

Shell flinched. "Why go back into that hell where you were assaulted and almost killed? They've got chaplains and prison ministries already. Charles Colson and that pastor named Cathon Burt from Senatobia started some in the state-run prisons."

"I'd be in prison if I didn't go. Maybe that's why I feel I'm still serving time. I feel called to do this. My legs haven't started yet, but they're gearing up."

"Now, you're making more sense."

As if Shell's comment was parenthetical, Cal continued. "This church will be different. It will be an actual church inside the prison with an Administrative Board, Council on Ministries—everything a normal church has including a pastor placed there by episcopal appointment. It will be comprised of guards and inmates, even prison staff if they feel led to join. I already have my first member."

"Your friend?"

"Yep. Chris Cruz. If it hadn't been for him, I might not be here. He's a big part of those 'legs.' And he has a following, not just in the prison. There's a new warden. New guards replacing the corrupt ones. It'll be a new day."

"That's gonna take a while," Shell added skeptically.

"This will only be the beginning," Cal continued. "A church in that prison could become a hub church from which others in other prisons would begin, throughout Mississippi, throughout the country," he paused. "Maybe even the world."

"What about Shelley and her world?" Shell questioned. "The DuBards may have something to say about it."

"I won't live in the prison," he said, his old confident voice back. "I can stay here in Little House. The conference would like that, not having to buy or build a parsonage, at least not right off. That prison's not far from here. I can take Shelley to school and pick her up each day."

"You didn't just come up with this."

"It's been on my mind," Cal said. "While I was serving time," and he smiled.

Shell returned the smile.

Cal adjourned to go to bed in the room with Shelley. But before he left, he laid a hand on Shell's shoulder. "Grandad, thank you for your legs, too. They saved me."

Shell continued sitting on the couch reviewing the day's events, observing the cut on his leg that could have been worse. Warden or not, he felt badly that he'd killed a man. Taking another's life was a sin, regardless of the circumstances. He would probably spend the rest of his life serving that time, asking for forgiveness.

He began feeling an unusual pain in the center of his chest. His breath grew shorter. It was probably nothing. After all, he'd had one long day, one long life, covered a lot of ground for a seventy-nine-year-old, lived beyond his own death. He was proud of his grandson, proud, too, of his great-granddaughter. She was going to be something someday, a chip off the old block and with that hopeful thought, he closed his eyes and went to sleep.

CHAPTER 46
AFTERMATH

A week after the Christmas hiatus, on New Year's Day, Shell "Jo Shelby" Ferguson had a massive heart attack. Emergency quadruple bypass surgery and aortic valve replacement saved his life. Six months after his recovery, back on his feet and looking for something to do, he received an enticing request from Director Garland Holifield.

The Reverend Cal Ferguson was exonerated and reinstated in his church with full conference membership and given permission by the bishop to start a church in the private prison where he had been incarcerated. The bishop and his cabinet concurred with his suggestion that the church be called The Church of God's Time. The corporation that owned the prison, Social Rehabilitation Agency of America, approved and offered its support.

Shelley Ferguson entered second grade in a county elementary school near her home in Rome. It was deemed prudent by her father that she undergo a psychological evaluation for the traumas she had experienced. She saw a female psychologist in Clarksdale who stated in her report that she was, "impressed by Shelley's maturity, resilience, bright-eyed candor, and gifted intelligence." Also in the report, she noted the dormant nature of Post-Traumatic Stress Disorder and cautioned regarding future triggers of the symptoms of PTSD and that those close to her should be vigilant.

The only eyewitness to the parsonage carnage, Shelley identified the two men she saw that night and later at the camp. She never knew their names, but her finger went straight to their faces in the assorted photos Inspector Bowen showed her, the MBI agent's prudence that an actual lineup and seeing the men in person would have been too traumatic for the small child.

The two men had survived the attack on the camp. Their fingerprints had matched those left in Doom's house, and one was the owner of the wide-bodied white pickup with the Mohawk mud tires and the round tread mark that turned out to be the butt of a spent rifle shell. Shelley also immediately identified Sadie Doom whom she said was, "This lady at my daddy's church," and continued unsolicited, "We went to her house one day a long time ago." When asked if Shelley had seen the face anywhere else, she said, "At that bad place, but only one time." In his report, Inspector Bowen theorized that Sadie would have known Shelley would recognize her and probably kept her distance from the small girl at the camp.

Sadie Beatrice (Bea) Doom, the queen bee of the Aryan Nations cell, recovered from her gunshot wounds to stand trial for federal terrorism, attempted murder, and conspiracy to commit murder along with other counts of illegal possession of firearms and dynamite, receiving stolen jet engines, and conspiracy to destroy three Mississippi River bridges, plus The Lorraine Motel Heritage and National Civil Rights Museum in Memphis, Tennessee. A "battle map," identical to the one found on the warden's body, was also found on her and noted those same targets. She adamantly, and consistently each time she was questioned, denied any involvement or knowledge of the parsonage fire that claimed the lives of Athen and Sally Ferguson as well as the abduction of Shelley Ferguson. She did confess, on the witness stand, that she did not have an affair with Cal Ferguson, which prompted, from the bench, the judge to level an additional perjury charge against her.

In her trial, prosecutors had requested the death penalty. A highlight of the proceedings was the testimony of her former boss, Cal Ferguson, who looked at her, told her that he forgave her, and pled for her life. Sitting at the table beside her lawyer, Sadie Bea Doom sobbed uncontrollably. Two weeks later, she committed suicide by hanging herself in her cell in the Sunflower County seat jail in Indianola, Mississippi before she could be transported to the private prison where Cal Ferguson had been incarcerated.

Before her death, Sadie Bea Doom confessed to having a love affair with warden John Culpepper. In her prepared statement, she stated the relationship had begun when she was in college, and she had successfully maintained the romance over the years. She also admitted that her husband had become aware of the affair, one of the reasons for his reneging on the jet engines deal. He had withdrawn from Aryan Nations before he was shot.

Chris Cruz, due to a letter from Governor DuBard to the Governor of California, was granted a pardon. Upon learning of his former cellmate's plans to plant a church in the prison, he requested that be able to remain in that prison, in his same cell and asked it be unlocked so he could move freely in being about "his Father's business." In his letter of gratitude to the Governor of California, he stated that he preferred solitude, and that the four walls offered him the privilege of "preaching to those who dwell in darkness from the prison, Isaiah 42:7."

Governor Byron DuBard served out his second term and returned to his former law firm in Jackson, Mississippi.

Under Governor DuBard's second tenure, Garland Holifield continued as Director of the Mississippi Bureau of Investigation. His next big case was dealing with militia in a place in northeast Mississippi called Twenty Mile Bottom. His unofficial undercover agent Shell Ferguson, whom he considered perfect for the task, had agreed to accept the challenge. "Why not," Shell had said. "Got nothing else better to do with my time."

FBI Agent Brent Chase received commendations for his part in uncovering the conspiracy and attempt to overthrow the government. He continued with the Bureau in Mississippi and, when in the area, would drop in on worship services at The Church of God's Time.

MBI Inspector Cavanaugh Bowen had an emotional breakdown, one related more to his marriage than the succession of traumas. Following his recovery, he made a pilgrimage to Rome to help celebrate Shelley's next birthday. Seeing her again, he stated, helped his recovery, "more than I can put into words."

Fain Durasmus kept his same position but his daughter Zell, who had been an assistant warden, was elevated to warden, one of the first females to hold that position in the Mississippi penal system. One of her first tasks, upon orders from SRAA headquarters, was to replace the double utility gate with a single gate, eliminating the gap that allowed Cal Ferguson's escape. Durasmus became one of the first members of The Church of God's Time. His daughter Zell and her children soon joined him.

Aryan Nations militia members arrested in the assault on Cessions Towhead were charged with federal terrorism and received life sentences without parole. Except for the two responsible for the murders of Athen and Sally Ferguson who were sentenced to death by lethal injection. Their appeal is still pending. Membership and influence in Aryan Nations had been waning, but this latest episode, the national attention it received in the media, hastened the decline of the domestic terrorist group. They continue to maintain a website and still remain on the FBI and Southern Poverty Law Center's hate group list.

Warden Culpepper's secretary, Diane Compton, was charged and convicted of perjury, conspiracy, and obstruction of justice. She had lied on the witness stand about Sadie Bea Doom's involvement with the warden, as well as having no knowledge of Aryan Nations when documents to the contrary were found in her locked desk drawer. Included in those documents were the names and phone numbers of militia members arrested at Cessions Towhead and addresses and phone numbers of members of the Aryan Nations Arkansas cell centered at Snow Lake, Arkansas. She was sentenced to twenty years without parole.

The Fisherman, real name Ricardo Guzman, was charged with federal terrorism and conspiracy. He had been incarcerated for an assault charge in Idaho. His ten-year sentence was increased to twenty years without parole

The Ferguson House was rebuilt by Cal as a halfway house for inmates returning to civilian status. Staffed by Moses Malone and Jefferson Lincoln plus mental health and vocational professionals from Clarksdale and Oxford, Mississippi and Delta State University. The facility services thirty inmates at a time.

The Camp and Schoolbus still exist. The vehicle has never been moved and is still there across the oxbow lake from Cessions Towhead. The area continues to be used by fishermen and hunters. Sadie Bea and her deceased husband, Ty Doom, had no children. Upon her death, the land and schoolbus reverted to the state, and a group of hunters purchased the land from the state. They decided to leave the bus as a testament to the triumph over domestic terrorism. The hunters' consortium refurbished and repainted the school bus and honored Cal's request—leave the "T."

The Panamanian Bank in Colon, Panama was investigated and an attorney, Julio Mendez, was questioned. No one ever claimed the money that sits today, unclaimed. Conventional and legal wisdom believe the money may never be claimed fearing it could be traced to its international terrorist source.

The two jet engines were returned to the United States Air Force Base in Little Rock, Arkansas and that case was closed. The alleged suspect who passed the lie detector test is still at large.

The Ranchero continues to serve its famous Bar-B-Q as it has since 1959.

The Levee along the Mississippi River still rivals the Great Wall of China. The Levee Road continues to serve as a travel option for the adventurous who want to drive on it from Illinois to Louisiana.

The Mississippi Delta is as flat and endless as ever and will always be "The Delta."

The prison—is everywhere.

ABOUT THE AUTHOR

Photo credit - Thomas Wells/Northeast Daily Journal

Joe Edd Morris is the author of the novels *Land Where My Fathers Died*, *The Last Page* and several non-fiction works including *Revival of the Gnostic Heresy: Fundamentalism* and *Ten Things I Wish Jesus Hadn't Said.* His short fiction has appeared in a number of literary journals with a nomination for the Pushcart Prize.

Thank you so much for reading one of our **Mystery** novels.
If you enjoyed our book, please check out our recommended title for your
next great read!

K-Town Confidential by Brad Chisholm and Claire Kim

"An enjoyable zigzagging plot." *—KIRKUS REVIEWS*

"If you are a fan of crime stories and legal dramas that have a noir flavor,
you won't be disappointed with *K-Town Confidential*." *—Authors Reading*

View other Black Rose Writing titles at www.blackrosewriting.com/books

and use promo code **PRINT** to receive a **20% discount** when purchasing.

Made in the USA
Monee, IL
22 August 2022

12222442R00163